Because sentence against an evil work is
not executed speedily, therefore the heart
of the sons of men is fully set in them to
do evil.

Ecclesiastes 8:11

Acknowledgements

How do you thank someone in just a few words for them giving you years of their heart and life?

My thanks to the Scott-Ross sisters, Poppy and Ang, for guiding me with patience and skill through writing kindergarten. My thanks also to Patricia Taylor and Graham Parks for continuing with my education. If I am a writer, it is only with your help.

'Special' thanks to Graham Parks and Rolf M Landaas for their assistance with the operational authenticity of this work.

And, of course, a big thank you to my fellow Skribblerz, for being there when I really needed you.

Sheep in Wolf's Clothing

George Maciver

Madison Sol

MADISON SOL LTD
Benview House, Brora
Scotland KW9 6QN

Published 2004 by Madison Sol

A catalogue record for this book is available from the
British library

ISBN 0-9548004-0-0

Cover design by pictii

Printed by printregister.com

Sheep in Wolf's Clothing

Chapter 1

The young woman stood framed by the doorway of the aircraft, her blue dress fluttering in the wind, the shadowed outline of a man beside her. There was a bright orange flash of a gunshot and she toppled from the aircraft, crumpling to the runway fifteen feet below. The man retreated and the door slammed closed.

Air rasped through respirators as the SAS men ran along the low gloomy tunnel leading under the runway from the hangar, MP5 sub-machineguns gripped tightly across their chests. As he ran, Corporal James Gilmour began to consider the rest of his life not in terms of years, but of minutes. His face was beaded with sweat and his blue eyes sparkled with the clarity of fear as he kept up with the bloke in front. Jostling for position, the assault groups reached the end of the passageway and bunched up under a steel manhole cover. Static cracked in his ears. 'All call signs . . . all call signs, this is Alpha, I have control . . . I have control.'

The police had handed over control to the SAS. Everyone in the tunnel tensed. The waiting was over.

The yellow lights in the narrow tunnel went out, plunging the sweating soldiers into utter darkness. The purpose-built padded manhole cover was eased noiselessly aside. Eyepieces reflected dull moonlight as upturned respirators stared out at the huge underbelly of the hijacked aircraft lying eerily silent in the faint glow of the lights of the freight terminal buildings. An arm beckoned and one by one they leapt out onto the runway.

Gilmour sprinted towards the huge starboard rear tyres. A hand was raised and the group stopped. Gilmour crouched down in the shadows. Static crackled in his ears again.

'Alpha . . . this is Blue One over. Blue teams at start positions over.'

'Roger Blue One.'

Black padded assault ladders were raised fore and aft against each side of the aircraft, their soundproofed legs silent against the fuselage. As his breathing normalised, Gilmour's mind wandered as he worried about a date he had the following day. Having already broken two dates with her, a third time would be unforgivable. What if he was killed? She'd get ready, not knowing, spending ages putting on her make-up, only to take a taxi into town to sit at an empty table in the pub by herself. The thought made him flinch. Then there was the cat. Who would feed it? How long would it be before old Scud gave up on him, forced into the trees behind the cottage to hunt for mice? A sly smile slithered over his slippery lips. Boy, would his bank manager be pissed off! *A sudden thought!* He'd only just bought the new Tomb Raider game for his PlayStation.

'Right,' he muttered to one of the huge tyres, 'that

does it.' There was no way on God's earth he was getting slotted. At least, not before he'd had some fun with Miss Lara Croft.

He glanced involuntarily over his shoulder. The pathetic, crumpled body of the young woman lay slumped on the runway where she'd fallen from the aircraft. *Why had they picked on her?* An SAS medic crawled warily over to her, making sure he couldn't be seen from the cabin, and checked for a pulse.

'All call signs . . . this is Alpha. Hold position . . . wait out.'

Damn! Gilmour thumped his new mate the tyre. Politicians, no doubt, more concerned about saving the lives of the hi-jackers than saving the lives of the hostages. Leaning back against the tyre, he rolled his neck and tried to control his fear. The man beside him turned in his direction and winked through the eyepieces of his black respirator. Yep, the others were just as scared as he was.

A torch beam swept round the cockpit. A warning barked over the radio net and everyone froze. The beam shone down at the runway as one of the hi-jackers tried to peer under the nose. Gilmour pulled his weapon to his chest and readied himself for the order to storm. Bile welled up in his throat, probably from the sausage sandwich he'd eaten earlier.

'That's all I need,' he moaned, swallowing to ease the burning.

In the distance, an aircraft roared away from another runway, navigation lights flashing. Distracted, the hi-jacker watched it go, then, after another quick glance down at the runway, he switched off his torch and disappeared back into the main cabin.

'Blue One, this is Alpha.'

'Roger, Alpha.'

'Proceed to Red positions.'

'Blue One, roger.'

Menacing shapes rose from the shadows under the aircraft and split into three groups. Gilmour ran towards the rear ladders in a group of eight men. Another hand was raised and his group split into pairs; two pairs to each double-width ladder. Placing a foot on the bottom rung of the starboard ladders, he looked up at the cabin. Five days of waiting was almost over. *Five days!* What it must be like inside was anyone's guess. A hand rested on his shoulder. Peter Black, his assault partner, a cheeky Cockney, gave him the wanker wrist shake. Gilmour tapped his respirator at the temple with his forefinger.

The arm rose again and Gilmour started climbing, Black beside him. Reaching the side of the emergency exit, he took two stun grenades from his belt and braced himself with his knees. From within he thought he could hear children crying. *Five days! It must have been hell in there.*

Black readied himself to punch in the emergency panel that opened the exit. Gilmour adjusted his feet on the ladder, bracing himself tighter with his knees, acutely aware of the treacherous fall below. The ladders shook as their back-up assault pair climbed up after them. One of them tapped his leg.

'Alpha . . . Blue Two,' reported Gilmour, speaking into the speech transmitter fitted to his respirator. 'In position at Red Two over.'

'Roger, Blue Two.'

The sick feeling in his stomach was making him nauseous. But it wasn't just fear. Things with his girlfriend hadn't been going well for some time. His thoughts were interrupted by static.

'Alpha, Blue Three . . . at Red Three over.'

'Roger, Blue Three.'

'Alpha, Blue Four . . . at Red Four over.'

'Roger, Blue Four.'

He loved her, of that he was sure, but he knew it was all slipping away. He didn't want to lose her.

'*Karen,*' he whispered, biting back pain, '*I'll make it up to you tomorrow sweetheart.*'

'Alpha, Blue One . . . at Red One over.'

'Roger, Blue One . . . all call signs, this is Alpha . . . Red on . . . Red on.'

Everything was set.

One of Gilmour's legs started trembling. Curling his toes in his boot, he pushed his foot down hard on the rung. *Make it up to her?* Not if there was a bullet waiting for him. His face was clammy. With the assault going in from either end of the aircraft, the assault groups working towards the centre, firing towards each other, it didn't exactly calm his nerves. But the Commander had felt the risk of being seen climbing onto the wings in bright moonlight too great. One of the blokes below put a hand on the back of his leg to stop it shaking. He'd never live it down back at Hereford.

If only he could go to his inventory if he got shot and use a medi-pak, like Lara Croft. Mind you, he observed, she didn't exactly have his body armour, even with her pixel tits.

Suddenly, two RAF Tornadoes swooped down over a copse of trees at the end of the airport and screamed along the runway, just a few feet off the ground. This was their cue. His leg stopped trembling.

'Stand by . . . stand by . . .'

Heavy feet pounded down the aisle above their heads towards the cockpit. Gilmour took the pins from his grenades. Pulling up at the last second, the Tornadoes shrieked along each side of the aircraft and thundered away into the night, afterburners glowing.

'. . . GO!'

Black punched the panel and the emergency exit thudded open. Moonlight spilled into the darkened cabin. The port exit opposite them opened and a head popped round the side of the door. Four stun grenades bounced inside. Ducking back outside, Gilmour braced himself. The aircraft rocked as the grenades exploded. A dozen searchlights stabbed the darkness, locking onto the fuselage, lighting up the entire aircraft. Gilmour flicked off the safety catch on his MP5, bit his lip so hard it started bleeding, and launched himself inside.

Through wreathing smoke, he glimpsed someone on his knees, someone holding a gun. Dazed eyes registered surprise as two small red holes appeared in his forehead. Black fired a long burst into the falling body. Gilmour got to his feet searching for another target.

'Blue Two,' he reported. 'X-ray down.'

'Roger, Blue Two.'

Shots rang out up near the cockpit. Gilmour could see nothing through the smoke.

'Blue Three, X-ray down.'

'Roger, Blue Three.'

Gilmour stepped over the body and paused by one of the toilet doors as the port assault pair went aft to check out the galley area. Black stepped up and readied himself. Gilmour nodded and Black kicked viciously. The door slammed open and Gilmour poked his weapon inside. Brown sludge and toilet paper dripped down the sides of the overflowing toilet bowl, forming slop on the deck. There was no one in there. Stepping back into the aisle, Gilmour became curiously aware that his fear had completely gone. Positioning himself by the other toilet, he nodded again and Black kicked out. Someone moved inside and a gun barrel glistened. Two shots caught the hi-jacker before he could fire and his body slumped into the filth on the deck. Black fired a few rounds into the man's chest.

'Blue Two, X-ray down.'

'Roger, Blue Two.'

'Blue Four, Green Two clear over.'

'Roger, Blue Four.'

'Blue One, Green Three clear over.'

The cockpit and aft areas had been cleared.

Gilmour started up the aisle, his MP5 swinging from row to row, searching desperately for terrorists among the screaming hostages. There would be a 'sleeper'. There was always a sleeper. A woman staggered towards him out of the smoke, doubled up and coughing. *Was she a hi-jacker?* She looked up, her face distorted with hatred, her lips curling with venom. Rounds whistled past his ear as Black beat him to it. Gilmour fired a few rounds into the falling torso just to be sure.

'*Lights out bitch,*' he whispered.

'Blue Six,' reported Black, glad to be on the score sheet, 'X-ray down.'

'Roger, Blue Six.'

Gilmour continued up the smoke filled aisle, searching among the hostages cowering in their seats, their faces twisted, their eyes screwed shut with terror. The stench of vomit, faeces and stinking bodies began filtering into his mask. A burgundy scarf worn by a woman seated next to the aisle caught his eye. The woman's deep brown eyes didn't flinch as his MP5 centred on her forehead. He moved on. She wasn't a threat.

Suddenly a little girl in a blue dress jumped out of her seat and pelted down the aisle towards him. She had no idea how close she came to death. Gilmour cursed as he snatched his aim away from her forehead. She slammed into his leg and wrapped her arms round him. Gilmour took a breath to steady himself as Black stepped past them. He stroked the blonde hair tumbling down her back, bloodied from a nasty gash on her forehead. She couldn't have been more than seven or eight. Glancing back over his shoulder, he nodded to the two men behind him. They bolted up the aisle after Black and quickly disappeared in the smoke.

The little girl's fingers were digging into him. Gently, he lifted her from the deck. She flung her arms round his neck and wrapped her legs round him, burying her face in his shoulder. Gilmour's heart crunched.

'Shhh, sweetheart,' he soothed, keeping his smoking sub-machine gun trained up the aisle. 'It's okay now.'

Empty words.

Things were far from okay.

Alerted by that sixth sense that makes a good operator, Gilmour spun round. A well groomed Asian man in his early thirties, lean and swarthy, dressed expensively in grey trousers, white shirt and gold watch, stepped into the aisle holding a green leather sports bag with a Jaguar motif. The man held the bag out in front of him, smiling and nodding his head in that funny Asian sort of way. Gilmour felt stupid. He'd walked right past him. This guy was good. But he held his fire. He had to be sure. The man stopped moving his head and his smile faded to sadness. Gilmour recognised the sadness. He'd seen it before. It was the sadness of a man who knew he would never feel the warmth of life ever again.

He fired and the girl tightened her grip, almost choking him. The Asian fell backwards, dropping the bag. Gilmour stepped forward, firing another long burst.

'Blue Two, X-ray down.'

'Roger, Blue Two.'

Gilmour stared down at the terrorist, whose last breaths were gurgling through blood beginning to froth from his nose and mouth. Then, inexplicably, a chill ran down his spine. Something wasn't right.

'Alpha, Blue One . . . Green clear . . . Green clear over.'

The assault teams had met up. The aircraft had been cleared.

'Roger, Blue One.'

Back in one of the hangars, where the SAS Command and Control Centre was located, the hostage reception team had already slipped their idling vehicles into gear.

Gilmour was deeply disturbed. There was something in the light fading in the Asian's eyes that terrified him. Then, in a terse, crystallised moment of sheer terror, his life, in monochrome shades of grey, flickered through his mind like forked lightning lacerating a flinching sky.

He was in a fight at school and felt the pain of a fist whacking his cheek; he saw his first breasts, his breath coming in gasps as he eased them from their school blouse; he was sitting at his school desk, staring listlessly out of the large windows; then it was the blimp at RAF Abingdon from which he'd made his first parachute descent, his heart stopping as he'd leapt into empty sky; startled monkeys screamed from the steamy jungle canopy, hurling abuse; a crippled submarine ploughed into a deep trough, green sea crashing over its bow; machine gun tracer flashed over his head, cracking into the wall of the house, showering him with splinters of red brick; it was pouring rain and he was on the Brecon Beacons, his legs staggering under him with the weight of the bergen on his back; his girlfriend reached out her hand, her gorgeous body silhouetted by the sun shining through her summer frock. The visions cleared. Now all he could see was the thin wisp of white smoke trailing from the sports bag.

Grabbing the leather handles, he started running. The girl sensed something was seriously wrong and dug her nails into his neck. The clamour and panic in the cabin seemed to grow heavy and listless as every molecule in his being focused its energy on propelling him forward. The white smoke thickened. Everything went into slow motion.

'*Blue Two . . .*' His scream sounded fuzzy and distant. '*Bomb!*'

There was a taut silence on the radio for a second.

'*What the fuck did you say?*'

Fizzing noises mixed with the smoke. The girl heard it too and started whimpering. Her arms tightened round Gilmour's neck, breaking the seal between the respirator and his skin. His eyepieces steamed up and he almost panicked. His arm muscles tightened, involuntarily tensing against the explosion that was going to blow them into sloppy chunks of dripping red meat. Indistinct patches of dull light gleamed through the dark cloudy haze. With every electron volt his body could generate, he reached his arm back and launched the bomb out of the starboard exit.

Turning his back to protect the girl, Gilmour smashed into the galley bulkhead. He crumpled under the impact with a grunt and collapsed to the deck. His arms covered the girl's head as the night sucked in its breath. With a last little fizz and a puff of ugly black smoke, the tumbling bag blew the sky apart. The starboard wing buckled and twisted and portholes cracked along the fuselage as the shock wave smashed into the aircraft. Across the runway, an abandoned service lorry burst into flames as the explosion ripped open its diesel tank.

Time went into cardiac arrest. To the shocked security forces watching, the aircraft had exploded. Stone faces stared disbelievingly at the huge pall of black smoke billowing high into the night sky. Then, through a torn curtain of smoke and flame, they caught a brief glimpse of the aircraft.

SAS Range Rovers bristling with automatic weapons erupted out of hangars. Uniformed police officers threw open a gate and an entourage of ambulances, fire engines, police vehicles and coaches rumbled onto the runway. Across the airfield, behind a chain link fence topped with barbed wire, a seething sea of journalists, cameramen and soundmen slipped and slithered in a muddy field, frenziedly capturing every detail for the millions of hungry viewers riveted to television screens around the world.

Within the cabin, it had gone deathly quiet. Passengers were slowly opening their eyes, touching themselves, checking for bullet wounds and blood, not really convinced they were still alive. A few people cried, their sobs somehow comforting within the ghostly silence.

Children hugged their parents, their eyes still screwed tightly shut.

The SAS men pulled their hoods back and slipped off their respirators, uneasy in the troubled hush. One of them walked up the aisle towards the cockpit, his feet crunching on broken glass and other debris, his shadow dancing grotesquely in the light of the flames still flickering in through the windows.

Gilmour got awkwardly to his knees and struggled out of his respirator.

'It's okay now sweetheart,' he gasped, wiping sweat from his face with his free arm.

The girl said nothing. There was more chance of the tide washing a barnacle from a rock than of her letting go of his neck. Grabbing the corner of a galley worktop, Gilmour pulled himself to his feet. Wispy fingers of smoke trailed out of the exits, vanishing on the night breeze. He glanced about, a little puzzled. Something had changed. The tension was gone. The whole world seemed strangely normal again. The hostages sensed it too. Deciding they'd had quite enough of that aircraft, they got out of their seats and headed for the exits.

Gilmour glanced up the aisle. The smoke was clearing. In the cabin, he could see Black and the others trying desperately to hold back the surging stampede. He limped over to the starboard exit. Floodlights blinded him and he blinked, putting up an arm to protect his eyes. Outside it was pandemonium.

Paramedics were sprinting from ambulances; SAS and armed police in riot gear were running around the aircraft, surrounding it; firemen were dragging hoses from their cradles, some spraying foam over the aircraft and its engines, others smothering the dying flames still licking the burned out service lorry; police officers and airport officials were barking orders into radios; and medical staff were setting up a make-shift theatre, ready to start operating, if necessary, right there under the stark glare of the searchlights.

'*Calm yourselves!*' screamed Black.

The bodies of the hi-jackers disappeared beneath the trampling mob. A gangway manoeuvred up to the starboard doorway and two heavily armed SAS soldiers bounded up the steps.

'Sorry lads,' said Black, his face flushed and sweating, his black hair matted to his scalp. 'You crap 'ats'll 'ave to wait till next time.'

The hostages, sensing freedom and smelling fresh air, surged forward. The dam burst. A few medical staff rushed up the steps but then fell back when they saw the human torrent bearing down on them. Hugging the little girl, Gilmour forced his way into the throng.

A group of paramedics were bunched round the body of the woman lying on the tarmac. The girl looked up anxiously. Suddenly, she struggled and dropped to the ground.

'*Mummy!*'

She pulled free of his hand and headed straight for the paramedics. One of them saw her coming and caught her, lifting her up off the ground.

'Hold up there young 'un, what's the rush?'

'She should be operated on immediately,' said one of the paramedics kneeling by the woman.

'We don't have the facilities here,' said another, getting a drip into her arm.

'Do you think we should take a chance and send her straight to hospital?'

'We have to know where the bullet's lodged before we touch her.'

Reluctantly, the others nodded. Lifting her carefully onto a stretcher, they rushed her to a waiting ambulance. Blue lights flashed and a siren stabbed the night.

'And how are you young lady?' asked the paramedic holding the girl, concern pursing his lips into a tight line. 'Here, let me look at you. Your mother will probably want to see you again when she gets better.'

'What're the chances?' asked Gilmour, surprised she was still alive.

'Depends on the bullet. We've no idea what's happened inside her head.'

'Did you hear that?' said Gilmour, smiling at the girl. 'Your mummy's alive.' It was the first time their eyes had met and Gilmour knew immediately that she could read him. 'What's your name sweetheart?'

'Angelina.'

'Hi Angel, I'm Jamie.'

Not Angel, you can call me Ang. I want my mummy.'

The medic sat the girl on a stretcher and Gilmour held her hand while she was checked over. One of the medics handed her a chocolate while he attended to the gash on her forehead. The chocolate hung in her fingers, unopened, and then dropped to the runway.

'She's fine,' said the paramedic, sticking a plaster on her forehead. 'You'll have to come with me now young lady.'

'*No!*'

She jumped into Gilmour's arms and buried her head in his shoulder.

'There are lots of nice people over there,' said the paramedic, turning to point towards a hangar, 'who—'

'*No!*'

'I'll take her over,' said Gilmour gently.

'Sure. By the way . . .'

'Yes?'

'Good job mate.'

The paramedics nodded their awed respects and then turned their attention to the other hostages, most of whom were being shepherded from the gangways to the waiting coaches. But there were others still on board, mostly elderly folk too weak to make it off on their own, and they went to see what they could do.

'Gilmour! *Move!*'

The Colonel's voice carried clearly through the bustle from the doorway of a coach. The rest of the lads were already aboard, waiting to be driven to a debriefing area.

'Last again Gilmour?' barked the Colonel, frowning under his bushy grey eyebrows.

'Sorry Boss.'

'Who's she?'

'The shot hostage's daughter, Boss.'

The Colonel gaped at him, his eyes angry rubies glinting in his weathered face.

'Say hello to the Colonel, Ang.'

She looked up with sad green eyes.

'Hello, Sir,' she said politely.

A few of the lads spotted the girl and a buzz rippled round the bus.

'Gilmour . . . I . . .' The frown softened and a faint smile cracked his lips. 'Why is it always you?'

'I said I'd take her to the holding area.'

'Of course,' said the Colonel, stepping aside to let them on, 'we'll drop her off on the way.'

Gilmour climbed aboard to a rapturous cheer. Compressed air hissed as the driver closed the door and let the brakes off. Gilmour found a seat and Angelina plopped down heavily beside him. As the bus drove out through the gates, he looked over his shoulder and watched the aircraft disappear behind the hangar that had been the Assault Team's base for the past five days. The flashing lights and the noise gradually faded away. It was over. Exhaustion dragged his chin forward.

'Jamie?'

A few of the lads had turned in their seats.

'Eh?'

'Thanks . . . you know . . . the bomb. If it wasn't for you . . .'

Gilmour shrugged.

'Yeah,' nodded another of them, 'cheers mate.'

Gilmour shrugged again, somewhat embarrassed.

'Well, someone's got to look after you wankers,' he said.

They all smiled and turned back in their seats.

'Are you my new daddy?' asked Angelina, looking up, her dishevelled long blonde hair falling over sullen eyes.

The question took Gilmour by surprise. They rounded a building towards a gate where a heaving tumult of television crews and reporters clamoured for pictures of anyone even remotely resembling SAS. A reporter ran towards the bus flashing a camera. Gilmour hung his head and put a hand up to hide his face. The coach crawled through the jostling throng, helped by police officers who understood the Regiment's need for secrecy.

'Bloody reporters,' someone moaned.

'Only doing their job,' said someone else.

'Should get themselves a proper job then,' retorted the first.

'If you were at home, you'd be glued to the telly just like everyone else.'

'Look . . . isn't that Kate Adie?'

'So it is,' said the bloke, waving out the window.

'About time she got her tits out for the lads, I reckon.'

The gate closed behind them and the coach picked up a little speed, headed towards a brightly illumined block of offices away from the main terminal. Dozens of excited faces peered out through the windows of a large office on the second floor.

'Heard the Prime Minister was about,' said one of the blokes to the guy next to him, his voice laced with awe.

Gilmour didn't feel like going into that office anymore than he wanted to answer Angelina's question.

'Why? Where's your daddy sweetheart?'

'He's dead.'

She looked up at him, her eyes questioning, her face sad. Gilmour couldn't hold her gaze and looked away. What could he say?

'Your mummy will be fine sweetheart. She'll be just fine.'

Angelina frowned and looked down at the floor. She knew when she was being lied to.

'C'mon Jamie,' scolded Black, turning round in the seat in front, his deep, throaty cockney accent uncharacteristically gentle. 'The girl needs a new dad for a while, awright.'

'Ang, it's not that simple,' said Gilmour gently, throwing Black a dirty look.

She searched his face, her legs kicking over the edge of the seat, giving him no way out.

'What's a wanker?' she asked innocently.

Black coughed and turned swiftly in his seat.

'I tell you what,' said Gilmour quickly, wriggling his way out of trouble. 'I'll talk to a few people and we'll see. Maybe I can come and visit you until your mum gets better.'

The bus drew to a halt outside the offices. Older men in suits and pretty young personal assistants were holding their hands up to the windows, trying to see out into the night. Compressed air hissed again as the door swung open. The bus juddered as blokes grabbed their weapons and kit and got up to leave. Gilmour, though, was in no hurry. Backslapping politicians ostentatiously spilling expensive champagne weren't his idea of a good night out. Angelina sat somewhat pensively beside him, thinking through his offer.

'Okay,' she said finally, deciding it was as good a deal as she was going to get.

Brushing her hair behind her ears, she stopped kicking her legs and waited, determined to show her new daddy what a good girl she was.

Chapter 2

Electricity crackled through the computer's circuitry as Gilmour fumbled in the dark for the power button. With heavy eyes, he sat at his desk in a corner of his bedroom and gaped at the flickering screen. Leaning his elbows on the desk, he stuck his head in his hands. Words came up on the monitor and he stared at them through his fingers. But as usual they were not there long enough for him to make any sense of. His bed creaked. He glanced over his shoulder at the restless bundle tucked up in his duvet. Had it really happened? Had he really done that back at the terminal?

His head went back into his hands. Why couldn't life just be simple? The Windows start-up tune sounded through the speakers and his Desktop appeared. It was an effort to lift his head. Staring vaguely at the screen, he moved the cursor to his ISP and double-clicked. He nodded at the monitor as if asking for its support. The modem dialled the number and fuzzy fax noise hissed from the computer.

'Welcome,' said the computer. 'You have e-mail.' Gilmour looked up tiredly. E-mail? But before he could click the icon to open his mailbox, the news headlines leapt out at him.

SAS Storm Hi-Jacked Aircraft.

A photograph of the tail of the aircraft just visible through billowing smoke and flame waited for a click of his mouse to transport him to the story. Janeway and the crew of Voyager had probably seen the footage out in the Delta quadrant. He didn't feel like reading about what a hero he was and clicked the icon to open his mail. It was from his girlfriend.

Hi Jamie
Sorry hun, I can't go on. I never get to see you and whenever we have a date, I never know if you're going to turn up. I know it's not your fault, but you must understand.

Gilmour stopped reading, his eyes burning. It had finally happened.

Was that you on the telly? I cried I was so proud! I also cried because I realised I could never have you, that your work would always be more important to you than me. I'm not complaining Jamie, I've never been so happy since I met you.
Please don't think badly of me. I hope we can still be friends. I'd like that more than anything. I'm sorry if this hurts you, but I just can't go on – worried sick every day, wondering if you are still alive,

wondering if you haven't turned up because you're dead. I'm always sick with worry. When that bomb exploded last night I thought . . . well, I just can't take any more.

> *I'm sorry I can't be stronger for you,*
> *Your good friend,*
> *Karen.*

Gilmour read the e-mail twice. It was all over? Just like that? An emotional shell whistled in and exploded. The pain was unbearable. Moving the pointer over the little cross in the top right corner of the screen, he clicked the mouse. A dialogue box asked him if he was sure he wanted to sign off.

'Damn right I do.'

He winced at the pain stabbing through his chest.

'Goodbye,' said the computer pleasantly.

'Fuck off,' he whispered with a groan.

He shut down the computer and the house went strangely quiet. So quiet, he could almost feel Angelina's gentle breathing behind him. The pain was dreadful. His career with the SAS would be over, that was for sure. Now what was he going to do? Go back to the Paras? The police would probably be looking for him too. And how was he going to sort out this mess with Karen? Taking a deep breath, he swung in his swivel chair, got up and left the bedroom.

Morning light glimmered through the cracks in the living room curtains. How long he'd been asleep in his armchair, he had no idea. Outside, birds chirped merrily, the only sounds in the stillness of the early dawn. He listened to them for a while, trying to figure out what the little bastards had to be so chirpy about. His head thumped and his feet ached in his boots. He ran a furry tongue along his split lip where he'd bitten it during the assault and wondered why he had a hangover when he'd not even had a drink. It didn't seem fair. Disgusted with life, he closed his eyes and tried to go back to sleep. It was no use. He groaned and sat forward massaging his neck. A glance at his watch told him Angelina would soon be up. Pain or no pain, he had to make sure they both had a damn good breakfast. It was going to be a long day.

Closing the living room door quietly behind him, he strolled across the kitchen towards the fridge. He toyed fleetingly with the idea of dropping Angelina off at his parents and jumping the country. He had an ex-SAS mate in Kenya with a few bob who was always offering him security work. A new life shooting ivory poachers seemed more appealing right then than facing the Colonel. *Karen!* Leaning his forehead against the top of the fridge, he clenched his fists and screwed his eyes shut. *This was shit!* Well, whatever it was, he had to get some breakfast on. Grabbing a pack of sausages, he closed the fridge door, walked over to the cooker and rattled the frying pan onto one of the rings. With a sharp knife, he separated the sausages and laid them carefully in the pan.

'What are you still doing here?' he muttered to himself, rummaging around in the breadbin.

Opening the kitchen window, he frisbee'd a stale slice of bread out into the back garden.

A few sparrows darted out of the hedges and hopped cautiously over the grass, keeping a wary eye out for the cat. A jackdaw, attracted by the twittering sparrows, swooped down onto the clothesline and bounced about awkwardly, struggling to keep its balance. Morning sun peeked over the horizon and bright sunlight streamed through the trees at the bottom of his garden. Gilmour looked up as two crows thundered in over the trees. The sparrows knew they were up against it and got tore into the bread as the crows thumped down onto the guttering above the back door. Gilmour leaned over the sink for a better view. The jackdaw, fed up bouncing about like a prick on the clothesline, dropped to the grass, scattering the sparrows. With a last look around for the cat, the crows decided to muscle in. The jackdaw though, was ready. Grabbing the bread in its beak, it took off and legged it over the trees. But it didn't get very far. A squawking seagull dive-bombed it and the startled bird banked away, dropping the bread. Like a squadron of scrambled spitfires, the sparrows flew off into the trees after the tumbling bread.

At least, thought Gilmour, watching a small feather drift round his garden, he didn't have to spend all day scrounging his next meal only to have some bastard crow nick it. Or did he? He saw a vision of himself at a petrol pump, a black-hooded politician sticking his sweaty fingers into his pockets as he filled up. *Bastards!* That was definitely his word for the day. With a last scout about for crumbs, the crows lumbered away and Gilmour closed the window.

Slicing open a pack of bacon, he laid a few rashers beside the now sizzling sausages. Another spasm of pain stabbed him. He was going to have to call Karen and get things sorted.

'Morning,' said a sleepy voice.

Angelina stood awkwardly in the doorway, watching

him with her sad green puppy eyes, her long dishevelled hair tucked behind her ears.

'Hi sweetheart.'

Gilmour suddenly felt incredibly guilty. Here he was feeling sorry for himself and yet there was a young girl with more problems than he could possibly imagine.

Angelina burst into tears.

'I want my mummy.'

Gilmour didn't know what to say. He didn't even know if her mother was still alive. She sniffed and bravely wiped away her tears.

'Are you crying?' she asked, looking up into his bleary eyes.

Gilmour shook his head dumbly and gave her a stupid smile.

'I hope you like bacon, sausages and egg,' he said, changing the subject.

'You *are* crying,' she said, somewhat bemused.

'Toast?'

'Smells nice,' she agreed reluctantly, looking at the cooker and deciding she was hungry.

'How's your head?' asked Gilmour, popping a couple of slices of bread into the toaster.

'Sore and I hope you have butter and not margarine.'

'I've got both and you can have peanut butter too if you like.'

She pulled a face.

'What's wrong with peanut butter?'

'Yuck.'

'It's lovely with tomato sauce.'

She stared at him in horror as if she'd just lifted a rock and found him crawling about underneath.

'*Yuck!*'

Gilmour pulled a face and reached into the fridge.

'Will we see my mummy today?'

'I don't know. Depends.'

Her deep eyes probed him, watching him, waiting for his next words.

'Okay,' said Gilmour, 'I'll phone the hospital in a minute and then my work. If everything's fine, we'll drive through to London straight after breakfast. Deal?'

She nodded.

'But you better be ready for the worst. Your mum might not make it.'

Somehow, he got the words out.

Angelina ignored them.

'Why did you hit that nasty man?' she asked.

The question caught Gilmour off guard. He'd never actually talked to an eight-year-old girl before, at least, not since he was eight, and he'd had some hazy notion they were stupid, giggly things that played with dolls all day. But this young lady could read him and he could feel her eyes. It was a good question.

Why had he hit him? Why had that stupid social worker pissed him off like that? Why did he have to try to take Angelina from him by force? He couldn't believe he'd actually thumped him and stormed out of the terminal with her tucked under his arm. She had given him a funny look as they'd jumped into an SAS Range Rover and driven off. The last thing Gilmour had seen had been the Colonel running after them, gesticulating wildly in his rear view mirror. A lot of people were going to be howling for his blood.

'Because,' replied Gilmour, thinking he was being clever.

'Because what?'

'Just because.'

Angelina struggled to pull a seat out from under the pine kitchen table. She was clearly not impressed. Gilmour turned the sausages one last time, switched on the kettle and turned to face her.

'Tea or coffee?'

'Juice.'

She didn't look at him.

'I'm out.'

'Milk then.'

She still didn't look at him.

'Okay,' sighed Gilmour, 'I didn't trust him and I didn't want you going off with someone I don't trust.'

She climbed onto the chair, a strange look on her face. Men had never fought over her before. Her feet started kicking under the table.

'I think I like you,' she said.

'Friends then?' said Gilmour, walking over and raising his palm.

'Friends,' she agreed, giving him a high five.

As their hands met, Gilmour felt a tingle run through him. He'd always believed he would one day meet a girl he could die for. He'd just never thought she would be so young.

The breakfast dishes piled in the sink for later and everything switched off, Gilmour grabbed a black leather jacket from a hook in the hallway and slipped it on. The mirror hanging on the wall next to his mounted stag's head reflected dark, lifeless eyes that stared back at him in dismay. He wondered if they would ever sparkle again. He needed a shower and some sleep, but it was going to have to wait. He hadn't had the guts to phone the Regiment. His life was over. His hand slipped into his pocket and switched off his bleeper.

Closing the front door behind him, he crunched the carbon steel, multi-point locking system into place. Angelina was already standing beside the car waiting for him. Her eagerness to get to the hospital poured from her eyes. Gilmour was feeling sick as he locked the front door. The news from the hospital had not been good. The doctor had not been optimistic either. But he couldn't face her with that one just yet. And after the hospital, there was still the Regiment.

Life!

Did it ever let up?

The orange indicator lights on his Isuzu Trooper flashed as he switched off the alarm. He'd return the Range Rover later. Angelina clambered in, pulled the seat belt around her and tried to click the end into the slot. She hated seat belts and just couldn't figure them out. *Why wouldn't the stupid metal bit just go into the stupid slot and stay there?* Gilmour climbed in, waited a few moments and then leaned over to help. She sat back exasperated and allowed herself to be belted in.

'What's the matter hun?' asked Gilmour.

'Oh nothing,' she said, folding her arms and lifting her chin to stare over the dashboard.

'Are we friends or what?' asked Gilmour patiently, keeping his voice very low.

She turned to look at him.

'Well, friends are supposed to tell each other when there's a problem so they can sort it out.'

She looked up into his eyes and wondered what was coming next. Gilmour leaned over and brushed her cheek with a finger.

'You don't like people helping you like that, do you?'
She shook her head.
'Tell you what. If you need help, you ask okay?'
'Okay.'
'Otherwise I'll leave you alone. Deal?'
She faced the front somewhat happier and Gilmour found himself suddenly longing for children of his own. He gunned the engine and pulled away from the cottage, his thoughts turning once more to the forbidding chasms ahead.

If he hadn't been so tired, perhaps he might have noticed the black Mondeo parked a little way down the road in the shadow of a large horse chestnut tree. If he hadn't been in such emotional turmoil, perhaps he might have noticed the tinted windows which prevented anyone from seeing the single male occupant behind the wheel. He should have noticed; it was his job. It was what he was trained to do, what kept him alive. Whatever the reasons, he drove on, oblivious to the cold eyes staring after them in the Mondeo's rear view mirror.

Chapter 3

As he looked through the large window into the ward, it occurred to Gilmour that Angelina's mother, whose pale cheeks were as white as the bandages swathing her battered head, looked about as dead as any corpse he'd seen. Had it not been for the beeping monitors and flickering lights on the equipment arranged around her bed, he'd probably have called for a nurse. Angelina stood on her tiptoes and peered in, her face streaked with tears.

'Why is there a tube sticking up her nose?' she sniffed.

Gilmour took a tissue from his pocket.

'Here.'

Angelina looked up at him.

'Well?'

A kindly hand rested on her shoulder.

'You'd better ask the nurse that when she comes back.'

'And what's that watery stuff in the plastic bag?'

She blew her nose and then used the windowsill to pull

herself up on her tip-toes for a better look.

'Well, your mum can't eat or drink, so that stuff takes care of it.'

'How does that work?'

'All the nutrients, the . . . er, you know . . . the vitamins and things . . . the stuff that's in food is in the liquid. It goes from there through the tube into her arm.'

'Why doesn't it go into her tummy?'

Gilmour sighed.

'You'd better ask the nurse that one too.'

Angelina stared at the rest of the equipment, determined to figure out what else they were doing to her mother.

The promised nurse suddenly breezed out of another ward.

'Hello again,' she greeted warmly, tucking a wisp of hair back up under her hat. 'You can go in now. Just for a few minutes.'

'I'll stay here,' said Gilmour.

Angelina followed the nurse through the door.

Gilmour was glad for some time to himself and watched Angelina through the glass as she walked slowly to the bed and lifted her mother's limp hand. Hurried footfalls echoed down the corridor.

'You must be Gilmour,' said a surgeon brightly, wiping his hands on his white coat as he strolled up. 'I came as quickly as I could.'

Gilmour turned and took the proffered hand without enthusiasm.

'We had a devil of a job getting that damn bullet out,' said the surgeon. 'She's stabilised somewhat, but her chances aren't good.'

'On a scale from one to ten?'

The surgeon stared through the glass.

'Two? Possibly three. But even if she survives, we don't know if any permanent damage has been done.'

'As bad as that huh.'

'Obviously, we're doing everything we can.'

'Thank you.'

'The little girl could be helpful.'

Gilmour toyed with the silent bleeper in his pocket. The Colonel would be going berserk.

'People need something to hang on to in situations like this,' continued the surgeon. 'You know . . . give them a reason to fight. Children often do the trick.'

Gilmour started, his mind replaying something. He was staring down at the corpse of a black African man. The dusty old boots on his feet had no laces and one of them had a hole in the sole. Life was cheap in Sierra Leone. He kept his weapon raised as he stepped over the body. That was when it moved. He bent down and waved the flies away. The eyelids flickered open and the man tried to say something. Gilmour put his ear closer to the man's mouth.

'My wife is having a baby,' said the man weakly, his voice barely a croak. 'Please, she needs me.'

The casualty evacuation helicopter roared away into the African dusk in a flurry of sand. Gilmour watched until it was but a speck in the shimmering heat haze. He sat down on a rock to ponder life. That the will to live had been so strong in someone with so little to live for had affected him deeply. He looked in at Angelina and her mother and finally understood.

'Are you okay?' asked the surgeon, looking at him closely.

'Yes, I'm fine. What other problems could there be?'

'Brain damage, paralysis – although that doesn't look likely now – coma, maybe even—'

'I get the picture.'

The surgeon's voice lowered with respect.

'Look, I know who the girl is and I've spoken to a few people. Were you one of the guys at the airport?'

'Yes.'

'Good job.'

Gilmour grimaced. The aircraft assault seemed like a million miles away.

'You don't think so? Well . . . a lot of people owe their lives to you.'

'I just did my job.'

'Like I said – good job.'

'Thanks.'

Gilmour nodded. Yes, things could have been a lot worse.

Down the corridor, a set of double swing doors clattered open and a trolley hurtled through being pushed by two frantic nurses. On the trolley, a young man writhed about in agony under a bloodstained sheet. The surgeon looked deeply into Gilmour's eyes, tilted his forehead perceptibly, then turned and strode off down the corridor. Gilmour watched until they all disappeared through another set of swing doors. Like the African man, his life would go on. And so would Angelina's – one way or another.

Another nurse came hastening down the corridor. She smiled at him as she rushed into the ward. Somehow, he managed a smile back. The two nurses exchanged a few words and then one of them walked over to Angelina and put a comforting hand on her shoulder. As Angelina stepped back from the bed, Gilmour opened the door for her and waited. She stepped out, her head down. Gilmour picked her up to let her watch through the window, but the nurses pulled a curtain round the bed. Angelina screwed her eyes shut, her delicate shoulders shaking with grief.

'C'mon sweetheart,' said Gilmour, putting her down. 'Let's go.'

She didn't argue and allowed herself to be led down the corridor.

Chapter 4

As they approached the outskirts of Hereford, Gilmour eased on the brakes, not wanting to wake a sleeping Angelina. He took a corner gently and her head lolled with the movement of the vehicle. Her long hair slipped from behind her ears and tumbled over her eyes. Gilmour felt the warmth of a smile softening his drawn face. Whatever happened when they got to the camp at Credenhill, he felt he was ready for it now.

'We're home,' he whispered, as they drove down the road towards the cottage.

As soon as the words left his mouth, he regretted them bitterly. Angelina lifted her head and stared sleepily out of the windows.

'Are we still friends then?' asked Gilmour, struggling to come to terms with his stupidity.

'Of course, silly,' she said, throwing him a reproving look. 'I'm hungry.'

'What do you fancy?'

'Hmm . . . McDonald's?'

'Bacon sarnies do?'

'Oh, okay.'

'With peanut butter?'

'Yuck!'

Gilmour winced as a chuckle skirmished up through the emotional barricades restricting his throat.

Sunlight filtered through the leaves of the horse chestnut, dappling the black Mondeo's bonnet. Gilmour eyed the heavily tinted glass suspiciously and peered in on the way past. But there was no one inside. He pulled up behind the Range Rover parked outside the cottage and stared thoughtfully into his mirror. Something was bothering him about that Mondeo. But before he could make any decisions, Angelina jumped from the car and bolted up the path to his front door. His fingers tapped the steering wheel. Putting the Mondeo from his mind, he stepped out into the bright sunshine.

He followed Angelina into his hallway, kicking the front door closed.

'Hello mate,' he said, slipping off his jacket as he greeted the stag's head.

Suddenly, he stiffened. The living room door was slightly ajar. He *never* left the living room door open.

'*Shhh . . .* Ang *don't move*,' he hissed.

The tone of his voice made her freeze.

He reached behind him for the SigSauer pistol tucked into the small of his back. Gleaming steel glinted in the dim light.

'*Stay here.*'

She saw the gun and put her hands to her mouth.

Gilmour stepped past her, his head cocked to one side, his mouth slightly open. He paused outside the living room. Blood pounded deafeningly in his ears. He listened, but all he could hear was the faint ticking of the clock in the kitchen.

Diving headfirst through the door, he rolled and came up on one knee, his aim darting round the room. Everything appeared as it should. *Could he have left the door open?* He'd been exhausted, his mind confused and wandering shell-shocked through the battle smoke of warring emotions. He couldn't be sure. Getting up, he stuck the pistol back into his waistband and strode into the kitchen. He tried the back door and it swung open. *He hadn't even locked the back door?* Peering suspiciously at the trees at the bottom of the garden, he made mental plans for upgrading the cottage's security. He was slipping. He thought about checking upstairs, but dismissed it.

'It's okay Ang,' he shouted over his shoulder.

A familiar shadow suddenly fleeted through the trees and a bundle of black fur darted across the grass and shot between his legs. Angelina stuck her head tentatively into the kitchen. Gilmour gave her a reassuring smile and headed for the fridge.

'Ooooo . . . *look!*'

Gilmour spun round, his hand reaching behind him for his pistol. Angelina was on her knees, a big smile on her face. The cat took one look at the outstretched arms and promptly forgot about its plate. Raising an expectant tail high in the air, it trotted over for some cuddles.

'Ooooo . . . what's her name?'

'Scud.'

'*Scud?*'

'And it's a *he*.'

The cat brushed itself against Angelina's legs, nudging her with its head as she stroked it. Gilmour relaxed his grip on the butt of the pistol and wondered what it must be like to live a normal life. He reached for the fridge and winced when he saw the yellow daffodil magnet on the door. Daffodils were Karen's favourite flowers.

'What a *silly* name,' said Angelina.

'Eh?'

'Look, he's all fluffy . . . you should call him Fluffy.'

'*Fluffy?*'

Gilmour opened the fridge and peered in. Back out in the hall, the phone rang. He hesitated, his fingers poised above the bacon. *Damn*. Knowing who it was, he closed the fridge, sucked in a deep breath and walked to his execution.

'Hello?' he said gingerly, holding the phone slightly away from his ear.

'*About bloody time!* It's the Colonel.'

'Yes Boss?'

'*Yes Boss?* Is that the best you can do?'

Gilmour nibbled unconsciously at his swollen lip where he'd bitten it the night before.

'Here are your Orders,' hissed the Colonel. 'Pack up and get back here, now. Bring the girl with you. Do not be late, do not stop anywhere and most of all, do not speak with anyone. Do you understand?'

'Yes Boss.'

'You still have the girl?'

'Of course.'

Gilmour tasted fresh blood.

'Where in God's *name* have you *been?*'

'Seeing the kid's mother.'

There was a pause.

'Then may I assume that you switched your bleeper off just so you'd piss me off? You have succeeded beyond your wildest expectations. Gilmour . . . have you *any* idea what you've *done?*'

'Yes B—'

'Get in here *now* and make sure she's with you.'

'Yes B—'

'If you're not here in half an hour, I'm sending the RSM . . . *you got that?*'

'Yes Boss.'

'Don't *yes Boss* me you bastard . . . out!'

The Colonel slammed the phone down.

Gilmour sucked his freshly bleeding lip. He'd never given much thought to what he was going to do after the SAS. He sauntered back to the kitchen with a rather haunted look.

'Sorry Ang, must go. We'll get something to eat at my work.'

'Aww.'

She wrapped her arms round the purring cat and gave it another cuddle.

'Bye Scuddy,' she said, getting to her feet.

'Suppose I'd better feed the little brute first.'

Gilmour reached into a cupboard for a tin of meat and the cat rushed to its plate.

'What's Scud mean?'

'It's a missile.'

'A *what?*'

'It's because of the way he catches birds.'

'Scud.'

She mouthed the word with little enthusiasm.

Gilmour took a clean plate from a cupboard and forked some meat onto it.

'We've . . .' started Angelina, then stopped, her face scrunching up.

'What is it?'

Gilmour picked up the cat and chucked it outside.

'We have a cat too.'

She stood in the middle of the floor, her head down, tears glistening in her eyes. Gilmour shoved the cat's food out onto the doorstep and closed the door.

As they pulled away in the Range Rover, Gilmour checked his mirror. The Mondeo had disappeared. But something told him he should have taken its registration number when he'd had the chance.

As they drove through the gates of the new SAS base in Credenhill, Gilmour spotted his mate and beeped the horn. Black smiled broadly and strolled over as he parked.

'Missed morning prayers,' reproved Black jokingly.

'Yeah,' said Gilmour, opening his door and glancing round nervously for police cars. 'Nipped through to London. Any trouble yet?'

'*Dick'ead*,' muttered Black under his breath. He ducked down to peer across at Angelina. 'Hiya gorgeous, 'ow you doing?'

She observed him coolly from the safety of her fringe.

'Anything I should know about?' asked Gilmour.

'Nope, it was all Presidential State visit security stuff,' said Black, considering a warning to keep an eye out for a white Transit van of insufficient interest to pass on. That it had been seen hanging around outside pubs in Hereford frequented by Regiment blokes didn't seem important. 'But the Colonel was quite animated when you didn't show. And I think the RSM wants a word.'

Gilmour unconsciously gripped the steering wheel a little tighter.

'See you later gorgeous,' said Black, throwing Angelina a little smile before strolling away.

'What's a RSM?' she asked, watching Black go.

'He's the Regimental Sergeant Major – the one man around here you *don't* want to mess with.'

'Oh,' she replied, not taking her eyes from Black until he disappeared inside a building and the door closed behind him.

The Colonel sat at his desk. A female sergeant stood at ease to one side.

'Good morning young lady,' greeted the Colonel affably from behind his desk as they entered his office. 'Did you sleep well?'

'Yes Sir.'

Angelina stood a little awkwardly, tugging at the sleeve of Gilmour's jacket. The Colonel studied her with his grave eyes.

'Would you like a drink? Or perhaps something to eat?'

'We've not had lunch yet,' said Gilmour, answering before she could politely refuse.

'Yes, well, it's . . . um . . . been quite a day,' said the Colonel, straightening himself. 'Not made any . . . well.'

He let the sentence go unfinished. Angelina was staring up at him with eyes that would melt a glacier. Suddenly his shoulders relaxed and the tension in his face seemed to ease.

'Sergeant Roberts,' he said evenly, turning to the female sergeant.

'Sir!' she replied, coming to attention and saluting.

Dark, smouldering eyes stared rigidly at the window ahead of her, their mystery accentuated by the dark brown hair tumbling out from under her hat, cascading off her shoulders and falling down her back.

'At ease Sergeant,' said the Colonel, not used to being called 'Sir' but obviously enjoying it. 'This is Gilmour and Angelina.

The stamp of Roberts' foot echoed round the office. Angelina looked up at the woman in her immaculate army jacket and skirt with some disdain. Roberts didn't move a muscle. She waited, her hands clasped behind her back, her feet slightly apart, her back straight and her chin up.

'Relax Sergeant,' said the Colonel with a wave of his hand. 'Would you please take Angelina for some lunch? And be back here by . . . let's say . . . fourteen hundred.'

'Fourteen hundred, Sir.'

She snapped back to attention.

'Dismissed,' said the Colonel.

She saluted, turned, stamped her foot down and stepped off.

Gilmour ran his eyes up the slim, elegant curves of her legs to the hem of her skirt. He was sure he'd seen her somewhere before, but couldn't quite place her. Angelina was not at all happy.

'Come along,' said Roberts a little nervously, offering her hand.

Angelina hugged Gilmour's leg.

'It's okay sweetheart,' said Gilmour, crouching to put an arm around her. 'You go get something to eat and I'll be along as soon as I can. Promise.'

Reluctantly she allowed herself to be led away, her face dragging along the floor behind her.

'Sit down Gilmour,' said the Colonel when the door closed.

Gilmour pulled a chair over and sat.

The Colonel tapped his fingers together on the desk in front of him.

'Hmmm.'

Gilmour lifted his head and held his eye.

Deep furrows appeared on the Colonel's silver-hair lined brow.

'Hmmmmm.'

'Am I binned?' asked Gilmour.

The Colonel suddenly sat back in his chair.

'*Binned?* You're damn lucky you've not been slotted!'

Gilmour was unable to hold the Colonel's fiery gaze.

'Social services are barking like wolves.'

'Fair cop.'

'We've also had a couple of Police Officers here looking for you. Ostensibly to help with their enquiries.'

Gilmour's shoulders collapsed. His career was in tatters.

'Not to mention distraught relatives telephoning every ten minutes.'

'Sorry.'

'*Sorry?* You'll see *sorry* when the RSM gets you – I gave him the responsibility of dealing with this.'

'*Oh shit.*'

'What?'

The Colonel stood up almost knocking his chair over. The veins stuck out on his forehead.

'I've even had *Downing Street* on the bloody phone. Have you any idea how difficult things are just now with the President arriving in a few days?'

'I'm sorry.'

The Colonel took a few moments to compose himself

before sitting back down.

'*Don't keep saying that!* What on earth were you *thinking?*'

Gilmour had never felt so wretched. He'd lost everything.

'However . . .' said the Colonel, sitting back.

Gilmour looked up, a little startled by the change in tone.

'. . . the Prime Minister has had a quiet word on our behalf.'

Gilmour felt his skin prickling as his drowning hopes clutched wildly at the lifebelt he'd been thrown.

'The image of the Regiment, of course,' explained the Colonel. 'In simple terms, social services have been told to wind their necks in, a substantial sum of money having been paid to the poor fellow you floored last night for his missing teeth.'

'Boss?'

'Much more than they were worth in my opinion. The police have, therefore, also dropped the matter.'

Relief flooded Gilmour like the rinse cycle of a washing machine.

'But there's still the matter of the girl.'

'Am I still in then?' asked Gilmour pathetically.

'Hmmm . . . I've left that one to the RSM. He's set on sending you back to the Paras. I'm afraid you will be RTU'd, 'returned to unit'. Quite frankly, God forbid my wife should ever hear me speak thus, you've pissed me right fucking off.'

The Colonel continued to study Gilmour closely, his fingers tapping together again. 'Any developments at the hospital?'

Gilmour shook his head.

'The girl's grandparents were finally located this morning, on holiday in the Far East. They had no idea their daughter and grandchild were even on that plane. They're being flown back to Brize Norton courtesy of the RAF and will be arriving here later this afternoon.' Gilmour lifted his head and tried to hold the Colonel's eye.

'They're not exactly enamoured of us either, but the RSM managed to calm them down over the phone by explaining to them in some detail the part you played in the assault. Roberts has been assigned to look after the girl until they get here.' The Colonel sat back, his hands behind his head. 'And you will assist her.'

Gilmour stared back at the floor.

'And remember,' said the Colonel, trying to enjoy at least some semblance of revenge, 'Roberts outranks you. There's a debrief on the hi-jack at fourteen fifteen. Be there. Dismissed.'

Gilmour got up hastily and headed for the door.

'And by the way . . .'

'Boss?'

'I'd try and stay out of the RSMs way for a couple of days . . . give him time to cool off. He doesn't have my kind temperament.'

Gilmour closed the door behind him and glanced about nervously for the RSM. The coast was clear and he legged it to the mess.

He found Roberts and Angelina sitting by themselves at a table in the corner of the mess hall. As he strolled over, the rich aromas from the kitchen made him suddenly very hungry.

'Were you part of the assault?' asked Roberts politely,

wiping the corner of her mouth with a napkin.

'Is that good?' asked Gilmour, looking at Angelina's plate as he sat. 'What is it?'

'Apple crumble and custard.'

Roberts lay her napkin beside her hat on the table and sipped from a glass of water.

'Looks good,' said Gilmour, 'what did you have for main course?'

'Are they taking me away from you?' asked Angelina, eyeing him pensively.

'Your grandparents are on their way.'

'I want to stay with you.'

Her eyes searched his face imploringly.

Gilmour pointed to the leftovers on another plate.

'What was that?'

'Stew.'

'Any good?'

'Bit chewy. The crumble's yummy though.'

'Think I'll have crumble then . . .' He turned to read the menu on the wall behind the servery, '. . . and curry.'

'Not on the same plate?' she asked seriously, remembering his penchant for strange food combinations.

'Maybe I'll chuck in a kipper too,' he added in a brave attempt at humour.

'Kippers! *Yuck*.'

'My name's Philippa,' said Roberts.

Gilmour had difficulty looking up at her.

'Hi, I'm Jamie.'

'The hi-jack was—'

He put a finger to his lips to cut her off and as he did so, the depth of passion and intelligence he saw in her startled him. Angelina stirred her spoon round the bottom of her plate making swirls in the custard.

'But you—' continued Roberts.

He opened his eyes wide to cut her off and tilted his head slightly at Angelina. Then with a supportive smile he got up from the table and walked across the mess, acutely aware of two pairs of eyes following him.

'Fit like Jamie?' greeted the bloke behind the counter in a thick Aberdeenshire accent.

'Shit. Curry and crumble please, mate.'

'We dinnae do shit curry. Fit's the matter laddie?'

'I'm RTU'd. Your curry is always shit.'

The bloke laughed.

'Och, sorry to hear it. Chips or rice?'

'Fried rice?'

The bloke nodded and pointed his ladle towards the table in the corner.

'Bonnie lass that.'

'Gorgeous,' agreed Gilmour. 'Swap places?'

'Ach, I dinna ken,' chuckled the Scotsman, sliding a plate onto a tray. 'Life's complicated enough.'

'Ta.'

The Scotsman ladled runny custard over a plateful of crumble and sneaked another look at Roberts.

'Mind you . . .'

'You're welcome mate.'

Gilmour turned to go and caught Roberts looking at him.

'So Philippa,' he said, when he rejoined them at the table, determined to make an effort, 'why did you join the army then?'

'Why, to learn how to kill,' she replied matter-of-factly.

Angelina looked up at her and Gilmour raised his eyebrows. It was her dark hair that made her so stunning, contrasting her fair complexion in a rather startling manner.

'Really?'

'You?' asked Roberts, noting his interest.

'Long story.'

Gilmour eased a forkful of curry past his sore lip.

'What's it like?' asked Angelina, fighting for his attention.

'Mmmm . . . lovely. Would you like some with your custard?'

'Is *she* going to be with us?'

'I'm sure you and Philippa will get along fine.'

'We have to talk,' said Roberts, feeling the awkwardness. 'Figure out how we're going to do this.'

'Yep, but I don't have much time.'

'Humphh.'

'Sorry Ang, there's a meeting I have to go to after lunch.'

'How long will that last?' asked Roberts.

'Don't know, it's a debrief. Shouldn't be too bad though, the main debrief isn't scheduled until tomorrow.'

Angelina started kicking her legs under the table.

'We have to go,' said Roberts, picking her hat from the seat beside her.

Angelina stared morosely at the pudding plate in front of her, reluctant to leave the table.

'Do I *have* to?' she sighed, looking up at Gilmour rather sadly.

He nodded and shrugged.

With a couple of glances back over her shoulder, she allowed herself to be led away. Gilmour watched her go, emotions he'd never realised existed suddenly fleeting through his heart.

Alone with his crumble, his thoughts turned to the debrief. It was going to be unpleasant. *Should he just keep his mouth closed?* With a groan he put his spoon down and pushed his plate away – he'd eaten far too much. What he was going to say wouldn't be popular. As he was already rock bottom in the opinion polls, he wondered if he should just sit quietly and shut up. He mind went back to the aircraft. Angelina's mother lay pathetically on the runway, her bloodstained dress fluttering in the night wind. With a philosophical sigh, he got up and headed for the door. Being popular had never been high on his list of ambitions anyway.

Chapter 5

Perched on the guttering above the closed windows of the crowded debriefing room, two sparrows cocked their heads and pondered what the deafening buzz of conversation emanating from the normally quiet room could possibly mean. Inside, unaware of the aroused interest of the camp's sparrow population, the men joked and laughed. Still high from the storming of the aircraft, they were revelling in its astonishing success. All of them that is, except Gilmour, who was hiding in a corner at the back of the room, cowering every time the door opened. Anxiety was etching premature wrinkles into his wearied features. He was not looking forward to his confrontation with the RSM one little bit.

Down at the front of the room, standing to one side of a large teak desk that had been freshly polished for the occasion, the Colonel glanced irritably at his watch. The door swung open and Gilmour cringed. The Colonel looked up curiously. Black strolled in, closed the door behind him and squeezed his way to the back through the packed chairs.

'Awright mate?'

'No,' said Gilmour unhappily.

'What's the matter?'

'Oh, you know . . . *life!*'

'Yeah,' replied Black glibly, settling his backside onto the seat next to him and stretching his legs, 'I know what you mean.'

'I doubt it.'

'Come on . . . can't be that bad.'

'Worse.'

''Eard the police were sniffing about, but it was sorted wasn't it?'

'Yep, they're no problem.'

'Sorted then.'

Gilmour turned to his friend, fighting to keep his emotions in check. His voice trembled.

'I've been RTU'd.'

Black dropped the smile and his flighty manner. Empathy suddenly oozed from the pores of his skin.

'What are you going to do?'

Gilmour shrugged.

'When did this 'appen?'

'When the RSM finds me.'

'Not binned yet then? Maybe there's 'ope.'

'Yeah right . . . you know what he's like.'

'You don't know 'im mate . . . e's 'ard, but fair.'

Gilmour slumped forward with the innocent sadness of an abandoned puppy. He put his elbows on his knees and his face drooped into his hands. Black decided to change the subject.

''Ow's the tart with the legs and the gorgeous tits then?'

'Karen?'

'Nah . . . 'ilary Clinton.'

'It's over.'

'*Wha . . .*'

'Yep.'

'*What?*'

Gilmour lifted his head and sat back.

'When did *that* 'appen?'

'She e-mailed me last night.'

Black decided to drop that subject too. There was no digging a man out of a hole left by a woman like Karen.

'Not your day mate. What're you up to later?'

'Looking after the ladies.'

Black was suddenly very interested.

'The sergeant with the kid?'

'Yep.'

'She's . . . um . . . a bit of a hunny.'

'Yep.'

Gilmour noted his mate could pronounce his *h*'s when he wanted to.

Black's mind slipped up a gear.

'Going shopping later? My motor's in for a service and I could do with getting some grub in.'

'Could nip down the supermarket in Hereford I suppose . . . I'll check with the ladies.'

'Awright!'

Without warning, the door flew open. Gilmour unconsciously gripped the edges of his seat. A sergeant marched in escorting two men wearing dark suits, one of whom was carrying a briefcase. Both men were in their forties, both had grey hair and both wore wide smiles.

The Colonel nodded a greeting and then motioned towards the chairs behind the desk. As the two men took their seats and calmly looked about them, the banter was gradually displaced by a silence that sparkled with expectancy. A few of the men sat forward in their chairs. The sergeant left, closing the door behind him.

'Good afternoon gentlemen,' said one of the new arrivals.

The silence became exquisitely tangible.

'My name is Peterson and I'm from the Home Office. You may call me Peterson. And this is my colleague, Jefferies.'

Peterson waited for the nods to subside before continuing.

'Good job last night.'

He undid the button on his double-breasted suit jacket and glanced round the room, holding each man's eye in turn until he got to Gilmour.

'*Good grief!*' he mouthed quietly.

Jefferies, the younger of the two men, though you wouldn't have known it from his lined features, raised a puzzled eyebrow.

The Colonel sidled over to the door, making himself as unobtrusive as possible.

'Stay alert,' mumbled Peterson, taking a minute to collect himself.

He'd been in politics long enough to know something was coming their way.

Suddenly he brightened. Sitting forward, he clasped his hands together on the desk in front of him.

'The Prime Minister has asked me to convey his personal thanks,' he smiled, warm wrinkles crinkling the corners of his eyes. 'And to extend a personal invitation to you all to join him and his wife at Number 10 for drinks – with partners of course.'

It was no less than the men had anticipated and he waited for the appreciative buzz to subside before continuing.

'The operation was a huge success.'

As his eyes once more met Gilmour's, his voice tailed away. Jefferies, realising something was up, followed the minister's gaze. Gilmour began to feel very uncomfortable.

'Is there a problem?' asked Peterson, deciding to take the initiative.

Gilmour coughed to clear his dry throat.

'Not so much a problem Sir, as a suggestion.'

Gilmour hesitated as everyone in the room turned in their seats.

'*Dick'ead*,' whispered Black under his breath.

'And you are?'

'Gilmour Sir, Corporal James Gilmour.'

The legs of his chair squeaked on the floor as he got stiffly to his feet. No one noticed the two sparrows fluttering off. Jefferies slipped a pen from the inside pocket of his jacket and took a notebook from his briefcase.

'With all due respect Minister,' began Gilmour, the rehearsed words tripping awkwardly from his clumsy lips, 'I believe government policy on the handling of aircraft hi-jacks should be reviewed.'

Jefferies stared at him incredulously. A few of the men muttered unintelligible remarks, their import legible only from their tone. Peterson seemed unmoved.

'You think the operation last night could have been *improved* on?'

'I didn't say that sir.'

'But we all just heard—'

Gilmour cut him off.

'The operation was brilliantly planned and executed.'

Peterson smiled like a procurator fiscal in the middle of a difficult case who'd just had irrefutable evidence slammed on his desk.

'I said I believe *government policy* should be reviewed.'

The silence in the room was complete.

'Re – viewed.'

Peterson chewed the syllables over. This wasn't what he'd been expecting at all.

Gilmour fidgeted with his trouser pockets.

'Yes of course,' said Peterson. 'There are always lessons to be learned.'

'No Sir, I don't mean the operation itself.'

'You can call me Peterson. I fail to see how we can possibly improve on *complete* success.'

'It wasn't complete.'

'Ah!' Recognition shone in Peterson's eyes. 'You mean the young woman who was shot.'

Gilmour nodded.

'Not much we could have done about that, I'm afraid.'

Peterson leaned forward over the desk and picked up a pencil. Jefferies slipped him a note. He looked down at it and nodded. The pencil started spinning in his fingers.

Gilmour drew a deep breath before embarking on his next rehearsed line.

'Had we gone in sooner—'

He didn't get to finish.

'Aren't you the soldier who assaulted a professional young man last night at the airport, without provocation, simply for carrying out his duties?'

Gilmour was taken by surprise.

'I'm trying to be helpful here.'

'And then kidnapped a young girl, one of the hostages?'

'*Kidnapped?*'

'For your information Gilmour, I am of the belief that last night government policy was responsible for saving the lives of over one hundred passengers and crew.'

'The success of the operation,' snapped Gilmour icily, stung by the minister's remarks, 'was down to the professionalism of the Regiment.'

The pencil stopped spinning.

'The girl's mother was shot by terrorists, not by government policy.'

'The girl's mother was shot *because* of government policy.'

The pencil clattered angrily onto the desk. The Colonel glowered in Gilmour's direction. Peterson kept his voice low.

'We do not storm an aircraft until a hostage has been shot because we consider that the *best* way of ensuring their safe release.'

'Well . . .' said Gilmour, holding the minister's eye, the words rattling up his dusty throat and clattering through his teeth like demolished bricks, '. . . you're wrong.'

A subdued rumour rippled round the room.

Peterson frowned.

The Colonel rolled his eyes. He'd been looking forward to a quick debrief and getting home early to some of his wife's nasi goreng, his favourite oriental curry.

'There's a lot of anger in your words Gilmour,' observed Jefferies, taking a break from scribbling.

'If you'd seen the girl on the runway beside her mother last night, Sir, or been with them at the hospital this morning, you'd be angry too.'

Peterson threw his arms up.

'You think we don't care?'

Gilmour felt a nudge against his leg.

'*Shut up*,' hissed Black from behind his hand.

'I didn't say that, Sir.'

Peterson sat back and put his hands behind his head. The Colonel thought of intervening, but instead leaned back against the door and folded his arms. Jefferies whispered something under his breath.

Gilmour continued.

'Things could be a lot easier for us.'

'Things are *never* simple in politics.'

Gilmour shook off the patronising remark.

'You couldn't possibly pick a worse time to assault.'

Peterson unconcernedly took a handkerchief from his pocket and patted his forehead. With all the bodies packed into the room, the air conditioning was losing the battle. Jefferies looked up from his shorthand.

'What is it you suggest?' asked Peterson.

'We should assault when the commander on the ground thinks we have the best chance of success.'

'Oh, we should just permit the SAS to do their own thing?'

Gilmour swallowed the irritation rising in his throat. Talking to politicians was like trying to wrap an eel round a bar of wet soap.

'No, Sir, I didn't say that.'

'Will you stop calling me *Sir*. And by the way, where was it you said you studied politics?'

'*Politics?* What do *you* know about assaulting aircraft?'

The Colonel made to intervene.

'It's okay Colonel,' said Peterson, slipping off his jacket

and hanging it over the back of his chair. 'I guess I deserved that. It's getting warm in here. Go on.'

'We should go in when *we* think it best – not when *you* think it politically expedient.'

Peterson sighed with exasperation.

'The hi-jackers know they're safe unless they shoot someone. It keeps their fingers off triggers. Nice and relaxed for as long as possible. That's how we like it.'

'*Relaxed?* What about the hostages?'

'What?'

'The hostages. They know one of them is going to be shot before anyone comes to help them. But they don't know who. What do you think that kind of mental torture does to people?'

'Your point?'

'We're ready. Everything is in our favour. It's a soft target. We have the best possible chance of successfully rescuing the hostages. But we do nothing.'

'A *peaceful* solution, we've been negotiating for a *peaceful* solution.'

'We wait until they murder someone. They've stepped over the line and now they've nothing to lose by murdering again. They're switched on and they're expecting us. It's not a soft target anymore. *Now* we get the order to assault. It's no longer a safe solution, but you already know that from previous hijackings. That's why you wait. Because you need a death to justify your actions. It's madness.'

'It's a dangerous situation.'

'It's a lot *more* dangerous than it should be and not just for the passengers either. And one of them is now dead.'

'The safe release of the hostages is our *primary* concern.'

'With all due respect, Minister, if that were true we would assault when we had the best possible chance of rescuing them. The political expediency of the hostages is your primary concern.'

'Going in before we've exhausted every avenue towards a peaceful solution just isn't democratic.'

'Oh, and what about the mother? What about her democratic rights? Doesn't she have the right to our protection? Are the rights of foreign criminals more important than the rights of British citizens?'

For once Peterson didn't have an answer.

'Taking out the terrorists when everything is in *our* favour,' asserted Gilmour, driving home his advantage, '*must* be the safest option for *all* the hostages.'

'That may be so,' conceded Peterson, 'but the political implications of a shoot-to-kill policy are incomprehensible.'

'That's bullshit and you know it. All you do is sit back and make no decisions. You wait for the terrorists to kill a hostage so that the decision is not yours to make. That way, if things go wrong, you can waggle your finger at the Regiment and say it was our fault.'

'Okay Gilmour,' said the Colonel, unfolding his arms and stepping away from the door, 'that's *enough!*'

'It's okay Colonel,' said Peterson with a tired wave of his hand. 'Is there anything else?'

A few of the men were beginning to shift about on their seats in the heat. Jefferies wiped his sweaty palm on his knee and loosened his tie.

'Your points have been noted Gilmour,' said Peterson, winding down the discussion, 'and an official acknowledgement will be issued by my Office in due course.

Thank you. Are there any other questions?'

Gilmour sat down, uncomfortably conscious of the wet patches that had grown under his arms. Jefferies clicked his tongue and looked up from his notebook. Peterson, anxious to get to the Officer's Mess before the next meeting, stole a glance at his watch. He needed a stiff gin and tonic.

'If there's nothing more?'

Heads shook, anxious for fresh air.

'Then that concludes our business gentlemen. Invitations will be forthcoming from the Prime Minister's private secretary shortly, though it won't be until after the President's little visit as we're all rather busy just now. That'll be all.'

Chairs scraped and the buzz of conversation again filled the room. Gilmour couldn't help but notice that the laughter was now conspicuously absent. Jefferies stuck his notes in his briefcase, slipped his pen into his pocket and stood up with Peterson to chat to the men as they left.

After the handshaking, the Colonel approached Peterson with a wan smile on his face.

'Dreadfully sorry about that Minister,' he said apologetically. 'I had no idea Gilmour was going to bring that up.'

'Not to worry, Colonel. Just because he has assaulted an aircraft doesn't make him an authority on the subject. And no one else agreed with him.'

'On the contrary, Minister. We all agree with him. He is right and you and your policy are wrong.'

'I beg your pardon?'

'I said, he is right and you—'

'I know what you said, Colonel. But surely you can't

agree with him?'

'Oh, but I do. Each time you delay, the risk to the hostages and the lives of my men increases. Sooner or later, if this wait policy of yours continues, we will lose men, hostages and an aircraft, probably all at once.'

'But—'

'No buts about it Minister. The rest of the teams agree with Gilmour, it's just that they know you don't want to hear it and are happy to head off for a drink in the Mess. Gilmour knows he's finished in the Regiment and has nothing to lose by speaking up. Now you are on public notice in respect of your policy, so, if something happens down the track the Regiment won't be blamed. The Home Office – specifically you – will be accountable. Gilmore has done us a favour. Now, shall we join them?'

A pale layer of stratus cloud washed the sky, gleaming with golden pools of light where the sun tried to burst through. Gilmour seemed deep in thought as he and Black wandered towards the Mess area. After the crowded debriefing room, it was wonderful to feel fresh air on his face.

For once, Black appeared speechless. Gilmour wondered whether his mate was thinking about the debrief or how he was going to get into Roberts' knickers. Just as he was about to ask, he heard a familiar clump of heavy boots approaching from around the corner of the next building. Gilmour almost fell in his panic to turn and run.

'*You haven't seen me!*'

'Wha . . . ?'

Black looked back with a blank expression, but Gilmour

was gone, ducked in behind another building. The next moment perhaps the most feared man in the British army crunched round the corner.

'Ah . . . *Black!*' bellowed the RSM.

He pulled up short, impaling Black to the ground with his dark gaze.

Black took an involuntary step backwards.

'Yes Billy?'

The RSM was struggling to control his temper, his bushy eyebrows bristling beneath a high forehead red with anger.

'Where's that little shithole mate of yours?'

'I . . . er . . . I . . .'

'*Speak up! Where is the 'orrible little bastard!*'

'I . . . I don't know.'

'Wasn't he at the debrief?'

'Yes Billy.'

'Well, where did he go?'

Black shook his head, his guilt spilt all over his face. The RSM leaned forward, his lips pulled back, and whipped a folded slip of paper from the top pocket of his combat jacket.

'*Well you tell that little shithole when you see 'im, I have a travel warrant for 'im. The poncy Paras can have 'im back!*'

'I . . . er . . . yes Billy.'

The RSM glowered at him for a few more seconds. Then, with a grunt, he marched off, his radar again sweeping the camp for signs of the enemy.

Gilmour waited until the heavy boots had clumped off into the distance before daring to sneak out from his hiding place.

Black was shaking.

'Jamie, pack your kit mate . . . you're binned.'

Wheeling a trolley round a supermarket on such a gorgeous afternoon wasn't exactly Gilmour's idea of fun. Neither, it seemed, was it Angelina's.

'Can we go to the pictures next?' she asked.

'Sorry sweetheart,' said Gilmour, trying to sound upbeat and cheerful, though his heart was heavy. 'We have to get straight back.'

'Humph.'

A couple of young boys hanging around a shopping trolley grinned at Angelina. Their mother was too intent on checking prices on shelves to notice they were blocking the aisle.

Black decided to make his move.

'So Philippa . . . where you from then?'

Roberts winced.

'Lichfield.'

'I don't like carrots,' said Angelina, looking with disdain at the rows of tinned vegetables.

'What vegetables do you like?' asked Gilmour.

'Baked beans, yum.'

'*Beans?*'

'Vegetables . . . yuck!'

'Oh I'm sorry,' said the mother suddenly, pulling her boys out of the way.

'That's okay,' smiled Gilmour, easing his trolley past the still grinning boys.

'Nice place Lichfield,' said Black. 'Where about?'

'One of the small villages.'

Roberts took a step away from him, finding the products on the shelves rather more exciting than the interest being shown in her.

'What? Not even brussells sprouts?' asked Gilmour, looking at Angelina in amazement.

She shook her head.

'I *love* brussells sprouts.'

'Yuck.'

'Cabbage? Broccoli?'

Her face screwed up.

Black persevered.

'So Philippa, d'you know 'ereford?'

'A little better than I did yesterday.'

She picked up a packet of cheese sauce and pretended to read the recipe printed on the back.

'I could show you about if you like?'

'Thanks, but I'm going home tonight.'

'Mushrooms,' said Gilmour, 'you *must* like mushrooms.'

Angelina paused, a little uncertain frown on her face.

'Sometimes on pizza. Oooooo *look!*'

She ran off down the aisle towards the pop videos at the far end.

Gilmour nodded and Roberts, glad for the distraction, chucked the cheese sauce back on the shelf and hurried after her.

'She's awright,' whispered Black, when he was sure they were out of earshot.

Gilmour couldn't take his eyes from the back of Robert's legs as she walked away.

'Suppose so,' he sighed, with a quick glance at the time.

As soon as he had a minute, he was going to phone Karen. The pain gnawing away inside must have meant something. Now that he was no longer in the SAS, she might be willing to try again. His eyes were drawn back

69

to Roberts. This was getting complicated.

'They've got a Boys Band video!' said Angelina, running back down the aisle.

'Have they?' said Gilmour, getting down on his haunches to be on her level. 'Would you like me to buy it for you as a pressie?'

She smiled stupidly.

'Okay, go and get it and chuck it in the trolley.'

Something very warm kindled within Gilmour as she pelted back down to the videos. Roberts looked over her shoulder with a smile.

'God, I'd make you smile,' whispered Black.

Roberts was still smiling when they returned.

'That was nice,' she said.

'I'll show you nice,' said Black.

Gilmour groaned.

Roberts lost the smile.

'Excuse me?'

Black gave her a wink and a wide smirk.

Roberts put her hands on her hips and glared at him.

'Okay you two,' said Gilmour.

Angelina placed her video very carefully into the trolley, making sure nothing would topple onto it.

A little later, Gilmour leaned over the trolley and tried to strike up a conversation with Roberts.

'Sorry about earlier.'

She seemed a little amused.

'What for?'

'You know, the . . . er . . .'

'You have a girlfriend then?' she asked.

With a toss of her head, she ran her fingers through her long dark hair, trying to fathom his interest. Angelina popped her head round the corner of an aisle.

'Can we go now?'

'Sure, sweetheart.'

Thankful for the intrusion, Gilmour turned the trolley and headed for the checkouts. He felt as if his heart had just been picked up off a dusty shelf and minutely examined.

Being a supermarket car park, it was busy. Cars growled around in low gears looking for spaces, avoiding clattering trolleys. There was a thrum of traffic from the nearby main road. Everything was so ordinary, Gilmour switched off. Roberts stayed close to his arm, keeping him between her and Black, which he found himself quite enjoying. Angelina trudged along behind them, absorbed in the photos on the back of her new pop video. So normal did things seem, Gilmour took absolutely no notice of the tatty white transit van backed up directly behind the rear of their Range Rover. The painted windows on the back doors, at least, should have raised a curious eyebrow.

Gilmour pressed the button on the car keys and the indicators flashed as he wheeled the trolley round to the back. Two stubble-faced, rather emaciated looking men got out of the transit. Manoeuvring the trolley, he turned his back to them. A leather boot scuffed the tarmac. He looked round, but already knew he was too late.

The driver of the transit put his hand over Angelina's mouth and thrust a pistol under her chin. Black grunted as a pistol poked into his ribs. Roberts froze, waiting for Gilmour to react. The back door of the transit flew open and a figure in a black balaclava pointed a handgun straight at Gilmour.

'*Get fucking in or the kid gets it!*' hissed a Belfast

accent.

It had happened so smoothly, so casually, that Gilmour thought it was just another SAS exercise. He wondered what was going to happen next. Angelina bit into a finger and the driver's face twisted with pain.

'You little *bitch!*'

The Irishman picked her up and hurled her into the back of the transit. She crumpled in a heap and lay still.

Gilmour went for his pistol at the same time as Black. There was a silenced shot.

Black fell to his knees clutching his half-drawn weapon in one hand and his chest with the other. Blood seeped through his fingers and he had a strange look on his face.

'*I wouldn't!*'

Gilmour stared straight down the barrel of a gun. Cold eyes sparkled inside the black balaclava. He weighed up his options as Black toppled over between the Range Rover and the next car.

'Okay,' said Gilmour, deciding he would be of more value to the women alive than dead.

Roberts was ushered into the transit.

Gilmour nodded and she complied, trusting him.

'*Drop the weapon.*'

He let it drop with a clatter.

A few startled folk pushing trolleys stared in their direction, but no one seemed to be running for help. Black stopped writhing on the ground and lay still, a sticky red puddle growing on the dusty tarmac beneath him.

'*Get in!*'

A filthy, mildewed hessian sack dropped over his head as he stepped up into the van. Powerful hands forced him to his knees, frisked him and then cuffed his hands behind his back. Doors slammed, the engine coughed and fired, gears crunched and the vehicle moved off. The driver turned to Roberts.

'*Who the fuck are you?*'

'Just top the slut and dump her,' suggested the bloke in the balaclava.

Roberts bristled.

'Who're you calling a slut, shit for brains?'

The barrel of a pistol clattered against her teeth.

'Any more and I'll shove this down your throat – best blow job you ever had.'

Gilmour was finding breathing difficult in the damp sack.

'We'll take her and let McCann decide,' said the driver.

'Aye, Jimmy'll know what to do.'

McCann!

Gilmour's skin crawled as if someone had kicked a nest of cockroaches all over him. He'd called it wrong. He should have taken his chances outside. *McCann!* He staggered to his feet and launched himself at the back door. They bounced over a kerb and he lost his balance, falling heavily against the side of the van.

'*Sort him out!*' screamed the driver.

Something heavy and metallic scraped off the floor. As Gilmour tried to get back to his feet, Roberts pushed the gun away and made her own move for the back door. Angelina recovered her wits and started squealing. The driver braked savagely and bodies fell everywhere. In desperation, Gilmour wrenched himself to his knees. But before he could concentrate his energy and lunge, a crow bar smashed down on his skull. His world exploded in a flash of bright light and then everything went dark.

Chapter 6

Peter Ellis stepped from his morning shower, the drops of water on his deeply tanned body sparkling in the sunshine glancing in through his bathroom window. Dripping on the carpet, he strolled unashamedly naked into his bedroom, towelling his tight black hair a little more vigorously than was necessary. He was not a happy man.

The towel landed on the duvet spread over his four-poster bed and he slipped on a deep purple dressing gown. It wasn't that he minded problems. Not at all. Sorting out problems was his business. Not the usual problems you would normally associate with everyday life perhaps – like folk on the wrong side of the law, or someone needing a doctor – but problems nonetheless. More often than not, they were the kind of problems that would have heads of state or royalty surreptitiously calling him at unsociable hours of the night. The nervous quivers in their voices were usually justifiable, but why it always had to be the middle of the night was beyond him. He was going to have to put his fees up again. Not because he wanted more money, but to put people off calling. He needed his sleep.

His leather slippers slapped his heels as he strolled through his small castle, a property he'd renovated from dereliction. Not for the first time, he found himself wishing there was a woman around the place. He padded down the stairs and crossed the main hallway to his study. Switching on his computer, he sat at his desk and laid his troubled brow on his hairy arms. His profoundly dark eyes stared at the motes of dust on the polished wood.

Of course he'd heard the news the night before. One SAS soldier gunned down in a supermarket car park, in broad daylight; another taken hostage along with a woman and child. *But in Hereford? On their own turf?* Being ex-SAS, he found that deeply disturbing. Even more disturbing was the fact that the American President's State visit was imminent.

It had been the Prime Minister himself who had phoned. At two thirty-seven a.m. The government wanted answers – fast. Apart from himself and his top cabinet, the Prime Minister had assured him, only the Director of Special Forces, the officer commanding 22 SAS and the heads of Mi5 and Mi6 would know he was involved. Ellis lifted his head and stared at the screen as his computer booted up. With the cabinet involved, the drug peddlers on the streets of Bogotá would probably be whispering his name by now.

The Prime Minister had been prepared too. Just as Ellis had been about to say something derogatory, put the phone down, turn over and go back to sleep, his front door bell had rung. It had been two forty-one a.m.

In a thin rain slanting through the glow of his porch lights, a tight-lipped courier had handed him a brief-case, jumped back into his car and sped off. Ellis had looked at the briefcase and then at the red taillights disappearing into the trees surrounding his castle before realising what had happened.

The climbing sun poked its cheery snout round the periphery of the study's turreted window and sunshine slanted onto the wall behind his desk, softening the luxurious dignity of the wood panelling. He reached down for the briefcase beneath his desk, lifted it onto his lap and opened it. One hundred and fifty thousand pounds sterling – his usual acceptance fee plus expenses. And, of course, one of the inevitable plain brown manila folders that seemed to smell of government.

It occurred to him that he didn't need the money. He could still walk away. But then, when had he ever done anything for money? This job bothered him though. No one, *but no one*, took on the SAS on their home ground. Would the Irish be so bold? If not, then who? He had the feeling that perhaps he was going to need some help with this one.

Setting his Mi5 firewall to maximum Internet security, he logged on and searched the latest news items for any developments on the kidnappings. There was nothing. He signed off and picked up the manila folder from the briefcase. A pile of photocopied documents spilled onto his desk – the complete dossiers on Gilmour and Black at his disposal. The top sheet was a photocopy of a supermarket receipt, the last known contact of both men before the shooting. Mi5 could move quickly when it wanted to. Having nothing better to do, he glanced down the list. Apart from the pop video, nothing looked out of place. His eyes scanned back up the list to the video. It had to be for the kid. A little smile told him he thought he would like Gilmour. Leafing through the rest of the documents disinterestedly, not expecting to find anything useful, he came across a number of photographs of the two men.

'Gilmour . . . hmmm,' he mused, trying to fathom his depth. 'What is it you've got? What is it they want? Was it you, the woman, or the child they were after?'

The mobile phone sitting on his desk rang. Grateful for the distraction, he picked it up, pressed the button and put it to his ear. It was the Director of Special Forces, a brigadier; an SAS fellow officer from the good old days when taking on the enemy meant you could shoot the bastards.

'Peter?'

'Yes.'

'It's John. We have the transit van old chap.'

Ellis sat bolt upright.

'*Already?*'

'Got the call last night.'

'*Last night?*'

'Thought that would please you.'

'Quite the contrary. Where is it?'

'You're a hard man to please.'

'Sorry, where did you say?'

'Still as impatient as ever, what.'

'*John!*'

The Brigadier laughed, exceptionally pleased with the effects of his teasing.

'Where would you like it?'

'Somewhere quiet.'

'Same as last time?'

'That'll do.'

'Already here.'

'Has the Prime Minister been calling you?'

'Not a happy chap.'

'Nor should he be.'

The Brigadier laughed again.

'It's not funny.'

'Of course not, old chap. I'll see you soon then?'

'About two hours.'

'I'll be here.'

Ellis ended the call and jumped up. Taking his Browning 9mm pistol from a drawer of his desk, he slammed a freshly loaded magazine up into the butt. Walking to the window, he opened it and lined up the barrel at a crow perched in a tree. It had been a while. He fired a single shot and the crow toppled from the branch, a bloodied mass of feathers. The thrill of the chase began to flow through his system. He'd found his starting point.

Ellis stood outside the porch of an immense property situated in a sprawling wood just off the M25 somewhere near Epping. He opened his double-breasted suit jacket, not because he was overly warm in the bright sunshine, but because he felt the need to know he could reach the pistol tucked into the small of his back in a hurry. He hadn't liked the sound of the voice on the intercom back at the main gate. Feeling decidedly uncomfortable, he walked up to the door and rang the bell. This job just wasn't sitting right with him at all. The transit had been found too easily.

The heavy oak front door swung open noiselessly. However, instead of being greeted by a well-mannered butler, as was usual, an unshaved ruffian dressed in jeans, shirt and trainers stared coldly at him. Ellis returned the unwarranted lack of simple etiquette by simply staring back, refusing to announce who he was or what he wanted. The ruffian's stare mutated into a scowl. Ellis waited patiently, relaxed in the confrontation, until the ruffian moved aside to let him in.

'After you,' said Ellis, refusing to compromise his tactical advantage.

The ruffian stalked off leaving him to close the door.

Ellis stepped from the sunshine into a cool elegance and sumptuousness that made his castle feel more like a rented suburban house. It didn't seem to matter how many magazines he leafed through, or how many interior decorators he paid vast sums to, his castle was still just a refurbished property. And it annoyed him. More than ever he felt the yearning for a good woman, someone he could share life with. To the majestic ticking of an antique grandfather clock, he padded through the plush pile carpet in pursuit of his escort. As they walked, he admired the old masters hanging on the walls and wondered if he should perhaps take up art. The ruffian opened a door and ushered him into the study. His scowl had noticeably darkened. Not in the least intimidated, Ellis took the pistol from the waistband of his trousers and pretended to examine it as he brushed past him.

'Ah Peter!'

Brigadier Jonathon Kennedy-Rushmore, Director of British Special Forces, was standing by a window, a carton of fresh orange juice in one hand, a glass in the other.

'Like some, old chap?'

'Yes please, John.'

'Did you see the new Constable in the hall?'

'Where's your butler?'

'Oh don't pretend you didn't see it!'

'Of *course* I saw it John. Set you back a bit?'

'A pressie old chap, by golly!'

'By golly,' parroted Ellis facetiously.

'The Butler? Perkins? He's helping out with the preparations at the Palace for the Presidential State visit.'

Ellis slipped off his jacket and followed the Brigadier through another door, his expensive leather shoes echoing on the stone-tiled floor of a luxurious kitchen panelled with walnut. Throwing his jacket over the back of a high chair pushed under the breakfast bar, he turned to the Brigadier who was smiling to himself knowingly as he poured some juice into another glass.

'You didn't like him, did you?' said the Brigadier, nodding towards the study.

'Where *do* you get them John?'

Ellis tucked his pistol back into his trousers.

'A nephew of mine old chap. My sister is down for a fortnight and she's hanging around hoping to meet the President at some point. Damned nuisance, what.'

'Oh,' said Ellis, realising his mistake.

The Brigadier strolled over and handed him one of the glasses.

'Yes, he . . . um . . . likes to look tough whenever I have guests.'

'Folk must expect a lot of him having you as an uncle.'

The Brigadier laughed again.

'Haw haw! Poor bastard, what!'

Ellis drank deeply, involuntarily shuddering at the sharpness of the juice.

'The transit?' he asked. 'Has anyone examined it yet?'

'There's an eager bunch of lads waiting to do just that.'

The Brigadier hoisted himself onto one of the chairs at the breakfast bar and lowered his voice.

'Have you *any* ideas at all?'

'None whatsoever.'

'Irish?'

'Maybe.'

'You don't think it has anything to do with the President's visit, do you?'

'I would doubt it,' replied Ellis. 'It's all a little too messy for an operation of that calibre.'

The Brigadier's shoulders seemed to relax a little. Ellis smacked his lips and eyed his glass approvingly.

'This is good stuff,' he said.

'Not bad.'

'What's its history?'

'Israel, I believe.'

'*Not the juice!*'

The Brigadier was clearly enjoying himself.

'Nothing important . . . self-employed plumbers van reported stolen last week in Manchester.'

'So, John, the Prime Minister's been harassing you.'

It was rhetorical, but the Brigadier considered it prudent to reply.

'Oh come now Peter,' he said, not really understanding Ellis' dislike of politicians. 'He is really quite a decent bloke. And with the State visit almost upon us, can you blame him for being a little cautious?'

'Where's the transit?'

'In the garage.'

'Was it wired or booby-trapped?'

'No. A couple of engineers, first-rate chaps, had a look at it and then we simply hoisted it onto the back of a lorry and brought it straight here.'

'Easy to find?'

'Yes. Actually, that surprised me too.'

'First impressions?'

'The kidnap?'

For once the Brigadier wasn't laughing. His expression said it all.

'Strange one this,' mused Ellis, now more uneasy than ever.

'Different certainly.'

'Gut feelings?'

The Brigadier put his glass down.

'Not good.'

'We had best get on then,' suggested Ellis. 'I don't think time is on our side.'

'Indeed, old chap,' replied the Brigadier, looking suddenly very much older than his sixty odd years. 'Indeed.'

Ellis stood well back from the transit as the back doors were eased open. The throng of forensic experts huddled together by the closed doors of the immense garage maybe didn't particularly understand the serious nature of why they were there, but they had no problem picking up on Ellis' purposeful stance.

The engineer who opened the back doors of the transit glanced at the Brigadier, a haunted glaze to his eyes. The Brigadier nodded and the guy gratefully shuffled to the relative safety of the garage doors. It was a few minutes before Ellis stepped towards the van. Something in the back had his attention, but he didn't want to believe what he was seeing. Just inside the door, placed deliberately where it would be found immediately, was a small cardboard box. In it was a pair of child's blood-stained knickers.

Taking a deep breath, he walked over and poked at the soiled clothing with his pistol. Underneath was a woman's freshly cut little finger. In a corner of the box was a folded scrap of paper. He picked it up and slowly unfolded it. The thick black lettering sent a shiver through him.

Come near me and I'll cut their fucking cunts out.

He folded the note and slipped it into his pocket.
'John,' he said quietly, 'we have a problem.'

Chapter 7

Ellis drove with both hands firmly on the steering wheel of his hired Cavalier. He dropped his eyes to the blood-spattered note on the dashboard. There was something about it that he liked. The note had been a serious mistake. It was giving him a feel for his adversary, a valuable edge he would otherwise not have had. And it gave him information. The finger told him the level of violence he could expect.

He slowed considerably as he hit a heavy build up of traffic. His mobile phone beeped on the seat beside him for the third time since leaving London. Picking it up, he read the number on the display and groaned. If he hadn't been so interested in forensics' examination of the transit, he'd have switched the damn thing off. The mobile bounced back on the seat, the call ignored. The Prime Minister was becoming a pain in the arse.

He wasn't entirely sure why he was even bothering to go and see the owner of the stolen transit. How many people ever knew anything about the folk who stole their stuff? Still, being a good operator, he knew better than to ignore the obvious. Noticing the middle lane was beginning to move a little more quickly than the outside lane, he indicated and barged his way over.

The mobile beeped again. He picked it up and checked the display. This time it was the Brigadier. He pressed the answer button and put it to his ear.

'Peter?'

'Yes John?'

'Would you *please* return the Prime Minister's calls, dammit man!'

'John, I'm trying to stay focused on the important issues here. I don't have time to reassure the PM every five minutes. That's your job. The more points of contact, the more chance of a leak. You know that and so does he.'

The Brigadier coughed.

'Will you please just return his calls; I haven't got time for all this skulduggery nonsense. He's a very busy man right now and he's understandably concerned.'

Ellis noticed with dismay that the outside lane was starting to move more quickly again.

'What is it with this traffic?'

The car that had been behind him before he changed lanes now pulled ahead of him. Wrenching the wheel round, he forced his way back over.

'What's the noise Peter?'

'Oh, just someone blowing their horn at me.'

'The PM doesn't want you approaching the transit owner.'

'Doesn't he now?'

'*Peter!*'

'The report?'

'Blood on a hessian sack has been confirmed as being Gilmour's.'

'The finger?'

'Sergeant Roberts – it's been confirmed.'

'What else?'

'That's it.'

'*That's it?*'

'I'm afraid so.'

'Nothing on the others?'

'Nothing.'

'Nothing *at all?*'

'Sorry.'

Ellis couldn't believe it. The whole thing was so professional it almost stank of government.

'Return to London,' said the Brigadier, 'there's a good chap.'

'No.'

Ellis could almost feel the officer having difficulty composing himself.

'The Prime Minister,' continued the Brigadier indignantly, obviously not accustomed to hearing such a word, 'is merely concerned about the press making more of the story than is absolutely necessary.'

'Is he now?'

'And, frankly, I share his concern. The last thing we need right now is the Americans cancelling the State visit because of sensationalist media reports.'

The congestion cleared and Ellis tucked the phone under his chin so he could change gears.

'I'm going to speak to the owner of the transit John, and that's final.'

'I've been told to order you to return to London.'

'Mi5 want him first eh?'

'Peter!'

His temper somewhat frayed, Ellis switched the mobile off and chucked it back on the seat, its display dark, its circuits dead. He gazed over at some distant low hills basking in the dull sunshine, their flanks shimmering with shades of gold and ochre. It would have been nice to drive over there and climb one of them. To him, sitting on top of a hill with the whole world at his feet was one of life's more exquisite pleasures. And he could have done with some time to think.

As he drove, he realised he had that feeling again, that estranged queasiness he disliked so much. Paranoid? But he *was* different to everyone else. He'd always known that, ever since he'd been a child. He just hated being reminded of it. Most of the time it didn't bother him and he could fool himself into thinking he was just like everyone else. The traffic slowed up again and he yawned like the mouth of a cave. It looked like being a long day.

Ringing the doorbell again and then clattering the letterbox for good measure, Ellis stepped back and checked the nameplate in the orange glow of the street lighting. It was the right address. The house though, was in darkness and the bloke could have been anywhere. He glanced over the garden fence and noticed a light on behind the curtains drawn round the bay window next door. The neighbours were always a good place to start.

Bzzzzzzzzzzzzzzzz

A young woman in a dressing gown opened the door. Long, dark, straight hair fell over sultry eyes. She smiled, greeting him warmly.

'Yes?'

'Hi.'

Ellis found himself smiling a little more broadly than was necessary.

'I'm looking for Gaz.'

'Gaz?'

'Gary next door.'

'Oh Gary.'

'If he'd told me what a gorgeous neighbour he had, I'd have popped round long before now.'

A beautiful smile lit up her face.

'Shhhh,' she said, putting a playful finger to her moist lips.

'*Hunny? Who is it?*'

She glanced back over her shoulder, the movement opening her dressing gown slightly.

'Someone for Gary.'

Ellis allowed his eyes to fall on the pale skin between her breasts.

'*He's down the pub!*'

The woman turned and caught him looking.

'He's down the pub,' she repeated, not attempting to close her dressing gown, her lips enjoying a curious pleasure.

'Pub?'

She pointed to a large red brick building at the bottom of the road, brightly illumined by thoughtful floodlighting.

'See you there later perhaps?' suggested Ellis, knowing he was perfectly safe.

Her face fell.

'I wish.'

'Another time then.'

'Sure.'

With a polite nod, the woman pulled her dressing gown together at the neck and closed her door. Ellis shut the garden gate and wandered down the street towards the pub, his hands in his pockets to hide the rather cumbersome bulge growing in his trousers. He really was going to have to find himself a girlfriend.

Warm air wafted into his face as he pushed open the heavy door and walked into the pub. At one end of the long bar counter, a group of young men in work clothes smoked and supped pints while they chatted. In a far corner, trying to look cool, a couple of youngsters posed by a pool table. An elderly drinker sat by himself at a dark wood table in the shadows of a poorly lit alcove. Feeding coins into a fruit machine at the other end of the bar was a bloke in a blue boiler suit. Ellis took all this in without moving his head or his eyes as he casually sauntered up to the counter to order a bottle of whatever good German lager it was they stocked.

Someone shoved a coin into a jukebox and an Oasis song oozed from the speakers, mingling with the jingles of the fruit machine.

'Sorry pal, nothing German in there,' apologised the barman, wiping his hands with a white tea towel.

To the clicking of pool balls, Ellis leaned over the counter to get a better look.

'Yeah,' said one of the young men near the bar, raising his voice to emphasize his point, 'you should have seen her face!'

A chorus of laughter decorated the pleasant ambience of the bar, an atmosphere only marred for Ellis by the cigarette smoke curling to the ceiling. Much to his chagrin, he had to settle for a bottle of Budweiser.

'Need a glass?' asked the barman, levering the top off.

'Oh yes,' nodded Ellis, who always went out of his way to avoid doing anything even remotely considered 'cool'.

Taking a deep mouthful, he turned to face the pub, licking foam from his lip. Tilting his head back, he took another swallow, enjoying the cool bite on the back of his dry throat. It was time to go to work. Figuring he may as well start with the easy option, he wandered over to the fruit machine.

'I'm not familiar with this one,' he said, nodding politely as the bloke turned. 'Do you mind if I watch, see how it plays?'

'Sure.'

The guy slipped a pound coin into the machine, thumped two flashing buttons below two bell symbols and delicately thumbed the start button.

'I'm Peter, by the way,' said Ellis, feeling his way forward.

'Gary.'

Ellis smiled. Another swig and his glass was almost empty.

'Would you like another drink mate?' he asked, motioning to the bottle on top of the machine.

The third bell dropped into place and the machine flashed wildly.

'Yes ta,' replied the plumber, enjoying the ridiculous tune the machine suddenly cranked out.

'Two more, please mate,' said Ellis.

The barman nodded and slipped the beers from the cooler as a few coins clattered out of the machine into the payout tray.

Ellis leaned over the bar, keeping an eye on the pub in the mirror behind the optics. He was mildly pleased at how easily he'd found his man. It wasn't always so. Three weeks and two continents it had taken him to find his last man. He could still feel that damned howling arctic wind as he peered through his binoculars over yet another frozen Alaskan glacier, finally seeing his man, a mere speck in the distance. Still, at least there wasn't much chance of anyone ever finding *that* body. He'd got what he wanted too and as far as he was concerned, the world was now a better place. At least, thinking that way allowed him to sleep at night.

Glancing round at the plumber, he pondered his next move. He couldn't very well start breaking the guy's bones, which somewhat hampered his style, so he was just going to have to adapt.

'There you go mate,' said Ellis, strolling back to the machine.

'Cheers. You from round here, then?'

'No, came up from Swindon to look at a transit van I saw advertised.'

'A transit? Now there's a coincidence.'

'Really?'

'Amazing. Second bloke in a week asking me about transits.'

The plumber slotted another coin.

Ellis restrained himself.

'Why did you hold the bar there and not the cherry with the two nudges?'

'Normally I would've,' said the plumber, scratching his backside through his boiler suit, 'but I'm feeling lucky and I'm a few quid up. How did it go with the transit?'

'Shed.'

'You'd have liked mine.'

'Would have?'

'Stolen.'

The other bars didn't appear.

'Oh dear,' said Ellis.

'All my bloody plumbing kit in it too. I was on my way to get insurance when it was nicked. Monday morning it was.' He took a sip from his bottle and hit the play button again. 'The insurance ran out on the Saturday, but as I wasn't using the van over the weekend thought I'd just leave it till Monday.'

'Bummer.'

The plumber laughed humourlessly.

'Yep, got a mate to run me into town and when we got back it was gone. And the insurance company don't want to know.'

Two pears fell into place and another few coins chugged out.

'Not like them,' said Ellis sarcastically.

'They reckon it was gone before the insurance began. I'm knackered.'

'What about the police?'

'The police?'

'No word on the van?'

The plumber laughed.

'Not their fault mate,' said Ellis with a smile. 'It's the one worlders. Criminals these days have more rights than victims.' He took the opportunity to step in. 'What did the other bloke want then?'

'Other bloke?'

'Asking about the transit.'

'Oh, the Irish prat I told to bugger off.'

Ellis nodded knowingly and then noticed the plumber had stopped playing the fruit machine and was looking at him suspiciously.

'Is this about the murder in Hereford? As soon as I heard the news last night, I knew. It was my van wasn't it? I've been half expecting a visit.'

Ellis knew it was pointless denying it.

'Forget about your transit,' he said. 'You'll get a new one. You'll get a nice cheque too, if you get ratty.'

'You a copper?'

'Just make sure it's convincing.'

Ellis finished his beer and placed his empty glass on the bar. It was time to go.

Outside it was raining lightly, cooling things down nicely, scenting the air with that fresh, damp smell he loved so much, that scent that was just so *England*. As he strolled to the car, he wondered how he'd blown his cover so easily. *Was he past it?* On the bright side, he'd found his man easily enough and he had the information he wanted. The Irish connection bothered him. That an IRA cell could have been operating on the British mainland just days before the President's State visit was rather unnerving.

Slamming the car door, he laid his head back against the rest. He was tired, and toyed with the idea of finding a hotel for the night. He reached for the blood stained note and picked it up off the dashboard. Easing the crinkled paper open, he read it again and shoved it into his pocket. He started the engine. There was no time for sleep. He had to get across the water to Belfast as quickly as possible.

Chapter 8

Ellis sighed with frustration. Credenhill, the nerve centre of the SAS, at fifteen minutes notice, without so much as raising an eyebrow, had calmly bundled him aboard a helicopter in the middle of the night and whisked him across the Irish Sea. By contrast, his Mi5 contact in Belfast was prevaricating and asking awkward questions, refusing to give him any information whatsoever. To add to his irritability, he badly needed a shower and a change of clothes. He glared at the middle-aged, overweight, balding man sitting behind the untidy desk. Shifting uncomfortably in his chair, he crossed his legs and ran a disapproving eye round the dingy office.

'But Peter,' objected the man, pushing paperwork to one side, 'what about the Good Friday agreement?'

'I don't give a *damn* about the Good Friday agreement,' replied Ellis bluntly. 'I've a job to do.'

'Even if that means threatening the whole process?'

'Frank . . . what *process?*'

The contempt in his voice was unmistakable.

'And, *of course*, you have authorization from some-one in government?'

'As a matter of fact, I do.'

Ellis considered dropping the Prime Minister's name, but refrained. If Downing Street learned that he was in Belfast he would probably wind up in a police cell for a day or two until they found out what he thought he was doing there.

'Frank, we—'

'Don't *Frank* me, what you are asking is *insane*.'

'Trust me.'

Frank laughed drily and ran a palm over the shiny part of his head.

'I'll trust the name – when I know *who* it is and *after* I've spoken to them.'

'I can't tell you.'

Ellis knew he had a fight on his hands.

'Don't give me that *deniable ops* bullshit,' said Frank, bristling, his surly eyes glowering from across his desk a little more brightly than they had for a long time.

Ellis sat for a moment, distracted by the sudden patter of rain on the window of the third floor office. Without Frank's help, he was stuck. Pushing himself from his seat, he strolled over to the window and stared out over the bleak city. He had seen better mornings. He turned from the window, his voice warm.

'Do you miss the Det?'

Frank sighed and sat back in his squeaky leather swivel chair.

'The old times? Sometimes. Actually I do. I just wish I'd tried for Selection now and maybe seen a bit more of the world than this shithole of a place.'

Ellis managed a wry chuckle.

Frank decided to go fishing and nodded towards a portrait of the Queen above a battered filing cabinet where he'd recently discovered a listening device.

'The old times . . . things were much simpler then.'

Ellis glanced at the portrait and nodded in return, acknowledging the gesture. He was starting to sweat under his arms, but he kept his jacket on.

'We didn't think so at the time eh.'

'Has this something to do with that shooting in Hereford?'

Ellis nodded affirmatively.

'No,' he said, for the benefit of those listening in to their conversation.

'Then I'm afraid I can't help you.'

Frank searched through the mounds of paperwork on his desk for a scrap of paper to scribble on.

'By the way?' he said. 'Does the Regiment still fly those helicopters they nicked from the Argies during the Falklands?'

'I came across in a 109, so I guess so.'

'Funny that, isn't it?'

Frank picked up a cheap ballpoint and poised himself to start writing. The pen twiddled in his fingers as he stared down at the blank paper. Ellis knew the man was struggling with his loyalties and turned and looked out of the window. It was time to shut up.

Weeping clouds swept low across the dismal city skyline. Ellis put his hands in his trouser pockets and stared down at the umbrellas going about their business in the street below. A woman hesitated in a shop doorway, unwilling to step out into the rain. She looked up at the building across the road. Ellis met her eye and didn't look away. She was young and pretty. He wanted her to smile, but she didn't. There was no greeting, no acknowledgement that she'd seen him, no nothing. How do you smile at a stranger who could be plotting your murder? The young woman ran to her car and jumped in. Ellis stepped back from the window and wished Frank would hurry up.

'You're right,' said Frank, still toying with the pen, 'things back then were not simple, they were horrendously complicated. Now they're just, I don't know – deranged, insane.'

Ellis looked at him, but said nothing. Frank hunched over his desk, heavy lines carved into his forehead. He knew he was in a corner; that he shouldn't have asked about the shooting. Ellis stole a glance at the clean scrap of paper. Without a word, he went back to his chair and sat down.

'We used to bitch about it all the time, didn't we?' said Frank, eyeing Ellis solemnly, looking for a way out.

Ellis gave him none.

'If we'd known what was coming,' continued Frank, 'maybe we'd have shot a few more of them, huh?'

Ellis stretched out his legs as Frank hurriedly scribbled something down.

'Who's got to you Frank?' said Ellis, getting to his feet quickly, playing his part for the benefit of those listening.

'Fuck you Peter.'

Ellis walked over to the desk and picked up the name and address before Frank could change his mind.

'Sinn Fein shagging you eh?'

'What?' said Frank. 'Just because I won't give you what you want, I'm in someone's pocket, is that it?'

Frank held his gaze steadily and leaned forward while Ellis folded the note without reading it.

'It's dangerous,' said Frank, sitting back again, sighing like an old actor tired of his lines, 'the criminals are politicians now . . .' A thoughtful finger tapped his lip. 'Or is it the other way around?'

'More pigs grunting in the trough down on Animal Farm. So, what's new? Are you going to give me what I want?'

'Like I said,' replied Frank, standing up to signal the end of the meeting. 'You give me a name to check this out with and I'll consider it.'

Ellis knew Frank was scared, but that was hardly surprising now that the traitors in Westminster had succeeded in slipping the enemy into the system.

'You'll regret this Frank. You'll be seeing me again.'

Frank pointed to his office door.

'Fuck off.'

Ellis slammed the door behind him and walked down the dimly lit hallway towards the stairs, conscious of hidden cameras watching his every step. He no longer trusted his safety within the government departments. Keeping his eyes on the threadbare carpet in front of him, his footfalls echoing dully off dark wood panelling, he decided this was the last job he was ever going to do for the British government.

It was still raining when he turned right and drove up the street between rows of parked cars. Finding the right road had been simple enough. Now that he was there, he didn't drive slowly as that would have raised eyebrows. Then again, neither did he drive so fast as to miss details. He drove just fast enough to look as if he was going somewhere. Thankfully, the houses were all clearly numbered.

What struck him most about number seventy-three

wasn't that it was a large detached bungalow, or that there was a new BMW sitting on the driveway, it was the large tree in the garden. It just didn't seem right. He'd gotten used to scum bags having nice things, but somehow he begrudged the tree. Tucked under a jacket on the parcel shelf in the back, the hum of the camcorder was making him distinctly uneasy. It was far too amateurish for comfort but he'd had no time to rig up anything more elaborate.

Across from the house was a covered bus shelter. Inside, taking refuge from the rain was a group of five or six young Irish hard men. He'd known they'd be around somewhere. The dickers always were. A yob with a shaved head and a gold stud in his lip threw him a dirty look as he splashed past. He was going to have to change cars. Following a route he'd memorised earlier from a street atlas, he turned right at the next junction and squinted through the rain-spattered windscreen for landmarks he would recognize at night.

Ellis slipped down in his seat and squirmed his buttocks around to find a more comfortable position. Sitting for hours in a lay-by in an unfamiliar car was murder. He was tired too, having missed a whole night's sleep. The miserable drumming of the rain on the car roof was starting to get to him. Grudgingly, he reached for the radio to drown out the noise.

'*Make sure you're there!*' sang some DJ, interrupting a decent song to hear the sound of his own voice, '*if you're lucky, you might even get the chance to touch me!*'

Ellis swore and hurriedly switched the radio off again. He was just going to have to put up with the pattering of the rain.

Watching the passing traffic in his rear view mirror, he began to have serious doubts. *What if his old IRA contact had changed sides again?* He glanced down at the keys dangling from the ignition. All he had to do was turn them and go.

A tatty old tan Ford Sierra, rusted round the wheel arches, indicated and pulled off the main road. He really wanted to turn those keys. The car drew up ahead of him and stopped, its engine still running. The driver was alone. His finger on the trigger of the pistol in his pocket, he drew a deep breath and got out of the car.

'*Chrissake* Peter,' said the driver of the Sierra as he jumped in.

'Hello Pat, been a long time.'

'Not long enough, you *bastard.*'

'Sorry mate, it's important.'

'It always is with you, so it is.'

Pat dropped a large brown envelope into his lap.

'This should cover your expenses,' said Ellis, reciprocating with bundles of bank notes.

'*Jasus, Mary and Joseph!*' whistled Pat, lifting the bundles with both hands, his eyes bulging.

Ellis opened his envelope and checked inside.

'*Jasus!*' exclaimed Pat again. 'How much?'

'Twenty grand.'

'*Twenty grand!*'

'My client is being generous.'

'*Jasus!*'

Ellis looked at him over the top of the envelope.

'If it's too much . . .'

Pat shoved the wads into his pockets and stared ahead through the windscreen. Ellis went back to sifting through the envelope's contents.

'Who's paying you?' asked Pat, a trickle of sweat running down his temple.

'The British taxpayer.'

Ellis slipped a large black and white photo half out of the envelope.

'When can I get near him?'

Pat took a pistol from his pocket and laid it in his lap. Ellis stopped what he was doing and peered over the top of the photograph.

'Don't fuck with me Peter.'

Ellis slipped his Browning carefully from his pocket and laid it on the floor.

'He has a date tomorrow night,' said Pat, looking down thoughtfully at the pistol.

'Dickers?'

'New girl, so they won't be around. He won't want to scare the shit out of her just yet.'

Ellis dropped his eyes back to the photograph.

'And where will you be?'

'Don't worry, I'll make sure the whole of Ireland knows where I am tomorrow.'

'Where's he going?'

'Dunno.'

'Any ideas?'

'You didn't need to do that.'

'What?'

Pat nodded towards the gun on the floor.

'He keeps first dates to himself,' he said. 'Security thing, but I heard he's picking her up about nine.'

'Uh huh, makes sense.'

'I thought you were setting me up,' said Pat, staring into the trees lining the lay-by. 'I thought I was going to die when I pulled in here.'

'Funny that,' said Ellis, slipping out another photograph. 'I was thinking the same thing myself. Is this the only car he has?'

'Yes,' said Pat, looking down at the BMW. 'Just the one. Sometimes he gets a taxi when he goes out.'

'Taxi, huh . . . from the phone book?'

'Don't be stupid. First date though, he'll want to impress. I reckon he'll take the car.'

'Hmm.'

'Things have changed Peter.'

'Sure have. How are Becky and the kids?'

'Doing fine . . . Janet's expelled from school, Catherine's fourteen and pregnant – little proddie fucker – and Tim's inside. Do me a favour.'

'What's that?'

'Don't *ever* contact me again.'

Ellis shoved the photos back into the manila envelope and offered his hand. Pat hesitated. His palms were sweating.

'Things are bad Peter. Every shite ever shat out of Irelands arse is back out on the streets.'

'Heard they're all queuing up for jobs as politicians.'

'Don't joke; you don't have to live with it, so you don't. You Brits have really fucked it up for us this time. And that McConnell's as bad as they come.'

'You sure about the dickers?'

'Would you want those bastards following you about on a date?'

'I'll see you around Pat and thanks for everything.'

Pat reached across and took his hand. The two men looked hard into each other's eyes. Ireland was no place for friends. As Ellis stepped out of the car, the Sierra was gone, its wheels spinning on the wet tarmac. He was alone again in the rain.

Chapter 9

An empty crisp bag blew up the dark, puddled street
and skittered past Ellis' parked Peugeot. A chill wind
blew in through the small gap left open at the top of his
window to stop the glass misting. It was getting cold
and he wished he'd put on a fleece under his black gore-
tex jacket. Through the rain trickling down the windscreen, the tree in McConnell's garden could be clearly
seen. He glanced across at the deserted bus shelter
and wondered why McConnell was late. Probably liked
to keep his girls waiting.

A shadow flitted behind a straggly bush in the scruffy
garden next to him. His heart raced as he slipped his
Browning from under his thigh and thumbed off the safety
catch. He checked over his shoulder, half expecting to
see masked men leaping hedges and fences. But apart

from parked cars, the street was deserted. Being alone, on a Catholic estate in Belfast, at night, was scary stuff.

A mangy tabby cat with a torn ear wandered from under the straggly bush, poked its head through the garden gate and glanced up the row of parked cars.

You little brute!' hissed Ellis, checking his mirror again while trying to calm his wildly beating heart.

The stray flicked its ears in the rain. Across the road, a black cat wearing a collar disappeared under a car. The stray didn't see it and stepped delicately through the gate, taking care to keep its paws dry. The other cat stuck its head out from behind a front wheel and glared across the road. The stray spotted it and crouched down, its chin almost on the pavement, its tail flicking.

Suddenly, the black cat darted across the road. The stray arched its back and hissed as the black cat made a lunge, swiping with its claws. The stray yowled and fled back into the scruffy garden. Curtains were pulled back and a scowling, unshaved face peered out into the night. A window banged open.

'Oi, *fuck off!'*

The cats legged it into the street and disappeared under cars. Somewhere, a child's swing squeaked in the baneful wind. The window slammed shut, the curtains were drawn and shadows returned to the garden.

Ellis slipped his gun back under his thigh and prised his trembling fingers from the keys in the ignition. He was not enjoying this one little bit. His gaze steadied on the large tree in the garden of number seventy-three. He still begrudged that bastard thing.

A car turned into the street at the bottom of the road and Ellis slid down in his seat. Somewhere a front door slammed. He slipped out his pistol and nestled it in his palm. The car splashed past and he lifted his head and peered carefully over the dash. A young couple closed a garden gate and hurried away down the road huddled under an umbrella.

For something to do, he reached across and slipped the photo of McConnell out of the envelope. The eyes surprised him. Everything he expected was there – the arrogance, the cruelty, the intelligence and the passion – but there was something else. Laughter. The guy enjoyed what he did. Ellis shivered again, though this time not from the cold. He looked back at the house. The BMW crouched patiently on the drive. It was almost nine thirty. He wondered if the weather had put McConnell off.

A hunched figure strolled round the corner at the bottom of the road, his hands shoved into his pockets, the hood of his jacket pulled over his head. There was something too deliberate about his manner, something about the way the hood moved from side to side. A light came on in McConnell's porch, the wet leaves on the tree shimmering under its gentle touch. McConnell stepped out into the wet night and closed the door behind him. He stood for a minute, sheltering under his porch roof, watching the bloke in the jacket walking up the street. Something seemed to draw his attention the other way. Ellis averted his eyes, knowing from the jungle that danger could often be sensed. McConnell seemed to hesitate, his hands fidgeting in his trouser pockets. Ellis tightened his grip on the pistol and reached for the car keys.

The bloke in the jacket nodded across the road as he drew level with the bus shelter. McConnell ran to his car and rain spilled from the bodywork as he jumped in.

Ellis turned the keys and the powerful engine kicked over and purred into life just as McConnell's BMW reared out of the drive like a stallion. When it turned the corner at the bottom of the road, Ellis switched on the headlights and pulled out.

The bloke in the jacket stopped and threw his hood back. Ellis accelerated hard, speeding past the bus shelter in a flurry of spray. The bloke whipped a handgun from his pocket as Ellis slammed on the brakes, throwing the car into the tight corner. Over his shoulder, he saw the bloke taking aim. A bullet punctured the bodywork. Ahead, he caught sight of the red taillights of the BMW disappearing round another corner. Another bullet punched a hole in his back window, starring the laminated glass. He dropped a gear and the car lurched forward.

As he took the next corner, the BMW was pulling up ahead of him at red traffic lights. He slammed his foot down and braced himself for the impact. McConnell saw him coming and took his foot off the brakes. But he was far too late. Ellis crunched into the back of the BMW with a crump that sounded like a bomb going off. His door was open before his face hit the airbag.

Yanking open the front door of the BMW, he hauled a dazed McConnell out into the street and coshed him across the back of the head with the pistol. Curtains opened along the street and frightened faces peered out into the night. Taking his arms, Ellis hoisted the slumped McConnell up over his shoulder and dumped him into the back of the BMW. Jumping into the front, he turned the key and the stalled engine caught first time. Crunching the car into gear, he checked his mirror. The bloke with the gun came sprinting round the corner. Ellis smiled, knowing the bastard would be losing his kneecaps for not doing his job properly. The back tyres spun on the wet road and the BMW darted forward. Ignoring the red lights, he took a left and headed for the dual carriageway out of town.

'Who the fuck are you?'

Ellis, a black balaclava pulled over his head, didn't reply. A gust of irritable night wind whistled out of the moody sky and rustled through the few stunted trees overhanging the disused quarry. Ellis pressed the steel barrel of his gun against the back of McConnell's head and forced him to kneel down in the mud close to the rock face. McConnell didn't seem to appreciate kneeling in cold mud with his hands cuffed behind his back.

'What do you want?' he hissed.

Ellis kept his finger on the trigger, hoping his man would show a glimmer of fear. He was disappointed. He had the feeling this was going to be a mucky one.

'Whoever you think you are,' said McConnell smoothly. 'It's over.'

Intrigued, Ellis clothed himself with an Irish accent.

'Over is it? And what would that be?'

'Your life.'

'Is that right?'

Ellis put his foot into McConnell's back and toppled him forward into the mud. Kneeling into the small of his back, he gripped the man's hair and yanked his head up. McConnell, his eyes screwed shut with pain, refused to allow even a grunt through his lips.

'Hard man are you?' hissed Ellis, hauling him back to his knees by his hair.

'You don't know who you're dealing with,' spluttered

McConnell, spitting mud from his mouth.

'Oh, I think I do.'

Ellis glanced at his watch. He wanted to be back on the mainland before first light. He didn't have much time.

'What do you want?'

'Just information,' said Ellis, dropping the Irish drawl.

On hearing an English accent, McConnell fell silent and shifted his weight nervously on his knees.

'Ah,' said Ellis. 'Respect, at last.'

The wind howled round the rock face of the quarry, tearing at the stunted bushes growing out of its cracks and crevices.

'Who are you?' asked McConnell, a note of anxiety creeping into his voice.

'You may have heard of me?'

'Peter fucking Mandelson?'

'I've been called many things in my life, but nothing quite so nasty.'

'What do you want?'

'Nice suit.'

'You said I might have heard of you.'

'Round these parts I'm known as The Terminator.'

McConnell's head fell forward as if to ward off a blow.

'I'll make a deal with you,' said Ellis, caressing McConnell's scalp with the gun barrel again. 'You tell me what I want to know and I'll make it quick.'

'Fuck you.'

'Remember that fat bastard Hegarty?'

'*Hegarty?*'

'We're old mates.'

'That was *you?*'

'Squealed like a pig the whole time.'

'What sort of information?'

Ellis suddenly glanced round at the bushes and trees surrounding the quarry. For some reason he had become distinctly uneasy. He leaned his mouth close to McConnell's ear.

'The dead soldier at Hereford?' he whispered.

'*Fucking Jasus.*'

'You know, you Catholics really should get together and figure that bloke out sometime.'

'That was nothing to do with us.'

Ellis sighed.

'Look, maybe you can wank off the British public with that splinter group bullshit,' he said. 'And maybe you can hold those spineless pricks in Westminster to ransom, but you *will* give me some answers.'

'We had nothing to do with it, I swear.'

'Look, I *know* the Real IRA is under the Sinn Fein umbrella.'

'Ah, little man, but you have no idea which umbrella Sinn Fein operates under.'

Ellis stepped back and cocked his head to one side.

'You have a unit operating on the mainland.'

'Kiss my ass.'

Ellis fired a round into the mud. The crack echoed round the stone quarry. The wind seemed to sense what was coming and howled down out of the black sky.

'What is its objective?'

'Run your tongue round my balls while you're there.'

Ellis bent down, put the gun to the back of one of McConnell's knees and pulled the trigger. McConnell screamed as his kneecap blew off.

'What is its objective?'

McConnell fell on his side and writhed in the mud.

'*You bastard!*' he screamed.

'Who's the commander?'

'*I've got immunity!*'

'Not from me.'

Ellis pushed the pistol into the back of his other knee and pulled the trigger again. Splinters of bone and blood spattered his jacket.

'The unit?'

McConnell thrashed about in the mud.

'Who's the commander?'

'*Andy fucking McNab!*'

Ellis fired a round into each of the man's ankles.

'What's the target?'

Using his heel, he ground it hard into the tortured man's knees.

'*I don't know anything about the dead soldier!*'

'What's the target?'

'*I don't know!*'

'Wrong answer.'

The bones in his elbows shattered as another two shots cracked round the quarry. McConnell's screams were becoming unnerving. Ellis glanced over his shoulder, conscious that even the shadows seemed to be cowering away from him. He stared coldly at the man on the ground. It was time to finish it. He put his heel back on McConnell's knees.

'How many kids have you done this to? Now what about that shooting in Hereford?'

'*I don't fucking know!*'

McConnell turned his head in the mud and looked up imploringly. Ellis took his foot away as the two men stared into each other's eyes. The bastard was telling the truth.

'Okay, just tell me who the commander is?'

McConnell hesitated.

'Just tell me and I'll make it quick.'

'McCann's your man. But this operation has been kept secret, even from me. This one is way out of your league, little man.'

Ellis turned him over and fired a single shot into the back of his head. McConnell's forehead exploded as his brains splattered into the mud. Ellis slipped off his balaclava and stood for a while, the Browning pistol hanging limply in his fingers, the wind clutching accusingly at his clothing. The whole thing looked close enough to an IRA execution to keep everyone happy. No one would mourn him, that was for sure. Except perhaps the girl he never got to fuck.

McCann!

The name chilled him like an arctic wind.

Chapter 10

It was totally dark. So dark Gilmour believed his eyes were still shut. A dull ache sank its molars into the back of his eyes and he blinked a few times, exaggerating the muscle movement to stretch and ease the tightness. The side of his face was damp from lying on a concrete floor in a pool of his own blood and saliva. Sweat matted his hair, stinging the wound on the side of his head where the crowbar had smacked him. A painful throb pulsed against the inside of his skull with an intensity that compelled the bile in his stomach to the back of his throat.

It was *impossibly* dark. He blinked a few more times wondering if the blow to his head had perhaps blinded him. His arms, numb from his shoulders to his fingers, were still handcuffed behind his back. His guts told him he was going to throw up. With a ferocity that left him imagining he could feel blood trickling from his ears, another throb thudded against the inside of his skull. His stomach hadn't lied. Before the reverberations in his head had finished rattling his teeth, he was sick. *That was all he needed.* Now he was face down in his own vomit and there wasn't a damn thing he could do about it.

Twisting his shoulders, he tried to get over onto his back. He didn't make it and rolled back into his vomit. A small lump sucked up his nose. Snorting frenziedly, he kicked out. Bright stars flashed through his skull. Spluttering in desperation, he kicked out again. His toes hit against something hard. Summoning his strength, he pushed and slithered forward a few inches, grazing the side of his face on the rough concrete. His head banged into a wooden crate and something metallic clattered to the floor. He wretched again but there was nothing left to come up. Although the floor was still damp against his cheek, he found he could at least breathe without inhaling any lumps.

Upstairs, a heavy key ground in a rusty lock and stuck. Someone cursed under his breath. With a hefty kick, a stubborn door creaked open on hinges that needed oiling. A switch was flicked and dull yellow light slanted into the room from a low wattage bulb hanging from old wiring half way up a dusty staircase. Footsteps hurried down the rickety wooden stairs. Silhouetted in the unfriendly glow of the light bulb was one of the stubbled blokes from the car park.

Gilmour found himself in a cellar littered with crates, hundredweight fertilizer bags and an assortment of rubbish. The musty smell told him that wherever he was, the place wasn't lived in. There was no sign of the women. An old screwdriver with a broken, oil-stained, green plastic handle lay on the floor where it had fallen. Somewhere, very faintly, a cow lowed.

'What's all the noise?'

The Irish drawl echoed round the large cellar. A torch flicked on and its beam stabbed into the shadows, hurting his eyes. As if terrified of walking into an SAS ambush, the Irishman shone his torch round the cellar, checking out the darkest recesses. Gilmour prayed he wouldn't notice the screwdriver.

'Enjoy your stay,' said the Irishman, his voice as cold as winter wind sighing through the broken headstones of a forgotten cemetery. 'And what's left of your life.'

The footsteps receded back up the stairs, the door creaked shut and the key grated in the lock as the darkness returned. Gilmour started shivering.

It was some time before he noticed he could still see the screwdriver. It was so dark, it must have been some strange trick of his mind. The clarity of the detail was astonishing. The image of the dirty translucent handle, the bent, rust-pitted shaft, and the head that was so worn it would never tighten any screws again was as clear as if the stair light still trespassed audaciously beyond the frame of the doorway. As a tool, it was worthless, but screwing things with it was not what he had in mind.

He pushed with his toes and slithered forward a few inches. Sweat stung his eyes and fresh blood oozed from his head wound. What was worse, he could feel his vomit soaking though his clothes as he wormed forward. To concentrate his mind, he thought about Angelina and Roberts. Exhausted, he rested his head on the floor. The concrete was no longer damp, but cool and dusty. *Sleep!* He lay still in the impenetrability of the cellar, his laboured breathing choked by the suffocating silence.

His mind went back to the car park. Black was on his knees, looking up with that perplexed expression, that strange expression that said, *this shouldn't happen – not out shopping*. Shaking off waves of nausea, he pushed again with his toes, found the screwdriver and picked it up in his teeth. With the last energy he could generate, he thrust himself to where he'd seen an open bag of fertilizer slumped beside a crate. His head spun in huge circles like he was drunk. The screwdriver was just going to have to wait. It slipped from his lips as his head sank to the floor.

Wraiths of night mist trailed among the tree trunks of a sinister wood. A cold wind bit into his exposed skin. *What was he doing in a wood?* Hooded figures crept towards him through the shadows, shotguns in their hands, their breaths misting on the night air. They were getting closer. He had to get away. For some reason, he couldn't move. He was lying on the ground and couldn't get up. A rotten branch crunched under heavy boots. They were almost upon him. The sound of their breathing chilled him. Branches parted and there they were, six of them, moonlight shining in heartless eyes that stared through slits in hoods. Without a word, they stepped into the clearing and formed a circle round him. He tried to speak but his lips wouldn't move. The ghostly figures stared down at him, saying nothing. One by one, they raised their shotguns and aimed. He screamed but no sound left his throat.

Shivering uncontrollably, he started from the vision. He was feverish and going down fast. His brain seemed to be trying to burst through the crack in his skull. Sweat poured down his face. He was soaking and desperately in need of water. His eyes closed irresistibly, heavy with the powerful magnetism of fatigue. Nudging the bottom of the heavy sack with his forehead, he rolled the screwdriver under it with his tongue. The base of the sack slumped over the handle and he gratefully lay his head down and drifted off to the warm fireside rug of unconsciousness.

Metal grating on rusty metal woke him. He lifted his head from the floor as the stubborn key turned in the lock. The door creaked open and the stark yellow light of the bare bulb once more filtered into the dusty cellar.

'Are you comfortable?'

Gilmour shivered in the icy hatred with which the words were clothed. The torch began an exploration of the shadows and then rested on Gilmour's crumpled form amongst the crates. For some reason the Irishman seemed reluctant to step into the cellar. Feet clumped down the stairs behind him.

'What's the crack?'

Another torch beam flashed round the cellar, checking out the corners.

'Just making sure, so I am.'

'Is he still out?'

Gilmour recognised the other stubbled bloke from the transit. Pistols in hand, the two men stepped warily into the cellar, using each other for courage. One of them covered Gilmour while the other walked over and nudged him warily with his toe.

'*Water*,' whispered Gilmour, his appeal little more that a croak.

'What *shitehole*?'

Taking an arm each, the Irishmen hoisted Gilmour to his feet and dragged him to the stairs. He was too weak to lift his feet and his toes trailed long lines in the dust. He forgot all about water as his shins skinned mercilessly on the rough edges of the wooden steps. In his effort to try and lift his feet, his head bumped the dangling bulb, sending shadows cavorting up and down the stairwell. He was dragged through another door into the kitchen of what he assumed was a disused farmhouse and dropped heavily, cracking his chin on filthy red tiles. He screwed his eyes shut, blinded by the bright sunlight streaming in the windows.

The Irishmen lit up a cigarette each and took a seat round an old pine kitchen table cluttered with newspapers and magazines, open cereal boxes and empty tins of stale food. Gilmour lay perfectly still until the sharp pain from his bleeding shins had subsided to a numb ache. The pain though had served a purpose – it had ignited his anger. Unnoticed by the Irishmen flicking their ash on the floor, he took in his surroundings, searching for the first fragments of an escape plan.

An old greasy cooker stood to one side of a filthy porcelain sink stacked high with black dusted crockery. Yellowing flowery wallpaper peeled from damp walls and the windows were cobwebbed and cracked.

'*Water*,' he croaked feebly.

One of the men peered at his watch. Stubbing his cigarette out in an overflowing ashtray, he took another from a pack on the table and lit up, sucking the smoke deep into his lungs. The bloke got up from the table and walked over, blowing smoke in a stream from his lips.

'You're thirsty eh?'

Gilmour knew he wasn't going to like what happened next.

'Here,' said the bloke, unzipping himself.

Gilmour squirmed away, pulling his neck into his shoulders as warm urine splashed on him. Shaking the last drops from his penis, the Irishman chuckled and did him-

self up. His mate laughed and picked up a puzzle magazine from the table.

Gilmour found himself forgotten for the time being as
the two men busied themselves with a crossword and
he retreated to his escape plan. He couldn't leave without the women. Or could he? He dismissed it. Maybe
Roberts was old enough to look after herself, but he
wasn't going anywhere without Angelina.

'*Cod!*' exclaimed one of the blokes. 'Thirty three down
is *cod.*'

'Hmmm,' replied with bloke with the cigarette, snatch-
ing the magazine from his mate, 'let me see that.'

'Well? Put it in then.'

'Dunno.'

'Dunno what? It's *cod.*'

'Could be *rud.*'

'*Rud?* What the fuck is a *rud*?'

'Not sure if it has one *d* or two *d*'s though. It's a fish,
you prick.'

'It's *cod*, put it in!'

'It might be wrong.'

'Well, what's thirty one across?'

'Um . . . a small house.'

'How many letters?'

'Seven.'

'*Cottage!* See, told you *cod* was right.'

'Hmmmmm.'

'Put it fucking in will you?'

A car approached in a low gear along what must have
been a worn track with deep potholes. The magazine
was pushed aside as the two men jumped up drawing
their guns. The one with the cigarette rushed to the window and peered out through the dirty glass.

'It's him.'

The car pulled up and the engine died. The car door slammed and footsteps crunched on gravel. A shadow flitted across the window and the men backed away from the table to the wall farthest from the door.

'*Jasus!*' said a voice from the doorway.

Jimmy McCann was having difficulty believing what he was seeing. Stepping slowly into the kitchen, he put a polythene bag down by the sink and took a pistol from the pocket of his worn tweed sports jacket.

'What's the crack?' he asked the other two.

'No trouble, Jimmy, no trouble.'

McCann put a foot on Gilmour and bent down to have a good look at him. His beer belly slumped over the belt on his trousers.

'They treating you right?'

Gilmour wrinkled his nose at the smell of stale whisky on the man's breath. McCann grunted, stepped back and took a seat at the table.

'I've got plans for you,' he said, taking a cigarette out of the packet on the table without asking. Striking a match, he sucked deeply and checked the end of the cigarette to make sure it was glowing properly.

'Get on with it then,' said Gilmour, already tired of the conversation.

'Oh I will, but I'm going to take my time.'

'Fuck you.'

'I don't think so. Mind you, the boys would like that, wouldn't you boys?'

McCann smiled crookedly, showing a gap in his stained teeth. The two blokes leered at Gilmour and McCann's smile disappeared.

'You two leave him alone until I say.'

The men flattened themselves back against the wall. Gilmour didn't like what he was hearing.

'What do you want?' he asked.

McCann laughed.

'Did the boy's wee on you?'

Genuine mirth sparkled in his eyes.

'Can I get the kid first?' asked the semi-intelligent one with the cigarette. 'Always liked virgins.'

His jealous mate scowled at him. McCann's tongue poked at the gap in his teeth, curious to see how Gilmour was going to respond.

'They weren't like this when they went inside,' he said eventually, as if apologising for his men. 'They were *good* lads. Believed in the Cause so they did. Loved their country. Auch, we get them back from youse changed men all right.'

'We could do the girl at the same time,' suggested the still scowling jealous one to his mate.

Gilmour's tongue was furry from lack of water. He'd lost a lot of blood, his split skull needed attention and the fever he had developed was draining him of what little energy he had left. He probably wasn't going to make it to whatever it was McCann had lined up for them. McCann got up from the table and peered through the dirty windows.

'Business first before we have our pleasure,' he said wistfully, then turned from the window and held up the polythene bag. 'Do you know what this is?'

Gilmour eyed the bag suspiciously. McCann rummaged around inside and slipped out a photograph in a silver frame.

'I found it in your living room.'

Gilmour paled when he recognised his family portrait.

121

McCann put the photo back into the bag, walked over and stooped to check Gilmour's head wound.

'Does that hurt?' he asked, running his fingers over the split in his skull.

Gilmour almost fainted. McCann squatted on his haunches and their eyes met.

'You have no idea how much this means to me,' he said, tilting his head slightly to one side.

'The girl is only eight,' said Gilmour pathetically.

McCann's voice creased sharply.

'Aye, and in twenty years she'll be *twenty*-eight. Another Brit slag cranking out arrogant little brats with nothing better to do then stick their noses into my country's affairs, presuming to tell us how to live our lives and throwing us in their faggot-infested prisons when we tell them to go away and leave us alone.'

'Jimmy . . . she's only eight.'

'Eight?'

McCann seemed to come out of a daydream.

'Auch, Brit women are all slags by that age, so they are. She'll be screaming for it, so she will.'

Outside, a dog barked. The two stubbled men drew their guns and bolted for the door.

'Good dog that,' said McCann thoughtfully, getting to his feet and walking to the window. He stared out over the fields and trees surrounding the farmhouse.

'What's with the photograph?' asked Gilmour.

'Huh?'

'And where are the girls?'

McCann looked over his shoulder, jolted from another daydream. Slipping a half bottle of whisky from his pocket, he took a slug and wiped his mouth with his sleeve.

'Ahhhhh,' he gasped, wandering back across the kitchen. 'That cut looks nasty.'

Fiery pain seared through Gilmour's head as neat whisky was poured into the wound.

'That should help,' said McCann. 'Don't want you getting infections and dying on us, so we don't.'

The two men returned and dumped a couple of dead rabbits on the floor.

'Well?' asked McCann.

'Only some poacher.'

'Yeah,' laughed the jealous one. 'You should have seen him run.'

'Where is he?' asked McCann, frowning at them.

'He'll no be back; the dog got a good bite at him.'

'Keep this bastard alive,' said McCann suddenly, lowering his voice. He burned his gaze into the men. 'I don't care what state he's in, just make sure he's alive until this is over. And don't touch him . . . you hear?'

The two men nodded vigorously, understanding the threatening nature of the command.

'I'll be back every now and then, so stay awake.'

The nodding continued. McCann looked down at Gilmour, dropped his cigarette on the floor and stubbed it out with one of his heavy brogues. Gilmour noticed one of the shoelaces was undone.

'By the way,' said McCann, heading for the door. 'You don't want to know what's going to happen to the sergeant. She's being shipped home. The boys want some fun with her.'

With that, he turned and left.

Shading their eyes from the sunshine, the two Irishmen peered out through the window until McCann had driven off down the track. They seemed relieved to have survived.

'Well, what d'you think?' asked the jealous one.

'Bout what?'

The bloke jerked a thumb at Gilmour as the car's engine gradually faded into the distance.

'He won't last till the weekend in that state.'

'Yeah, lets clean him up.'

Gilmour decided he needed suitable names for them. *Attila and Hitler?* Didn't sit right with him. Too manly. *Jessie and Jean?* Didn't sit right with him either. Too feminine. *Bill and Ben, the bendy men?* Yep, that would do nicely.

'Let's give him some grub,' suggested Ben, the semi-intelligent one.

'Let's just untie him for a bit and do the job right,' suggested Bill, wringing his hands a little nervously.

'Go and run the bath will you.'

Bill ducked out into the hallway and disappeared.

'Hmm . . . suppose he has a point,' said Ben. Pulling Gilmour over onto his side, he unlocked the handcuffs. 'I get any aggro,' he warned, 'you'll regret it.'

Gilmour didn't even notice the barrel of the gun caressing his forehead. From somewhere down the hall came the sound of running water. The Irishman untied his feet and stepped back to a safe distance, both hands steadying his pistol. Gilmour tried to pull his arms in front of him, but they wouldn't respond. With a grunt, he wrenched his shoulder round and his right arm flopped uselessly in front of him. Dragging his other arm out from under him, he lay on his back and cuddled himself as the circulation returned.

Ben laid some food out on the table and the delicious aroma of fresh bread almost lifted him from the floor.

Quickly, before the Irishman changed his mind, he rolled over onto his stomach and pushed himself to his knees. Using a cupboard for support, he got groggily to his feet. A pistol pointed straight at him, but all he could see was the food on the table. A banquet of fresh bread, sliced meat, cheese slices and bottled water beckoned. The table was only a couple of paces away, but he wasn't sure if he would make it. Recklessly, he pushed himself from the worktop. Catching the corner of the table just in time, he pulled out a chair and sat down heavily. Grabbing a couple of slices of ham, he shoved them straight into his mouth with his fingers. Before the food was properly chewed, he washed the food down with half the bottle of water. Stuffing another couple of slices of ham into his mouth, he set about buttering bread with a vengeance. Like a starved hyena at a stolen carcass, he ripped into the food.

'Tea would be nice,' he mumbled arrogantly through a mouthful of food, knowing the Irishman's hatred for him cowered in the shadow of his fear for McCann.

A dirty kettle filled up at the sink and a steaming mug of tea soon slammed down on the table beside him.

'Ready,' said Bill, stepping back into the kitchen a few minutes later.

'Enough,' said Ben, dismayed at how quickly their food was disappearing.

Gilmour forced another cheese slice into his stuffed mouth, poured some cold water into his tea and drained the mug.

'*Get up!*' barked Ben, nodding towards the door.

At gunpoint, Gilmour was ushered from the kitchen. A spider crawled for cover behind an old picture frame hanging on the crumbling plaster of the hallway.

'In here.'

Gilmour looked with dismay at the dust and dead flies floating on the water in the grimy enamelled bath. The stench of vomit on his clothes though, kept him to the task. Without even kicking off his trainers, he stepped into the filthy water.

'Two's up?' said Bill, turning to Ben with his eyebrows raised.

'Hmmm . . . maybe if you're good to me later.'

'You're a sick bastard, but okay then.'

Gilmour ignored them as he splashed and grunted in the quickly discolouring water. He made sure his head wound was taken care of and then scraped and washed the vomit from his clothes. When he stepped out of the bath, he felt a little better.

Even when he was handcuffed and tied up, he didn't feel so bad. If anything, the knots on the ropes weren't as tight as before. When he was dragged back down to the cellar, he was gratified to see one of them throw an old blanket on the floor for him to lie on. He felt almost comfortable when they dumped him down and left.

Later, as he lay in the dark listening to the kitchen table creaking in rhythm upstairs, he felt strangely confident. One of the Irishmen groaned and the table stopped creaking. The thought of those two humping him made him squirm. From that moment on, he never considered it again and thought only of escape.

Chapter 11

Conscious again, and the now customary blinking ritual over, Gilmour shifted his weight about on the blanket in a futile effort to get comfortable. He doubted he had ever stunk so badly. Not being able to scratch his itches was driving him crazy and he was convinced he could feel bugs crawling over him. Angelina and Roberts were heavy on his mind. If he'd believed the women would be spared a lingering torture, he might have just accepted things, as men in hopeless situations often do, but the thought of the sweating faces of Bill and Ben grunting into them soon had his ankles chewing at the ropes.

At first he didn't notice this new pain, so insignificant it seemed amongst the others, but its passion steadily intensified until it could no longer be ignored. Eventually, he stopped fighting the ropes. Injuring himself any further was stupid. What he needed was a plan. He had to *think!*

Some time later, a resigned sigh sneaked out between

his lips and slunk off into the darkness. There was no plan. What? He was just going to magic the handcuffs off, do a couple of karate chops, nick one of their pistols and sort them out? The silence and darkness crowded over him. His eyelids drooped and he fought in vain to keep them open.

He started from sleep, disturbed by the stubborn door getting a couple of hefty kicks and creaking open. Heavy boots clumped down the stairs. The two Irishmen glanced round the cellar, allowing their eyes time to accustom to the gloom. Gilmour stole a peek at the handle of the screwdriver poking out from under the fertiliser sack and checked his bearings.

'Cover me,' said Ben, stepping cautiously into the cellar, his pistol grasped in both hands.

'Is he okay?' asked Bill, his voice heavy with concern.

Ben poked his pistol into the soft flesh of Gilmour's neck.

'Dunno, I'm not a doctor.'

'Let's just do it.'

Slipping their pistols into their waistbands, the Irishmen hoisted Gilmour from the floor and helped him carefully up the stairs. It was dark outside and a light rain pattered against the window. He was forced to his knees on the kitchen floor and untied. Gilmour felt his buttocks tighten. To hell with his plan. If they tried it on he was going to rip someone's balls off.

'Come on, hurry up,' said Ben, ushering him to the table with his pistol.

Gilmour got up slowly. However, instead of forcing him to bend over the table, Bill took three fish suppers from a carrier bag and started unwrapping them. The smell of the food almost buckled his knees.

Stuffing another handful of flaking cod into his mouth, Gilmour sucked oily batter from his fingers and then gulped down some dirty looking tap water. A disturbing thought occurred to him. He didn't know where the women were so he was going to have to keep one of them alive long enough to find out. His jaw slowed. That complicated things a bit.

The Irishmen stood to one side of the kitchen, munching their suppers, somewhat amused by the pig grunting at the table.

'Nice of McCann to bring us some proper grub,' said Bill.

'Where are the women?' mumbled Gilmour through his food, not expecting an answer.

He didn't get one.

'Are they still alive?'

'Shut the fuck up.'

Oh well, he was just going to have to do it the hard way.

'I could do with a crap,' he said, shovelling a few more chips into his mouth. Half turning in his seat, he stared down the barrels of two hastily drawn handguns. 'You'll want me clean for the party.'

Bill and Ben looked at each other and then back at him. They hadn't thought of that.

'Finish your grub,' said Ben.

All too soon, Gilmour was dragged back down to the cellar. As the door slammed and the key rasped in the lock, he lay back enjoying the full feeling in his stomach and the empty feeling in his bowels. He had stopped shivering and sweating. The fever had broken.

Some time later, he became aware of a scratching sound over in a corner of the cellar. He was not alone. A mouse twitched its whiskers and scurried along the side of a crate. He recalled a story he'd once heard about rats nibbling through a prisoner's ropes. Suddenly he felt very alone and his thoughts slunk off to the comfort of childhood memories, to a cave he'd once explored.

He shone his torch down from the end of the low passage in the cave, lighting up the rocky floor of the chamber. It was only about a six-foot drop, but to a nine year old it might as well have been a cliff. His mate crawled up beside him and shone his torch along the rock face.

'It's sheer,' whispered his mate, afraid that the ghosts were listening.

Gilmour could hear the gurgling of the underground stream. It sounded close. Shining his torch to the back of the chamber, he imagined he saw an opening behind a pile of boulders that had fallen from the roof. Having come so far, he wasn't about to give up now. Slipping his legs over the edge, he lowered himself down until he was hanging by his fingers. His mate leaned over and shone his torch down. Gilmour checked below him, picked his spot and slithered down the slightly sloping rock. His mate dropped him his torch and Gilmour flicked on the yellow beam and shone it towards the far wall, lighting up the rock fall. He hesitated.

'*What is it?*' asked his mate.

'Nothing.'

Gilmour walked cautiously towards the rocks, flashing his torch round the small cavern as he went, picturing all sorts of monsters lurking in the shadows. He thought he heard something behind him and whipped round.

'*What is it?*'

'Nothing.'

He took another few steps towards the rock fall, half expecting to see mad staring eyes peering out at him from the blackness beyond. An overwhelming desire to get back outside into the tropical summer afternoon heat stopped him momentarily. But he'd come too far to turn back now. He crept a little closer to the rocks.

As he poked his head round the rock fall, he heard the stream clearly. His torch shone into the passageway. And then he saw it, black water trickling seemingly out of the rock itself and then disappearing down a hole. Disappointed that the passage didn't lead anywhere, but relieved he'd completed his mission, he ran back to the ledge.

'*Did you see it?*'

'Yeah.'

'Does it go anywhere?'

'Nuh.'

He stood back from the rock face and shone his torch along it, wondering why he hadn't thought about how he was going to get back up. His mate reached his hand down. He jumped up and tried to pull himself up, his flip-flops slithering about on the soles of his sweaty feet.

'It's no use,' he said, dropping back to the cave floor. He checked out the rock again, exploring for crevices or tiny ledges. It was like running his fingers over the walls in his bedroom.

'What are we going to do?' asked his mate, more frightened than ever.

Gilmour's torch flickered and the beam became noticeably dimmer. He switched it off to conserve the batteries.

'It's my lunch time,' said his mate, a tremor in his voice. 'I'll get in trouble if I'm late.'

He started crying.

'Can you get a rope?' asked Gilmour.

'I'm off.'

His mate wiped his eyes and scuttled off along the low passage on his hands and knees. Gilmour watched the torch beam disappearing down the passage walls. Then it was just him and the trickling of the stream. He was alone.

Sitting down with his back to the rock, he switched on his torch to make sure there was nothing creeping up on him. The rushing of the stream echoed eerily round the chamber. He wondered how much longer his torch would keep the ghastly darkness away.

He'd never needed to be rescued before and he wondered what it would be like. Everyone would be mad at him. The police would scold him. Maybe he would even be in the newspaper. His mum would cry. She always cried when he got in trouble. The torch flickered again and he banged it with his palm a few times.

When the torch was no longer powerful enough to pick out the far wall, he switched it off. How long he had been sitting there he had no idea, but it was *ages!* Someone should have been back by now. His mate only lived ten minutes away. Why he hadn't returned with a rope yet was beyond him. His mum would have stopped being mad by now, and started crying.

When he finally realised that no one was coming, that

no one even knew where he was, he wasn't frightened – he just became very lonely. In years to come, some kid would wriggle in through the tiny entrance, crawl to the chamber and shine a torch down. He wondered if the kid would scream when he saw the pile of mouldy bones. Switching on his torch, he looked about for a sharp stone with which to scratch his name in the rock so people would know whose skeleton it was. As he got to his feet, the stream seemed to call to him and he shone the torch towards it. It occurred to him that he'd not really explored the passage that well, so he wandered over for another look.

The cold water made him shiver as it sloshed round his ankles. He crouched and shone his torch downstream. To his surprise, there *was* a passage. It was low though, and he was going to have to get down on his hands and knees. Holding the torch in his mouth, he got down into the water and started crawling. His knees skinned on sharp stones, but he didn't cry out.

The torch was now so dim the beam was no more than a reflection on the surface of the dark water, with not the strength to pick out the stones on the bottom. He knew no one would ever find his bones now. But there was nowhere else to go. He crawled on.

After a while, he found he could crouch. Trembling with cold, he closed his eyes and dreamed for a minute of warm sun beating into his skin. Rubbing his bleeding knees, he moved on, keeping a hand above his head to protect him from the jagged rock.

Suddenly, he bumped into a rock face, hurting his nose. He felt around with his hands for a passage, but the stream disappeared under a ledge. To go on he would have to put his head under the water and hold his breath while he wriggled through on his belly. Drowning didn't appeal to him. He banged the torch, but the batteries were dead. He found some dry rocks to one side of the stream and climbed ashore.

As he nursed his knees, waiting for death, he became aware of a patch of darkness ahead of him and slightly to his right that seemed a little less intense than the rest of the cave. He squinted, but couldn't be sure. Groping his way forward, he found there was a passage leading away from the stream. He followed it; hardly daring to believe it could lead anywhere. Rounding a corner, the darkness ahead softened to indistinct shades of grey.

Clambering out of the cave mouth, he put a hand to his eyes and squinted in the brilliant sunshine. He was in a graveyard. Early evening sun slanted through the tangled undergrowth round the entrance to the cave. He stood for a while, his face turned to the warmth. Not far away was an ornamental pond with colourful carp swimming lazily amongst the green floating leaves of water lilies. A feeding fish grazed the surface and leisurely waves rippled to the sides of the pond. He looked around at the tall gravestones, some etched in English, some in Chinese, and understood that one day he would lie beneath one. But not yet. With a little laugh, he ran up a path towards the road, dreaming up lies he knew his mother would never believe anyway.

Gilmour stared into the darkness of the cellar. He'd been here before. All he had to do was get moving, just like that time in the cave. If he didn't give up, he would feel the sunshine on his skin again. It was time to get the screwdriver. The food and the rest had given him strength and he made good progress. The smell of his vomit was the pole star by which he navigated. He wondered if the mouse was still about. It was probably tucked up in its cosy nest with the wife and kids, scaring them with stories of the big bad bastard shuffling about outside. His head began to swim and he felt sick again. He laid his temple on the dusty concrete, just for a second, and dozed off into a dream.

He looked about him. The room was empty. It was strangely hot for the time of year. And why was he lying face down, breathing in fluff from a dirty carpet? Suddenly a door burst open, slamming back against the wall. Masked men stormed into the room dragging a young screaming child. It was Angelina. *Angelina!* The men ripped her clothes from her body, cutting her skin, bruising her legs and arms. He struggled, but couldn't move. The men lay her down and yanked her legs apart. One of them unzipped himself. The vision was so startling and so real, Gilmour struggled awake and pushed himself to go on. His sweat had turned cold.

His forehead nudged the cool polythene sack just as the kitchen table started its familiar rhythmic creaking. With the screwdriver in his teeth, he kicked out and started the long haul home. Arranging the blanket under him as best he could, he rolled over onto his back and worked the screwdriver up his sleeve. Upstairs, the table was threatening to collapse.

The screwdriver felt good against his skin. He tried to think through his plan one more time, wondering if he'd forgotten anything. But he was exhausted and soon drifted off to a land of ugly chimneys and black smoke, rattling chains and dungeons, where evil men whipped myriads of weary workers along the bleeding roads of a life that shouldn't be and yet was.

Chapter 12

Every muscle in Gilmour's body was bruised from lying on the pitiless concrete. There were no comfortable positions remaining to him. His mind began to grapple with the problem of what day it was, how long he had been held in the cellar. It seemed like a week since he'd last seen light. Under him, he could feel his arms growing cold again from lack of circulation. He couldn't afford that; he was going to need them. His face contorted with effort as he twisted over onto his stomach and he lay for a while, enjoying the tingling in his fingers.

The screwdriver nestled comfortingly up his sleeve. It was his only tangible contact with the world outside. *Angelina!* He could still see the strained smile on her face as she got down on her knees to stroke the cat. He longed to hold her hand, to whisper to her that everything was going to be fine. She was like his own daughter. The concrete floor sank its teeth into him with such ferocity he wondered how much more he could take.

He struggled with the ropes for a while, but his mind soon wandered off down a dark alley of whispering voices. No longer capable of resisting, he drifted off into unconsciousness.

For some curious reason, he was wet round his groin. Saliva dribbled from his mouth as he tried to reason where the wetness had come from. He was not sweating or feeling feverish. He sniffed and turned his head away. He'd simply pissed himself while he'd been sleeping. That was comforting. No new injuries.

'What day is it?' he suddenly asked aloud.

The silence ignored him.

'Okay, DON'T answer.'

Hearing sound again was wonderful and he raised his voice.

'What's on at the movies then?'

A disturbing thought interrupted him. *What if Bill and Ben didn't know where the women were?* He hadn't thought of that.

Upstairs, the key grated in the lock and stuck. Someone kicked the door and rattled the handle.

'*Fucking thing!*'

The door flew open, cracking back against the wall. The light came on and the stairs creaked. Gilmour rolled about on the blanket, flexing his arms and legs to get the blood pumping round his body. Two torch beams shone into the darkness and swept the corners.

'You know,' muttered Ben, shining his torch directly onto Gilmour, 'I don't know what we're so afraid of – this guy's a shite.'

'Yeah,' chuckled Bill bravely.

'Must be all those SAS stories you listen to as a kid,'

said Ben, switching off his torch as he stepped into the cellar. 'Let's have some crack.'

'What about McCann?'

'Fuck McCann,' said Ben, who had obviously been drinking. 'We'll wash him and put him back nice and clean as you like.'

'What if he tells him?'

'Oh shut up and come on.'

Gilmour was hoisted from the ground and dragged to the stairs.

'We too rough with you?' asked Ben, his breath stinking of beer. 'You'll soon see what rough is.'

Gilmour's shins caught the first step, ripping a scream from his throat as the fresh scabs tore away. He felt the handle of the screwdriver slipping. His shins scraped another step and a vicious splinter pierced his skin. The screwdriver handle nudged the plasticuffs. If he dropped it, it was all over.

The glare of the electric lighting stabbed his eyes as he was dragged into the kitchen. They dumped him on the floor and his head struck the tiles. A little dazed, he rolled over, slipping the screwdriver back up his sleeve. It was dark outside.

Ben picked up a can of Guinness from the table and drank deeply. Smacking his lips, he crunched the empty can and rattled it into the sink.

'Thought we'd break you in gently, so we did,' he said, reaching for another can. 'And tonight's your lucky night.'

Gilmour wiggled his toes to make sure they were working. The Irishman cracked the can, burped loudly and started massaging his groin. Bill untied Gilmour's feet and chucked the rope into a corner.

'Get up!' he barked.

Gilmour turned onto his side and struggled to a kneeling position.

'Turn round.'

Gilmour shuffled only so far. The handcuffs fell from his wrists and were chucked over beside the rope. He turned his back away from the two men and let the screwdriver slip down his sleeve into his fingers. Feeling the weapon in his hand gave him strength.

'C'mon,' said Bill, 'on your feet.'

'I feel sick,' said Gilmour, getting up on one knee.

He ran his free hand through his hair to draw their attention away from the screwdriver. Grabbing the corner of the table, he hauled himself to his feet. Ben was the one he wanted, but Bill was the closest.

His hand flew from behind his back. The screwdriver punctured Bill's neck, pierced through his head and burst out of his ear. Warm blood spurted into Gilmour's face as he tried to pull the screwdriver back. But it was wedged fast and the handle slipped through his fingers. He dived to one side as a shot exploded, almost bursting his eardrums. Bill slumped to his knees, one hand on the screwdriver, a dumb look on his face.

Gilmour rolled as another round splintered the tiles near his head. Slamming into the cupboard under the sink, he braced his feet against the skirting and pushed himself away. A bullet grazed the top of his head and splintered a cupboard door as he clattered into a rusty steel pail. Grabbing the handle, he sent the bucket sailing through the air. Ben threw up his firing arm to ward off the blow. It was the vital second Gilmour needed.

One of the heavy pine kitchen chairs caught Ben's ankles and sent him sprawling. Gilmour dived on top of him, reaching for the gun. Ben though, was tough and wiry, and brought the butt of the gun down hard against the side of Gilmour's head. In the bright flashes that followed, Gilmour lost his bearings. *The gun! He had to get the gun!*

He clawed desperately for it but was thrown off with surprising ease. The Irishman tore his firing arm free and brought the muzzle towards Gilmour's eyes. Seizing Ben's greasy hair, Gilmour yanked the man's head down and sank his teeth into the unprotected nose. Hot air, blood and snot snorted into his mouth as his teeth crunched through the bone and clamped together.

The gun was almost at his head. His hardened knuckles punched the soft skin of Ben's forearm and the gun skittered across the tiles. The Irishman wrenched himself free, leaving most of his nose in Gilmour's mouth. Throwing himself to one side, he rolled away. Gilmour rolled the other way and leapt to his feet. For a few seconds the two men faced each other, bloodied, sweating and breathing heavily, their eyes glaring like rabid dogs. Gilmour spat the filth from his mouth. On equal terms, he knew the Irishman was already dead. He beckoned provocatively with his hand.

'Come on then you faggot bastard!'

Still kneeling upright and oblivious to the life and death struggle around him, Bill gave a last gurgle of air from his punctured neck and toppled forward onto his face. Blood stung Gilmour's eyes and he blinked to clear his vision. A mixture of emotions traversed Ben's bloodied face. First, it was disbelief, then rage. There was a flicker of uncertainty in his eyes. Just a flicker, but it was enough for Gilmour. The blow, when it came, was no surprise.

Stepping to his right, Gilmour blocked the punch with both arms. The back of his right fist, then his left palm smacked the side of Ben's jaw, pitching his head back. The Irishman staggered away swinging wildly; the uncertainty in his eyes now a wild fear. He stood for a moment holding his face and looked down at his dead lover. Catalysed by the booze, his heated emotions suddenly reacted violently. A maelstrom of rage and revenge burned in his eyes. So terrible was the effect, Gilmour stepped back. With a yell, the Irishman came at him. Gilmour blocked the punch and slammed his knee up into his groin. The Irishman buckled. Slipping an arm round him, he threw him over his shoulder, slamming him down hard on the tiles. Dropping his knees brutally onto his head and into his ribs, he took an arm, twisted it and forced it down over his thigh. The Irishman screamed as the bone splintered. He finished the move with a blow to the side of the temple.

Gilmour got up and casually strolled across the kitchen and picked up both guns. Ben curled up in a ball, dragging his broken arm to his side. Gilmour slipped out the magazines and checked them.

'Where are the women?' he asked quietly.

There was no reply.

'Are you deaf as well as stupid?'

Gilmour slammed the magazines back in and pocketed one of the pistols. He pointed the other at the Irishman's legs and fired. Ben screamed as one of his ankles shattered. Gilmour shook off the noise. The ringing in his ears would be a long time going away.

'Where are the women?'

He fired again, shattering the other ankle. Ben whimpered and pulled his jacket over his legs for protection.

The next time Gilmour fired, there was a different sound as the bullet struck the man. He groaned, took a shattered mobile phone from the pocket of Ben's jacket and hurled the useless equipment angrily across the kitchen.

'*Where are the women?*'

There was no reply. McCann had picked his men carefully. *McCann!* He glanced nervously out of the window, expecting to see headlights approaching. Deciding to quickly check out the rest of the house, he hurried into the hallway. Kicking open the first door, he peered in at an empty room of peeling wallpaper, crumbling masonry and broken floorboards. Out in the hall the picture frame fell from the plaster, the glass shattering as it struck the floor. He hit the deck and rolled over, his pistol searching for a target as a now homeless spider scuttled along the wall.

He picked himself up and ran down the hall, past the bathroom and into the living room. Sleeping bags lay rolled out and personal belongings tumbled out of army kit bags. There was a reek of body odour and stinking socks, but there were no women. He was just going to have to ask some more questions.

Back in the kitchen, he cleared the sink and filled it with water. He took a quick look at himself in a cracked mirror and winced as he dabbed gingerly at his scalp with a wet tea towel. There was a lot of blood on his face but most of it just wiped away. He spat into the sink, nauseated by the taste in his mouth. Hitching up his trouser leg, he eyed the splinter thrust angrily into his raw flesh from where he'd been dragged up the stairs. He wrenched it out and jammed the bloodstained cloth onto the wound to suppress the pain. There was not much else he could do for himself.

Holding the cloth to the side of his head, he turned to the Irishman. Ben blinked at him, his eyes cold. Gilmour smiled nicely.

'Tell you what mate, I'm not such a bad bloke. Tell me where the women are and I'll make it quick.'

He aimed the gun at various parts of the Irishman's body, lingering around his genitals. The eyes continued their blinking.

'You know I'll get you to talk eventually.'

More blinking.

'I'm not interested in your operation, just the women.'

Ben thought about that for a moment.

'They're in one of the barns,' he said.

'Which one?'

'The big one with the corrugated roof.'

'Anything else?'

The blinking resumed. Gilmour slipped a watch from the dead Irishman's wrist. It was nearly 10:00 pm. *A Rolex? Where did they get the money?*

'Well?' asked Ben, no longer blinking.

'So, I lied,' said Gilmour. 'I think some friends of mine will want to ask you a few questions.'

'*You fucker!*' hissed Ben, his hatred spewing from his eyes.

Gilmour walked to the door and looked back. The kitchen was a mess. There was even blood on the ceiling.

'*Good job,*' he whispered to himself, and stepped outside and closed the door.

It was raining lightly, but plenty of stars peeped through large breaks in the clouds. The almost bare autumn trees behind the house creaked gently. There was no mistaking the barn. Silhouetted against the night sky, it was by far the largest building on the farm. He hobbled quickly across the driveway. The track leading to the barn was heavily rutted, making walking treacherous, and he stumbled in the dark, almost twisting his ankle. It began to sink in. A rush of elation swelled within him. *He'd escaped!*

Climbing a large rusty gate into a field long gone to seed, he approached the barn from the rear. His pistol raised, he ran across the field. He was taking no chances. Reaching the side of the barn, he listened for sounds from within. Suddenly, a deep growl rushed out of the darkness behind him. Too late, he spun round. A huge German shepherd leapt for his throat. Instinctively, he threw out his free arm. Teeth clamped onto him, piercing deep into the flesh. Still growling, the dog shook its head viciously, trying to drag him to the ground. Shoving the pistol into its neck, he looked away and pulled the trigger. Blood spattered his face, but the dog didn't let go. He fired again and with a yelp, the dog fell to the ground, dead. Biting back tears of frustration, he sat back heavily against the barn and nursed his bleeding arm. *How could he have forgotten about the bastard dog?*

Headlights appeared in the distance. Hauling himself to his feet, he started running, clutching his injured arm to his chest. Tripping in a rabbit hole, he sprawled in long grass. The headlights got closer. Picking himself up, he ran on. The massive barn doors were shut. A heavy chain looped between them was clasped together by a huge padlock. He pointed the gun at the lock, but held his fire. A gunshot would alert whoever was in the car. His mind went blank.

The moon appeared from behind a cloud and the new

chain glimmered with pale light. He turned to face the headlights. He was just going to have to go back to the farmhouse and take this on. He started running. The headlights were too close. He was never going to make it. Diving into a hedge, he wriggled through and settled down. Anyone coming up the track was going to get a fright.

The car pulled up outside the house and the lights died. Someone got out and stretched like he had been driving a long time. A whistle cut the night.

'Here boy!'

McCann's voice carried clearly on the night air. When the dog didn't immediately appear, he stiffened, sniffing the air as if he could get the wind to tell him its secrets. Whipping a pistol from his tweed jacket pocket, he stalked to the backdoor of the farmhouse and disappeared inside. He was not inside long. There were two shots and he ran back out into the darkness, pointing his pistol around him at the shadows. He started up the track towards the barn and then seemed to hesitate. Taking a mobile phone from his pocket, he jabbed a button, mumbled a few hurried words and then headed to his car.

'*I'll be back,*' he screamed, somehow sensing Gilmour was listening. '*I'll be fucking back!*'

Jumping into his car, he drove off, knocking the shit out of the underside of the vehicle. Gilmour wormed back through the hedge and sprinted to the farmhouse. Ben had been shot twice through the back of the head. Socketless eyeballs glistened in the bloody pulp that had been his face.

Gilmour searched the kitchen frantically, but there were no keys. Not on either dead man, not hanging on a nail, not in any drawers, nowhere. He ran outside and raced off back up the track. He was about to fire at the padlock when he noticed the small door set into the side of the barn. Aghast with his stupidity, he ran over and pushed. The damn thing was open. Inside it was pitch black.

'*Ang! Philippa!*'

His voice echoed round the disused barn. Something glassy glinted in the dull moonlight slanting in through the door. He grabbed the torch from a workbench and switched it on. He found Roberts in a far corner, gagged and unconscious, staked down on bales of hay. Working swiftly, he untied the ropes and removed the dirty cloth stuffed into her mouth. Gently, he lifted her to a sitting position and put his good arm round her.

'It's okay sweetheart,' he said softly.

'Is that you Jamie?'

'Yes.'

'I thought you were dead.'

'You okay?'

'No, I'm not,' she moaned, nursing her chaffed wrists.

'What happened to your hand?'

'What does it look like?'

Gilmour pulled her close to him to get some body heat into her.

'Where's Angelina?' he asked.

'How should I know?' she hissed, pushing him away. God, you stink!'

Gilmour put his arm back round her shoulders.

'Are we safe yet?' asked Roberts, looking up at him with sad eyes.

'No, not yet.'

'*Fuck!*'

'Where's Angelina?' asked Gilmour again.

'I don't know.'

'Stay here.'

'Where are you going?'

'Can you walk?'

'No.'

'Well, you'd better learn.'

'Fuck you.'

'Ever heard of Jimmie McCann?'

She sat bolt upright.

'Belfast McCann?'

'Yes, that's who we're dealing with. He plans to ship you back to Ireland for the lads to have some fun with.'

Roberts clutched at him, her eyes wide.

Gilmour nearly fainted as he prised her fingers from his injured arm.

'He'll be back soon,' he said, getting up to check out the rest of the barn. 'So could you please learn to walk again.'

The disused pens and stalls were all empty. Of Angelina, there was no sign. Roberts was on her feet when he got back, hobbling about taking tentative baby steps.

'Can you manage?' he asked, taking her hand while she tested her legs.

She hobbled a few more steps and he gently led her towards the patch of light spilling in through the door. He switched off the torch as they stepped outside.

'Which way?' asked Roberts.

'I've no idea where we are.'

'Where's the road?'

'McCann will be coming back that way. I'm going to look around for a bit, try to find the girl. You stay here and get your legs working.'

'We were split up when we were taken from the van.'

Gilmour headed off towards a ramshackle outbuilding. Headlights appeared in the distance.

'*Shit!*' hissed Roberts, beginning to panic.

Gilmour slipped the pistol from his waistband. This time there were two sets of headlights. He glanced into the trees behind the barn. With McCann on his tail, no survival kit, map or compass, and no idea where they were, things did not look good.

'We're going to have to run sweetheart,' he said.

Taking Roberts' hand, he helped her over a barbed wire fence. Stealing a nervous glance back at the approaching headlights, he led her quickly into the forest.

Chapter 13

Gilmour lost his footing and sprawled headlong, scratching his face in a thorny thicket. He lay for a minute, his chest heaving, his filthy shirt stuck to his sweaty skin. Inside he felt hollow and empty. Leaving Angelina behind had torn his heart out. Roberts blundered out of the shadows and collapsed to the forest floor beside him, her slim frame shaking as she fought for air. *At least*, he thought wryly, *he wasn't going to lose her*. She was making more noise than an outing of school kids munching crisps at the movies. He touched the side of his head and grimaced at the fresh blood on his fingertips. Tearing the lining from a pocket of his trousers, he sat up and dabbed gingerly at his head.

As he sat listening to the forest, he tried to come to terms with his decision to leave Angelina. He looked up at the night sky, but found no comfort there. The beauty of the moonlight glistening on the drying branches of the silvery forest was cold and meaningless. The breeze breathing through the trees drifted against his skin like cold threads of spider's web on a damp morning. Somewhere in the trees an animal snuffled about. It must have caught their scent, because the snuffling stopped and he never heard it again. A faint barking leached through the forest from the direction of the farm.

'Shit,' said Gilmour, helping Roberts to her feet. 'Let's go, he has another dog.'

He ran blindly, keeping the moon behind them to their left. Roberts loped along after him, her breathing now controlled and steady, determination glistening in the sweat on her forehead. She wasn't making much noise now either. She was a quick learner. He wanted to say something encouraging, but couldn't think of anything that didn't sound pathetic.

Hearing running water, he leapt a patch of heavy undergrowth and ducked under a low branch. The ground fell away and he lost his footing and slithered to the bottom of a steep gully. He got up quickly, waded into the middle of a shallow stream and sat in the deepest bit. Roberts scrambled down the bank and dropped to her knees by the stream.

'Don't drink that,' warned Gilmour.

'Are we lost?' she asked, splashing her face and then washing her wounded hand carefully.

'We should have found a road or a path by now,' he said, holding the side of his head.

'What about the dog?' asked Roberts, with a pained expression. 'Have we lost it?'

'No.'

'Shouldn't we run in the water for a while?' she asked, staring up the side of the gully at the dark shadows of the forest overhanging them.

'Eh?' said Gilmour, splashing water over himself as

he tried to scrub the stink from his body.

'Isn't that how you escape dogs?'

'In movies.'

'Don't patronise me.'

Gilmour crawled ashore and slumped down on a large gnarly root growing out of the bank.

'Sit down will you,' he said, patting the root beside him.

Roberts stood in the middle of the stream, her hands on her hips, the water eddying round her knees.

'It's okay,' said Gilmour, 'I don't smell quite so bad now.'

Roberts waded out of the stream and sat, but not on the root beside him.

'What is it?' asked Gilmour.

She ignored him.

'Look, walking in streams *can* confuse a dog, you're right, but it slows you down too much.'

'How so?' she asked, pulling strands of straw from her tangled hair.

'How long would it take us to scramble a mile down that?'

She glanced down the rocky watercourse overhung with heavy bushes.

'Ages, I suppose.'

'And how long would it take a dog to run down the bank after us?'

'So what are we going to do?'

'Well, the dog can only go as fast as the bloke holding the leash.'

'Unless they let it off.'

Gilmour patted his pistol.

'McCann's not that stupid.'

'But we have to do *something*.'

'I know what I'm doing.'

'Oh, aren't you the *clever* one,' she said, her eyes smouldering. 'So what are *you* going to do then?'

'Put you over my knee in a minute.'

Roberts glared at him and then noticed with some alarm blood on the side of his face.

'What happened to you?' she asked.

'It's nothing.'

'*Look at your arm!*'

She reached out to help, but he pulled away. She got down on her knees in front of him and working quickly, slipped off his jacket and pulled up his shirtsleeve. Gilmour didn't have the guts to look.

'Will I live nurse?'

'Hmmm . . . the muscle is punctured, but the bruising makes it look worse than it is.' She took the pocket lining, washed it in the stream and dabbed gently at the punctures. 'It'll keep till we get you to a doctor,' she said when she was satisfied the wounds were clean.

Gilmour winced as her fingers ran through his hair, checking the side of his head. She pressed the cloth against the gash on his scalp and placed his hand on it to hold it in position.

'What are we going to do?' she asked.

Gilmour sighed, but figured he had better start explaining himself. She wanted to learn, he could see that.

'The dog will be finding it easy, so we're going to run in circles for a bit, back and forth across the stream, leaving trails everywhere. Then we'll take off in a different direction, and, hopefully, confuse the dog.'

Roberts nodded, a little happier, but not much. She thought she heard something in the trees and jumped to her feet. Her reaction sent fear coursing through Gilmour and he levered himself from his root.

'Then let's start now,' suggested Roberts.

'That should do it,' said Gilmour, hanging and dropping from the low branches of an oak.

'You're a mess,' observed Roberts, checking the side of his head again.

'Later,' he said, pushing her hand away.

'You think climbing those trees will help?'

He glanced at the moon and picked a new bearing.

'I hope so.'

'If not?'

Gilmour thought about it. Walking over to her, he took her hands in his. She didn't pull away.

'If it comes down to it,' he said, looking deep into her eyes, 'I'll hold them off and take out the dog. That'll give you time to leg it.'

She had the good sense not to argue.

'You know what to do,' he said, giving her a small smile.

'Please,' she whispered, 'let's go.'

With a squeeze of her shoulders, he turned and set off into the forest, this time with the moon behind them to their right. As they ran, he tried to make sense of what was happening between them. This woman, padding along behind him now as silent as a prowling panther, was already entrenched in places he hadn't even known existed.

Gilmour stopped and held up a hand. Roberts barged straight into the back of him, almost knocking him over.

'*Watch it!*' he hissed.

She pushed him away.

'Why didn't you warn me you were going to stop? *Idiot!*'

Gilmour sighed heavily.

'When I hold up my hand like this, it means *stop*.'

'Really?' she said, her voice weighted with sarcasm. 'And my middle finger raised like this means—'

Gilmour stepped towards her menacingly and leaned forward until the tip of his nose touched hers.

'You're beginning to piss me off.'

'Is that so?' she said, putting her hands on her hips, staring right back into his eyes.

'From now on,' said Gilmour, his voice dripping with controlled menace, 'you will do *exactly* as I say.'

'Oh yeah?'

'Or else I'm going to leave you right here.'

Gilmour watched the fire in her eyes slowly dim, then led her down a steep hillside where they heard the sound of rapids. When they came to the river, they concealed themselves in the shadows of bushes by its banks.

While he listened to the roaring of the rapids, Gilmour found it hard to believe that things could be so wrong. Life could be so beautiful; yet drip with ugliness. It could be so peaceful; yet scream with pain. It could take his breath away; yet choke him with horror. It didn't make sense. Something was seriously wrong with the world. Roberts pointed downstream.

'What's that?'

Hidden in the shadows of the forest were the ruins of an old cottage. Its roof had long fallen in and tangled briars grew out of empty windows.

Gilmour didn't reply.

'Are you okay?' she asked.

Gilmour looked at her, having noticed something different about her tone.

'What is it?' he asked gently.

'Oh . . . you.'

Pain swirled briefly through the deep pools of her eyes. It reminded him of a time when he was a boy. He was kneeling by the side of a river peering down into dark water. Suddenly, before his startled gaze, a fish darted up from the bottom, turned with a flash and disappeared back into the depths. Gilmour knew she had wanted him to see her hurt.

'Here,' he whispered, handing her one of the pistols. 'Use it if you have to.'

Using the shadows of a fallen tree for cover, they picked their way down to the banks of the river. With scarcely a ripple, they slipped into the black water at the tail end of a quiet pool. The water gurgled round their necks as they remained motionless for a while, watching the trees on the far bank.

Stuffing the pistol into his mouth, Gilmour led the way across, using the weedy stones on the bottom to pull himself forward. His eyes never left the trees on the other side. The bottom shelved away and he tucked his legs under him in the deeper water. Upstream, something moved. He froze. On a mossy rock beside the rapids cascading into the head of the pool, an otter was watching them, its whiskers bristling with curiosity. The moon disappeared behind the clouds, plunging the riverbank into darkness. The otter dived into the dark water without a ripple and disappeared.

Crawling out of the river between two large boulders, Gilmour peered carefully over the lip of the bank. The chill breeze cut through his wet clothes. Suppressing a shiver, he edged into the trees, his pistol firmly gripped in his good hand. Tucking in behind a thick tree trunk, he controlled his breathing and listened. He was tuned to the night now. He slipped round the trunk and set off once again into the night, Roberts close behind him.

Gilmour stumbled across a ditch, lost his footing and tumbled down a short grassy slope. He picked himself up at the bottom, hugging his arm.

'I can hear water,' said Roberts. 'I'm thirsty.'

'It's not safe,' he said, and turned and headed away from the sound of the water.

'Oh, stuff you,' croaked Roberts through her parched throat and headed for the stream.

Surprised at how quietly she was now moving, Gilmour checked back over his shoulder and pulled up.

'*Women!*'

He found her on her hands and knees in the stream, washing sweat and dirt from her face and neck.

'You're *impossible!*' he muttered heavily.

She leaned down putting her lips to the water and drank deeply.

'Oh bollocks,' said Gilmour, kneeling down beside her. 'If we get the runs, I'm holding you responsible.'

'You can put me over your knee,' she said provocatively.

Gilmour stopped drinking to give her a hard stare and she turned away to hide a smile.

Suddenly, some way behind them in the forest, a gunshot rang out. A dog yelped. They both leapt to their feet. Gilmour drew his pistol. Roberts clutched at him. Gilmour groaned and prised her tightening fingers from his injured arm.

'I wish you'd stop that,' he said.

'*What was that?*'

'The dickhead's got pissed off with the dog and shot it. Our little ruse has worked better than I'd hoped.'

A scream cut through the forest, clear and dreadful, terrorising the night.

'*Gilmooooooour!*'

He felt his blood chill.

'*You're fucking DEAD!*'

There was a shocked silence, which even the stream feared to break.

'*And so's that little fucking shite bitch!*'

'Is that so?' hissed Gilmour, taking a step across the stream.

Roberts grabbed his good arm. Gilmour tried to shake her off, but she flung her arms round his neck and forced her legs into the bank to hold him back.

'*Stupid bastard!*' she hissed.

Gilmour levered her hands from him and threw her off. Somehow, she managed to keep a grip of his jacket. In the struggle, Gilmour tripped over a large mossy rock and the two of them fell into the stream. She struggled on top of him, pinning him down. He looked up into her frightened face and tried to get up, but she was strong. Lying there in the stream, unable to move, his hatred of McCann flowing through his veins like acid, madness suddenly sprang into his eyes. He nipped the insides of her thighs viciously and slammed his fingers up under her armpits. Roberts grunted, her vision clouding with pain. Throwing her backwards, he used his right leg to force her thighs apart, pulled his arm back and clenched his fist.

'Jamie . . . *no!*'

She held up an arm to ward off the blow.

Gilmour, his lips curled back over his teeth, no longer saw her. He saw only terrorists and explosions and McCann and Angelina being raped. He blinked as the storm passed. His vision focused and he slowly unclenched his fist. Roberts was shaking, blood trickling from the corner of her mouth. Twigs and bits of moss stuck out of her hair and her face was bruised and dirty. Gilmour sat back in the water and screwed his eyes shut. Roberts got painfully to her knees and stared at him, not sure what to do.

'You don't understand,' said Gilmour. 'You don't know what they're going to do to her.'

Her arms went round him and he felt her head on his shoulder.

'I think we should go,' she said.

Gilmour wiped his sleeve across his eyes. She stayed close, her arms round him, holding him together. He hung his head and listened to the stream. He had never cried in front of anyone before.

'I'm sorry,' he said softly.

'I know.'

Gilmour noticed that the slow dripping of raindrops from the forest canopy had finally stopped.

'I thought I was going to die just now,' said Roberts quietly.

'When you heard the shot?'

'When you were going to hit me.'

'Ah.'

'You always so rough with your women?'

Gilmour dropped his eyes. Moonlight danced in the swirling water of the stream. He'd never watched moonlight on moving water before. It took him a long while to answer.

'If you knew what McCann's going to do to Ang, you'd understand.'

'Maybe.'

Gilmour pointed at the reflections on the water.

'Isn't that amazing?'

'The moon has no light of its own,' said Roberts, following his finger.

'I watch Star Trek,' said Gilmour, 'but that's about the extent of my science knowledge.'

He got up and took her hand, lifting her from the water. She allowed herself to be helped up and wondered why she found herself enjoying the experience.

'Star Trek?' she asked.

'Well, Voyager mostly.'

'Is Spock in it?'

'No, but there's a cool Vulcan.'

'I liked Spock, he was so sensible.'

'I like Seven.'

'Seven?'

'You've not heard of Seven of Nine?'

'Is it another sci-fi programme?'

'No, she's a Borg with gorgeous . . . er . . . rather nice, well you know . . . tits.'

'You mean breasts?'

Gilmour struggled up the bank and reached back a hand.

'We can take it a bit easier now,' he said, 'and by the way . . .'

'Yes?'

'. . . you're no sergeant.'

Gilmour hauled her up the bank and waited.

'No,' she said, 'you're right.'

'You going to tell me?'

'I was a captain before working for the Secret Service. The sergeant bit is a cover to stop a lot of the wrong people looking twice at me.'

She touched her toes to stretch her calves and when she straightened up, Gilmour found he couldn't pull his eyes from her.

'What?' she asked, aware of his eyes.

Gilmour shook his head, checked his bearings and set off into the forest at a gentle trot.

'It's no use,' said Roberts, pulling up. 'I can't go on.'

Gilmour looked around them. It was just past midnight and dawn was still hours away. Why they hadn't found any signs of civilisation yet was beyond him.

'We must have passed trails in the dark,' he muttered under his breath. 'I'll build us a little shelter and then we can maybe get a couple of hours sleep.'

'Mmmmmmmm . . . sleep,' she sighed, sitting down on a tussock and massaging her legs.

Gilmour left her to it and went to work. He didn't want to stop, but as he saw it, he had little choice. As he rooted about looking for fallen branches, he found himself looking back at the lithe form of Roberts silhouetted in the shadows of the trees. The thought of her cuddling into him for warmth suddenly seemed rather appealing. Exhaustion gripped him and he felt giddy. Angelina was just going to have to forgive him.

'Is that it?' asked Roberts, looking down her nose with some disdain at the tiny shelter.

'What's wrong with it?' asked Gilmour, somewhat affronted, thinking the latticed structure of branches and leaves leaning against the dead trunk of a fallen tree one of his better efforts.

With one of his trademark sighs, he crawled under the low roof, taking care not to disturb the bed of moss he'd taken such great pains to gather.

'You getting in or what?'

He pushed himself to the back of the tiny structure and opened his arms for her. Cooled down now, Roberts was beginning to shiver in her wet clothes. She got down on her hands and knees and crawled in.

'Closer,' said Gilmour, 'shared body heat is all we have.'

'Keep your hands to yourself, please,' she retorted. She wriggled about to find a comfortable position and then turned her back to him. 'This ground is so *hard!*'

'Please yourself,' said Gilmour, nodding off.

He hadn't been asleep that long when he was woken by Roberts fidgeting.

'What is it?' he asked.

'Don't be so grumpy,' she moaned. 'I'm frozen.'

Gilmour rolled onto his side, put his good arm round her and pulled her into him. Her face gratefully nuzzled into his neck and he lay back absorbing her warmth, enjoying her soft breath on his skin.

'Is that better?' he asked gently.

'Mmmmm.'

'The tighter you cuddle, the cosier it gets.'

She cuddled tighter, wrapping a leg over him and he pulled her closer, laying his head against hers, luxuriating in the delicious heat they were sharing. Her knee slid up his leg towards his groin and he felt himself stirring.

'Life is certainly different around you,' she said drowsily.

Gilmour found himself developing a bulge in his trousers.

'How so?' he asked.

'What?'

'I was thinking . . .'

Her leg slid a little farther up his and he didn't have time to stop her. Her knee slid quickly down again.

'I'm sorry,' he said, a little embarrassed.

'*Men!*'

'You're kinda . . . well, overpowering at close range Philippa.'

'Go to sleep.'

'Sure.'

'What were you thinking?' she asked, half opening a sleepy eye.

'You just told me to go to sleep.'

'Don't be obtuse.'

'I was just wondering . . .'

'Yes?'

Gilmour looked up at the twigs poking down into his face from the low roof. He wasn't sure how to put it into words.

'What?' she asked, both eyes open now.

'It doesn't matter.'

The eyes closed again.

'Mmmm . . . this is so nice,' she said, snuggling into him.

Gilmour couldn't believe he was afraid of a woman. 'Actually, it does matter,' he said softly.

'I'll buy one tomorrow . . .' she whispered incoherently as she drifted off to sleep.

Gilmour hugged her close to him, the bulge in his trousers now so hard it ached.

Should I ask her out? asked his head, struggling to find the courage.

Sounds good to me, replied his heart.

The conversation developed into an argument.

But what about Karen?

Karen?

You haven't even phoned her yet.

As he drifted off to sleep he knew he had fallen for her.

Chapter 14

The mood in the Colonel's office was sombre. Ellis, still soaked to the skin from the quarry in Northern Ireland was hunched up over a steaming mug of coffee, clutching it close to his chest with numb fingers.

'Would you like a blanket while we find you a change of clothes?' asked the Colonel who had not long been dragged from his bed. He sat forward, his elbows on his desk, his chin resting on his interlocked fingers, and gazed interestedly at Ellis' clothing.

'Are you sure none of that blood is yours?' he asked. 'Would you like a medic to take a look at you?'

Ellis shook his head, ignoring the annoying drip on the end of his nose.

'Thanks for the lift, Colonel,' he said, 'but next time try not to leave me standing about in the rain for over two hours, eh.'

'You getting soft?' asked the Colonel with some amusement. 'It couldn't be helped. We had a compromised observation post down in Crossmaglen and we had to reroute your chopper. A couple of the lads needed a rather hasty evacuation.'

'They okay?'

'A drunk young lady staggering home from the pub they were watching decided she couldn't wait. She squatted down to relieve herself behind the particular bush they were concealed in.'

'She *saw* them?'

'I believe one of our chaps giggled.'

'Well, no offence Colonel, but in future I think I'll travel a little more comfortably thank you.'

'That blanket?'

'If you don't mind,' said Ellis, wiping the drip from his nose with the back of his hand.

The Colonel picked up his phone and pressed a couple of numbers. While he waited, he raised an eyebrow and motioned a finger towards Ellis' clothing.

'No doubt there's a peculiar story behind all that blood.'

'No doubt.'

'Anything I should know?'

'How long till Peterson shows up?'

The Colonel spoke briefly into the phone and replaced the handset.

'Another hour or so, I should imagine. I authorised a highly irregular return flight to Ireland for you, at the tax payers' expense I might add.'

'*Please*, Colonel. I'm required to report to my client first.'

'Peterson got quite agitated when I mentioned you were here.'

'Did he now?'

Ellis shifted uncomfortably in his damp clothing. He was dreaming of a long hot shower and something to eat. A disgruntled politician was the last thing on his mind.

The phone rang.

'Yes?' The Colonel listened; his face registered surprise. '*Really?*' Suddenly, he sat back. '*Good lord!*'

Ellis tried not to look interested.

'Yes . . . yes, of course.'

The Colonel put his hand over the mouthpiece and leaned forward.

'Are you still here?'

'Who is it?'

'Peterson.'

Ellis nodded.

The Colonel took his hand away and spoke into the phone.

'Yes, he's here in my office.'

Ellis felt a tightening in his stomach. Something was seriously wrong. Uncharacteristically, the Colonel replaced the receiver very gently.

'That was Peterson.'

'So you said.'

'He's *ordered* me not to let you leave until he gets here.'

'Did he have anything intelligent to add?'

'Under *any* circumstances. Ordered me to detain you, *by force,* if necessary.'

The mug dropped slightly from Ellis' lips.

'He also mentioned that the body of a senior IRA man has been discovered in a quarry on the outskirts of Belfast and did I know anything about it?'

Ellis checked his watch. It was less than five hours since he'd left the quarry. The body had been found too quickly. He was in trouble.

'From the body?' asked the Colonel, pointing to the bloodstains again.

There was a knock at the door.

'Come in!' said the Colonel, sitting forward at his desk; ready, as always, to handle any problems that might come through the door at him.

An NCO stuck his head in and looked across at Ellis.

'Your clothes mate,' he said, chucking over a bag and a blanket.

'Appreciate it,' said Ellis, grabbing them as they sailed through the air.

'Catch you later.'

Ellis looked at the Colonel as the door closed, a solemn expression on his face.

'Am I being detained?' he asked.

'Yes, of course!' exclaimed the Colonel, looking up with amazement. 'Have you a problem with that?'

'You didn't tell anyone about me being across the water?'

'No.' The Colonel pushed his chair back and stood up. 'Now, if you don't mind, I have pressing things to attend to.'

Ellis frowned.

'I think I have a problem,' he said tiredly.

His concern seemed to intensify as he stepped out of the office into the night-lighting of the empty corridor.

Scrubbing the last of the blood from his skin, Ellis closed his eyes and tilted his head into the steaming jets, appreciating the shower as only cold, tired, dirty, wet soldiers can. McConnell had not been lying, of that he was certain. Many years of listening to men and women dying in great pain had taught him to recognise the truth when it finally came out. McCann was now starting to really bother him. Delicious water cascaded down his skin, radiating welcome heat to his chilled muscles and bones, and he allowed his thoughts to drift off with the steam.

It was early winter and his breath clouded before his face. Frost glistened in the moonlight, crunching under his boots as they patrolled cautiously along the edge of a forest. Two shots rang out somewhere in the trees. The patrol commander barked an order and the four soldiers clambered over the fence. As they ducked under branches and leapt irrigation ditches, Ellis wondered what a high velocity round thumping into his chest would feel like. McCann? The name didn't mean anything to him yet. All he knew was that three men had been disturbed planting explosives in a culvert under a country lane and that they had run off into the night.

It wasn't long before they stumbled across a couple of bodies. Two young IRA men lay on the frosted ground, their bodies still warm, their moist eyes staring vacantly up through the branches. To Ellis, their blood seemed a little too black against the sparkling white frost. *But who had shot them?* There were no other Army patrols in the vicinity. SAS? Paras? The RUC? 14 Int? *But where were they?* They went into all round defence and waited while the patrol commander sent his report over the radio.

It was the following morning before they learned the truth. The third man had escaped; a young IRA recruit who was showing great promise, a man so ruthless he had shot his men to save his own skin. The clever bastard had made sure the SAS was credited with the kills too.

Ellis turned in the shower to allow the water to flood

down his back. McCann had come a long way since those inauspicious beginnings. He slicked down his hair and put his head back under the jets. He still had a few minutes with which to think. His mind on the killing, he recalled the first time he'd encountered the SAS.

He was lying behind a stone wall, getting wet in the rain, his rifle covering a farm cottage. Suddenly, a bloke leapt from behind a shed, bringing an AK-47 rifle to his shoulder. Someone screamed a warning. Bodies dived for cover as Ellis loosed off two rounds and dropped the bloke stone dead.

As he walked over to the twitching body, a tremendous sense of being alive had flushed through him. It was his first kill, but he felt no remorse or guilt. To his surprise he found he was exhilarated. Every pore of his skin tingled. He kept his rifle locked into his shoulder, aimed at the man's head as he approached warily. The face seemed still alive and its twitching made him giggle. His section commander bawled at him to shut up, but it only made it worse. He stuffed his fist into his mouth, but it didn't help. The other soldiers gathered in a nervous group, staring at him as if he was mad.

An officer talking into a radio walked over to a large clump of bushes nearby and spoke to it. To Ellis' surprise, it rustled violently and two scruffy, longhaired blokes crawled out. They dusted themselves down, picked up their rifles and kit and sauntered over. They were stinking and had obviously been in the bush a long time. Through his tears, Ellis saw that they were both laughing as well. One of them told him he should join the SAS. That had shut him up. A car hurtled down the lane to the cottage and slewed to a halt in a cloud of dust. The blokes ran over and jumped in, the tyres skirled, and they were gone.

The SAS? Joining them had been fun. Rain lashed his young face, driven by the blustery wind howling across the desolate Brecon Beacons. His heavy bergen was breaking his collar bones and his boots had long scraped the raw blisters from his feet. He thought he could feel blood squelching between his toes. He looked up at the forbidding mountainside ahead of him, its peak lost in the mists. He knew he couldn't go on, that he was a beaten man. Beyond that mountain too, he knew, there was yet another. All he had to do was sit down in the wet grass and it would all be over. The SAS directing staff would take him to the train station. No one would say a word to him. They would drop him off and drive away and that would be that. He would become just another inked name in the great register of SAS failures. He looked back up the mountainside and started climbing. It was only pain.

Ellis turned in the shower and soaped himself one last time, lathering his arms and chest. Putting his face right up to the showerhead, he let the force of the water massage his skin. He knew many people were terrified of him and hated him. But they didn't understand. They believed that properly trained soldiers abhorred war and hated killing. What did they know? If the pacifists wanted to roll over and have their bellies tickled every time a slavering wolf snarled at them that was their fucking problem.

But how had McConnell's body been found so quickly? No one would have been in the disused quarry at that time of night in *that* weather. Not unless he had been followed. *But who?* Perhaps it had been someone out poaching who had stumbled across the grisly find and phoned the authorities. He liked that idea, but somehow he knew it was not that simple. His skin was starting to turn red. It was time to get out of the shower.

Back in the Colonel's office, tired but refreshed and comfortable in a crisp shirt and freshly laundered trousers, Ellis was pleasantly surprised to find a tray with a plateful of curry and rice waiting for him.

'For me?'

'At this time of morning,' smiled the Colonel, 'I much prefer sausage and egg rolls myself.'

'Thank you,' said a grateful Ellis, the aroma of the succulent curry making his mouth water. 'I'll be outside if you need me.'

Plate in one hand, fork in the other, he turned and left the office.

There were hardly any clouds. He looked up at the dawn sky and wondered if Gilmour was still alive. His involvement was an enigma. What was his role in this puzzle? He took a mouthful of curry and stopped to savour the tang of the spicy sauce. If there was one thing the SAS was good at, it was curries. It felt good to be back amongst men who cared.

A few stars twinkled away happily in the twilight. He felt no enmity from them. He had no regrets about McConnell and felt sure that if there were a God, he would be a much happier God that morning as the world was now a better place. He sank his teeth into another chunk of juicy meat as a shiny new black Jaguar pulled up and parked, the round headlights shining against the wall of a building. The engine died and the lights went out. Curious to see who was behind the tinted glass, Ellis ambled over in its general direction.

'Good morning,' said Peterson, getting out of the car and stretching.

'Yes it is,' replied Ellis, poking his fork into another piece of meat and running it round the creamy juices on his plate.

'Ellis, you're slipping.'

'Am I still under arrest?'

'You're lucky you're still alive.'

'Mmmm . . . gorgeous,' said Ellis, stuffing the forkful of food into his mouth.

'The BMW was a silly move, Peter.'

'Hmm?'

'McConnell.'

Ellis swallowed what was in his mouth without chewing it properly.

'I think we had better go inside,' said Peterson.

'Good morning Colonel,' said Peterson, striding into the office with his hand out. 'Good of you to see me at such short notice.'

The Colonel shook his hand warmly and waved the two men towards the chairs he had hastily arranged round his desk.

'Coffee gentlemen?'

'Fresh?' asked Peterson.

'Instant at this time of morning, I'm afraid Sir.'

'That'll do me,' said Ellis.

'Instant will be fine.'

As the Colonel picked up the phone, Ellis noticed Peterson quietly shift his chair to the opposite end of the desk from him. The Colonel ordered the coffee and replacing the receiver, turned to Peterson.

'Pleasant drive, Sir?'

'Most agreeable, thank you Colonel,' he replied. 'That new Jaguar is really quite exhilarating.'

Ellis found the mood in the office tense, but not uncomfortable. The Colonel was eager to get things going but Peterson seemed unperturbed, content to wait for his coffee. Like a boxer before a bout, Ellis sat quietly in his corner. Peterson may have known things he didn't know, but he knew things that Peterson didn't. This was going to be interesting. It was an impatient Colonel who rang the bell.

'Peter . . . your appearance last night. An explanation?' he asked.

'To be honest, Colonel, I think our good friend from the Home Office might be able to throw a little light on that.'

'I can understand your reticence Ellis,' said Peterson smoothly, 'especially after my earlier remarks.'

Peterson seemed a little too pleased with himself, thought Ellis, but kept his annoyance from his face.

'McConnell's car was wired,' explained Peterson at length, tiring of the game.

'*What!*'

'That's right.'

'But who?' Ellis was stunned. '*Mi5?* They wouldn't dare! Surely the—'

Peterson cut him off.

'Oh, not by *us* Peter. By his own people, at *his* request. It was a personal security measure.'

'You mean . . . I was followed? By *them?*'

'Precisely. It wasn't very clever of you driving off in the man's car like that.'

Ellis dropped his eyes to the desk. He was not enjoying what he was hearing.

'And *you* followed *them?*'

'We had a tip off.'

'Pat?'

The minister nodded.

'You saw everything that happened then?' asked Ellis, watching the Minister very closely.

He thought there was something a little odd about his manner but wasn't able to put his finger on it.

'Oh, much better,' said Peterson, actually smiling. 'After taking care of a couple of Irish rascals for you, we filmed the whole thing. Infra red of course.'

'Of course,' sighed Ellis.

He knew what was coming next. McCann was now his problem, whether he liked it or not.

'I'm sure you two know exactly what it is you are discussing,' said the Colonel with some frustration.

'I'm sorry,' said Peterson. 'Ellis here, for reasons quite beyond the British government and the intelligence agencies, interrogated and executed John McConnell last night in a quarry on the outskirts of Belfast.'

'*Good Lord!*'

'All part of the job,' added Ellis, looking for effect.

'This has something to do with Gilmour and Black?' asked Peterson, his anxiety at last showing itself.

'Yes.'

'*What is going on?*' asked the Colonel, struggling to contain himself.

'Is there any word on Gilmour yet?' asked Ellis, looking from the Colonel to Peterson, but was met by shaking heads.

The coffee arrived, and he gratefully took a mug.

'There is something else,' said Peterson quietly as the NCO left and the door closed again.

'Oh?' said Ellis, thinking he didn't like the sudden change in tone of voice.

'The rather quaint appellation of *The Terminator* was overheard on a monitored telephone call to the offices of Sinn Fein late last night.'

Ellis spluttered into his coffee.

'Yes, I thought that would get your attention.'

'*You!*' started the Colonel, so surprised Ellis thought his eyes must pop out of his head and hang down his cheeks. '*You're* The Terminator?'

Ellis looked at the two men in turn; he was beginning to feel sick.

'McConnell's body was wired too?' he said weakly.

Peterson nodded and stared hard at Ellis.

'He wasn't going on any date. That was just a cover for his *real* reason for going out that night, a reason which, thanks to you, we will now never know.'

Ellis composed himself and sipped his coffee. McCann would know he was onto him now, making things even more impossible than they already were.

'I think an explanation would be in order,' said Peterson.

The Colonel sat forward on the edge of his seat.

'I've made a mistake or two,' said Ellis heavily.

'Be that as it may,' retorted Peterson irritably, 'but I am still no nearer to learning anything I didn't already know.'

The Colonel tapped his lips, wondering where this was all heading.

'Jimmy McCann was behind the shooting,' said Ellis simply, as if that was explanation enough.

'*Good Lord!*' said the Colonel.

'*My God!*' said Peterson.

Ellis picked at a thread on the cuff of his shirt.

Peterson raised half out of his seat.

'*You have to stop him!*'

'You bastards let him out of the Maze,' said Ellis quietly, lifting his eyes from his cuff. '*You* stop him.'

'Whatever . . .' said the Colonel, sensing unresolved resentments surfacing, '. . . but whatever he is up to concerns us all.'

'Agreed,' said Peterson quickly. 'We require someone to deal with him.'

'That's not my particular field, Minister,' said Ellis, tapping the side of his mug and watching the tiny ripples converging into the middle.

'You did a fairly comprehensive job last night with McConnell,' said Peterson.

'Black mail?' asked Ellis, his dark eyes surveying the politician suspiciously over the top of his mug.

'Call it what you like.'

'I'm tired,' said Ellis.

'Were it not for us,' continued Peterson, clearly enjoying himself, 'it would have been you lying stretched out in the mud this morning.'

'And if I refuse?'

Peterson sat back with a crooked smile.

'The way you remove your balaclava, the pistol still smoking in your hand, is really quite dramatic.'

Ellis stifled a yawn.

'If Sinn Fein finds out who I am,' he said, 'I'll hold you personally responsible.'

Peterson tried to sound brave.

'Is that a threat?'

The edge was gone from his voice though and Ellis knew it. He slipped out his pistol and clattered it onto the Colonel's desk.

'Call it whatever you fucking like,' he said quietly.

'Of course,' said Peterson, quickly squirming his way out of trouble, 'you will be appropriately remunerated.'

Ellis sighed and got to his feet. He knew he had no way out. He might as well do it willingly and take the money.

'I guess I'm going to be working with you for some time then, Colonel.'

'I'll sort you out with everything you need,' said the Colonel. 'It'll be good to have you back.'

Ellis thought for a moment.

'I trust the security measures surrounding the Presidential State visit are adequate.'

'Impregnable.'

'Yes, quite' mused Ellis reflectively, picking up his pistol and heading for the door. Almost as an afterthought, he turned to the Minister. 'My fee will be five hundred thousand pounds sterling.'

Quickly, he stepped outside and closed the door before Peterson could recover his wits.

Chapter 15

It was light outside and a glance at his watch told Ellis he had been sleeping for over five hours. He lay for a while staring at the ceiling, wondering why he had an erection.

'This is stupid,' he whispered, taking his hand from himself.

He never could get excited about masturbating.

While his erection softened, he stretched his legs, gradually working the aches from them. Then he remembered what Peterson had said and he sat up in bed. *Sinn Fein knew about The Terminator!* Life had suddenly become very dangerous. Throwing off the duvet, he leapt out of bed, pulled on his trousers and strolled to the window to see what the weather was up to. He was making far too many mistakes. Perhaps it was time to retire.

'Ellis? *Peter?*'
Ellis looked up from his late breakfast, a forkful of

scrambled eggs near his mouth. A piece of egg tumbled from his fork and fell to his plate. He put his cutlery down, picked up his napkin and wiped his mouth.

'Hello Brian,' he replied, getting to his feet and gesturing to a chair on the other side of the table.

Brian Munro, B Squadron's sergeant major took off his beige beret and ran his fingers through his thinning hair.

'Not eating in the officer's mess?' he asked.

'Not when I can help it,' replied Ellis, resuming his seat.

'You're an ugly bastard,' chuckled Munro as he sat at the table. 'Did you have bad acne as a kid?'

Ellis observed the bright scar running from Munro's right ear across his cheek to the side of his mouth, a wound courtesy of an Argentine 7.62 mm high velocity round, and doubted any woman alive would have found him attractive. Making fun of good looking men was just his way of dealing with it.

'Wouldn't do to be too noticeable in my game,' he reflected drily.

'Don't worry,' said Munro, 'it doesn't matter to the Hereford ladies. Being ugly doesn't put them off as long as you're SAS.'

'Lucky for you.'

'And they seem to be able to smell us a mile away too, canny wenches.'

'You should tell the men to clean behind their foreskins more often then,' said Ellis, getting on with his breakfast.

Munro laughed.

'Wouldn't want to spoil things for them – they seem to like it mucky.'

Ellis chewed thoughtfully, pondering the erection he'd had earlier. For the first time in his life he was starting to feel lonely. *Retiring?* To what? Sitting in an empty castle reading books by himself? A bit of mucky sounded good.

'What is it Peter?'

Ellis stuck his fork into a chunk of sausage and dipped it in a blob of brown sauce on the side of his plate.

'Nothing important.'

'Never were the chatty type, were you.'

'How's the family?'

'We have a pub now, the Clown and Dagger. You know you're always welcome to pop round. Shirley is a fantastic cook.'

Ellis looked across at him sadly.

'And risk getting you all murdered?'

Munro lost his smile.

'Hannah still asks about you,' he said.

'Gosh, Hannah, she must be grown up now.'

'She's nearly twenty one.'

'Doesn't time fly.'

'The wife's sister is down for the week too, and she's hot! Bloody nipples always poking through her clothes. Keeps pestering me to set her up with a date.'

Ellis avoided the obvious hint and pulled the sausage from the fork with his teeth. There had always been somewhere to go, always something to do. Now there was nothing and no one.

'Going to be around for a while?' asked Munro.

'Couple of days, maybe. Actually, I could do with a little help. You interested?'

'*Me?*'

'I need someone I can trust, someone who can handle

himself. Preferably someone with a brain.'

'I'm a *soldier*, Peter.'

'We're talking McCann here.'

'Belfast McCann?'

'Interested?'

Munro took a deep breath and ran a hand round the back of his neck.

'Like I said, I'm just a soldier. Besides, I'm extremely busy with the security arrangements surrounding the Presidential State visit. I'm the SAS liaison officer for the whole operation.'

Ellis thought as he put the last of his breakfast into his mouth.

'Brian, is there any way to get to the President?'

Munro shook his head confidently.

'No chance.'

Ellis picked up a mug of tea and sipped.

'I've given up tea,' said Munro.

'You've *what?* Isn't that an RTU offence?'

'I was getting these terrible headaches some days and then I discovered it was the tea, or rather, the lack of it.'

'Really?'

'Yeah, I found that if I didn't have tea in the morning, I got the headaches come lunch time.'

'Caffeine?'

'I thought it might be the tannin in the leaves.'

'You're still into all that conspiracy stuff eh.'

Munro grinned.

'Now that you mention it, what do you make of the pyramids on the back of American dollar notes?'

Ellis took another sip of his tea and looked into his mug, wondering if there was anything behind the headaches theory.

'Did you know there are eye's in them?'

'Eyes?'

'Well . . . an eye,' said Munro, looking very grave.

'And?'

'Dunno, just never noticed before. Thought you might know something.'

'Not me.'

'Oh come on Peter, everyone knows you're into all that secret society shit.'

Ellis grimaced. People really did have the wrong idea about him.

'Only because that's where all the scum bags I'm looking for seem to hang out,' he said.

'You don't know anything about eyes and pyramids then?'

'Nope.'

'And I suppose you hadn't noticed that there's an eye and a pyramid in Mi5's logo?'

Ellis shook his head.

'Lying bastard. And I suppose you've never heard of the Illuminati either.'

Ellis put his mug down and dropped his napkin onto his plate.

'You'll be bringing up the CFR and Chatham House next.'

'So you *do* know something?'

'It's not a nice world out there.'

'Don't patronise me Peter.'

'The Illuminati were founded by the Roman Catholics,' said Ellis. 'Weishaupt was a Jesuit priest.'

'Wise who? Tell you what though.'

'What?'

Never could understand . . .'

'*What?*'

'Impatient bugger aren't you.'

With a shifty look round the Mess to make sure no one was listening, Munro leaned across the table and lowered his voice.

'I think Concorde was *shot* down,' he said, his voice almost a whisper.

Ellis watched him closely, wondering what was coming next. Munro sat back quietly, as if he had just revealed the secrets of the Universe.

'Really?' said Ellis at length. 'Is that possible?'

'Sniper – two shots just before the aircraft took off.'

'Why two shots?'

'Had to take out a tyre to make it look accidental.'

'You think it was the Illuminati?'

Munro sat back and stretched his legs under the table, his scar pulling his satisfied smile into a grimace.

'Why not check with the Colonel? He'll know if he can spare someone. But don't get your hopes up, we're stretched.'

'I might just do that. What motive?'

'The Colonel?'

'Concorde.'

'Ah, now that's where the story gets interesting.'

'Hmmm, what is it you're digging around in?'

'I couldn't kill men the way you do, Peter. In battle or on operations is one thing. But the way you do it?'

'Is it so different?'

'Yes.'

'I'll take your word for it.'

Munro suddenly turned very serious.

'Don't get me wrong; I'm glad there are guys like you

out there. I just couldn't do it, that's all.' He sat forward and put his hands on the table. 'By the way, I meant what I said about coming round. You'd be very welcome.'

Ellis had no idea what to say to that, but he appreciated the gesture. Munro pushed his chair back, got to his feet and pulled his beret over his head. Looking deeply into Ellis' eyes, he gave him a slight nod, turned and left.

Peterson stood by the window in the Colonel's office, his hands behind his back, staring up into the sky. The Colonel sat at his desk, tapping a pen on his notepad. Ellis sat by himself, off to one side of the room, watching the two men disinterestedly. Peterson pushed himself up on his toes a couple of times, then turned from the window and addressed his colleagues.

'Even conjecture would be very welcome at this juncture, gentlemen.'

'There is no more we can do,' said the Colonel in exasperation. 'This is getting us absolutely nowhere.'

'By the way Ellis,' said Peterson. 'I learned something quite interesting this morning.'

'Oh?' replied Ellis, catching a hint of excitement in his voice.

'Yes, a very curious link between Gilmour and McCann.'

'Indeed?'

Peterson wandered over and lowered his voice to a whisper.

'You're quite sure?' said Ellis, his eyes widening.

Before he could say anymore, the telephone rang. The Colonel picked it up.

'Yes?'

Peterson walked back to the window and stared back up at the sky, his hands wringing nervously behind his back.

'*Gilmour!*' exclaimed the Colonel, leaping to his feet and knocking his chair over backwards in the process.

Peterson spun round. Ellis lifted himself half out of his chair. The Colonel's face registered a mixture of conflicting emotions.

'It's . . . it's Gilmour,' he said in wonder, putting his hand over the mouthpiece. 'He's *alive!*'

Chapter 16

As Gilmour drove through the gates into the SAS camp at Credenhill, a few sparrows darted across the sunlit road, narrowly missing the bonnet of the Ford Escort he'd nicked from a car park on the edge of the forest.

'It's okay for you little bastards,' he whispered tiredly.

He glanced in the rear view mirror at a bedraggled Roberts. She caught his eye but didn't smile. She had not said a word since they'd left the forest. With a heavy heart, knowing that he couldn't put off his confrontation with the RSM any longer, he pulled up and switched off the engine.

A few men ran towards the car and one of them yanked open the door.

'You okay?' asked a concerned voice.

'I'm fine Doc,' said Gilmour.

With practiced fingers the medic firmly tilted Gilmour's head to one side and parted his hair.

'You had better come and see me when you get a minute,' he said, 'or you won't be fine for much longer.'

Gilmour grunted and pulled his head away. The Colonel made his way to the car and ducked down to peer inside.

'Where's the girl?' he asked, his fear and concern very evident in his eyes.

Gilmour wrestled with his guilt.

'I had to leave her, Boss. McCann still has her.'

'Gilmour . . . I . . .?'

The Colonel peered disbelievingly into the car and then stared down at the ground. He was a very troubled man.

Strong hands helped Roberts from the car.

'Are you okay young lady?' asked the Colonel.

'Yes Sir.'

'Better let the Doc take a look at your hand.'

The medic hurried away and she hobbled off after him, leaning on a soldier's arm for support.

'What about you?' asked the Colonel.

'I'm fine, Boss.'

'You don't look it.'

Gilmour could hardly find the strength to lift his legs over the doorsill.

'Check with the Doc,' said the Colonel, 'and when you've sorted yourself out, report to my office.'

Gilmour got wearily out of the car.

'What a mess!' sniffed the Colonel disapprovingly. 'And make sure you take a long shower.'

'Something to eat and a good sleep is all I need.'

'The sleep will have to wait but I can get you something to eat . . . what about the girl?'

Gilmour clunked his door shut.

'I don't know. We were all separated.'

The Colonel sighed and then strode away with a purposeful gait. Gilmour took a long look around the camp.

It was time to face the RSM and get it over with.

A few minutes later, a bergen slung over his shoulder hurriedly stuffed with a few personal effects, he headed back to the car park and strolled quickly to the Escort. The boot was difficult to open, but it finally jerked up and he dumped the bergen inside. As he slammed it shut, someone stepped out of a nearby building and stared at him.

'Are you going somewhere?' asked the bloke in some surprise.

Gilmour ignored him.

The bloke hurried over, a puzzled expression on his face.

'You must be Gilmour,' he said.

'And you are?'

'Ellis . . . Peter Ellis.'

'You Regiment?'

'I'm here on behalf of Her Majesty's government.'

Ellis smiled as if that was the most revealing information he had ever divulged about himself in his entire life.

'You don't say,' said Gilmour.

'Have you a problem?' asked Ellis, sensing something wasn't quite right.

'Well, I have to go,' sighed Gilmour, and headed for the RSMs office. 'Nice meeting you.'

'Go?' said Ellis. 'The Colonel is expecting you.'

'It'll have to wait. I have an appointment with the RSM.'

'Ahhh,' said Ellis, finally figuring it out. 'You're the bloke who's being RTU'd. Could I perhaps interest you in some work?'

'*Work?*'

'In return I could sort out your little problem with the

RSM for you.'

Gilmour looked up at him, his face askew.

'You have a problem,' explained Ellis, 'and I solve problems. It's what I do. You help me with McCann and I'll sort your problem.'

Gilmour didn't know what to think.

'My standard contract fee is one hundred thousand pounds,' said Ellis, 'plus expenses, of course. You work for me and I'll fix your problem for free.'

Gilmour stared vacantly into the distance.

'Have we a deal?' asked Ellis.

'A deal? What deal exactly? And if I refuse?'

Ellis laughed.

'Now that *would* be silly. Trust me. Put your stuff in my car – that's it over there. Have a shower and something to eat, then meet me outside the Colonel's office in, say an hour?' He quickly checked his watch, and added, 'I need to organise someone to meet with us.'

'That's not my concern,' said Ellis calmly, running his finger through the dust on the windowsill of the disused office.

'*What!*' shouted Peterson, glowering at him.

'If McCann is still my responsibility, then so is Gilmour. The two are indivisible.'

Gilmour stood with his back to a wall and shifted his weight uneasily from one foot to the other.

'Look—' continued Ellis, who was in no mood for arguments.

'Don't *look* me Mr Ellis,' interrupted Peterson, trying to make sense of Gilmour's body language, but coming up with no answers. 'I'm paying your fee, so I have some say in this!'

'*How* I do things is *my* business,' said Ellis, turning from the window.

'You *expect* me—?'

'I don't *expect* anything from you.'

'Ellis—!'

'It's final.'

Peterson stood for a moment, pondering his position.

'We don't have much time,' said Ellis, forcing the issue.

'Alright,' sighed Peterson in frustration. 'You can have Gilmour.'

'You'll okay it with the Colonel for me? And keep the RSM off our backs?'

'You're out on a limb, Ellis, if it breaks under you, do not expect any support from me.'

'When have I ever expected *anything* from you?'

Peterson stalked out of the office, almost knocking over Roberts who was about to knock on the door.

'Would you be Mr Ellis?' asked Roberts, trying to catch the Minister's eye as he brushed past her.

'Ah, yes!' said Ellis admiringly, looking the woman up and down. 'Yes, please come in.'

'So,' said Ellis, sitting back in his chair and looking at Gilmour thoughtfully. He was looking happier than he had for some time. 'Do I have this right? One of the bodies in the farmhouse was killed by *this* Browning pistol?'

'No,' said Gilmour, glancing nervously through the window at a police car pulling up in the car park. 'I left him alive. McCann killed him.'

Ellis turned the weapon over in his hands.

'Ah yes. But you can't remember how many times

you shot him?'

'Not exactly.'

'Hmm.'

'Shouldn't we be going?'

'Would you please leave the thinking to me?'

'Colonel,' said Ellis gently, trying to pacify the outraged officer. 'I *can't* tell you any more.'

The Colonel rose darkly from behind his desk.

'You do not just waltz in here and *demand* one of my men without offering me an explanation. You may ask me for my support and I am entitled to refuse in which case, some form of arbitration is necessary. But you demand nothing of me in my Regiment. Is that clear?'

Peterson brooded by the window, his hands behind his back.

'Furthermore, you do not *tell* me,' continued the Colonel, 'that I can't even *speak* to him!'

Ellis calmly absorbed the anger, which only seemed to infuriate the officer further.

'Who do you think you are, *mister?*' cracked the Colonel.

'With all due respect Colonel,' said Ellis, 'why I need Gilmour is really none of your business. You know what my task is and you know I need help. Gilmour is the very help I both need and want.'

The Colonel's face became sterner.

'Oh, and the girl?' he said, his shoulders twitching with resentment. 'Is she none of my business either?'

'She was . . . until you lost her.'

'*Get out!*'

The Colonel pointed to his office door.

'Will you keep the RSM away from Gilmour for the

time being?'

'*Get out!*'

Peterson turned with a resigned expression.

'Yes, Ellis, whatever you want,' he said. 'Just stop McCann.'

With a nod, Ellis turned and left.

'Is everything okay?' asked Gilmour as they walked towards the car park. He pressed a tentative finger into his bandaged forearm and then gently fingered the stitches on the side of his head.

'No,' said Ellis heavily, climbing into his car and slamming the door. 'Everything is not okay.'

'So what now?'

'Please! I'm trying to *think!*'

'Listen mate,' said Gilmour quietly, 'if you and I are going to work together, you'd better begin changing your lone wolf attitude. I wrote the fucking book.'

'Is that right?' said Ellis, throwing him a curious sideways glance.

Whether it was the grassy track, the fields long gone to seed, the rusted fencing overgrown with weeds, or just the tightening in his stomach, Gilmour wasn't sure. But somehow, he just knew that this was the right farm.

Ellis braked and brought the car to a halt.

'What's the matter,' asked Gilmour.

'You tell me; you're the one fidgeting. Is this it?'

'Nothing definite, just a feeling.'

Gilmour pored over the dog-eared road atlas on his knees for the hundredth time.

'Well,' said Ellis, slipping his pistol from his pocket and wedging it under his thigh, 'it has to be one of these damn farms. You ready for this?'

Gilmour folded the map, chucked it onto the dash, palmed his pistol and peered ahead through the windscreen. Ellis let out the clutch and the car lurched forward. Rounding a bend in the track, Gilmour spotted the roof of the barn above the trees.

'*This is it!*' he said, becoming quite agitated.

'What's the matter?' asked Ellis.

'Shouldn't we . . . er . . . you know, be sneaking up quietly?'

'What for?'

'McCann.'

'Do you honestly think he is still going to be here?'

The bonnet of the car lurched into the air as the wheels bounced out of a rut.

'I guess not,' said Gilmour.

'Trust me.'

They cleared the trees and the filthy windows of the farmhouse smirked at them, as if the house knew they were already too late.

'Is that the dog?' asked Ellis, pointing across a field. Gilmour nodded and gripped his pistol in one sweaty hand and grabbed the door handle with his other. Ellis drove right up to the cottage and pulled up outside the kitchen window. Gilmour threw open his door, dived out, rolled and came up on one knee, shifting his aim from window to window.

Ellis stepped out of the car and gawped at him in disbelief.

'*What are you doing?*'

Gilmour stared at him blankly.

'Look,' said Ellis, 'if you're going to be a wanker, I'll drop you off at the nearest bus stop.'

'But—'

'Do something useful. Go and see if the back door is booby trapped.'

Feeling like a scolded school kid, Gilmour got up, dusted himself down and dragged his heels round to the side of the building. His nose wrinkled at the stink wafting through the wide open door. Flies lifted from the bodies as he stuck his head carefully round the doorframe.

'When we get inside don't touch anything,' said Ellis, his pistol hanging loosely in his hand.

'They sure left in a hurry,' said Gilmour.

'Stay behind me and do exactly as I say.'

The disturbed flies lifted from their feast, buzzing with annoyance as the two men stepped into the kitchen.

'Where's all that fertilizer you told me about?' asked Ellis, his eyes darting round the kitchen.

Gilmour gagged at the smell and jerked a thumb at the door leading down to the cellar.

'Has anything been moved?' asked Ellis.

Gilmour glanced meticulously round the kitchen, taking the time to absorb the details. He pointed to bloody footprints on the tiled floor.

'I don't think so, but they've been in here.'

'What about the bodies?'

Gilmour waved flies from his face.

'No . . . that's how I left them.'

'Okay, we'll check the kitchen for booby traps, but forget the rest of the house. Be careful. I'll do the bodies.'

Gilmour stared at a thick drop of blood that had congealed on the end of the screwdriver sticking out of Bill's ear. Ignoring the flies, Ellis crouched beside the other body.

'Good job,' he said. 'I'm impressed.'

Gilmour walked carefully round the kitchen, checking for explosives. The glistening eyeballs in the bloody pulp that had been Ben's face seemed to watch him wherever he went.

'You did this?' asked Ellis.

'What?'

Ellis indicated to the splinters of bone poking through Ben's trousers.

'You took your time with him.'

'I needed to know where the women were.'

'Did you enjoy it?'

He watched Gilmour's face closely for a reaction.

'*Enjoy it?* I wasn't thinking about anything except the women.'

'Hmmm . . . you had the right idea. But it's very amateurish.'

'*What?*'

'For a start, you didn't find out where the girl was. Neither did you find out what they were up to.'

'I'll read up on it,' said Gilmour sarcastically.

'Next time . . . here and here,' said Ellis, pointing to various spots around the knees and elbows. He looked up to see if Gilmour was paying attention. 'You can always step on the wounds too. That can be very effective.'

Gilmour stopped what he was doing and took note of the instruction, a little disturbed by the direction in which his career seemed to be heading.

'Good,' said Ellis simply, getting back to his work.

'There's nothing here,' said Gilmour, walking over to the window.

The sight of the dead dog made his forearm ache terribly beneath the bandages.

'Impressions?' asked Ellis, ignoring the flies crawling in his hair as he rummaged through pockets.

'Eh?'

Ellis glared at him.

'Would you please switch on! Anything damn it, just think out loud!'

'McCann left in a hurry.'

'No, he didn't.'

'But he's made no attempt to cover his tracks.'

'Right observation – wrong conclusion.'

'Oh . . . and what's the *right* conclusion?'

Ellis flipped open a wallet.

'McCann's made absolutely no attempt to cover his tracks. Identification, money – it's all still here.'

'So?'

Ellis plucked a wad of notes from the wallet.

'There's over a thousand pounds here,' he said. 'What kind of criminal would leave a thousand pounds lying about?'

'Like I said, he was in a hurry.'

Ellis kneaded his temples as if he was in pain. He suddenly flapped the heavy wad of notes in his hand.

'It would have taken just seconds to strip the bodies of money and ID,' he said. 'Doesn't that suggest anything to you *at all?*'

Gilmour leaned back against the sink and folded his arms defensively.

'It's no wonder no one will work with you,' he said.

Ellis pointed to the back door.

'If you don't like it, beat it.'

Anger burned Gilmour's cheeks.

'You could do with learning some people skills, mate!'

Ellis gazed at him dispassionately.

'I've heard that before,' he said, slipping the wallet into his pocket. 'And you need to learn to put your emotions to one side.'

'Tell you what,' said Gilmour, trying desperately to contain himself. 'You make an effort to be more human and I'll make an effort to think.'

'That may be difficult,' muttered Ellis, turning back to his work.

'Being human?'

'No, you thinking.'

Stung by the remark, Gilmour stepped away from the window.

'Oh?' he hissed through his teeth. 'And when was the last time you had sex?'

Ellis stopped what was he doing and frowned.

'Been a while eh? I'll bet you've not had your dick in a woman's mouth since you left school.'

The frown became a steely gaze.

'Tell you what,' said Gilmour. 'You leave my intelligence alone and I'll leave you and your unused dick alone.'

'Okay, so you're not as stupid as you act,' said Ellis. 'And now that I know you can think, I could do with some help here.'

'How?'

'McCann left the ID on the bodies because he's confident we can't trace him in time to stop him. The money is a conundrum though. Who would pay so much to the likes of McCann as to make a thousand quid not worth picking up?' The flies settled quickly back on the bodies as Ellis got up and walked to the sink. 'I was rather hoping,' he said, 'that another mind would be helpful.'

As the depth of the compliment sank in, Gilmour began to feel a little guilty for his outburst.

'Another major problem I have,' said Ellis, 'is what did he want with you?'

Gilmour felt like a boy scout going for his first badge.

'Hostages?'

'Why SAS? Why Roberts and the girl? Are there any others?'

'I see,' said a perplexed Gilmour.

'No, you don't, and I'm beginning to wish I'd left you to the RSM. Can't you come up with anything at all?'

'You don't think it was a personal thing with me then?'

'Hmm, interesting.'

'What?'

'That you would take it personally.'

'Angelina is still alive,' said Gilmour, having difficulty keeping a tremor from his voice.

'You had best keep your emotions out of this,' warned Ellis, 'or I'll be dropping you off at that bus stop.'

'I'll be fine.'

'I hope so. The best thing you can do for the kid is stay clear-headed. Let's finish off here. I'm going to spend some time going through this place. Think you can be useful?'

'What am I looking for?'

'Anything – use your head.'

Gilmour picked up a torch from the table and skulked off towards the cellar on the prowl for clues.

'By the way?' said Ellis, as an afterthought. 'How did you know about the sex?'

Gilmour thought about it for a few moments, not really knowing what to say.

'I mean is it really *that* obvious?' asked Ellis.

'Yes, do you want me to set you up with a date?'

'And risk getting the girl killed?'

Gilmour saw deep pain in the man's eyes and his heart was heavy as he creaked his way down the rickety stairs.

Nothing in the cellar had been moved. He doubted McCann had even bothered to come down. He picked out the blanket with the torch. The cellar was going to be a black hole in his dreams for a long time. He flashed the torch round the shadows and headed back up to the kitchen.

'The fertilizer's untouched.'

'As I'd expected.'

'Did you find anything?'

'Yes,' said Ellis.

'And?'

'I'm just making sure I've not overlooked any details.'

'You sound confident. What did you find?'

'A phone number scribbled on a scrap of paper. It was tucked into the wallet very discretely.'

Ellis took his mobile phone from his pocket and tapped in a number from memory.

'Brigadier? It's Ellis. I've a phone number I need checked out.'

When he finished the call, he strolled outside waving the flies away.

It was less than five minutes before his phone rang. It was so quiet around the farmhouse that Gilmour could just make out the conversation.

'Ellis? It's John.'

'Hello, Brigadier.'

'You're still sore at me eh, haw haw.'

'John, what did you come up with?'

'I was offered a painting at a ridiculously low price this morning Peter, a Monet, but I'm a bit strapped just now, what with a new Aston Martin being delivered next week.'

'How ridiculous?' asked Ellis.

'Very. Shall I put a reserve on it for you?'

'Hmmm . . . please. And the phone number?'

'It's a fishing lodge on an estate in the Highlands of Scotland.'

'Scotland?' Ellis' eyebrows creased with surprise. 'You're sure?'

'Absolutely old chap, but the owner was not helpful at all. He says the lodge was booked through an agent and that he was paid a lot of money to stay away from the place for a couple of weeks.'

Gilmour didn't think he liked the expression on Ellis' face.

'Any ideas?' asked Ellis.

'None whatsoever, but I've spoken to the Colonel and we're inserting a small patrol tonight to set up an observation post to watch the lodge. Did you find the farm?'

'Yes, I'll let the Colonel know where it is. I want Gilmour on that patrol.'

'*Oh don't be ridiculous!* He's going to be RTU'd!'

'John, you're not listening again.'

'But—'

'I haven't got time for bullshit, John. Just okay it with the Colonel for me please.'

Gilmour took a few involuntary steps backwards into the forest, his mind stunned at how Ellis was talking to the Director of Special Forces. Ellis tapped the phone thoughtfully as he ended the call.

'You ready to do some proper work now?' he asked,

slightly amused at the expression on Gilmour's face.

'I . . . er . . . yes, I am.'

'Good, then let's go. You're off to Scotland.'

Chapter 17

A red light blinked on above the open door in the fuse-lage of the Hercules C-130 aircraft and glowed through the gloomy interior.

'*Red on!*' screamed the RAF crewman by the door, trying desperately to be heard above the deafening noise of the engines.

Four men shuffled towards the door, struggling beneath their heavy loads. The aircraft lurched and banked to port, drawing curses from the men being thrown around inside. Gilmour hung on grimly to the worn leather strap dangling above his head and wiped away the sweat drip-ping down his face. His steel helmet was pressing pain-fully into the stitches on his scalp. He leaned back in a futile attempt to ease the weight on his shoulders. One of the blokes behind him groaned.

It was pitch black outside. Not a star to be seen. Not a single light twinkling anywhere below them. The air-craft hit another pocket of turbulence and then climbed, the fuselage vibrating to the strain of the engines.

Gilmour's sweaty grip was almost wrenched from the leather strap. With his injured forearm, he hung on, willing the green light to come on so he could get away from the noise, pain, and sweat, and out into the cool, clean, quiet night outside.

The Hercules was flying low. Skirting hills and thundering up misty glens, it lumbered through a dark Scottish night towards a secret drop zone. Seated in the cockpit, looking like something from an alien movie, the Flight Lieutenant peered ahead through the night glasses draped over his head. He knew this was an important mission and not just another exercise as he'd been briefed. The two sinister looking characters hanging around at the back of the briefing room, saying nothing as the Squadron Leader talked, had convinced him of that. '*A quick flight up to Scotland,*' the Squadron Leader had said, throwing furtive glances towards the two men at the back of the room. '*One stick of four Paras to jump into the hills of Sutherland – nice and simple.*' Sure. Under two hundred feet. Flying at night through the mountains of Scotland. Nice and simple.

The aircraft cleared a low ridge and through his night glasses the Flight Lieutenant made out a long glen stretching away into the night. With a shake of his head, he eased back on the throttle and nosed the aircraft down to a hundred and fifty feet. He'd been flying Special Forces missions for some time and he'd recognized one of the blokes in the back. What were SAS doing kitted out as Paras? Why the remote Scottish Highlands? Why not a helicopter insertion? This was no exercise. Exercises were never as irregular and dangerous as this.

A dark mountainside loomed ahead. With practiced calm, he banked the aircraft steeply to starboard and levelled out on a new bearing. The navigator tapped him lightly on the shoulder. This was the final run. He throttled up, preparing to climb sharply to five hundred feet. All he had to do was switch on the green light in the back and their cargo would be floating silently towards the ground.

'*The sooner the better*,' he muttered under his breath.

As the aircraft roared up the glen, he stole a quick glance up at the dark mountains and craggy peaks frowning down at him on either side. This low level, cloak-and-dagger night stuff just wasn't his thing anymore.

Gilmour's legs began to buckle under the weight he was carrying. It didn't matter how many operational jumps he did, they never seemed to get any easier. Gritting his teeth, he hauled himself up by the strap with both hands and tried to force his mind to other things. His fingers began to cramp. He was losing his grip. He couldn't hang on any longer.

'What's the matter Jamie? Can't handle it?'

Gilmour looked up.

From the doorway, his mate Andy Taylor grinned like a crescent moon, his teeth unnaturally pale in a face blacked with cam cream. Gilmour being the only ex-Para in the patrol, he was needled.

'Crap hat,' he mouthed back.

'Dickhead,' replied Taylor, his grin broadening.

Gilmour forced a smile – if his ex-crap hat mate could hang on, so could he. Breathing deeply, he clamped his teeth together and tightened his grip. *'For fucks sake,'* he whispered, *'let me out of this damn crate!'*

The Hercules vibrated intensely as the engines throttled up. Suddenly, the nose lifted sharply as they climbed to jump height. His fingers began to slip from the strap. There was no way he could handle any more of this. The aircraft levelled off, the red light went out and the green light glowed.

'Green on!' screamed the RAF crewman by the door and then slapped Taylor hard on the shoulder. *'Go!'*

Taylor launched himself forward and fell clumsily out into the night. Adrenaline rushed through Gilmour and his pain was gone. He hauled himself forward, grabbed the door rail with his right hand, put his injured arm over his reserve and braced himself.

'Go!'

The hand thumped his shoulder. He tried to jump, but it was impossible with the weight he was hauling. A grunt tore from his lips as he toppled forward. He exited the aircraft, bumped down the slipstream, heard the crack of his chute opening and the night closed around him.

One thousand, two thousand, three thousand, he counted silently . . . *check canopy.*

He looked up. The parachute billowed as if collapsing and then opened fully. He craned his neck in every direction, kicking his legs wildly to twist himself round to check for chutes which may have been too close. He was on automatic now. He'd done this so many times it was instinctive. The drone of the Hercules faded away and a pleasant silence washed over him like the cool waters of a moonlit beach on a sticky night.

What now?

Drop the bergen.

He pulled the strap on his leg and his kit fell, jerked at the end of the rope and started swinging from side to side. He wondered if Angelina would be at the fishing lodge. Looking down between his feet, he couldn't make out any details on the ground. It was too dark. The Hercules was gone, the noise, everything. It was just him and the night.

The shadowy ground loomed up at him. Far too quickly, it seemed. He hoped there were no rocks about. Clamping his feet and knees tightly together, his knees slightly bent, he pushed his chin down into his chest, tucked his elbows in and pulled down on the rigging lines behind his head to slow his descent. His bergen hit the ground with a thump and a second later he piled in heavily, his fall broken by deep, springy heather. A sigh of relief hissed through his tightly pursed lips. He was down.

Hitting the quick release on his harness, he rolled onto his stomach, pulled in the rigging lines and collapsed the fluttering canopy. Within moments, he was on his feet, rifle at the shoulder, peering into the shadows. He heard the metallic click of a weapon being cocked. His oppo's were on the ground. Although the light in the Hercules had been subdued, he still had to squint while his night vision adjusted.

'Jamie, is that you?' growled a deep, gruff voice.

'Yes, it's me Mike.'

A burly figure loomed out of the darkness. Mike Mitchell sniffed the air and lowered his rifle.

'Smells like rain,' he said. 'You all right?'

'Heavy landing, but I'm fine,' said Gilmour.

'Yeah,' said Mitchell, 'like landing on a mattress. Give me heather any day.'

Two more figures appeared out of the darkness.

'What's going on Mike?' asked the last member of the patrol, Charlie Jones, a hardened Welshman who had seen too much.

Mitchell didn't reply. Gilmour took off his steel helmet, stuffed it into the folds of his parachute, pulled a Red beret out of his pocket and stuck it on his head.

'Come on Mike,' said Jones, kicking his toe into a clump of heather, sending lumps of damp peat flying in his direction. 'What's going on?'

'You were at the briefing, same as me Charlie.'

'Come on Mike, something's bothering you – I've known you too long. I noticed you weren't happy before we jumped.'

Mitchell ignored him and set about finding their exact position with his satellite navigation set. With a sigh, he stopped what he was doing and looked round.

'Hide the chutes will you and make yourselves useful.'

When he was satisfied they were busy, he got their position, checked his map, looked around him and nodded. They were *precisely* where they should have been. The RAF never ceased to impress him.

'Mike?'

'What is it now?'

He turned to face the Welshman.

'We should have M-4s,' said the disgruntled soldier, holding up his SA-80 rifle with disdain. 'You know, short-ened American rifles, red dots on foreheads, that sort of thing.'

'Yes, and we should have been inserted by chopper. For this operation we're Paras, remember, and Paras use public transport and only get to play with crap weapons.'

'Appropriate,' said Taylor.

'Dickhead,' said Gilmour.

Jones fell silent, but his frown had deepened. Gilmour looked about him trying to pierce the shadows. For some reason, his pulse had quickened.

'Right, let's go,' said Mitchell, hoisting on his bergen. 'I'll lead, Jamie you follow me. Charlie, with a name like that you've got to be tail-end.'

'Ha ha.'

'Actually, it's so I can't hear any more of your honking.' He paused. 'And keep your eyes open,' he added as an afterthought.

Something in his tone caught Gilmour's attention and he felt his skin prickle. Something was definitely bothering Mike.

Mitchell set a blistering pace, head down, arse up, attacking the ground. It was difficult going, small gullies and ditches abounding. Tripping over clumps of wet peat, wading through knee-deep heather and stumbling into holes soon had them all sweating. In silence they tabbed, covering the ground as only SAS men can. They had fifteen miles to cover before dawn, only a few hours away, but that didn't bother them, that was the job. As they marched, Gilmour's mind wandered through the possibilities lying ahead, but the more he pondered, the more unsettled he became. He wondered what was bothering Mitchell. He looked around at the lonely moors and then glanced up at the starless sky. In his heart, he knew something wasn't right.

The weather was pleasant enough, with a chill late autumn breeze pushing them along. Not having to fight the elements made a welcome change. Visibility wasn't good though, and a heavy layer of thick cloud obscured the sky, threatening rain.

'Bastard!' hissed Mitchell, tripping and landing in the heather with a thump.

Someone giggled as he struggled back to his feet.

'Okay, let's take five,' he said, easing the bergen from his shoulders.

Gilmour slipped his bergen off and sat back against it, determined to enjoy every second he could get. Taylor came over and slumped down beside him.

'What do you make of it?' he asked quietly.

'Dunno, mate,' replied Gilmour.

'I don't like it,' said Taylor.

Jones heard them whispering and crawled over.

'What's so important?' asked Mitchell, sensing a little discussion brewing.

The whispering tailed off.

'C'mon Mike,' said Jones softly, stretching his legs. 'A little bit of empathy eh? How would you like it?'

'Okay,' said Mitchell resignedly, and sat down heavily beside them.

He looked grim.

There was a pause while he studied their faces. No one spoke. They didn't need to. Gilmour leaned forward expectantly and looked into his dark eyes. What he saw unnerved him.

'Just before we jumped,' said Mitchell at length, 'the Headshed told me over the radio they'd contacted the agent. It was a Colombian that booked the lodge.'

Jones sucked in his breath. Mitchell watched their faces first register surprise and then shock. Fear tingled down Gilmour's spine. Taylor's mouth dropped open. Their reaction made Mitchell look even grimmer.

'Yeah,' he said tiredly. 'Let's get to our lying-up point before it gets light and sort this out then, eh.'

He pored over his map, checked his bearing and got up. Gilmour checked his new Rolex. It was just after midnight. It would be getting light in a few hours and they still had quite a way to go. The rest of the patrol got up and fell in behind Mitchell as he led off into the shadows.

As they threaded their way through a misty glen, an ominous hush settled on the patrol. For the first time in his SAS career, Gilmour began to wish he was somewhere else. He wasn't the only one.

Some time later, Mitchell stopped and waited for them to gather round. The four of them stood steaming in a circle.

'You know the brief,' said Mitchell, keeping his voice low. 'The lodge is in the next glen.' He ground the heel of his boot into soft peat as if squashing a slug. 'We'll set up an observation post and watch their movements from a distance, then move in closer tomorrow night.'

Somehow, his voice carried little conviction. Gilmour looked up at the dark sky. Taylor shook his head slowly.

'Colombians?' muttered Jones uneasily. 'Why not send in Mi5 to pick them up, or the police?'

'C'mon,' said Mitchell under his breath, 'let's go.'

With that, he turned and set off up a steep hillside, forcing the others to trot to keep up.

The sky darkened perceptibly and the wind freshened. Over the hills ahead of them, a huge black cumulonimbus cloud reared its ugly head. An uncomfortable tension began to grow in the air. Mitchell checked his map one last time and contoured cautiously round the brow of a hill, taking care not to silhouette them against the night sky. A dark glen lay far below them. The heather began to wave in the freshening breeze. Mitchell sniffed the air again.

'Rain's coming,' he said.

Gilmour took off his beret and wiped his brow.

'Where's the Lodge?' asked Jones.

Mitchell pointed to a dark copse of trees up the glen near the banks of the river.

'It'll be light in an hour,' said Gilmour, pulling his beret back on and checking his watch.

'Right,' said Mitchell, 'find somewhere to lie up.'

'Over here,' said Taylor, pointing to a rough hollow sunk into the hillside.

'Fine,' agreed Mitchell, slipping his bergen to the ground. 'Let's get it done.'

It didn't take them long to fashion a comfortable little hide with a couple of heather-strewn ponchos stretched over it for camouflage and protection. Soon they were inside sorting out their kit and getting settled in.

'Jamie,' said Mitchell, nodding to the back of the hide. 'Get a brew on mate.'

The sound of water gurgling into aluminium mess tins was comforting, but the welcome brew did little to lift the heaviness hanging over them. Taylor sat to one side of the hide wrapped in his own glum thoughts, his steaming plastic army mug cupped in his hands. Jones lay beside Mitchell, setting up the radio. There didn't seem to be too much to do or say for the time being, so Gilmour got his sleeping bag out, stuffed it inside his Gore-Tex bivvy bag and laid it out at the back of the hide.

'Good idea,' said Mitchell, handing the scope to Jones. 'Jamie, Andy, get some gonk.'

Gilmour needed no further prompting and wriggled into his sleeping bag.

'Andy?' whispered Gilmour, as they lay snugly under the lightly billowing ponchos.

'Yeah?'

'Is everything okay? You've not been looking too happy lately.'

'Yeah, fine mate,' lied Taylor.

'How's the missus?'

'Fine.'

'No, really.'

Taylor's face saddened and he lay for a moment deep in thought.

'I think it's all over,' he said.

'But you were so happy.'

'Yeah.'

Gilmour felt pangs of genuine sorrow for him. After all, he'd been at his wedding.

'What happened?'

'You know . . .'

Taylor looked embarrassed and Gilmour tried to look sympathetic. Taylor lowered his voice to a barely audible whisper.

'Got pissed at the weekend, shagged some tart in town, and the missus found out.'

Gilmour turned on his side and propped himself up on an elbow.

'Yes, I can see how that would ruin things. Can't you put it right?'

Taylor turned to him.

'How?' he asked. 'How can I put it right?'

It was Gilmour's turn to go quiet. He lay down again. He had absolutely no idea how he could put it right. He felt close to his friend though, and wanted to help. He'd had no concept of real friendship until he'd passed Selection. Sure, he'd had mates in the Paras, but he didn't keep in touch with any of them. The SAS was different. The world had been such a lonely place before Selection.

'Jamie?'

'What?'

'Thanks for caring mate. It means a lot.'

'Wish there was something I could do. Would you like me to talk to Sue when we get back? Perhaps take her out and try to tell her what a great guy you are?'

'Nah, she'll be at her mums with the kids when we get back.'

'Eh?'

Gilmour sat up, somewhat startled. Taylor smiled weakly.

'Yeah, she's leaving me mate.'

Gilmour lay back down, gob-smacked.

'How's it going with the Sergeant?' asked Taylor.

'Roberts?'

His mate offered him a weak grin.

'She's fiery,' said Gilmour, wondering where she was and what she was doing.

'Will you two tossers get some gonk!' barked Mitchell, turning for a moment to stare at them.

As Gilmour was dropping off, he thought he heard a roll of distant heavy artillery, but couldn't quite pull himself awake. He dropped off into a sound sleep as the first drops of rain pattered on the hide and a roll of thunder rumbled through the night.

Chapter 18

Someone was poking him with the toe of a heavy boot. Gilmour opened a tentative eye and peeked out from the cosy warmth of his sleeping bag.

'Wakey wakey tosser.'

'The Red beret quite suits you Charlie,' he said sleepily. 'It's a pity you didn't earn it though.'

'It makes an excellent arse wipe, I'll give you that,' retorted Jones, stripping off to reveal tattooed arms rippling with muscle. He took his beret off and offered it to Gilmour. 'Want a sniff?'

'Shut it!' moaned a disgruntled bivvy bag. 'Some of us are trying to sleep.'

Gilmour yawned and then savoured the scent of damp heather and peat as he wriggled out of his sleeping bag. As the Welshman disappeared inside his bivvy bag and zipped himself up, Gilmour ran his fingers through his hair and pulled his beret onto his head. Rain was still drumming lightly on the ponchos, but it was reasonably dry in the hide. He crawled over beside Mitchell and an involuntary whistle escaped through his teeth.

'Will you look at that!' he exclaimed, overawed by the sheer rugged beauty of the glen.

Far below them, the river meandered its way downstream, the odd almost leafless tree overhanging its banks. Farther up the glen, a small forest of pine trees marched down a hillside and tramped across the moor to the banks of the river. In the midst of the trees he could just make out the roof of the lodge poking into the damp sky. A thin wisp of smoke curled lazily from one of its chimneys. From the lodge, a dirt track cut through the forest to an old wooden gate set into a deer fence and from there wound down the glen until it was lost behind the foothills of a mist-shrouded mountain. The rain looked on for the day. He glanced back at the wisp of smoke. Seeing the lodge ventilating into the cheerless sky reminded him of why they were there.

'Okay Mike, what's happening?'

Mitchell eyed him solemnly, his face devoid of expression. Gilmour sensed his uncertainty.

'Come on Mike, what's the story?'

Mitchell turned away, lifted his binos and swept the glen. He was not a happy man. Gilmour frowned and became restless.

'What is it Mike?'

'Dunno, I just have a real bad feeling.'

Mitchell returned to the binos. Gilmour looked down into the glen and followed the riverbank upstream. There was no one to be seen.

'In for lunch or something?' he asked.

'Huh?' said Mitchell distantly.

'There's no one on the river.'

'There hasn't been anyone out of the lodge since we

got here.'

'This ain't no fishing trip then, as we suspected. What do you reckon?'

'I don't know,' said Mitchell. 'I just don't know.' He sounded drained. 'With Colombians and Irishmen involved, drugs most likely. But I've got a bad feeling.'

A tremor ran down Gilmour's spine. This was getting worse by the minute.

'What did the Headshed say the last time you radioed?'

'We get in close tonight and watch the place.'

'Is that it?'

'Get yourself some grub,' said Mitchell, changing the subject quickly.

Gilmour thought about saying something else but changed his mind. His misgivings would just have to wait.

Rain pattered on the hide as he sat munching biscuits and sucking something from a silver sachet. He was having trouble coming to terms with their situation. Jones snored, grunted and turned over in his bivvy bag.

'Jamie?'

Mitchell was looking at him closely with his deep, doleful eyes.

'Yes?' he replied through a mouthful of oatcakes and cold stew.

'If you were a Colombian working for a Cartel, you know . . . doing whatever it is they're up to, what precautions would you take in a place like this?'

Gilmour thought for a moment, took a mouthful of water and swallowed.

'I'd carry a 9 milly at least,' he offered, wiping his mouth with a sleeve.

Mitchell looked exasperated.

'I know that you dickhead,' he said. 'I mean, what little *extra* things would you do? You know, over and above the obvious.'

Gilmour looked at him. He had a few ideas, but they frightened him. He licked his lips as a list of things raced through his mind. But he was damned if he was going to answer and risk being a dickhead again. A lone midge drifted into the hide. Chewing thoughtfully, he kept his eye on it. When it strayed a little too close, he suddenly pinched it between his finger and thumb. He peered at the tiny squashed insect for a moment and then wiped his finger on his smock. *Life sure could end abruptly*, he thought.

'Chinese parliament time, I guess Mike,' he replied eventually, taking the diplomatic way out.

'Hmmm . . . that's a damn good idea.'

Gratified by his promotion from dickhead, Gilmour took another sip of water and returned to his meal.

'Want one?' he asked, offering a biscuit.

'No thanks mate.'

Mitchell fell quiet again and went back to watching the glen. Gilmour ate his cold meal slowly, wishing he could shake off his unease. He was not enjoying the clammy sense of foreboding that was gathering on him.

The afternoon passed uneventfully into evening, with only the changing of watch disturbing the quiet routine. Apart from the plume of smoke wafting from the lodge, the odd midge droning about near the hide and the drizzle dampening the bleak moorland, nothing stirred.

Gilmour lay watching the lodge through the binoculars. Across the glen, upstream of the forest, a small herd of red deer wandered down a hillside and slowly picked their way across the moor to the river. The sky began to lose light. The time for decisions was approaching and the tension mounted. They all felt it. Mitchell called them together and they bunched at the front of the hide. He started things on a very sober note.

'I expect they will be armed,' he said. 'I suspect that if we don't get this right, things could turn hot.' He paused for effect and got plenty. 'Any questions before we continue?'

Three voices broke out in unison and then fell silent. The tension thickened. Mitchell turned his eyes on them one by one, holding each man's gaze for a few seconds. His respect for them was unquestionable and those few moments were all that was needed to convey it.

'Nothing from the estate owner yet?' asked Gilmour, wiping his nose with his sleeve.

Mitchell shook his head.

'So,' said Jones, 'we have Colombians, McCann and a bunch of Irishmen, a hostage, and we've no idea what they're up to.'

'Something like that.'

'This stinks,' said Taylor.

'Any word on McCann from our mates across the water?' asked Gilmour.

'The way things are with this Northern Ireland 'peace' crap, we're not sure. We can't exactly phone up Gerry Adams and ask either.'

'His mate Tony could ask him for us,' suggested the Welshman. 'Invite him over to number 10 for more tea and sticky buns at the taxpayer's expense.'

'Cut it out Charlie,' warned Mitchell.

'Well, this job sucks.'

'Granted,' said Mitchell, pointing out through the door of the hide, 'but you don't have to be here.'

'C'mon Mike,' said Gilmour, 'Charlie has a point. Mi5 should be dealing with this until we know what's going on. We shouldn't even be here.'

'Look,' said Mitchell, 'what I need is support.'

There was a brief pause.

'I'll make us all a brew,' said Gilmour, reaching for his bergen.

An uncomfortable silence pervaded through the hide. Mitchell cleared his throat and waited for someone to speak. He didn't have long to wait.

'So what do you reckon?' asked Jones. 'Drugs?'

'Yes,' said Mitchell, 'that's what I reckon.'

'Then there are probably more of the wankers on their way here.'

'Probably.'

'Anything on the Colombian who booked the lodge?' asked Taylor.

'Cartel. Drugs and murder mostly. Nasty man. He's known as The Weasel to his mates.'

'You better explain Mike,' said Jones very unhappily. 'I'm getting real confused here.'

The scent of a fresh brew wafted round the hide.

'Look,' said Mitchell patiently. 'There's a lot at stake here.'

'That's for sure,' muttered Jones darkly.

'Good grief!' sighed Mitchell, starting to lose his cool. 'We *know* McCann is good. That's why each of us was specifically picked for this job. If four of the best blokes from B squadron can't handle him, then I don't know – might as well go home and join the boy scouts. Is that what you want?'

'What I want,' retorted Jones, 'is to be lying on a beach somewhere with some drop-dead gorgeous babe brushing her hair over me while she sucks my cock. And that's not going to happen if I'm dead.'

Mitchell glared at him with a face of granite as Gilmour handed the brews round.

'Charlie's right,' said Taylor. 'We're going in totally blind and that's just asking for trouble.'

'Maybe Charlie's slapper will get her tits out for the lads,' said Gilmour, ducking to avoid a lump of peat lobbed at him.

'Well?' said Taylor, pressing Mitchell for a reaction.

Mitchell nonchalantly poked at his boots with a sprig of heather.

'What's the problem?'

'*What's the problem?* Are you serious?'

Gilmour leaned back against his bergen and sipped his tea.

'I don't like it,' said Jones. 'We're going to have to adapt how we do things.'

'I know,' said Mitchell, picking at the sprig of heather.

'Cut the bullshit Mike,' snapped Jones irritably. 'What's bothering you? Things have a habit of going pear-shaped on half-baked jobs like this.'

Mitchell thought for a moment before replying.

'The Headshed reckons,' he said deliberately, 'that we couldn't wish for a better location to confront them and take them into custody. Do we all agree on that?'

Three heads nodded reluctantly.

'Right, so we have the ideal place.'

'Mike?'

Jones was eyeing him warily.

Mitchell eyed him back.

'You're not telling us everything,' said the Welshman. Mitchell sighed.

'Our orders have changed,' he said, throwing the sprig of heather away.

The others all leaned a little closer.

'I've had a long chat with the Headshed on the radio. Under no circumstances is anyone in the lodge to leave this glen until we know what's going on.'

'I *knew* it,' said Jones with a shake of his head.

'I don't know about any Colombians,' said Gilmour, 'but if McCann is here, he certainly won't go without a fight.'

'I've discussed that with the Headshed,' said Mitchell, running a hand over his face. 'If anyone draws a weapon – we slot them.'

Gilmour almost dropped his mug.

Jones stared at him in disbelief.

'I know,' said Mitchell, 'but that's from the top. Apparently, the order came from Downing Street itself. Seems we have a lot of jumpy politicians who are rather concerned about the American's cancelling the State visit. They want to know who's going around shooting SAS men, and why.'

'Can't say I blame them,' muttered Gilmour, the shooting at Hereford still very fresh in his mind.

'If the worst comes to the worst,' continued Mitchell, 'and bodies fall, we call in a chopper, dump them on board and leg it.'

The finality of his words sank in.

'We . . . we can't just go around shooting people in Scotland!' stuttered Jones.

'We can if they start it,' said Mitchell.

'What if there are witnesses?'

'That's where the Para kit comes in handy.'

Jones looked at him blankly.

'The only people who would see us out here,' explained Mitchell, 'would be poachers or hillwalkers. To them we're Army on exercise. If they hear shots, they'll assume we're firing blanks.'

'Oh, and if someone sees bodies fall?'

'That's the worst-case scenario. We call in a chopper and leg it with the evidence. The Paras will be grilled, but they'll only scratch their heads and look bewildered.'

'What if one of us gets slotted Mike?' asked Taylor, looking at him seriously.

'No one asks questions when SAS come home in body bags mate. We're on exercise. SAS die on exercise.'

'Bollocks,' snorted Jones. 'What about back-up?'

'We're on our own until tomorrow night.'

'Oh shit,' muttered Taylor quietly, finally getting the message. 'So if anyone tries to leave in the meantime, we have to deal with it, right?'

Mitchell nodded.

'Okay,' he said, 'as soon as it's dark we'll bug out. Any more questions?'

Three heads shook. The talking was over. Last light wasn't far away. Mitchell turned for another look at the lodge through the binos.

'Okay, get yourselves sorted out and get ready to move.'

Gilmour glanced up the glen as the last light dimmed behind the hills. The small herd of deer had climbed back up the hillside and were disappearing over a ridge, being briefly silhouetted against the grey clouds. The lodge was in darkness, but that wasn't right. There should have been a light on. Someone should have been out of doors doing *something*.

'C'mon Mike,' he asked quietly, 'is there anything else?'

'I don't like it any more than you do.'

'You sure there are no more surprises?'

'No more surprises,' assured Mitchell, taking a last long look through the binos. C'mon, let's move.'

The hide was quickly dismantled and all signs of their stay were soon gone. In single file, they picked their way carefully down the wet hillside. Gilmour wiped rain from his face with his sleeve. He knew they were going in unprepared but the live round up the spout made him feel a little better. In his heart, he knew he would have no problem shooting anyone if he had to. He also knew the bad guys would have no second thoughts about shooting him either. But that wasn't what was bothering him. It was the lack of intelligence and planning. Knowing who everyone was and what they were doing was fundamental to the success of any operation. It was a heavily subdued patrol that wound down into the glen and disappeared into the shadows.

Chapter 19

The sound of rushing water increased alarmingly as the patrol filed down the dark hillside and crossed the moor towards the river. When they reached its banks, Mitchell crouched down on his haunches and wiped drizzle from his face. For a long while he stared with dismay at the angry torrent, trying to gauge the depth and strength of the current. The others remained silent behind him, twitching nervously in the shadows. Eventually, he convened a hasty parliament.

'Damn rain,' he whispered. 'River's rising quickly. Anyone any idea's?'

'Did anyone bring a rope?' asked Jones.

The silence told its own story.

'I *knew* I should have brought a rope,' said the Welshman.

'We'll just have to tab upstream until we find someplace safe to cross,' suggested Taylor.

'If we do that,' replied Mitchell, 'we could lose a night and have to lie-up for another day somewhere.'

'What other options are there?' asked Gilmour.

'We have to be in position tonight.'

'C'mon Mike,' said Jones, 'be serious.'

'We can't cross that without a rope, surely?' said Taylor, jerking a thumb at the river.

'Why not?' asked Mitchell, nonchalantly scratching an ear.

'The sensible thing would be to go upstream,' said Gilmour, now seriously scared, 'find a safe place to cross and recce the joint tomorrow night.'

'The *sensible* thing,' countered Mitchell, 'would be to phone Mi5 and go home.'

'You've already made up your mind,' observed Jones, 'so why the chat?'

A wry smile cracked Mitchell's lips.

'I just want you guys to understand why I'm taking you across this thing.'

Gilmour noticed his mate was flapping.

'Crap hat,' he whispered, nudging him with his elbow.

Taylor smiled warmly and nudged him back.

They were all very aware that more Regiment men died from drowning than any other single factor.

'I still fancy going upstream and lying up for the day somewhere,' said Jones rather forcefully.

'And if the bad guys bug out in the meantime?' asked Mitchell.

'Tough shit.'

Mitchell ignored him and stepped into the river without even bothering to look for a wading stick. He strode forward powerfully, rifle at his chest, his thighs sending a bow wave rippling across the choppy surface. A couple of times he stumbled and waved his arms wildly, but he somehow managed to keep his feet. As he reached the main stream the water slopped up to his waist and it looked as if he would be washed away. But with a couple of strong lunges, he surged through the worst of it and splashed safely ashore.

'That didn't look *too* bad,' said Jones, beginning to flap big time.

'Yeah, but we don't have his height or weight,' observed Taylor, who was seriously considering walking back up the hill and going home.

Gilmour stepped off the bank next. The cold made him shiver. He pressed forward, feeling with his boots for the next safe step in the broken water. It wasn't too difficult to begin with, but as he approached the middle the current surged into him ferociously. He gasped as the freezing water sloshed around his groin. When he reached the main current, the water rushed into him with such force his feet began to slip. He took another step, but the bottom was shelving down. Taking a deep breath, he jumped forward through the swirling water. His toes grounded and he jumped again, grunting with the effort. Somehow, he managed to stay upright. The power of the current subsided and he found his feet. Dripping like a bout of bad flu, he waded to the bank and staggered ashore.

'I thought you were gone, you tosser,' said Mitchell, helping him from the river.

Gilmour turned to watch the other two ploughing through the rapids, weapons above their heads. They took a different route to him, avoiding the hole he'd stepped into. As they sloshed ashore, Taylor giggled through his nose.

'*Shut it, dickhead!*' hissed Mitchell.

The giggling soldier clamped his hand over his mouth

to stifle it.

'So *that's* how the Paras do it,' remarked Jones glibly.

Gilmour was in no mood for humour.

'Okay girls, let's move,' said Mitchell.

Making good use of the dark cover afforded by the many large rocks strewn along the riverbank, they slipped silently from shadow to shadow, unseen by anything other than the most inquisitive night animal. Creeping past dark pools and thundering rapids, they picked their way through tangled bushes and scrambled over gravel beds, making their way cautiously upstream towards the trees surrounding the lodge.

'Listen up,' whispered Mitchell, going to ground and waiting until the others huddled around. He pointed up the banks of a gushing tributary. 'We'll head up this stream and come down into the trees from up there. This spot,' he said, indicating to where the stream joined the main river, 'is ideal as an emergency rendezvous. Easy to find in the dark and plenty of cover. Any questions?'

Gilmour had none and no one else said anything. He thought he caught the scent of wood smoke on the night air.

'Is everyone happy?' asked Mitchell.

'What if there are too many of them for us to handle?' asked Jones, voicing their unanimous concern.

Mitchell shrugged. The Welshman fell unhappily silent.

'Look,' said Mitchell patiently, 'we've no choice. So let's stop moaning about it eh, and just get on with it.'

Gilmour slipped off his bergen and pulled a black fleece from one of the side pockets. Once he'd slipped it on and was back into his windproof, he felt a lot better and a lot warmer. He struggled into his webbing, hoisted his bergen onto his back and jumped up and down a couple of times to make sure he wasn't rattling.

'How's my face cam?' he asked.

'Fine,' replied Mitchell. 'Mine?'

Gilmour checked him over and stuck a sprig of heather into his webbing to break up the lines of his shoulders.

'Right, let's go,' said Mitchell.

Not far away, a startled rabbit crouched down at the entrance to its burrow, its ears laid flat along its back. It watched fearfully as the four soldiers crept by and disappeared into the dirty night.

Gilmour was the last to wriggle through the hole Mitchell had cut in the deer fence. As he got to his feet and took a few steps into the musty forest, the hairs on his neck prickled. Danger was close.

He could see nothing in the gloom. The trees had been planted so close together that their top branches blocked the sky. As he stepped farther into the forest, the gloom became impenetrable darkness. Dead lower branches, left behind and forgotten in the rush to reach the sky, poked him as he pushed forward. One of them whipped back noisily.

Dickhead!' hissed Mitchell. '*Be careful!*'

'Ooops.'

'Where are you anyway? It's like the bloody jungle in here.'

'I'm right here.'

'I can't see you.'

'I can't see any of you,' moaned Jones.

'We'd better crawl,' said Mitchell. 'Don't lose me.'

Mitchell programmed their position into the illuminated face on his hand-held GPS, put it back in his pocket and got down on all fours. Following the luminous needle on a compass, he led them deeper into the trees. It was slow work, much too slow. Crawling through the inky darkness, Gilmour lost track of time.

He was beginning to think they were lost when suddenly he crawled into the back of someone. He stiffened and peered past him. A faint patch of grey light filtered through the trees from the dirt road leading down from the lodge. After being in darkness for so long, the night seemed almost bright despite the moody sky and the rain. Keeping well into the trees, they turned and followed the track until they rounded a bend and the lodge hove into view. It was in darkness. Not a chink of light anywhere. They crept stealthily through the trees until they could see the whole lodge.

'I think they've blacked out the windows,' whispered Mitchell, settling down in a hollow behind a tree.

'Why would they bother doing that out here?' asked Jones.

Gilmour's trained eye soaked in the scene. A black Range Rover brooded on the gravel courtyard near the front door, its heavily tinted glass dripping with rain. The lodge itself was two converted cottages knocked into one. Off to one side was a wooden shed with no windows, a black electrical wire stretching to its roof from the lodge.

'Shall we have a look out back?' suggested Jones.

'Let's just sit here for a while and watch,' replied Mitchell warily.

The wind stirred the trees with growing anger as rain fell steadily from the murky sky.

Suddenly, glass shattered and light streamed down from an upstairs window. The four of them jumped with fright.

A heavy metal object crunched onto the gravel and a woman screamed. There was a muffled crump and the scream choked. A blanket was hastily pulled back across the broken window, plunging the courtyard back into darkness. Mitchell caught Gilmour's arm and looked at him in horror.

'*What the—*'

'*Shhh!*' warned Jones, pointing to the window.

The blanket was pulled back and yellow light streamed back down into the courtyard. A drawn, weasel face peered out for a moment and then rearranged the blanket. Everything went dark once more.

'Easy seeing where the Colombian gets his name from,' observed Jones.

'*What the fuck is going on?*' hissed Mitchell.

They lay for a long while, but there wasn't another sound.

'What are we going to do?' whispered Taylor eventually, completely at a loss.

'*Shhh . . . shut up!*' whispered Mitchell, raising his rifle slowly.

Gilmour looked. *Were his eyes deceiving him?* The front door was slightly ajar. His skin crawled. Someone was standing just inside the lodge, listening out at the night. His palms began to sweat.

The door opened and a shadow stepped outside. It was the Colombian, wearing a combat jacket and an evil snarl. A Browning pistol hung loosely in his fingers. The black wire stretching to the shed drew a moan from the lacerated wind. The Colombian looked suspiciously at the trees and then walked quickly to the dark lump lying on the gravel, picked up a hammer and disappeared back inside. The door closed noiselessly behind him and the lodge went back to sleep.

'This is what we're going to do,' said Mitchell a few minutes later. 'We'll lie up right here in the trees. The next time we have someone in the courtyard, we step out and challenge them. If anyone draws a weapon – we slot them.'

There were a few uncomfortable moments as they digested his plan.

'Just like that?' said Gilmour unhappily.

'Once we have them secured,' continued Mitchell, throwing Gilmour a funny look, 'two of us will enter the building and check it out. Any questions?'

'I'm getting too old for this,' sighed Jones.

'*Are there any questions?*'

'You're knee-jerking,' cautioned Gilmour.

'What about the woman?' asked Mitchell. 'Can she wait?'

'If we go in unprepared we're asking for it.'

Mitchell rubbed his troubled brow.

'Let's just do it,' agreed Taylor reluctantly. 'It's a simple scenario and we must have practiced it a thousand times.'

Gilmour knew it was the awful scream still echoing in their heads that had swayed the decision. In silence, they stashed their bergens and sorted themselves out under the trees, preparing to spring their trap. Gilmour found himself a spot behind a tree, with a clear view of all the lodge windows, and made himself comfortable on beds of damp pine needles. Now and again, he imagined he heard, or rather felt, muffled thuds coming from the lodge. But he shrugged it off. He felt prepared and ready. However, he wasn't even remotely prepared for what was to come. None of them were.

Chapter 20

Gilmour lay in an electric silence, his thumb on the safety catch, watching the lodge from the cover of the trees. The night passed and dawn touched the black sky with the faintest of grey hues. The black Rover stood ominously by the lodge, like a silent sentry, raindrops running in little rivulets down its windscreen. The bloody thing was giving him the creeps. Behind it, the lodge remained impassive, its dark windows revealing no secrets. The smell of damp pine needles seemed to hang in the dank morning air. Although the topmost branches of the trees were rustling belligerently, there wasn't a breath of air within the forest. It was stifling under the trees, as if the forest was holding its breath. Mitchell wormed his way over.

'Jamie?' he whispered.

'Yes?'

'I want you to stay in the trees when we step out and challenge them.'

'Eh? What for?' asked Gilmour, his eyes narrowing

with suspicion.

'I want someone to stay in cover and watch our backs when we step out. You know, keep an eye on the lodge in case someone takes a pot at us from a window or something.'

'Makes sense,' agreed Gilmour. 'Expecting trouble?'

'What do you think?'

Gilmour nodded.

'I thought so,' said Mitchell, reading his expression. 'If anyone so much as breathes too deeply – slot them.'

'What if a woman shows her face?'

Mitchell threw him a derisory scowl and Gilmour realised he'd just been demoted to dickhead again.

The miserable dawn light grew and the night began to crawl away under mossy stones and rocks. Hues of dark brown and green began to form amongst the blacks and greys of the forest. The drizzle continued to fall in a light curtain, occasionally swirling round the courtyard. Ragged shreds of grey cloud trailed across the lowering sky, threatening heavier rain. A fresh morning chill brushed Gilmour's cheeks. A dull stiffness had crept into his limbs from lying on the damp ground and he tensed and relaxed different muscles to keep the blood flowing. Apart from the wind moaning in the wires and the stirring of the trees, nothing moved. Not even a bird.

And then it was day. As usual, he'd noticed the first tinge of dawn in the sky and had watched the shadows sneaking away, but it had been so gradual he'd missed the event yet again. And still nothing happened. He wondered what Mitchell was thinking. There would be no more talk now, that was for sure.

A scraping sound suddenly emanated from the lodge and Gilmour's senses flared like a lighted match to petrol. The front door opened and two men stepped out, dragging a woman's body lightly wrapped in a blood-soaked sheet. *They'd killed her?* Their breaths clouding on the cold morning air, the two men looked nervously over their shoulders as they dragged the body to the rear of the Range Rover.

The front door of the lodge swung a little on its hinges. Someone was standing in the hallway, watching and listening. The two men opened the boot of the car and dumped the body inside. Rain spilled off the vehicle as it juddered under the weight and they slammed the boot shut with a resounding clunk. The Colombian stepped out into the rain, pulled a pistol from his combat jacket pocket and peered suspiciously at the trees.

'*Don't fucking move!*' screamed Mitchell, his voice dreadful and menacing, chilling even Gilmour's bones.

Three figures loomed up, weapons at the shoulder.

'*Move and we'll fucking drop you!*'

'What is—?' started the Colombian.

'*Shut it prick!*'

The tone in Mitchell's voice drove the point home. Gilmour's gaze darted from window to window.

'If any of you so much as *breathe* too hard,' hissed Mitchell icily, 'we will shoot you! Do you understand?'

There were a few uncomfortable moments when neither side moved. Gilmour knew Mitchell was giving them an opportunity to fight. If they took it, there would be three dead men lying on the gravel. Mitchell took a step forward keeping his weapon firmly trained on the Colombian.

'Drop the weapon, asshole.'

The pistol fell and crunched on the stones. Mitchell stepped out from the trees flanked by the other two and stopped to take in his surroundings with his peripheral vision. Sweat trickled down Gilmour's back. Even the trees seemed to tremble. Mitchell took another wary step. Gilmour switched his aim from the lodge to the men in the courtyard. Something wasn't right. The Colombian had dropped his weapon too casually. Mitchell edged forward until the muzzle of his rifle jabbed into the soft flesh behind an ear.

'Who are you?' asked the Colombian. 'Can't a we go a fishing in peace?'

'Get those two sorted,' said Mitchell, nodding at the other two.

Taylor and Jones moved swiftly, their weapons into their shoulders, and marched the two men to the side of the lodge. Jones pushed them into the stress position, palms flat against the wall, legs apart.

'They're clean,' he said after searching them, and stepped back.

Mitchell prodded the Colombian's scalp with the muzzle of his rifle.

'Up against the wall.'

The Colombian rubbed his head as he walked to the building. Jones picked up the fallen pistol and covered him while Mitchell searched him. Gilmour relaxed a bit and let the pressure off the trigger.

'Get them in the Rover and cover them,' said Mitchell quickly. 'I've only one set of plasticuffs.'

Jones quickly searched the car for weapons.

'It's clean,' he said confidently.

'What about the boot?' asked Mitchell?

The Welshman wiped rain from the glass and peered in through the rear window.

'Only the woman as far as I can see.'

Taylor covered them as the Colombian clambered in first. Jones stood by the open door with his rifle pointing into the vehicle.

'Andy, check the boot,' said Mitchell, sounding a little unsure of himself.

The dead woman was really bothering him. Taylor walked round but was reluctant to open it.

'Get on with it man,' barked Mitchell.

Taylor fumbled with the door catch.

'It's the body of a young woman,' he said, pulling back the sheet and feeling for a pulse. 'She's dead. Didn't die very quickly either. She's been smacked about. Burns, bruises, and cuts – she's been tortured. Looks like a hammer to the back of the head finished her off.' He choked as he turned her body round. Her injuries were appalling. For a moment he stared at her and then let the sheet fall back over the body. It was a pity he didn't think of checking to see what the body was lying on.

Mitchell eyed the lodge. The blanketed windows were disconcerting, but someone had to go in and check it out. He was worried. The dead girl was something he hadn't bargained for. He walked quickly to the car and peered in.

'Fishing eh?' he hissed, eyeing the Colombian coldly.

The man ignored him and kept his eyes on his lap. Mitchell looked at each of the lodge windows in turn. Someone had to go in there, but who? It was a two-man job, but he couldn't leave just one of them covering the vehicle. Gilmour was back up and there was no way he was going to reveal him just yet. He knew it was lack of preparation that was letting him down. But what else could he have done?

'Andy, go and find something to truss these pricks up

with.'

Taylor trotted off round the back. Bending down slightly, Mitchell glowered at the Colombian. He was too angry to notice that the other two men were sweating rather more profusely than they should have been.

'What's with the dead girl?' he asked.

When he was ignored, he pushed his beret back and rubbed his troubled brow. Slowly, the Colombian lifted his head and turned towards him.

'What a you want?' he asked, his voice low and soothing. 'Money?'

Gilmour felt the hairs on the back of his neck prickling. The Colombian was too smooth, too much in control. Jones shifted his weight from foot to foot.

'This'll do Mike,' said Taylor, wandering back with some rusty fence wire.

The Colombian looked furtively at the trees.

'Charlie, call the Headshed and get a chopper in here quick,' said Mitchell.

Jones ran for his bergen.

'You don't a know what's going on,' said the Colombian suddenly, staring straight into Mitchell's eyes. 'You don't a know jack shit.'

Mitchell kept his eye, but the man saw his uncertainty. Jones stepped out of the trees and dropped his bergen on the gravel. The Colombian leaned over towards Mitchell and lowered his voice.

'You want to know about the woman?' he asked, malice dripping from his lips. 'You should be here while she still warm and twitching. English woman is great fuck.'

Mitchell recoiled in horror. It was precisely the reaction the Colombian had hoped for. He kicked open his door and rolled out onto the gravel. Jones looked up from the radio and shouted a warning. The other two men in the Rover panicked and scrambled for the doors. Getting to his feet, the Colombian darted for the side of the lodge. Taylor sprinted after him. Gilmour whipped up his rifle, but he was far too late.

There was a blinding flash and the Rover was blown apart as a huge car bomb detonated. Gilmour threw an arm over his eyes as the vehicle erupted into the air. The shockwave hit him and he was hurled backwards into the forest like a piece of dried camel dung in a desert storm. He smashed into the trunk of a tree and everything went black.

Chapter 21

Ellis propped his foot on a large rock, leaned on his knee and looked back down the steep mountainside. He'd almost reached the low clouds obscuring the summit. His steely gaze swept the valley far below. If he hadn't been preoccupied by recent events, he might even have been enjoying himself.

It wasn't that the problems were unduly concerning him; it was just their sheer magnitude that was giving him cause for concern. He shook his head as if it would somehow dislodge thoughts that might make sense of the whole thing. Problems, he was discovering, liked to lurk under each other. Sweep up dead leaves and you find something nasty crawling around in the gutter underneath.

He noticed the climb was leaving him a little more breathless than it should have been. Keeping fit was becoming more and more of a chore. One of these years he knew he wasn't going to be able to haul the weight over the distance any longer. He cocked his head, thinking he felt the distant thrum of a helicopter beating the air somewhere. He didn't hear it again and put it from his mind. With a sigh, he allowed himself a few more seconds rest. Then, with a pull on the bergen straps, he continued up the steep hillside and soon lost sight of the world below as he was swallowed by the clouds.

Before he reached the summit he sensed someone was following him. He glanced back down the hillside but saw only grey mist. It started to rain lightly but he kept his hood down. Reaching into his waistband for his Browning pistol, he thumbed off the safety catch. Below him, a disturbed rock clattered. His skin prickled and he whipped round, his pistol raised. His pulse raced, though not with exertion. Fear was something he was used to seeing in others and he found he wasn't enjoying the experience. He looked hurriedly around him but there was nowhere to go, nowhere to hide.

Slipping the weighted bergen from his shoulders, he threw it back down the steep track. As it bounced and tumbled off into the mists, he set off along the hillside at a run. Without the bergen he could move quickly, but the ground was treacherous and he wasn't familiar with the mountain. For a moment, he thought he'd lost whoever was following him.

Then he heard the beat of a helicopter's rotors thumping the air. *It was in radio contact with the man on the ground!* They were using heat-imaging equipment. *They could see him!* Running recklessly, he started down the hillside. He had to get down out of the clouds. He knew he wasn't going to make it.

A shot rang out.

At the same instant, he stumbled and twisted his ankle. A bullet grazed the top of his head as he fell and the breath was knocked from him as he hit the ground. He rolled a few times and smacked into a rock. Fighting for breath, he pointed his pistol back up the hillside. A complacent shadow sauntered down out of the mists, a pistol hanging loosely at his side. Ellis didn't wait for the man to realise his mistake and fired two quick shots.

The man gasped and fell, slithered and bounced a few times and lay still. Ellis got awkwardly to his feet, put his hand to his head and limped over to the body. The unshaved, swarthy complexion of the man was unmistakably European, probably Italian. A gold crucifix and the earpiece of a covert radio dangled round his neck. The helicopter seemed to hover undecidedly and then banked away. As the sound of the rotors faded, he tried to calm his wildly beating heart.

He took his hand from his head, his fingers red with blood. He knew there would be no identification on the body and there wasn't. He sat down and nursed his twisted ankle. The crucifix hanging around the dead man's neck disturbed him.

When he clambered painfully to his feet, he breathed deeply, relishing each exquisite moment in a way he'd never done before. A drop of blood trickled behind his ear, but he didn't care. He was alive and he shouldn't have been.

Chapter 22

Ellis crouched on one knee beside a small bush and waited for the moon to disappear behind a cloud. He was desperate for a piss and his twisted ankle ached terribly. Over the top of a nearby stone wall, the roof of a country manor house gleamed in the bright moonlight. Dressed completely in black, a balaclava pulled over his head, a small black waterproofed operations bergen on his back, he was darker than the shadows around him. A rifle with night scope hung in his hand and a short black lightweight assault ladder lay on the ground beside him.

Finding out who his Italian would-be assassin had been hadn't been too difficult. The Brigadier had his uses, especially when he needed access to Mi5 computers. But why would an English Lord employ such a fellow? Did the Jesuits know one of their Swiss Guard was an assassin? Did this have something to do with McCann? He was going to find out. The pale face of the moon slipped behind a cloud and the shadows deepened.

Soundlessly, he got up and limped towards the stone wall surrounding the manor.

Placing the ladder noiselessly against the stonework, he climbed a couple of rungs. Resting his elbows on top of the wall, he nestled the rifle into his shoulder, peered through the scope and fired a single silenced shot. A Doberman slumped to the lawn at the rear of the house. Through a lighted window he could see a few men playing cards in the kitchen. He wondered if they were missing their Italian mate. He doubted it. Judging by the intensity of their expressions a lot of money must have been on the table. He checked his watch and had the unnerving feeling that his life, like the time, was running out on him.

Pulling thick sacking from inside his jacket, he wrapped it round the barbed wire running along the top of the wall. Propping the rifle up beside the ladder, he had a last cautious glance around him before slithering over. He dropped to an herbaceous border on the other side and fell painfully onto his side. As he sat nursing his swollen ankle, he saw one of the men in the kitchen chuck his cards on the table in disgust. There was no mistaking the holstered gun under his arm. Not caring about the footprints he was leaving in the mud, he set off along the wall.

The first floor study window was open and he was secretly thankful that the weather was warm for the time of year. He thought he heard arguing from the kitchen. He hobbled across the lawn and took a firm grip of the ivy that covered the entire side of the house. It took his weight easily so there was no need to go back for the ladder. Quickly, he shimmied up to the window and clambered inside.

Arranging the heavy velvet curtains behind him, he glanced at his watch again and was startled to see he'd lost another fifteen minutes. From his pocket he slipped out a small mag-lite and shone the beam round an opulent office. On the far side he picked out a computer on a large mahogany desk. Shadowed portraits frowned at him as he padded silently across the plush carpet. His head tilted slightly to one side as his trained but nervous eyes flicked through the CD-Rs lined up beside the computer. Dropping his bergen, he stuffed them inside.

In the distance, a dog barked faintly. He stiffened involuntarily and glanced at the curtains, half expecting to see returning car headlights warming the rich velvet. The curtains remained dark. Unable to contain himself any longer, he unzipped himself and sighed with relief as his pee trickled down the side of the desk forming a dark stain on the carpet.

Apart from the CD's, he found nothing of interest in the office. Still, at least he'd annoyed a few people. He switched off his mag-lite and hoisted on his bergen. Limping to the window, he eased the curtains open a crack and peered down.

His heart stopped.

A dark figure was standing in the garden below looking up at the window. Ellis reached for his pistol and thumbed off the safety catch. A light came on in the hallway outside the office, shining in the crack under the door. The figure in the garden looked around a little hesitantly and then wandered off towards the back of the house. Ellis waited until he'd disappeared round the corner and slipped out onto the window ledge, hurriedly rearranging the curtains behind him. As he lowered himself over the sill, the door to the office opened and a light came on. When he hit the lawn, he ran for the cover of the shrubs along the stone wall.

'*Oi!*' shouted the bloke who'd wandered round the back. '*The bloody dog's been shot!*'

Ellis lay flat on the ground, using the shrubs to conceal him. The curtains of the office were thrown back and cold eyes peered down. He recognised the shaved head and the gold stud in the lip immediately.

It was McConnell's dicker from Belfast.

'What the—?'

Somewhere, a door banged open. A torch flicked on and two men with drawn pistols ran across the lawn and stared dumbly at the dead dog. The cold eyes at the office window disappeared. Ellis thought he sensed a movement on the other side of the manor and turned to see a black shadow flit behind a tree. His skin prickling, he got to his feet and ran.

'*There he is!*'

A bullet smacked into the wall near his head, showering him with splinters of stone. He turned and fired a few rapid shots and the three men dived for cover. Then, like a dark ripple on a black pool, he limped along the border and disappeared over the wall.

Chapter 23

The first grey light of dawn filtered in through Ellis'
study window and he leaned back at his desk and
stretched. His ankle was killing him and he was exhausted. Sleepless nights were becoming an unwelcome
habit. Taking the last stolen CD-R from the disc drive,
he closed down his computer and switched it off. Draining what was left of a mug of lukewarm coffee, he
pushed back his leather swivel chair and got gingerly to
his feet. He leafed through the many pages of scribbled
notes scattered about on his desk, searching for something that had been puzzling him. When he found it, he
left his office and strolled through his small castle towards the kitchen, his leather slippers slapping his heels.
He needed some breakfast.

As he padded along the plush carpeted hallway, he
was warmed by the richly exuberant emotion of the
Monet the Brigadier had bought on his behalf. He had
no idea what it was about old paintings that made people spend such vast sums on them, but it did seem to

brighten the old place up a bit. Dull morning light filtered in through the turreted windows on either side of his heavy oak front door and gleamed on the wood panelling of his hallway. Before he got to the kitchen, the doorbell rang.

He frowned and gripped the butt of the pistol in his pocket. When he opened the door, a rather stern Sergeant Roberts glared at him. She tossed her head and settled her profoundly deep eyes on him. For the first time in his life, Ellis was speechless.

'Well, what was it you stole from the manor?' she asked.

'Hmmm . . . you're not what you seem, young lady.'

'Don't *hmmm* me Mister Ellis.'

'Ah, that was you sneaking behind that tree, wasn't it?'

'Are you going to invite me in?'

'No.'

'I'm sure the police would be very interested in your nightly pursuits.'

Ellis looked her up and down and decided that he liked her.

'It would seem we have quite a lot to discuss, young lady.'

'I'll be keeping an eye on you, *Mister* Ellis.'

'It would appear you've been doing just that. Please, call me Peter.'

'You can call me Roberts.'

Ellis laughed.

'So what brings you here? A citizen's arrest?'

'Curiosity.'

Ellis suddenly thought of something.

'Have you any dealings with Peterson?'

'Peterson? The Minister?'

He knew from her reaction she was hiding something.

'Hmmm . . . if I were you, young lady, I wouldn't let him know you were here.'

With another toss of her head, she turned and strolled back to her car.

'You take care now,' he said, and closed the door.

He wasn't laughing anymore.

Munching cornflakes and milk, he tried to make sense of it all. A spoonful of cornflakes near his mouth, he suddenly stiffened and grabbed the page of scribbled notes. He put the spoon down on his plate and stared at the sheet. Shaking his head, he stared dumfounded out the window at the trees swaying listlessly in the cool morning breeze.

'*No, no,*' he said repeatedly, '*surely not. It couldn't be?*'

Leaving his unfinished cereal, he walked quickly back to his study. He didn't even notice his new painting. The door clicked shut behind him as he sat at his desk and switched on his computer. Fumbling through the CD-Rs, he tried to remember which one he was looking for. His computer couldn't boot up quickly enough. He slapped the CD into the disc drive and quickly scrolled through the documents until he found one entitled aQ.

'al Qaeda?'

The document opened and he quickly skimmed it. It was just a list of United Nations and Red Cross vehicles that were being shipped to Afghanistan and Iran. It said nothing he didn't already know but he hadn't expected it to. When he reached the end of the document he stared dumbly at the screen. The page ended with three little Latin words.

Novus Ordo Seclorum

He began to tremble. He was back to eyes and pyramids again.

Chapter 24

There were many curious things about Peter Ellis but perhaps one of the most talked about among those who thought they knew him was that he didn't actually own a car. For someone who could afford to buy any car on earth with his pocket money, it only fuelled the speculation that he was mad. He knew what people thought, but it didn't bother him. If he was honest, he enjoyed his eccentric status. It kept folk away. However, little did they know that he was prone to stealing the odd admiring glance at Aston Martins. Once he had even parked up beside a showroom and stood outside the plate glass windows, jangling the loose change in his pocket as he eyed a V8 Vantage. Twenty minutes later, after much arguing out loud with himself – to the consternation of people passing in the street – he'd torn himself from the Aston Martin and dragged himself away. Driving around in the same car all the time, especially one so head turning, was just too much of a security risk.

Around mid morning, he locked the front door to his

castle, waited until his security system stopped beeping, picked up his hastily packed suitcase and strolled quickly to the hired Cavalier parked on his forecourt. He was in a hurry. He'd done a little research and had not liked what he'd found. He was a seriously worried man. His brow was so furrowed, he didn't notice the tiny speck of a helicopter way up in the sky as it darted behind a cloud.

As was usual, he checked underneath the car for explosives. Having dumped the suitcase in the boot, he jumped in the front. His mobile phone bounced on the seat beside him and he started the engine. He drove through the trees surrounding his castle to the main gate, turned left and headed down the country lane to the village. Suddenly, his skin started prickling. Yanking up the handbrake, he threw the wheel round. The tyres skirled as the car lurched and slewed round facing the other way. The front wheels smoked as he floored the pedal.

As he sped past his gate, a large black Mercedes careered round the next corner coming towards him. He didn't wait to see what it was going to do and kept the accelerator hard down. The Cavalier sank into its suspension in the tight bend and shot out into a long straight. He was going so fast the overhanging trees were a blur. No one knew these roads like he did. The Mercedes was never going to catch him now.

A few miles farther on, he took a right into a narrow lane, intending to cut across country to the M4 and head for Hereford. He desperately needed to speak with Munro. He checked his mirror and pushed his misgivings to one side. Suddenly, a rifle bullet punched through his side window, nicking the back of his neck. Putting the boot down, he threw the car from side to side as he sped down the single-track road.

When he reached the junction with the main road, he turned right and headed for the motorway. Almost immediately, he spotted a black Mercedes in his rear view mirror. He leaned forward and glanced up through the windscreen at the tiny speck of the helicopter hovering way up in the sky.

'Hmmm . . . so you want to play rough eh?' he muttered, reaching into his pocket for his Browning pistol.

With the needle pushing 120 mph, he swerved past a slow moving articulated lorry. The Mercedes pulled out to follow. An oncoming line of traffic was fast approaching so he knew the Mercedes was committed. As he pulled in, he braked hard and slammed the car down into third gear, leaving no room between him and the lorry for the Mercedes. The lorry driver thumped his palm onto his horn and held it there. Ellis elbowed out the shattered glass in his side window. As the Mercedes sped past, he fired two shots and the car skidded off the road. Putting his foot down, he accelerated away, leaving the lorry and a few cars skidding to a halt in a cloud of smoke. He leaned forward. The helicopter had come down for a closer look. He was going to have to ditch that thing.

Round the next corner was a busy petrol station. Most of its pumps whirred with activity and its shop was alive with custom. He pulled in under the protective canopy, pocketed his phone and got out. Taking his suitcase from the boot, he walked smartly over to a green Ford Ka about to pull away. He opened the door, threw his case on the back seat and jumped in. A startled young lady stared at him in horror.

'Let's go,' he said, resting his pistol on his lap.

The woman was too shocked to move.

'Let's go!' said Ellis forcefully, staring hard at her.

'*Get out of my fucking car!*'

'Hmm,' said Ellis, his brow wrinkling.

'*Get out!*'

He slipped his pistol into his pocket.

'You're not scared of my gun then.'

'Scared? You . . . you . . . arsehole!'

'Hmm.'

'*Get out!*'

'Look, I'm one of the good guys and I'm in trouble. I need your help.'

'You think I'd help you because you show me a gun?'

'It usually works.'

Ellis held the eye of the young lady. She was really quite gorgeous. Short light brown hair, lovely curves and deep eyes. For some strange reason, he pictured himself kneeling behind her head, easing his penis between her moist lips while he played with her nipples.

She observed him coolly for a few moments, glanced over at the smashed window of the Cavalier, put her car in gear and pulled out of the forecourt.

'What's the problem?' she asked, barging her way into the traffic.

'That helicopter up there,' replied Ellis, indicating to the machine hovering around trying to see under the forecourt canopy. 'It's been following me and they're not very nice people.'

'I don't think you're a very nice person.'

'I've heard that before.'

'I'm Chrissy.'

'Hi, I'm Peter.'

'I'm working and I'm late for an appointment.'

'Drop me off in the first place we come to,' said Ellis, wiping blood from his neck with a handkerchief, 'and I'll be out of your life.'

The young lady fell thoughtfully quiet at that and concentrated on her driving. Ellis checked behind him. They turned a corner and he lost sight of the helicopter behind some trees.

'You a secret agent or something?' asked the young lady.

'No.'

'Military?'

'No.'

'You don't speak much.'

'I guess not.'

'It's illegal to carry guns you know.'

'Is that so?'

'Yes.'

'Well I find them very useful.'

'They're illegal.'

'Especially when folk are trying to kill me.'

'Does that happen a lot?'

Ellis sighed and wished she would shut up.

'What do you know about guns?' he asked, taking the offensive.

'They're illegal.'

'So you keep saying.'

'Well . . . they are.'

'The IRA have them.'

'Excuse me?'

'Making guns illegal doesn't take them away from the bad guys, does it? It merely leaves good people defenceless.'

'Don't patronise me,' said the young lady, throwing him a reproving look.

'Okay,' sighed Ellis, 'there's an organisation out there determined to take over the whole world and set up a one world government.'

'Yeah right.'

'It's true.'

'So what's stopping them?'

'American gun laws.'

'Oh spare me!'

'Shall I go back to patronising you?'

'And they're trying to kill you right?'

'Something like that.'

'Because you've stumbled on their little plot?'

'Their little plot is rather well known.'

'Really?'

'Where are you heading for?'

'Swindon.'

'That'll do me.'

'I'm not a taxi.'

'This'll do here then,' said Ellis, reaching for the door handle.

'Don't be so stupid!' said the young lady. 'I can't just dump you in the middle of nowhere.'

'You like me, don't you?' said Ellis, settling back in his seat.

'Pretty damn sure of yourself, aren't you?'

'Am I wrong?'

'This organisation . . . have I heard of them?'

'Oh yes, but I'm having difficulty figuring out where Jesuit priests and Rhodes Scholars fit into the big picture.'

'Priests and Scholars?'

Ellis looked across at her.

'You don't believe me, do you?'

She smiled across at him.

'You're absolutely mad Peter, but I think I like you.'

Ellis suddenly tucked his chin down and frowned.

'Would you mind dropping me in this town?' he asked, nodding to the next junction.

'Have I upset you?'

'No, not at all, I've just thought of something important. I need to get to Hereford to speak to someone and I need to speak to them now. I don't suppose you're heading that way?'

The young lady indicated and they headed into a built up area.

'This'll do here,' said Ellis, pointing to a used car lot on the outskirts. 'And thank you.'

She looked crestfallen.

'Is that it then?' she asked.

Ellis got out and reached into the back for his suitcase.

'Is what it?'

'You could at least invite me to dinner or something.'

Ellis hesitated.

'What's the matter?' she asked.

'Nothing,' he said, unable to stop himself stealing a glance at her breasts. 'I'm just not very good at things like this.'

She handed him a business card.

'Here's my number. I'll expect a call.'

She reached across and pulled the door closed, reversed into the sales lot and headed back out of town. Ellis quickly scanned the skies for helicopters.

'I'll bet I've got just the thing!' beamed a salesman strolling through the rows of shining cars.

He was dressed in a blue double-breasted suit, white shirt and bright yellow tie festooned with cartoon characters.

'Have you now,' said Ellis turning to meet him, pondering whether he was going to cut all the commission out of the bloke's sale or not.

Chapter 25

Gilmour cracked open an eye and blinked a few times. Above him, leafless trees jutted alarmingly into an overcast sky. As he tried to sit up, an excruciatingly sharp pain stabbed through his head. He lay down again feeling sick. *That was strange!* The trees were all blasted and splintered. He put his hands to his head to try to shut off the ringing in his ears. Then, like a thundering tsunami, the memories flooded back, devastating the shores of his mind.

With a grunt, he rolled over and forced himself up on one knee. *Where was his damn rifle?* It was lying half covered in pine needles and brown earth beside the trunk of a tree. With a colossal surge of self-preservation, he got up and stumbled over to it using tree trunks for support. He fell to his knees, picked up the weapon, cleared the muzzle of soil, slipped out the magazine, checked it, whacked it back in, cocked the rifle, got back to his feet and turned towards the lodge. The magazine fell off and thudded to the ground.

Muttering darkly, he bent quickly to pick it up. Rattling the magazine about to make sure it was secured; he pulled the rifle into his shoulder and looked around. The acrid smell of burning rubber drifted into the forest and wisps of black smoke stung his eyes. Feeling dizzy, he stumbled forward. Through the trees he could see the charred, twisted shell of the Rover lying in a mangled heap beside a smoking crater. Small fires littered the courtyard, flickering in the morning wind. Lumps of smouldering debris were scattered everywhere. He ducked under a branch and something brushed the top of his head. He waved it aside but it fell back again. He reached up and grabbed a piece of cloth. Something heavy fell out of the branches and thumped to the ground.

He recoiled in horror. A severed arm lay at his feet, blackened and bleeding, broken bone poking from the soggy end. Barely visible on the charred skin, the tattoo of a nude woman smiled up at him. With his rifle raised, alert for trouble, he walked quickly to the edge of the trees. He could see only two bodies. Of the Colombian there was no sign. He stepped over a smouldering wheel blown off an axle. Realising the Colombian would have been long gone, he allowed the rifle to drop from his shoulder. As he did so a torn nail caught on his clothing, almost ripping it off. He squeezed his finger to stop the fresh blood oozing from the wound. Dark thunderclouds loomed behind the hills and the cool scent of heavy rain drifted down the glen. He stared at the bodies and tried to think. He knew it was pointless but he had to check them.

'Mike? Is that you?'

He walked over but there was no response. Mitchell's

stomach had been ripped open and his guts lay strewn around on the gravel. A couple of flies were buzzing about on the raw flesh. Tears welled into Gilmour's eyes as he trudged wearily over to the other body. Jones lay near the trees, face down and lifeless. Both his arms were missing and his brain lay exposed to the cold grey light. Blood seeped from the terrible head wound, forming a red pool on the damp gravel. Gilmour gently nudged him with the toe of his boot.

'Charlie?' he whispered pathetically.

The only answer was the wind in the wires.

He looked around for his mate Andy, but couldn't see him anywhere. He figured the explosion must have blown him into the trees. The two men who had been in the vehicle were in bits, which explained most of the sloppy lumps lying all over the gravel. His fingers shook as he knelt to rummage through Charlie's shredded bergen for the radio. It was wrecked. For a long while he knelt there beside the bergen, his head bowed, the rifle hanging limply in his grasp. Cold fingers of rain trickled down his neck until he eventually struggled back to his feet.

Curtains fluttered from gaping dark holes behind piles of rubble where the windows of the lodge had once been. The front door was splintered and hung at a crazy angle. It creaked as a gust of wind caught it. Heavy clouds rolled overhead and the rain became heavier, hissing on the hot, twisted metal of the wrecked car. His head spinning, he went to look for Taylor.

As he rounded the edge of the building, his heart fluttered. Taylor was sitting with his back to the wall, trying to squeeze a bag of clear fluid into his arm through a needle.

'Andy!'

Taylor looked up in surprise, his face streaked in blood. Gilmour choked and couldn't get any more words out.

'Give us a hand mate,' whispered Taylor weakly, a desperate, frightened look in his eyes. 'I'm in shit state.'

His head lolled forward and the bag of fluid slipped from his fingers.

Gilmour lay him down gently and squeezed the rest of the fluid into him. His mate had lost a lot of blood and his breathing was shallow. There was a horrendous hole in his right thigh. As the last of the precious fluid disappeared into his veins, he plucked a field dressing from a strap on Taylor's webbing and packed it into the wound. Blood quickly soaked through the dressing and he ripped his own off and packed it in as well, pressing it with his fist as hard as he could until the bleeding stopped.

The rain was starting to teem down and they were both getting wet. Sheets of rusty corrugated iron lay in a heap beside a pile of logs near the back fence and he got up and limped over. The tin screeched as he lifted a few sheets. When he'd finished building a small lean-to against the side of the lodge and he was happy there was no more he could do for his mate, he went to look for a phone. As he approached the front door, he faltered. His head swam with dizziness. He really didn't want to go in there. Steeling himself, he lifted his rifle to his shoulder and stepped in through the shattered doorway.

It was eerily hushed inside the lodge. The dark, stuffy silence was suffocating. Outside, he could hear the rain hissing in dying flames. Four doors led off the hallway and a flight of stairs led up to a landing. Light streamed in through a shattered window towards the end of the hall, sparkling on the broken glass on the floor. He walked cautiously to the nearest room and pushed. Debris scraped over the carpet as he forced the door back and squeezed his head through the opening. The living room had been superbly furnished but the explosion had destroyed it. Velvet curtains waved limply in the cold air blowing in over wet rubble. Side tables, chairs, books, ornaments, pictures and other furnishings lay scattered and broken, covered with dust and fallen plaster. The phone lay in a pile of fallen masonry, smashed. He hoped there was another.

Back out in the hall, he turned the handle of the next door. It swung open effortlessly and he walked into the dining room. Apart from a few fallen ornaments and pictures, it was untouched by the blast. A stag's head stared at him with glassy eyes from the opposite wall. A large dining table set for six took up most of the space. Pictures of stags, grouse, salmon and smiling sportsmen dressed in tweeds, adorned the walls. *Set for six?* Gilmour looked quickly over his shoulder, half expecting a blow. His heart hammered in his chest. The next door was a little tight. A slight shove with his shoulder and it swung open. His eyes darted round the spacious kitchen. His palm was sweaty as he reached for the last handle. He eased the door open and cast a cursory glance into a small toilet.

A movement outside caught his eye and he spun round. A small bird had landed in the middle of the courtyard and was looking inquisitively at the lodge. He had it in his sights and his finger trembled on the trigger. Suddenly, with a flutter of wings, it was gone. He started sweating and took a few controlled breaths to steady himself.

Just inside the front door, a smashed vase lay in pieces

beside a small broken side table. Amongst the shards of china lay a business card. He walked over and picked it up. *Fred Dillon – specialist cars*. There was an address in Manchester and a phone number. He stuffed the card into a breast pocket of his smock and turned towards the stairs.

Easing a foot onto the bottom step, he put his weight down carefully on the side of his boot. The stair didn't creak. Keeping his back to the wall, his weapon firmly locked into his shoulder, he eased himself up the stairwell. The horror of the carnage outside was briefly forgotten as his entire mind focused on the job. This he could handle. This he could do. This he'd been trained for. Another step took his weight without creaking.

He paused as his eyes drew level with the landing. There was a long passageway with four doors leading off. Three of the doors were slightly ajar.

His footfalls muffled by thick carpet, he inched towards the nearest open door at the rear of the lodge. With his toe, he gave it a little push and poked his rifle inside. A spacious, tiled bathroom swung into view. His heart beat a little faster. There were six toothbrushes sticking out of a glass on the windowsill. The toiletries caught his eye. It was mostly women's stuff. Dread swamped his heart like a cold sea rushing into a sinking ship. He wiped the sweat from his face and turned to the door opposite. The silence was bursting his eardrums. He inched the door open. It was a small bedroom. Fallen plaster, dust, splintered wood and broken glass was everywhere.

The next room at the front of the lodge was where the scream had come from. Dull daylight spilled out through the crack between the door and jamb. Motes of dust twinkled as they danced in and out of the narrow beam.

Sweat dripped back into his eyes and he took the time to wipe his forehead with his sleeve. He licked his lips, tempted to go back outside and leave the rest of the house to someone else. A gust of wind moaned dismally up the stairwell and the door creaked. He took a couple of steps and eased the muzzle of his rifle into the crack. Fresh sweat trickled down his temples. Very, very slowly, he nudged the door open with his toe.

As the room swung into view, he choked and staggered backwards, an arm up to cover his eyes as if warding off a blow. He threw down his rifle, clenched his fist and hit the wall so hard he cracked the plaster. *No one had said anything about dealing with stuff like this when he'd proudly stuck his beige beret on his head.* With a titanic effort, he picked up his rifle and stalked into the room.

Two upright wooden chairs sat in the middle of the floor with a blanket spread under them. Broken glass, fallen plaster and splinters of wood covered everything. A limp, naked woman's body was slumped over the back of a chair, her bleeding wrists tied cruelly with wire to the front legs. Cigarette burns, horrendous bruises, punctures and deep knife cuts disfigured her young body. The back of her skull had been smashed in. A rag stuffed into her mouth had vomit seeping through it. One of the other chairs had bits of twisted wire lying on it. A couple of knives lay on the blood-stained blanket. He forced himself over and touched her with trembling fingers. She was stone cold.

Then he thought he heard something. Running back out into the hallway, he grabbed the last door handle. It was locked. Taking a step back, he unleashed a powerful kick. The door held. Raising the rifle, he loosed off a round and kicked again. Timber splintered and the door flew open. Apart from the furniture, the bedroom was empty. There was a door on the other side of the bed. He leapt over the bed, yanked the door open and sprang into the en suite bathroom with his rifle at the hip. Lying in the bath, bound and gagged, her bedraggled long blonde hair stuck to her face where she'd been crying, was Angelina.

'It's okay sweetheart,' he soothed. 'It's okay, don't be afraid.'

He reached for the cord holding the gag in place and eased the rag from her mouth. She gasped, spluttered and coughed violently. Gilmour took a survival knife from a sheath on his webbing, slipped his hands behind her, cut the ropes and lifted her gently from the bath. She threw her arms round his neck, looked deeply into his eyes for reassurance and then fainted. He carried her into the bedroom, laid her gently on the bed and covered her with the duvet. She was almost blue with cold. He tried to think but his mind was a typhoon.

'What the *fuck* is going on?' he cried aloud.

As if in answer to his distraught cry, there was a sudden flash at the window followed by a grumble of thunder. It grew even darker outside and then the rain hammered down. This was not a good day out.

Chapter 26

Gilmour felt strangely isolated as he listened to the rain beating against the window. Angelina moaned. He sat on the bed beside her and gently shook her awake.

'It's okay,' he whispered, putting his hands up as she shrank away. He wasn't sure if she was hearing him.

Sad green eyes peeked out at him from the safety of the duvet, her puppy eyes searching his. He lightly brushed her cheek with the back of a finger.

'We need to go sweetheart.'

'I thought you were dead,' she said, staring up at him.

'You hungry?'

'I'm cold.'

'It's not very pretty outside,' he warned. 'Stay close to me, okay?'

As they left the room, he stepped across the hallway and quickly closed the door to the front bedroom. She gazed past him at the door.

'Don't even think about it,' said Gilmour, nodding towards the stairs.

She complied without arguing. When she stepped outside and saw the bodies, she put her hands to her mouth. A few wisps of steam scurried away on the damp wind, but most of the fires were out. A heavy smell of burnt flesh and rubber hung around the courtyard. Gilmour grimaced as a sudden stab of pain shot through his head. Grabbing Angelina's hand, he led her past the rear of the bomb crater and headed to the side of the lodge.

Lifting one of the corrugated iron sheets, he checked Taylor's pulse. It was weak, but steady. The hole in his thigh looked bad but at least the bleeding had stopped. First priority was to get to a phone. The metal sheet scraped back against the wall and he headed off to get his bergen.

He groaned as he hoisted on the heavy back pack. The pain in his head brought sweat to his brow. Gingerly, he fingered his stitches and checked for blood. He felt nauseous and unsteady on his feet. With a last glance around the courtyard, he set off down the track towards the glen, pulling a trotting Angelina after him. When they lost sight of the lodge, she let go of his hand.

'What did those men do to those ladies?' she asked. 'They said they were our friends.'

'I . . . er . . .' started Gilmour uncomfortably, trying to put it into words she could understand. 'They're what you call wolves in sheep's clothing.'

She looked up at him blankly.

'They were terrible men,' he explained, 'wolves, but they were dressed up to look nice, like sheep.'

A gust of wind blew through the forest, rustling the branches on either side of the track as it came. Gilmour fastened her jacket up for her, took her hand again and led her towards the open glen.

As they approached the gate, he stepped off the track, pulling her after him into the trees.

'Wait here.'

She stumbled over a rotting branch and clutched his arm.

'You said you wouldn't leave me!' she squeaked in alarm.

'Don't worry, I'll be back.'

With that, he pushed through the trees and was gone.

The glen was deserted. Somehow he'd half expected to see police cars and ambulances bumping up the dirt road, soldiers running everywhere and helicopters buzzing towards him. But the glen was empty. It looked no different to what it had from the hide. A herd of deer crested a shoulder and started down a hillside for a drink and a graze at the river. Life was getting on with it. The deer did it for him and he headed back through the trees.

'Right, let's go,' he said, when he got back to the gate. 'It's a long walk.'

She looked at him with a pained expression.

'I'm tired.'

Gilmour thought about it for a moment.

'Okay, I'll heat us up some curry first.'

'How's my mummy?'

'I don't know sweetheart.'

'And Scud?'

'Oh, he's fine,' smiled Gilmour, and gently pulled the hood of her jacket right over her head. 'He can't wait for another cuddle from you.'

At the first stream they came to, Gilmour stepped off the road and dumped his bergen down. Reaching into a side pocket, he rummaged about for his small army stove. He was faint with hunger and needed something inside him. Scratching a match over a sandpaper strip, he watched gratifyingly as the protective wax fell from the match head and the sulphur ignited. Cupping his hands round the flickering match, he crouched and lit a hexamine block on his little stove. Soon the curry was sizzling away in a mess tin, sending comforting wafts of delicious hot food scurrying away on the wind. Even Angelina began to look interested as the warm smells drifted in her direction.

'I missed you,' she said.

Gilmour studied her drawn face and felt a strong urge to wrap his arms round her and tell her everything was going to be fine. She must have noticed, because she gave him a brave smile. He emptied half the curry into a black plastic army mug, stuck a spoon in it and handed it to her.

'I don't know if I can eat anything,' she said, poking at the food with the spoon.

Gilmour put another hexy block on the stove and started to boil some water. As he munched his curry, he watched her out of the corner of his eye. She poked at her food for a while longer and put the mug down. She was going to slow him down and he wondered if he should perhaps leave her with Taylor while he went for help. Credenhill would note their missed radio report, but they would wait until a second missed report before sending in a patrol to find out what was up. It would be hours yet before anyone came looking. By then Taylor could be dead.

He turned his attention to the little bubbles forming in the mess tin and dropped in a couple of tea bags, watching as the brown brew leaked out and drifted round the tin. When it was boiling, he sprinkled a couple of sachets of sugar in with some powdered milk. Fishing out the tea bags with a small stick, he chucked them in the stream.

'Here.'

She took the sweet tea gratefully and cupped her cold hands round the mug.

The brew gave Gilmour a few minutes to think. Laying his rifle down, he stretched his legs. Perhaps now was a good time to talk.

'Did you find out anything at the lodge?' he asked in a soft, encouraging tone.

She sipped her tea a few times and then shook her head. Gilmour kept his steady gaze on her.

'How did you get here?'

'We drove here. It took forever. This tea is awful.'

'Who drove you? Another Irishman?'

'No, he said he was an Arab.'

Gilmour dropped his mug and spilt his tea.

A raghead?

Angelina searched his expression and became agitated. What is it?' she asked.

Gilmour stared at her, open-mouthed.

'What? *What is it?*' she asked, becoming distraught.

Gilmour tried to collect his wits.

'Was there anything else about him?'

She turned to look at the lodge and Gilmour's eyes followed. Over the treetops, he could just make out shards of jagged chimney jutting into the sky like broken teeth. He felt a strong urge to run. Instead, he stared down at the rushing water in the stream.

'Did anyone mention anything, or talk about anything?' he eventually asked.

'No.'

Gilmour gazed past her at the lodge again. Who had put the car bomb together? McCann? But what had been the target? It was time to get going and he started to get to his feet.

Something stirred behind him. He knocked over the stove and reached for his rifle. Angelina jumped up and her mug clattered down the bank into the stream. Cold razor steel bit into Gilmour's throat. He froze, his whole body rigid. The knife bit cruelly. A drop of blood trickled slowly down his neck.

'*Drop a the rifle or you dead man,*' hissed a cold, thin voice.

Chapter 27

Gilmour arched backwards in an effort to ease the pressure on his throat. The knife was biting and breathing was excruciating.

'You sit down child,' hissed the Colombian, turning to the girl.

Angelina stood with her hands over her mouth, the colour completely drained from her face. The Colombian reached for the rifle with his free hand, then stepped back and checked it had a round in the chamber. Gilmour wiped the blood from his throat with his sleeve. Powerful hands frisked through his clothing searching for a handgun, then the Colombian backed away keeping the rifle up.

'Who are you? What a you want?' asked the Colombian, and then aimed the rifle at Angelina, who promptly sat down.

'I was going to ask you the same thing,' replied Gilmour, playing for time while he tried to think.

'I waiting for friends.'

'Friends?'

'You very sharp mind. Where they find you?'

Gilmour eyed the stream and wondered how long he could hold his breath underwater while the current washed him downstream.

'You jump, no?' said the Colombian, guessing what he was thinking.

Gilmour's shoulders relaxed.

'What a you know about me?' asked the Colombian. When Gilmour didn't reply, he raised the rifle to his shoulder. 'Ah, you know nothing.'

Gilmour's mind raced.

'Fred put us on to you,' he said, recalling the name from the business card he'd picked up in the lodge.

The Colombian lowered the rifle a little.

'Who is Fred?'

It was a gamble, but Gilmour was out of options.

'We traced the Range Rover here from Manchester.'

The rifle lowered even further.

'Where is others?'

It was time for some truth.

'The explosion destroyed the radio, but they will be here soon.'

'How you find Fred?'

At the mention of others, Angelina lifted her bloodshot eyes and looked for some kind of reassurance. When Gilmour eventually returned her gaze, she knew from his expression there were no others. The Colombian had been watching and he saw her face fall.

'You lie, you know nothing.'

Gilmour turned very cold. Steeling himself, he eyed the stream. He might as well at least have a go. His blue eyes sparkling with defiance, he got slowly to his feet and turned to face the rifle. The Colombian took up the pressure on the trigger and Gilmour braced himself for the bullet. Just then he heard something stirring faintly on the wind, like the drone of a distant bee. The Colombian heard it too. The droning faded and then returned, perceptibly louder. This time it was unmistakeable. A car was racing up the glen in a low gear. Angelina pricked up her ears and searched Gilmour's face. He shrugged apologetically.

'*Oh no*,' she whispered, pain clouding her eyes.

The Colombian seemed undecided about something.

'Sit down,' he said.

Gilmour threw an encouraging smile at Angelina, but it blew away on the wind, unnoticed. He complied and hung his head.

It soon became clear there were two vehicles approaching.

'How could you have known there were no more of us?' asked Gilmour, wondering why the Colombian hadn't tried to warn them.

'I didn't,' he said. 'But I do now.'

Round a bend in the track came another two black Range Rovers, identical to the one at the lodge. When the vehicles were close, the Colombian stood up and waved. The cars pulled up and doors slammed.

'What's the crack?' shouted a thick Belfast accent.

On hearing McCann's drawl, Gilmour became horribly afraid. He tried to see as much as possible while keeping his head down. Apart from McCann, the others were all Arabs. He'd seen enough. A quick round through the head suddenly seemed appealing. A pair of brown brogues stepped up in front of him.

'*Fucking Jasus!*'

McCann couldn't believe what he was seeing. The cold steel of a pistol nudged Gilmour's scalp behind his ear. Silence fell on the Arabs when they spotted a British soldier.

'Watch your language in front of the kid, dickhead,' hissed Gilmour.

He sensed something coming and a brogue caught him full in the mouth. He fell backwards, tasting fresh blood.

'*Leave him!*' shouted the oldest Arab, running over.

McCann grunted and stepped away.

Gilmour struggled back to a sitting position.

'What has happened?' asked the Arab.

By far the oldest of the group, well into his fifties, with a balding head and greying moustache, it was obvious he was in charge.

'He is soldier,' said the Colombian, 'I kill the others. They are no good.'

'He's SAS,' said McCann.

At the mention of SAS, a few eyes widened.

'There is explosion,' said the Colombian, throwing Gilmour a queer look. 'The bomb is no more. I do good job. Now we must a go, quickly.'

'Where are the others?' asked the Arab, studying him coldly.

The Colombian swept a hand round the remote glen.

'You say that here we are safe for a few days. You are wrong. I put right *your* mistakes.'

The Arab thought for a moment.

'So what you suggest we do?'

'With them?'

'What does he know?' asked the Arab, nodding towards Gilmour.

'I think he know nothing.'

'You *think?* Then why he here?'

'You are the leader, you tell me.'

'And you hired *expert!*' hissed the Arab, glaring at him. 'And the girl?'

'Ask him,' said the Colombian, throwing McCann a knowing smile.

The Arab didn't take his dark gaze from the Colombian. The other Arabs stood in a little huddle, scanning the moor nervously as if expecting to see SAS creeping up on them.

'Okay, we go,' he said. 'And we take them.'

'SAS?' complained one of the younger Arabs, obviously from London. 'Ee's dangerous. We should kill 'im.'

'No, he come.'

'Why?'

'I say so.'

The younger man stood his ground, not at all happy.

'You think I wrong?' asked the older Arab. 'And if the SAS know our plan? He come so we make him talk.'

'No, he die!' said the Colombian, spinning round with the rifle.

Before he could fire, McCann smashed the butt of his pistol into the side of Gilmour's head.

'Auch, he's not dangerous anymore, so he isn't,' he muttered, as Gilmour slumped over in the wet heather.

Chapter 28

Angelina curled up as McCann stepped towards her, the pistol butt raised.

'Leave girl alone!' shouted the Arab, walking briskly over.

'She could be a nuisance,' said McCann warily.

'She travel with me,' replied the Arab, looking at him with disdain. 'I pay you to make bombs, not make decisions.'

McCann stared down at the cowering girl.

'They were saving you for me sweetheart,' he whispered, his tongue poking at the gap in his teeth. 'Maybe later.'

Gilmour's webbing was torn from his limp body, the pouches emptied and the contents strewn in the heather. One of the young Arabs opened a tobacco tin and a condom dropped out along with a few other bits and pieces.

'The SAS are always prepared,' he laughed, holding the condom aloft for everyone to see.

Then someone found the bergen. For a while it seemed as if Angelina and Gilmour had been forgotten as the bergen was plundered and the spoils fought over. The older Arab kept his distance, but every time something caught his eye, he pointed and someone would bring it over. The Colombian tried to spirit a couple of items away, but the others didn't let him get away with it. More than once his face fell as expensive shiny things were taken from him.

'What was that?' asked one of the young Arabs, as McCann slipped something into a pocket of his worn tweed jacket.

'Mind your own business.'

The Arab took a step towards him. McCann pulled his pistol and pointed it at his head. Everyone stopped what they were doing. The older Arab mumbled something and the young man backed off. McCann laughed, put his gun away and went back to rummaging.

Angelina lay in the rain feeling very miserable. No one was paying her any attention so she crawled over to Gilmour and laid her head on his chest. As she lay listening to his heartbeat, she was reminded of her father. She'd done the same thing when she'd found him collapsed on the floor. She'd crawled over and laid her head on his chest and listened to his heartbeat while it faded.

'*Please, Jamie, please don't die,*' she whispered.

Blood trickled from the side of his head, so she wiped away her tears, took a damp tissue from her jacket pocket and dabbed at the wound. His chest kept rising and falling steadily, which made her feel a little better.

The older Arab looked at his watch and glanced round the hills. Someone ran over to him with a night scope and McCann watched it go a little sadly. When the bergen was emptied and its contents scattered, the Colombian walked over to McCann and offered him a cigarette.

'What you have there then?' he asked politely.

'Never you mind,' said McCann, eyeing him distrustfully as he took a cigarette and lit up.

The Colombian sucked hard, inhaled deeply, then waved the match out and flicked it away.

'C'mon, let a me see.'

'What did you get then?'

The Colombian showed him a GPS satellite navigation system. McCann caught his breath.

'Jasus! What is it?'

'It look like mobile phone.'

'Auch, I think you're right,' agreed McCann, blowing out a long stream of smoke and wondering how he was going to get it off the stupid bastard.

'Okay, we go,' urged the Arab, wiping rain from his brow.

'Let's move!' shouted McCann, stepping towards Gilmour.

'Leave him alone!' said Angelina defiantly, wrapping her arms round him.

McCann kicked her away.

'Leave her,' said the Arab. 'She come with me.'

McCann turned and eyed him.

'Okay, but the soldier comes with me,' he said flatly, daring the Arab to argue.

He didn't.

McCann put his hands under Gilmour's armpits and tried to hoist him up.

'Oi, give us a hand Weasel.'

Strong arms helped Angelina from the moor.

'We must go,' said a kindly voice.

She looked up into a somewhat weather-beaten face. The Arab was quite distinguished and his smile seemed warm. She brushed her tangled hair behind her ears.

'You come my car,' he said softly.

She nodded and walked stiffly behind him. McCann and the Colombian dumped Gilmour in the back of one of the vehicles, clambered in beside him and set off. Angelina was ushered into the back of the other car. The Arab sat in the front, tapped the dashboard with his finger and pointed through the windscreen. The driver started the engine, turned and sped off after the other Range Rover.

They bumped hurriedly down the glen, splashing through muddy puddles and crossing rough wooden bridges over swollen streams. Angelina was thrown around uncomfortably, but she put up with it. It was better than being clubbed unconscious. Every so often the nice Arab turned to smile encouragingly, but it did little to lift her spirits.

The lead Rover set a furious pace, bouncing through rain-filled holes and scattering sheep. Mud splattered the windscreen, but the wipers coped with the help of the rain. The moody sky frowned menacingly, showing no signs of improving. She looked out through the rain dripping down the windows. Her heart sank and a single tear ran down her cheek. *Jamie*, she mouthed silently, *please come and get me*. The tear trickled to her chin and dripped onto her jacket.

At times, the Rover ahead of them was barely a couple of yards away, splashing uncomfortably close and at other times she had to strain to catch sight of it way ahead of them in the mists. She looked out over the moors, hoping to see soldiers closing in on them. Surely they would come looking for Jamie. If they came for him, they'd help her too. She wondered if he was still alive. He hadn't looked it when they'd dumped him in the back of the car.

They closed up behind the other Rover and she made out the shadowy forms of two men through the heavily tinted glass. Of Jamie there was no sign. The driver braked hard and the older Arab swore as they almost ran into the back of the other vehicle. They sped down a steep hill, rumbled over a cattle grid and stopped by a single-track road. When they pulled out, the ride suddenly became incredibly smooth.

'How you do girl?' asked the Arab courteously, obviously a lot happier now they were out of the glen.

'Please let us go,' said Angelina. 'We won't tell anyone.'

His face saddened.

'I cannot,' he said simply.

She looked into his eyes with longing.

'Why?'

The Arab faced the front and fell quiet.

They pulled into a passing place to allow an oncoming car to filter past. Nearby was a croft. She saw a girl out walking a dog. The girl turned with a smile and waved. A strange mix of despair, fear and hopelessness clouded her heart as the Arabs beside her waved back. A mobile phone rang. The older Arab pressed a button and put it to his ear.

'Yes,' he said. 'Hello?'

He pressed another button, put the phone on the dashboard and muttered something to the driver. The signal had gone.

'Why can't you let me go?' asked Angelina innocently.

The Arab stopped talking to the driver and looked into her eyes.

'I wish you not here,' he said, 'but you here.'

'Why?'

The Arab thought for a moment.

'If I let you go,' he said, 'would you tell the police?'

Angelina felt a lead weight forming in her stomach. She knew she would tell the police everything.

'Don't worry,' said the Arab, seeing the fear in her eyes. 'Once mission over, you may go.'

'Are you a terrorist?'

'Terrorist?' questioned the Arab, raising his bushy eyebrows. 'I think you watch much TV.'

He turned, picked up the phone, tapped a few buttons and waited for some kind of tone. When he didn't get one, he sat tapping the illuminated face. Angelina looked out over the moors, her sight blurring with tears.

They were driving along beside a large river. A light curtain of rain swept down from the hills. The driver mumbled something and pointed. They drove past a couple of crofts and into a village. An old woman hurried along the side of the road under an umbrella. At a junction, they turned right onto a main road with two-way traffic. She looked longingly at the passing cars and lorries. Then she saw the sea and a small harbour. Fishing boats were tied up alongside the quay. A boat chugged in through the breakwaters, seagulls wheeling overhead.

The Rover in front swerved a little. The phone rang and the Arab answered it. He listened, grunted a few times and then put the phone down.

'We stop for petrol soon,' he said, turning to Angelina

with a pained expression.

He searched her face and sighed.

The road followed the coast, furrowing the narrow strip of fertile land between the hills and the sea. Even though she was despairing, Angelina couldn't help but notice the beauty of the Highlands. A village sign greeted them, but she had no earthly idea where they were. The leading Rover slowed, indicated right and turned onto the forecourt of a small petrol station. She looked around quickly for someone to shout to for help. A pistol poked into her ribs. One of the young Arabs smiled lewdly, exhaling foul breath through bad teeth as their driver got out.

'Please not try something,' said the older Arab, raising a bushy eyebrow as a warning.

The Colombian got out of the Rover ahead of them and grabbed the pump.

'Is Jamie still alive?' she asked, trying to dry her eyes.

'Yes,' said the Arab brightly, enjoying giving her some good news.

'Will you let him go with me after your mission?'

He shrugged.

'Maybe.'

Chapter 29

When Gilmour regained consciousness, he wished he hadn't. His head throbbed like the pistons of an old rusty ship pounding through a heavy sea. He cracked open an eye and then snapped it shut. He was wedged between two men in the back of one of the Rovers. No point in letting them know he was conscious. They'd probably only break his head open trying to knock him out again. Saliva and blood dribbled from his swollen lips where McCann had kicked him, staining the front of his smock. *Let it dribble*, he thought, as his head lolled from side to side with the movement of the vehicle. The car braked hard, forcing him forward and he almost passed out with pain.

'Slow down,' ordered the Colombian.

The driver mumbled something unintelligible.

Fine, thought Gilmour – he knew who was beside him on his right and one of the Arabs was driving.

'Auch, that would be grand,' agreed McCann to his left, his breath reeking of stale whisky.

Gilmour's thoughts fled to escape. His only option was to go for the door and launch himself out. If the Colombian was asking the driver to slow down, that meant the other vehicle was behind them.

The car hit a deep hole in the road and the jolt almost tore a scream from his throat. Fresh blood dribbled onto his smock. He'd bitten through his tongue. McCann unscrewed a half bottle, took a mouthful of whisky, gasped and then burped.

'You are animal,' said the Colombian.

The Irishman lifted his arse and squeezed.

'Jasus!' he sighed happily as his foul smell wafted through the car.

The Colombian pressed a button to let his window down. Gilmour sensed resentment brewing in the front as McCann sniffed contentedly.

It soon became clear they were on a single-track road. He found it amazing how much information he could pick up with his eyes closed. The vehicle was constantly slowing down and accelerating hard, sometimes pulling over and stopping to allow on-coming traffic to pass. Escaping from the car just yet would be pointless as a single-track road meant open country. Better wait until they hit a town somewhere. For one thing, there would be folk about he could run to for cover.

He cracked open an eye again, barely enough to let in a little light. The butt of his rifle was nestled between McCann's feet, but the magazine had been removed. He knew the Irishman had a pistol, so fighting was out of the question. He was just going to have to leg it. *But were the child locks on?* No point trying anything until he knew that.

'I don't a know what the speed limit is in your country,' said the Colombian provocatively, 'but here it is less than 70 miles a hour.'

Hostility welled up in the front like magma in the crater of a volcano. There was no murmuring this time, a sure sign the Arabs were pissed off. However, the car slowed down. Gilmour felt a rush of fresh spring water bubble up through the cracked earth of his hopes. This lot was at each other's throats!

'Jasus, lifesh grand!' slurred McCann, taking another swig from his bottle.

'You are getting drunk,' warned the Colombian, eyeing him with his weasel eyes.

'Well, to be sure,' said McCann.

'We have not been paid yet,' cautioned the Colombian. 'You put a the whisky back in your pocket.

McCann grunted and screwed the top back on.

'You infidels have no honour,' spat the driver suddenly.

The car went deathly quiet.

McCann stiffened.

'What did you say, raghead?'

'We fight the great enemy, the great Satan,' said the driver deliberately, forcing the words through his teeth. 'We are warriors. We fight for Allah. You murder your brothers for money.'

Gilmour realized with a rush of enthusiasm that the Arabs were feeling sorry for him.

'Sure Allah can kiss my bum . . . and the Pope's too!' exclaimed McCann, forcing out another fart. 'I fight for the mother church, so I do. And your Allah can kiss my bum.'

The tension was sharpened by the rancid smell filling the car. Gilmour held his breath as someone let a window down.

'*Infidel pig!*' hissed the driver.

'*Shut it!*' shouted McCann, starting to lose it.

The driver jabbered to his mate who punched some numbers on a mobile phone. He tried a second time, but shook his head and put the phone down. *A phone!* Gilmour almost cried with frustration. The jabbering became heated and then stopped. McCann tried to catch the driver's eye in the rear view mirror.

'What was that all about?'

The driver didn't reply.

'What do you think, mishter Weashel?'

'I think you drink too much.'

'Auch, do you now?'

McCann didn't sound quite so happy anymore. He took his pistol from his pocket and poked it viciously into Gilmour's ribs. He was pissed off and getting suspicious.

'He should be awake by now, so he should.'

The Colombian seemed to agree and yanked Gilmour's head back roughly by the hair. Gilmour allowed his mouth to fall open. He moaned and opened his eyes, but screwed them shut again at the sudden brightness of the daylight.

'Don't do anything stupid,' warned McCann, sticking the barrel behind his ear.

Gilmour opened both eyes.

'Angelina?'

'Youse can have me, sure you can,' laughed McCann, lifting his arse and trying to force out more wind.

Gilmour noticed they were driving through a village. He tried to wipe some of the bloody saliva from his lips with a sleeve. The Colombian yanked his head back further. McCann leaned over.

'We'll have us some fun later,' he whispered, his breath reeking of whisky. 'Youse and me and that little shite bitch.'

'Fuck you,' said Gilmour weakly.

The Colombian threw his head forward and something heavy crashed against his temple. Just before he passed out, he caught sight of a tree-lined river flowing under an old bridge. He recognized it. He'd been here before. It was a small fishing village in the Highlands some-where. He couldn't quite remember and slipped back into darkness.

The next time he came too, the car was drawing to a halt. Bile choked the back of his throat. Sharp searing pains stabbed through his head. He was tempted to close his eyes and forget everything. His head swam with pain. He was sinking. A boy's face smiled at him. Laughter shone on his face. It was him. *The boy was him!* The sun was warm and birds were singing. The sweet waters of the ocean tumbled mellifluously against the shores of a sandy beach. Trees swayed gracefully, danc-ing to the singing of the surf. He was swept up into the sky. He could fly! In a valley far below he saw a beau-tiful young lady with dark flowing hair. His pain was slipping away. He swooped down and the young lady smiled at him. A gentle stream tumbled down a mountainside and gurgled across a green meadow. He'd seen her before somewhere. She was *so* beautiful. She reached out her hand, smiled and then ran away, her long hair waving in the breeze. The pain was gone. He ran after her. She looked back and laughed.

Then the atmosphere changed. The air became cooler. Dark clouds brooded on the mountain. Her name was Philippa. That was it! *Philippa?* The mountain shook.

She turned and held out her hand towards him again. Why was she crying? She was so beautiful. He looked up at the sky and then at Philippa again. But she was gone. Now it was young Angelina standing there. The sky turned blood red and filled with swirling black clouds. Foul smelling creatures crawled out of slimy holes and slithered towards her, groping for her ankles. She began to scream. It was getting darker. He had to help her. It was getting so dark. She was fading. His fingers reached out and the pain began to come back. But he wasn't afraid of it anymore.

Gilmour regained consciousness and swallowed the urge to vomit. The car drew to a halt and the engine died. His mind cleared instantly and electricity surged through him. *They were at a petrol station!*

Everyone stay in car until I get back,' said the Colombian curtly. He nodded towards Gilmour. 'If he move,' he said to McCann, 'you shoot him.'

The door clunked shut and a pump nozzle clattered in the filler pipe. Gilmour knew he had to move now. There would never be another opportunity like this. But what about Angelina? Leaving her in the shit was becoming a bad habit. But it was their only hope. If he could get away, he could have the boys airborne in minutes. He opened his eyes but kept his head down. An adrenaline rush eased the thumping in his head. He got McCann into his peripheral vision. The stupid bastard was dozing with his head back. The Arabs in the front seemed totally disinterested. How far would he get? Didn't matter. His mind readied itself.

The petrol pump stopped humming and the nozzle clattered back onto its cradle. He waited to give the Colombian time to get to the counter. He pictured him walking across the forecourt and into the shop. A few more seconds. *Surely he'd be there by now*. Every muscle in his body tensed.

Now!

His clenched back fist smashed into McCann's throat. The Irishman doubled up choking for air, his eyes bulging. Gilmour grabbed the door handle and launched himself out, falling backwards onto the forecourt. There were cries of dismay. He rolled over and looked quickly around. The other Rover was parked behind them at another pump. An Arab standing beside it had a petrol hose in his hand and a stupid look on his face.

His driver started to get out. The bastard had a gun. Kicking out with all he had, he caught the door full, trapping one of his legs. There was a crack of splintered bone and a piercing scream. The horrified Colombian stared out at him through the shop window.

He thought he saw Angelina's startled face through the windscreen of the other Rover. Forgetting about her, he leapt up and started running. He couldn't feel his feet, but somehow his legs responded. Any moment now there would be a shot and a bullet would thump into him, knocking the shit out of him.

It didn't, and he ran faster than he'd ever run in his life before.

Chapter 30

Angelina sat slumped in the rear of the Ranger Rover as the Colombian rattled the petrol pump back onto its cradle. He then strolled across the wet forecourt into the small shop where a girl behind the counter smiled and took his money. The Colombian smiled back. Angelina hated him. How could such a horrible man exist?

Suddenly, Gilmour tumbled out of the other Rover onto the forecourt. She gulped and wiped away her tears. He rolled over and looked about him, then kicked the car door as an Arab was getting out. She heard the crack of bone breaking as his trapped leg took the full weight of the door.

The Colombian rushed out onto the forecourt brandishing a pistol, his face black with rage. The screaming Arab was thrown into the back of the Rover and the Colombian leapt into the driver's seat. Gilmour jumped a garden wall and disappeared behind a row of bungalows. The older Arab got out, but thought better of it and climbed back in.

'The SAS good, no?' he said.

The look on his face told her that McCann and the Colombian had just fallen out of favour.

A terrified woman rushed to the large front window of her bungalow and hurriedly closed her curtains as the Rovers squealed to a halt outside her gate. The Arab twitched nervously and tapped the dashboard gently with his gun as the Colombian leapt the wall into the garden. Angelina's fingers clasped and unclasped as she tried to think of a prayer.

After a while a shot rang out, then another one. She wrung her hands. The Colombian returned, flushed and out of breath. He leapt into his Rover and screeched off in a foul mood. Their driver stuck his foot down and sped off after him. They raced through the village and were soon out in the countryside. The phone rang.

'What is happened?' asked the Arab.

He nodded a few times and then ended the call.

'He is escaped,' he said in astonishment.

The Arab turned, the benevolence completely wiped from his face.

'Our mission more important than is your life,' he said, studying her reddening cheeks. 'You will now be part of our sacrifice.'

'Sorry?'

'Things change,' said the Arab. 'Now we need hostage.'

The finality of his tone and the set look in his eyes numbed her excitement. She gripped the edge of her seat as they sped round a sharp corner. They just made it. She searched his eyes frantically.

'But you said you would let me go.'

'I'm sorry,' said the Arab simply, and turned to face the front.

Her euphoria sank like a slimy stone in a dank well. Gilmour was gone and now she was more alone than ever. Her shoulders slumped. Despair gripped her with skeletal fingers. The Arab looked over his shoulder, but said nothing.

The phone beeped. He let it ring a few times before turning to pick it up. A dark scowl clouded his face. He ended the call abruptly and clattered the phone onto the dashboard in disgust. The heaviness in the car seemed to stifle thought. The phone beeped again and he put it to his ear.

'I think your fee much big,' he hissed. There was a pause. '*My* fault?' he bellowed, almost choking on the phone. '*You* who let him to escape!'

He threw the phone back onto the dashboard and stared at the road.

Angelina closed her eyes and thought about Gilmour. What would he be doing? Surely, he'd have contacted his base by now? Soldiers would be on their way! She searched her mind for images of them storming the aircraft. Mysterious black men with machine guns who came from nowhere to save them. They would come for her. If they could get her out of that plane, one silly little car wasn't going to be a problem.

'Put rescue from you mind,' said the Arab.

She looked up into his smoking eyes.

'Your friend escape, but mission still succeed.'

His face had a strange set to it.

She found some spirit to fight with.

'I don't like you,' she said defiantly.

The phone went again. The Arab picked it up and listened, still eyeing her solemnly.

'Wait,' he said icily, turning to fumble in the glove compartment. He fished out a road atlas and leafed through the pages until he found what he was looking for. 'Yes, we go now to target . . . yes . . . we be at, how you say, RV? In three days, yes.'

His head continued to nod as he pored over the map.

Angelina looked out the windscreen. Through the wipers slithering quietly backwards and forwards she saw a few oilrigs moored in a large inlet of the sea. The driver pulled out to overtake and followed the leading Rover past a row of cars. When they pulled in again, she went back to staring at the world outside.

The rain seemed to be easing off and she was sure the sky was brightening. She looked round the countryside and tried to take the improving weather as a good sign. But in her heart, she felt doomed.

After a while she noticed that the driver seemed a little nervous. With increasing frequency, he would look up and search the sky.

'What are you looking for?' she asked.

She was ignored. His increasing agitation lifted her spirits a little though. The phone beeped again. The Arab's head began nodding in its slow, self-assured manner as he spoke.

'Yes . . . okay . . . yes.' His voice had regained some of its composure. The atlas rustled as he turned a few pages. 'We must be there two days.'

The phone went back onto the dashboard, but in a more orderly fashion. He checked his map and then stared straight ahead as if looking for something. They were skirting the shores of the large bay. Through the drizzle, a long bridge appeared across the inlet. The Arab picked up the phone and punched some buttons.

'I have,' he said. 'Yes . . . we follow.'

He held onto the phone as he studied the atlas.

The car slowed as they approached a roundabout, but not enough to prevent Angelina being thrown around as they hugged the tight bends. The first exit led onto the bridge and was clearly signposted to Inverness. They carried on and took the next exit. The Rover lurched as it left the roundabout and straightened up. They took a corner too fast and she was thrown into one of the young Arabs beside her. He pushed her away with a curse. The older Arab turned and stared at her. Angelina sucked in her breath as the muzzle of a handgun poked round the side of his seat.

'We should just kill 'er,' said the driver. 'We don't need 'er.'

The Arab didn't reply.

The driver pressed him.

'We'd be much better off without 'er.'

Angelina became horribly afraid.

'We need hostage,' said the Arab.

'A hostage was not part of our planning.'

'SAS not part of planning either,' he countered quickly, putting his gun away. 'With hostage, they not attack maybe, if find us.'

The driver nodded slowly, reluctantly agreeing the point.

'Too many things are going wrong,' he said hesitantly.

'What you suggest?'

'Perhaps we should call it off.'

'Over twenty million American dollars has cost this mission. You think we stop?'

The driver didn't reply.

'Allah Karim,' said someone softly from the back.

The Arab nodded his appreciation for the remark.

'Allah Karim,' said the driver, accepting his lot.

'Something more,' said the Arab, pulling at an earlobe, 'if we kill girl, what that do to soldiers . . . um, resolve?'

The driver nodded again, acknowledging that point also. But he was still unhappy.

'Perhaps they only search for us *because* of the girl?'

The Arab looked at him briefly and sighed.

'Perhaps.'

'So why risk it?'

'If SAS come, I think you glad for girl.'

It was the driver's turn to sigh.

The Arab went back to his map as they sped into a small Highland town. Angelina watched for a police car in the hope she could wave to it, but there were none. The other Rover turned right at a junction, but they carried straight on.

As they left the town, the Arab barked a few directions and eventually they turned right onto a single-track road. Finding some overhanging trees, the driver pulled onto the verge and switched off the engine. It went very quiet and still. Nobody made any move to get out. *Now what?* They sat without speaking until she couldn't stand it.

'Why have we stopped?'

No one replied.

'Why have we stopped?' she asked again.

The driver let out an exasperated breath and put his hands over his ears.

The Arab spun round.

'Why you not shut up?'

He glared at her and then turned away.

She was not intimidated.

'Why have we stopped baldy?'

The driver reached across and put a hand on the Arab's shoulder.

'You see?' he said. 'Perhaps you should think again.'

The Arab turned to face her.

'We stay here until dark.'

'What does *Allah Karim* mean?' she asked, searching his dark gaze.

'It mean everything God's will. Everything . . . um, happens, is will of Allah.'

She couldn't get her head round that one immediately. When the Arab turned away, she looked out through the misting windows. *Everything that happens is God's will? Even all the nasty things?* That didn't sound right.

Dejected shades of brown and ochre shimmered on the few wet leaves still clinging to the trees around them. Silent raindrops dripped to faded grass, glistening as they fell. A rusty barbed wire fence, broken down in places, ran along the side of the lane, briars twisting through the scruffy grass along its length. On the other side of the fence, the trees stopped abruptly beside a field that stretched to the feet of a steep hill. Sheep grazed contentedly in the field, occasionally lifting their heads to throw curious glances at the car. Mists shrouded the peak of the hill, reminding her of her gloom. A sheep looked at them and bleated as a shaft of bright sunlight, a finger of yellow in a sea of grey broke through the clouds and lit up the hillside.

It all seemed so surreal. Here were these sheep grazing away quite happily as if nothing had happened. Didn't they know she was going to be murdered? The sky brightened perceptibly and another finger of soft light broke through the clouds, tinting the field with a fragile warmth. Then the rain stopped. She looked forlornly at the hill, wondering if she would ever walk across a field again.

With an effort, she dragged her thoughts back to the car. Everyone was staring through the windows, scanning the sky. *Of course!* The soldiers would be searching for them in helicopters. Her heart raced and she listened for the thumping of a helicopter's blades. But there was nothing but the unnerving sound of men breathing and the clicking of the cooling engine.

Then she understood why they were hiding under trees. A rush of blood burned through her veins bringing colour to her cheeks.

'When they come,' she said calmly. 'You are all going to die, just like those bad men in the airplane.'

The finality of her words brought a chorus of curses. The Arab turned and the gun reappeared. He was shaking.

'*You shut up,*' he hissed, madness swirling in his eyes.

'Allah Karim,' she said quietly.

The mood in the car became very subdued. Her words were weighing heavily on them. The driver put his hand on the Arab's shoulder again and the gun lowered. Her thoughts turned to her future. Was her life over? She pictured Gilmour's face and tried to recall the tenderness in his voice. She touched her cheek where he had gently brushed her with his finger. If only she could feel his touch again, hear his soft words, see the care shimmering in his eyes. Would anyone ever touch her like that again? The thought left her feeling strangely sick inside.

Chapter 31

As Gilmour sprinted from the garage forecourt, he seemed to be out of phase with the world around him. The road felt spongy as he ran. Sounds were muffled. His eyes darted left and right. The only sanctuary was a row of small bungalows. He leapt a low stone wall into someone's garden, raced across the lawn and sprinted round the back. A few startled sparrows flew off in different directions, chirruping madly. He charged across a vegetable plot and fell over a fence into a patch of briars. Car doors slammed. The briars tore his skin as he scrambled to his feet.

After dashing across a piece of waste ground, he sprinted along the side of a small industrial unit and out into a large open car park at the front of an old school building converted into flats. The main road was only yards away. His boots slid on loose grit as he turned and ran for the rear of the building. He cleared a low wooden fence beside a small electricity sub-station and found himself in a row of neat little gardens hemmed in by a high dry-stone dyke. Hurdling the fences, he took off through the gardens. As he ran, he felt his scabbing head wounds opening. He hurdled the last fence and threw himself at the dry-stone dyke. His momentum tumbled him over and he fell heavily onto a pavement on the other side. Winded and dazed, he closed his eyes just for a second. Broken glass tinkled behind him in the gardens. He forced himself up and staggered across the road.

Running past a church, he came to an open field. Across the field, about a hundred yards away, was the back of a row of houses. *A hundred yards? Would he make it?*

He scrambled over a barbed wire fence, ripping his smock. The houses seemed so far away. His eyes misted over as he set off across the field. Air wheezed into his lungs and the mists became impenetrable. Only a few more seconds he promised himself. It was a lie but it kept him going. Pain stabbed through his head. There was no more adrenaline. He felt his stitches tearing open. Sweat and blood poured down his face.

A shot cracked out and a round tore into the ground at his feet. Another bullet whined past him and smashed into a concrete coal bunker with a puff of dust. Astonished faces peered out of windows. He threw a glance over his shoulder. The Colombian was kneeling by the barbed wire fence taking deliberate aim. With a grunt, he dived headfirst into the nearest garden. A dustbin clattered noisily as he rolled into it and a startled cat bolted off with a yowl. Someone opened their back door to see what the racket was about.

'What's going on?' shouted an angry gentleman.

Holding his ribs with an arm, Gilmour crawled towards

the front of the house. Sweat and blood stung his eyes. A funny thought crossed his mind. He'd endured hell getting into the SAS and for what? *Move, you crap hat!* He screamed the words at his body and struggled to his feet.

Across the road was open ground with a small industrial estate beyond. He looked up and down the road, but there was nowhere to go. Swaying from side to side, he limped along the pavement until he caught the eye of a young couple in their garden.

'Please,' he pleaded, stumbling in their front gate. 'I need help.'

'*Go away!*' exclaimed the distraught woman, clutching her husband's arm.

Gilmour's legs buckled, but he somehow managed to reach their doorway before collapsing. On his hands and knees, he crawled into their hallway.

'*John!*' shouted the woman hysterically. '*Get him out!*'

Gilmour sat with his back to the wall and felt in his back pocket for his wallet. His brass SAS winged dagger gleamed dully against the black leather as he flipped it open.

'Please,' he pleaded, 'I'm with the security forces.'

The husband nodded and closed the door.

Gilmour crawled into the living room and settled down behind the curtains, blood dripping from his chin onto the carpet.

'Get us an old towel or something mate,' he asked, turning to the husband.

'Would you like a cup of tea?' asked the woman, who was in tears.

Her husband chucked him a towel.

'A cup of tea would be simply wonderful love,' replied

Gilmour, mopping the blood from his face.

'Milk and sugar?'

'Eh?'

Everything felt so strange. Some of the hardest criminals in the world were hunting him and here he was being offered tea in someone's living room. He nodded and the woman disappeared into the kitchen.

Gradually his breathing returned to normal and the pounding in his head subsided somewhat.

'Have you a phone?' he asked, turning to the husband.

The man pointed across the room.

'I don't suppose you've a shotgun about the place?'

The man paled.

'Nuh.'

In the kitchen, a kettle filled with water.

'I'm Jamie by the way.'

'John. My wife's Helen.'

Gilmour punched the number from memory. The phone rang once and was answered.

'Yes?'

'It's Gilmour; I need to speak to the Colonel.'

'Wait one.'

There were a few mumbled words, a rustling of papers and the squeak of a chair being pushed back. Just then, the two black Range Rovers sped past the end of the road. Gilmour almost collapsed with relief.

'Yes?'

'It's Gilmour, Boss.'

'You have an annoying habit of telling me things I already know. Is something wrong with the radio?'

'Mike and Charlie are dead. Andy needs casevac'ed.'

'Wha . . . ?'

'There was a car bomb at the lodge and it exploded. Andy needs a medic. He's lying by the side of the lodge. You can put a chopper in, the area's safe.'

'Wait one.'

The Colonel barked some orders.

'Chopper's on its way. What's your situation?'

Gilmour took his time and spoke slowly and clearly.

'*Arabs!*' exclaimed the Colonel, not enjoying his day. 'Where are you?'

Gilmour put his hand over the mouthpiece and turned to the husband.

'Where are we, mate?'

The man told him and Gilmour repeated it into the phone.

'Got it,' said the Colonel. 'Any ideas what they're up to?'

'No, but they just headed south from here a minute ago. Oh, and there's another body in the lodge.'

'An Arab?'

He turned to see if Helen was listening.

'A young woman,' he whispered.

'Good Lord!'

'I'm going after the Rovers.'

'How?'

'I'll find a vehicle.'

'Roger that . . . wait one.'

There was a lot of noise of blokes coming and going.

'Right,' said the Colonel, 'Let me know when you're mobile. Out.'

The line went dead.

Gilmour's eyes were still on the end of the road. A car turned in and stopped a couple of houses away. A middle aged man dressed in a grey pinstripe suit got out, opened the back door of his car and lifted out a brief-case. Everything was so ridiculously normal.

'Your tea's ready,' said the wife, poking her head round the kitchen door.

She brushed her shoulder length brown hair behind her ears.

'Cheers love, I'll be there in a minute.'

'I've put some lunch on for you. Would you like a bath?'

A bath! Soaking in delicious hot water! A wave of exhaustion swept over him. But there was no time. Food though . . . he needed food.

'Something to eat would be wonderful.'

She managed a weak smile.

With a last look down the road, Gilmour got to his feet and hobbled into the kitchen to clean himself up.

'Can I use the sink?'

She regarded him dubiously for a moment.

'I'm a bit of a mess,' he explained.

She nodded and then cracked a couple of eggs into the frying pan. He lifted out a few dirty dishes, stuck in the plug and turned on the hot water. Clouds of steam rose into the kitchen as lashings of hot water splashed into the sink. He almost yelped with delight as he held his hands under the water. Cleaning himself up though was easier said than done. Dabbing at his wounds with the wet towel didn't really accomplish very much. In the end, he took off his smock and stuck his head in the sink. His head wounds stung ferociously and the water soon clouded with blood and dirt. Helen looked up a few times and eventually came over and took the towel from him. She emptied the sink and filled it with fresh water.

'Stand still,' she said, starting on his wounds.

'Ouch!'

Gilmour tried not to move, but the pain was fearsome.

'*Ouch!*'

'Oh, don't be such a baby.'

When she'd finished, the bloodied towel went straight into the bin. She fished around in a drawer for a tube of antiseptic cream and smoothed some into the wounds.

'Better see a doctor,' she said.

He looked longingly at the frying pan. She noticed and smiled. She was warming to him.

'Seat yourself at the table,' she said, and busied herself serving the food.

As Gilmour gratefully shovelled bacon, eggs, beans, tomatoes, mushrooms and toast down his throat, his thoughts turned to Angelina.

'Have you a car?' he asked.

'Aye.'

'Can I borrow it?'

'John!' she shouted, bursting into tears again. 'He wants to take the car!'

Her husband didn't reply.

'Will you replace it if you damage it?' she asked, drying her eyes with her apron.

'Of course. What is it?'

'An old Audi.'

'Reliable?'

'Aye, it's just been serviced.'

She rummaged around in her handbag and handed him the keys.

'Thanks love.'

It wasn't long before he wiped his plate with the last piece of toast and drained his mug. Back in the living room, the husband was on duty at the window.

'John, is there any petrol in the car?'

'Aboot a tenner – enough to get you doon the rod tae Inverness anyways.'

Gilmour stuffed his beret into a pocket and combed his hair with his fingers. He scribbled a few words on a piece of paper, signed it and handed it to him.

'If you don't hear from me within a few days, call that number and tell them they owe you a new car, okay.'

The husband read the note and nodded.

Gilmour picked up the phone and pressed the re-dial button.

'Yes?'

'It's Gilmour.'

The Colonel came on the line.

'Yes?'

'I'm one up in a dark blue Audi 100,' he said, looking out at the car sitting in the street.

'Registration?'

He read it out.

'It's an old bugger. Will it do?'

'Think so, yes.'

'Anything else?'

'ETA chopper?'

'Blue Team's airborne . . . out.'

Gilmour held the phone away from his ear and stared dumbly at it. The Colonel wasn't the most talkative man he'd ever met.

John put his arm round his wife's shoulder and they both waved him goodbye from their doorway as he climbed into their car. Determination gleamed in his eye as the engine roared into life. The front tyres squealed as he let out the clutch. When he turned onto the main road, he spotted a policeman running along the pavement chattering into a radio. No doubt the village would be talking about this day's events for a long time to come. When the policeman was out of sight, he stuck the boot down and the bonnet rose as the car surged forward.

As he flew over the new bridge into Inverness, he hit the brakes. There wasn't a Range Rover to be seen. His heart sank and his frustration was overwhelming. He'd lost them. An orange light flickered on the dash. He needed petrol.

Startled people stared at him while he queued to pay for his fuel. It wasn't surprising really, the state he was in. With his hands full of sandwiches, chocolates and drinks, his face cut and bruised, his military clothing filthy and bloodstained, he stepped up to the counter. The young guy at the till gingerly took his card. Gilmour smiled at him.

'I've had a real shit day,' he said.

'No kidding mister,' said the youth, hurriedly handing him back his card.

Before he left, Gilmour headed for the loo. After a good piss, he checked himself in the mirror. The blood-crusted wounds on the side of his head looked ready to burst open, his lips were purple and swollen and he had a black eye. With a grimace, he turned and headed out to the car, clutching his food and drink.

When he was back on the A9, he pushed the Audi to its limits, hoping against hope that he'd spot the Rovers on the road ahead. Eventually, though, his foot eased off the pedal and his speed began to drop. The concentration he'd used during his high-speed chase had com-

pletely drained him. A green Cavalier he'd already over-
taken passed him. The driver threw him a dirty look on
the way past. Gilmour wound down his window and
gulped in some fresh air to shake off the drowsiness
creeping up on him.

The Arabs confused him. What would they be doing
mixed up with the likes of McCann? Was McCann
working for them? It seemed the most likely option. One
thing was for sure though, there were no Range Rovers
on the empty road ahead. A Little Chef appeared on
the right and he pulled into the car park. When he walked
in, the buzz of conversation was displaced by an uncomfortable hush. He walked over to the phone feeling
very conspicuous. As he punched in the numbers, he
turned and a dozen eyes quickly looked away.

'Yes?'

'Gilmour.'

'I've been expecting you,' said the Colonel.

'I'm in a Little Chef about 30 klicks south of Inverness. They've gone to ground in the hills somewhere,
probably north of Inverness.'

'We're still looking.'

'How's Andy?'

The Colonel went very quiet.

'Is he . . .?'

'No,' said the Colonel, 'but it's not looking good. We're
just about to enter the lodge. Is there anything we should
know?'

'The dead girl is in the main bedroom upstairs, second
on the left. Better send someone with a strong stomach.'

'I could do with you here.'

'I'll head on south at a steady 60 until you pick me

up.'

'Roger that, I'll divert a chopper, out.'

The walk back through the diner was very uncomfortable. Every kid in the place was staring at him or tugging on their parent's sleeves and pointing. The clatter of plates and cutlery from the kitchen seemed somehow incongruous in the hushed dining area. *How not to be the grey man*, he thought ruefully, glad none of his mates could see him. *His mates!* Mike's wife and kids didn't even know he was dead yet. And Charlie could forget about his blowjob on the beach. He climbed into the car and slammed the door, anxious to escape the stares from the large windows of the diner. Small stones crunched under the tyres as he pulled out. He checked the road was clear and turned right. At least Andy was still alive. It was something.

The road had been climbing up into the hills for some time. Looking round at the bleak moorland, he knew he was up a fair bit. Visions of the dead girl tied to the chair kept flashing through his mind. He could still smell the vomit. His knuckles whitened on the steering wheel. McCann wandered into the vision and he whipped up an MP5 and emptied the magazine into him, laughing as chunks of his flesh blew off. He knew he was starting to lose it.

After the inhospitable ruggedness of Drumochter Pass, the road wound down through some of the most breathtaking scenery in Scotland. How could such things be happening here? He'd felt the same sense of disbelief the first time he'd gone to the Balkans. *It couldn't be happening*, he'd kept saying. Here he was with that same feeling again. Only this time he was in Scotland.

What were the Arabs up to? The question passed through his mind for the thousandth time. Britain and Bosnia suddenly became very similar. Northern Ireland was on the brink, despite the ridiculous peace process, or whatever it was they called it. The world was becoming a very dangerous place.

A couple of crows hopping awkwardly along the road picking at dead rabbits flapped away as he approached. A blue patch appeared in the clouds and the sun made a brief foray through the grey stratus. The warm light did little to cheer him.

Thump, thump, thump, thump.

He felt, rather than heard the helicopter. His eyes darted round the countryside. It sounded like it was behind him somewhere. He jerked his head round and searched folds of broken ground to his right. A couple of cars were approaching going the other way. They sped past and quickly disappeared in his mirror.

Thump, thump, thump, thump.

The helicopter rose from dead ground and sped towards him, nose down. The Audi shuddered as it flew low overhead. He stopped by the side of the road as the chopper pulled up. A bloke in black kit jumped out and ran towards him carrying a bag. As the chopper lifted away, one of the boys leaned out of the open door and gave him the wanker wrist shake.

'Hello Tom,' said Gilmour, recognising the bloke as the back door was yanked open. 'That was all very dramatic but shouldn't I be on the chopper?'

'What a mess! You all right, like?'

'Doesn't the Colonel want me in Creden?'

The soldier's eyes crinkled with concern.

'The only bloke looking for you in Creden, mate, is the

RSM. He asked me to give you this.'

Gilmour took the travel warrant and shoved it in his pocket.

'What did the Headshed tell you?' he asked.

'Typical,' muttered the soldier, unzipping his bag. 'Dragged away from the pub, chucked on a chopper, dumped in Scotland and no one knows what's going on.' He paused for a moment. 'This isn't a wind up, is it?'

'This is no exercise mate.'

'Here you go.'

Something hard and cold prodded Gilmour in the neck as he drove. He reached a hand back and the welcome feel of beautifully machined steel slapped into his palm. He stuffed the pistol under his right thigh where he could get at it in a hurry. Something heavy thumped onto the front seat beside him.

'Much better,' said Gilmour, eyeing the MP5.

'So what's up like?'

'McCann.'

'Belfast McCann?'

'And a sprinkling of Arabs.'

'Here, give the Headshed a dog and bone.'

Gilmour took the mobile and punched the numbers.

'Yes?'

'Gilmour.'

'Wait one.'

The familiar sound of scraping furniture came down the line.

'Gilmour, what's your situation?'

'Just passed a turn off for Pitlochry, still on the A9.'

'Splendid.'

'Wasn't I supposed to catch the chopper?'

'Couldn't spare it.'

'Oh.'

Gilmour wasn't sure what to say next.

'Hinckley's a relief driver,' explained the Colonel.

'Ah.'

'What is it now?'

Gilmour sighed. Well, at least he wasn't walking.

'Can I fill him in Boss?'

'Might as well, the lid's off this one. Look, I'll call you back. Out.'

'Got some fresh clothes for you mate,' said Hinckley. 'Pull over will you. Let me take a look at you.'

'You a medic?'

'No, a mechanic. I want to lubricate you with grease, dickhead.'

A mile or so down the road Gilmour parked up in a lay-by. He got stiffly out of the car, picked up the pistol and clambered awkwardly into the back. Hinckley examined him briefly, taking particular care to check his head wounds. At one point, he looked into his eyes with an expression that scared him. But the seriousness passed.

'Don't do that,' said Gilmour.

'Can't understand . . ,' said Hinckley, rummaging in his bag, '. . . why the Headshed didn't tell me you were such a mess.'

Gilmour grunted as a lump of grit was dug out of a cut behind his ear.

'*Ouch!*'

'That's it,' said Hinckley, dabbing the freshly bleeding wound with a cloth. 'I'm done.'

Gilmour lay back on the seat feeling nauseous as Hinckley clambered over the seat into the front. He fought to keep his eyes open, but almost immediately drifted off into a deep sleep. He didn't hear the phone ring a few seconds later. It was probably just as well. The helicopters were faced with an impossible task. The terrorists had disappeared and no one had the slightest idea where to look.

Gilmour was snoring as Hinckley put the car in gear and pulled away. The helicopter pilots donned their night glasses and were kept flying in the failing light. Detailed reports came in from the lodge. Some bloke's voice kept breaking as he described the dead girl's injuries over the air. The Regiment trembled as the full horror hit home. Hinckley lost the colour in his cheeks. They just had to find those Rovers.

Chapter 32

Afternoon dragged into evening, but, unlike Angelina's hopes, the daylight showed no signs of fading. They just sat there under the trees. Not even speaking. The men were beginning to smell too and she needed the toilet. The windows were misted over so there was little to see outside. The older Arab let his window down briefly for some fresh air and she imagined she heard helicopter blades thumping in the distance. No helicopter appeared though, the window closed and the day dragged on.

One of the Arabs beside her wiped his sleeve over his window and she peered gratefully out into the world. The rain had now stopped completely. A yellow shaft of sunlight burst through the clouds and the dewy field sparkled with a million tiny diamonds. She longed to run barefoot across the field, laughing and singing, like she had done when she'd been little. Her dad smiled, picked her up and swung her round and round until she was dizzy. My, how she had laughed and laughed. She missed him. The sun disappeared behind the clouds and the world was plunged back into dreary shades of grey. She wondered if her mummy was now dead like her dad. The window gradually misted over again and her dream fell apart.

The driver nodded off, which seemed to please the older Arab who was poring over his map pondering his next move. Angelina tried to make herself as small as possible, avoiding touching the men on either side of her. She dreaded falling asleep in case her head slumped onto one of their arms. The smell was getting worse. She had to get outside or she was going to scream.

'I need the toilet,' she mumbled, keeping her eyes on the floor.

She was ignored. A wild light sprang into her eyes.

'I need to *pee!*'

The older Arab turned to stare at her. His face was grim and his eyes were cold. He nodded to one of the men beside her.

'You stay behind car. This man go with you.'

With a wave of a pistol, she was ushered outside. Stiffly, she eased herself over the leather seat.

As her feet touched the grass, she took a deep breath. Another shaft of sunlight broke through the clouds. The wind had died away and a more gorgeous evening she couldn't have imagined. Through the trees she could see the hill basking in the late sunshine, its flanks aglow with hazy hues of autumn. So near and yet so far. A few sheep lifted their heads, but quickly lost interest and went back to their grazing. It was so nice to breathe clean air. She reached towards the sky and stretched her lithe limbs. The young Arab leered at her and she promptly folded her arms.

'Well?' she enquired, 'are you going to turn your back?'

The man stood his ground, grinning inanely. She marched round to the front window and tapped on the glass. The electrics hummed and the Arab looked down suspiciously from his map.

'Will you please tell him not to look.'

She returned his stare until he nodded and barked an order.

Almost crying with relief, she squatted behind the Rover. Underneath the car she saw a worm wriggling in the grass. A tyre had squashed its head and it couldn't burrow anymore. She felt sorry for it. The worm was better company than she'd had for a while though and she made the most of it, talking quietly to her new wriggly friend. When she stood up, pulling up her jeans at the same time, something in the back of the Rover caught her eye. On tip toes, she looked through the rear window and spotted a few cables and different coloured wires partially hidden under a jacket. As she tucked herself in, she was drawn to the wires.

'Okay!' said the young Arab, waving his pistol around. 'Enough.'

With a last longing look at the hill and a brief smile at the sheep, she turned and climbed sadly back into the car. It was the cue for everyone else and soon they'd all been out to relieve themselves.

Another couple of hours dragged interminably by and it was still broad daylight. She sighed with exasperation. This couldn't be right.

'What time is it?'

The driver looked at her in the mirror.

'You can see the clock,' he said, pointing to the dashboard display.

'It doesn't seem to be getting dark,' she replied haughtily.

'It won't be dark for another hour,' said the older Arab.

Angelina slumped back in despair.

Another hour!

'I'm hungry.'

The driver pricked up his ears at the mention of food.

'We get something when move.'

'What are the wires in the back of the car for?'

The Arab spun round. The look of grave concern on his face sent terror coursing through every nerve in her body. Her heart fluttered with panic. The bodies of the dead soldiers leapt on her. The Arab held her eye and didn't as much as blink.

'It's . . . it's a . . .' she stuttered, unable to say the words.

The Arab smiled.

'It is bomb,' he said, relishing each syllable.

Angelina thought she was going to pass out. Then anger surged through her and she pounded the back of his seat with her fists.

'*You're going to blow me up!*' she screamed. '*You wankers! You wankers! You . . .*'

She grunted as the muzzle of a pistol poked hard into her ribs. The sharp pain brought her back to her senses and she quietened down. The gun left her side and she nursed the bruise.

'You *shut up!*' hissed the Arab, fixing her eyes with his smoking gaze.

'You're a loony,' she said, keeping her voice low.

'I am *warrior*,' he burst out. 'A warrior who strike at heart of great Satan. Allah my God! I warrior in holy war, Jihad! You not possible understand. Three days,' he whispered ominously, 'all world will learn. I warrior and what I do will of Allah.'

Angelina held his eye.

'Does Allah like his warriors to murder little girls?'

The Arab took a small black object from his pocket.

'If I press button,' he said, holding up the object for her to see, 'bomb explode. If SAS come, I press button like true warrior.'

'You're a loony.'

'Loony? *Loony?* What is loony?'

He turned to the driver, who whispered something and his face turned a deeper red.

'Perhaps if you see dead people in my village, you not think so. The British . . .' He paused as dark memories pained him. 'The British and Americans kill my people.' The corner of his mouth developed a sneer as he spoke. 'My wife . . . my children . . .' His voice fell to a whisper. 'Dead . . . now dead.' Revenge burned his tears away. 'The British have no honour. They are spear that pierce hand when lean on for support. They will pay for treachery.'

Angelina found no words. All she saw was the madness glowing in his eyes. The Arab put the detonator back in his pocket and picked up his map again.

Slowly, inexorably, the light faded from the sky and the little hope she had left faded with it. How could Jamie possibly get her out of this? Even when he found her, this lunatic was going to blow them all up. She wondered what the Arab's wife and children had been like.

Patches of dull orange sky faded behind the hill and the inky blues of twilight gradually evanesced to shades of deep purple and black. A lone star twinkled and then another. Night was almost upon them. The Arab turned to the driver and muttered something. The engine roared into life. She turned to her friends the sheep and waved a quick good bye. But they were too busy resting after their hard day to take any notice. The Rover juddered as it slipped off the verge and set off down the lane. Gilmour reached through her clouded thoughts. He was coming for her with all his mates, just like on the plane. That was all she knew anymore.

Chapter 33

The bomb absolutely petrified her. Every time the car lurched, Angelina screwed her eyes up and clenched her fists, waiting for the explosion that would rip her to shreds. Her nails dug into her palms. She was so tense, her calf muscles suddenly cramped. She doubled over and clamped her fingers round the muscles. Only then did she notice the blood where her nails had cut into her palms. She sat back breathing heavily. The smell of body odour in the car was stifling. Sweat trickled down her back. The Arabs had the heater on full and it was unbearably hot. And so it went on, hour after interminable hour.

Occasional headlights passed silently in the dark as they drove on through the small hours. Where they were or where they were going she had no idea. She no longer cared. There was plenty of food, sweets, chocolates and drinks, but she had no appetite. Now and then she cast a secretive look at the door handle and thought about trying to throw herself out. It was suicide, but it appealed from time to time. One of the Arabs beside her dozed off and she thought about trying to grab his gun. But she dropped the idea as she wouldn't know what to do with one anyway.

Colour brushed the horizon at last and the light grew. The older Arab growled a few directions and soon they were driving along a country lane looking for somewhere to park up. Eventually they pulled off the road and stopped under the overhanging branches of a natural forest. The engine died. The mood in the car was grim. The driver settled back immediately and fell asleep. With a heavy heart, Angelina peered through the misting windows at the distant world outside. Despair gnawed at her. Her lip began to quiver uncontrollably. They were going to be there *all day!* She cried until her head fell forward and she sank into an exhausted sleep.

The clouds darkened as the sun fell behind the forest. The trees turned to grey in the failing light. Angelina shifted her weight on the seat, but it did nothing to ease her discomfort. Gloomy shadows gathered in the forest. She nibbled on a chocolate and sipped from a can of juice. Sleeping had been the only way to pass the day. But each time she started from her restless naps, instead of feeling refreshed she was becoming progressively more exhausted.

The driver fiddled with the radio and found some irritating DJ who laughed and joked between bad songs. The light continued to fade until she couldn't make out the bark on the tree trunks anymore. She thought she saw a squirrel run along a branch, but it was too dark to be sure. The Arab tapped the dashboard and the engine roared into life. The car bumped out of its hide and they moved off into the night, their headlights white on the road ahead.

The driver lowered his window and fresh air wafted in. Angelina breathed in the soft scents of the forest. Would she ever walk through a wood again? Would she ever stop to pick a wild flower and hold it to her nose? She had no more strength to cry. The phone went and the Arab picked it up. He was still frosty.

'We moving now,' he said, 'but need more time to reach . . . um . . . yes, RV. I know it day of . . . um, operation,' he said, getting quite animated. 'We go from RV to London. It is simple.'

His head nodded a few times as he listened to whoever was on the other end. The driver swerved to hit a rabbit caught in the headlights. Angelina winced at the dull clunk under the vehicle.

'No, you follow us now!' commanded the Arab, tapping his hand on his knee with exasperation. 'We stay together.'

He nodded a few more times, ended the call and went back to poring over his map.

The night passed even more slowly than Angelina could possibly have imagined. Every time she looked at the dashboard clock, she was shattered to see that only four or five minutes had passed. She cried a few times out of sheer pain and frustration. The Arabs seemed impervious to her plight. Twice they stopped at deserted lay-bys so everyone could get out for a few minutes, stretch and relieve themselves. To Angelina it was like heaven getting out of the car. She even learned to ignore the gun being held to her head as she squatted in the darkness. All too soon though, it would be time to go and she was forced back into the car at gunpoint.

On they drove, headlights shining on strange roads, the radio re-tuning itself to different stations as they travelled. But the music and up-beat chat did nothing to improve her spirits. She began to wish they would just put a bullet through her head. At least it would be quick. Waiting to be blown up was eating away at her. Death began to seem like such a lovely way out. And still they drove on into the night that had no end.

At some point, they stopped at a service area for fuel. She pulled herself from her stupor and stared at the people in the shop. A couple of laughing kids ran around the Arab while their mother scolded them fruitlessly. Loneliness brimmed in her eyes. The Arab returned and passed a large bag round.

'You must eat,' he said curtly as he got in.

She didn't hear him.

'If you are rescued you will need strength to escape,' smirked the driver.

Something stirred her. *Escape?* The word floated through her despair and she looked up at him. He was blurry, but gradually his features came into focus. Yes, she must think about escape.

It was a turning point for her. As they drove out of the station, she kept her mind on Gilmour. He was out scouring the country for her and he would find her. Somehow, he would get her out of this. She went over the storming of the aircraft in her mind, replaying every detail she could remember. She pulled out a sandwich. The driver was right, she must think about escape. She peeled off the cellophane wrapper and started nibbling.

Sometime later that night, she began to slip in and out

of consciousness. Her world had become one long rest-less dream punctuated by snarling moments of reality. She lost all track of time. At one point she noticed they were parked up and it was daylight. The next time she opened her eyes they were travelling down a motor-way in the dark. A couple of times she made an effort to pull herself together, but it didn't last. She tried to picture Jamie's face but saw only the dead soldiers lying outside the lodge.

Looking up through the clouds, she caught glimpses of the silvery moon. She wished she could fly away and burn across the sky like a shooting star. She wanted to be at home in bed, her mother tucking her in, giving her a kiss and telling her how much she loved her. She wanted to smell her perfume. She wanted to feel the warmth of her lips on her cheek, the soft caress of her hand on her skin. She wanted to see the soft twinkle of love in her eyes. Fresh tears rolled down her cheeks and she hung her head as her heart broke.

Chapter 34

When Ellis got to Hereford it was early evening. He parked up outside Munro's pub, the Clown and Dagger, and delicately checked the scabs on his head and neck. He hoped Munro was around. It was cool but smoky in the bar when he pushed through the doors and limped over to the counter. A pretty young barmaid with short black hair smiled at him. A group of young men huddled round a table in the corner threw him a few hard stares. It was early yet and they were the only customers.

'Half of lager please,' he said pleasantly, sliding onto one of the red leather bar stools.

In the mirror behind the optics, he watched the young men in the corner and from reading their lips already knew they were discussing sex. The barmaid stuck a glass under the tap.

'Is Brian about?' he asked quietly, as the cool crisp lager swirled under a creamy head.

'Is he a friend of yours?'

'Yes, we go back a long way. Tell him Peter's looking

for him.'

The barmaid looked at him strangely.

'Uncle Peter?'

Ellis realised with shock that it was Munro's daughter.

'Hannah? Is that you?'

She smiled and handed him his lager.

'It's been a long time uncle.'

'Gosh, yes. My, you've grown up. I never was your real uncle, you know.'

'I'm twenty one next month.'

'Has it been that long?'

He swallowed a mouthful of lager and smacked his lips.

'Would you like me to call Dad?' she asked.

'Is he at home?'

'Yes, with Mum.'

'I think I'll surprise them.'

She smiled deviously and picked up a tea towel to dry some glasses.

'The Regiment doesn't make them like they used to,' she said, nodding towards the table in the corner.

'The puppies coming on too strong?'

'They're full of shhh . . . oops, excuse my language Peter.'

Ellis laughed and noticed it had gone very quiet behind him.

One of the young men wandered over to the bar.

'Two pints of bitter and two lagers please love.'

Hannah winked at Ellis and reached for fresh glasses.

'So,' said the young off duty soldier, smiling at her, 'you thought anymore about that concert then?'

'Yes,' she replied, 'you're very sweet, but no thanks.'

'I'm afraid I don't take "no" for an answer,' he replied smoothly. 'It's not part of our training.'

'No thanks anyway,' she said, swapping glasses under the tap and turning to Ellis. 'So Peter, sweetheart, where are you taking me later? Tell me you brute.'

Ellis watched the creamy foam dripping down the sides of the glass and wondered where the conversation was going.

The young man was visibly shocked.

'You can't possibly fancy this old fart, surely?' he scoffed, obviously with a little more beer in him than was good for him.

'Crap hat,' whispered Ellis, just loud enough for him to hear.

The young man blinked a few times.

'Okay over there Bob?' shouted one of the other young men from the corner. 'Is that prick giving you any aggro?'

'Watch your step, old timer,' warned the young man and wandered back to his corner, his hands full of pints.

'Don't worry about them,' said Hannah.

'You sure turned out gorgeous,' sighed Ellis. 'Am I really too old for you?'

She leaned across the bar, pulled his head forward and kissed him full on the lips. The sudden silence from the corner table was deafening. Ellis ran his tongue along his lips.

'I think I'd better go,' he said, and drained his glass. 'I'll maybe catch up with you later, young lady.'

'See you sweetheart,' she waved.

Ellis couldn't help himself and winked over at the table in the corner as he walked out.

He was just about to reach for the doorbell of the cottage when he thought he heard a muffled cry from within. He put his ear to the door and heard it again. His senses flaring, he reached for his pistol and stole silently round to the side of the cottage. Cautiously, he peered round the curtains of the living room window. Munro's wife was tied to a chair, naked and gagged. The chair rocked back and forth as she desperately fought to get free.

Ellis ducked under the window and composed himself. There was no time to call for back up. He was going to have to go in alone. Taking a few deep breaths to get his blood pumping, he hurried round to the back door. It was unlocked and he eased himself carefully into the kitchen. The muffled cries from the living room were becoming more frantic and the chair was threatening to collapse. Upstairs a floorboard creaked. He crossed quickly to the living room and thumbed off the safety catch.

The door slammed open as he unleashed a powerful kick. Diving headfirst into the room, he rolled up on one knee. Shirley Munro stared at him in horror through her dishevelled hair. Her wrists were red from where she'd been struggling with the ropes. Ellis noticed her breasts were bruised.

'What the *fuck* is going on down there?'

Brian Munro stomped down the stairs wearing only a leather waistcoat and an erection. He stopped half way down and stared at the pistol pointed up at him.

'Peter?'

'Brian?'

'*What the fuck?*'

'Oh shit.'

'You never heard of doorbells?' asked Munro, quickly losing his erection.

Ellis pulled the gag from the poor woman and untied her.

'*You bastard,*' she coughed, and fled up the stairs.

'Um . . . I think I'll wait in the kitchen,' said Ellis, hanging his head as he wandered from the room.

A few minutes later, Munro and his wife wandered sheepishly into the kitchen and sat with him at the table.

'You owe me a new kitchen fucking door,' glared Munro.

Ellis was too embarrassed to think of anything intelligent to say.

'Thank you Peter,' said his wife with a smile, bravely pushing her awkwardness aside. She pulled her dressing gown together at the neck. 'That was . . . er, very noble of you.'

'You still owe me a new fucking door,' said Munro dourly, his scar pulling his scowl into a crooked smile.

Suddenly, Munro's wife giggled.

'Shut up woman,' moaned Munro.

'The look on your face Peter!' Tears sparkled in her eyes as she got up from the table. 'I need a bath, I'll see you later.'

The giggling woman clumped upstairs and locked herself in the bathroom.

'Okay Peter, it must be *damn* important to bring you round here. What's up?'

'Eyes and pyramids.'

Munro looked at him for a long moment.

'What happened to your head?'

'Brian, I need a big favour.'

'How big?'

'The security surrounding the President's State visit. I need information.'

'Too big, sorry mate. And you should know better than to ask.'

'Hear me out Brian.'

'I'm listening.'

'What do you have on Secret Societies?'

'Hang on, I've a folder here somewhere.'

Munro got up and walked over to a large pile of paperwork sprawled messily on top of the fridge and shuffled through them.

'Here it is.'

He slapped the folder on the table and slipped on a pair of reading glasses.

'Bad business in Scotland eh,' said Ellis.

'I've not heard the details yet, but we've lost two good men. You think this is all connected to the President?' Munro took off his glasses and squinted across the table. 'What's going on Peter?'

'I could do with a coffee. You still off the tea then?'

'Ach, I'm getting headaches with the coffee too. Bloody migraines!'

'Caffeine then?'

Munro shrugged and filled the kettle at the sink. When the kettle whistled, he poured boiling water into two mugs. Upstairs, his wife started singing in the bath.

'Where's this sister with the nipples then?' asked Ellis, gratefully accepting his coffee.

'Hit the town last night and didn't come home.'

'Ah, some bugger got her then.'

'I'm still listening.'

'Brian, I've a problem. Certain Americans aren't quite what they seem and I'm having a bit of trouble getting my head round it.'

'What sort of problem?'

'Patience Brian, patience. You've heard of the Round Table?'

'Yes.'

'I have your attention now?'

'Undivided.'

'Between the ages of 24 and 26 Cecil Rhodes made seven wills. The first will established a secret society which became the Round Table, while the seventh will established Rhodes Scholarships.'

'Hang on a minute,' muttered Munro, shuffling through his paperwork for a clean sheet to write on.

'By the beginning of World War One,' continued Ellis, 'there were secret Round Table Groups established in seven countries – The United States, The United Kingdom, South Africa, Canada, Australia, New Zealand and India. After the Paris Peace Conference the seven Round Table Groups were formally established as the Institute of International Affairs at a meeting held at the Majestic Hotel in Paris.'

'Was this after the war?'

Ellis slipped out a small notebook to check his dates.

'March 19th, 1919, to be precise. In 1920 the American Group broke off from the other six because of anti-British feelings in America caused by the War. The American Institute took the cryptic name the Council on Foreign Relations.'

'The CFR!' exclaimed Munro, looking up with wonder. 'So we'll be getting to the United Nations soon?'

'Oh yes,' nodded Ellis, 'this plot is most definitely thickening. Communism wasn't defeated during the Cold War. It mutated, it changed, it grew; it became more sophisticated, more intelligent, more devious and more treacherous. Today we call it Internationalism.'

'*Peter!* Will you get to the point!'

'The CFR runs the State Department and the CIA, as you know. They work together to misinform and deceive the President into acting in the best interests of the CFR and not the American People. The CFR members that surround the President are 'the Secret Team'. They help carry out psycho-political operations scripted by CFR members in the State Department and the Intelligence Organisations. The psycho-political operations are coordinated by a group of Council on Foreign Relations members called the Special Group, which evolved from the Psychological Strategy Board. The Board was run by CFR members Gordon Gray and Henry Kissinger. Anyway, the American people became wary of the Psychological Strategy Board so Eisenhower issued an executive order changing its name to the Operations Coordination Board. The OCB was bigger and more powerful than anything before it and Gray and Kissinger ran that too. And you'll like this next bit.'

'I'm pretty breathless as it is mate.'

'President Kennedy abolished the OCB.'

Munro looked up, somewhat startled.

'Kennedy?'

Ellis nodded, a little smile on his lips.

'After that it became an ad hoc committee called the Special Group, which exists today, and it always has CFR members running and sitting on it. Remember, these are unelected officials who continue from administration to administration regardless of any elections or their outcomes. Democracy no longer exists.'

'So who was this Wise bastard you were on about?'

'Adam Weishaupt was a Jesuit priest and professor of law. He founded the Illuminati on May 1st, 1766.

Since the Reformation, the Roman Catholics have been determined to get the world back. To accomplish their goal, they need to set up a one world government first. To this end the Jesuits devised a new concept in political thinking – Communism. Weishaupt was the brains behind the Jacobin clubs that sprang up all over France just prior too, and which fomented and were responsible for, the French Revolution.'

'Hang on Peter, I'm trying to write some of this down.'

'In 1785, one of Weishaupt's men was struck and killed by lightning and a few important documents were picked up by the Bavarian government. They immediately ordered the police to raid the headquarters of the Illuminati in Germany and Weishaupt fled for his life. Illuminati became a dirty word and they went underground. Some time later they changed their name to the League of the Just and had a noteworthy man join them – Karl Marx. In 1842 Marx was charged with updating the writings of Weishaupt. The Communist Manifesto appeared in 1843 and the Illuminati changed their name again, this time to the League of Communists. In the 1890's, a certain Vladimar Ulyanov joined them and travelled to Russia on an American passport.'

'Who?'

'Ulyanov. He later changed his name to Nicholai Lenin.'

'Ah.'

'The British police tried to stop him, but the Illuminati in the States, under the influence of Albert Pike, had become strong. Using the same principles they'd learned in France, the Illuminati overthrew the Tsar and founded the first Communist superpower. Under the guise of human rights and world peace they have been systematically overthrowing governments, stealing countries and murdering millions ever since.'

Munro looked at him queerly.

'Is the President in danger mate?'

'Hear me out Brian. After the first world war and their success in Russia, the Illuminati set up an organisation called the League of Nations with its headquarters in Genev—'

'The League of Nations? So the Roman Catholics are behind the United Nations?'

'Yes, and the World Bank, the Royal Institute of International Affairs, the Trilateral Commission, the Council on Foreign Relations, the Department for International Development, the World Health Organisation, the Red Cross, Greenpeace, CND and a host of other subversive organisations all working together to make the whole world a Communist state with the United Nations as its governing body. And that brings me to the purpose of my little visit.'

'At last,' said Munro, looking up expectantly.

'I've tracked McCann through McConnell to a Lord in Lichfield, who just so happens to be a Rhodes Scholar and a member of both Opus Dei and the Royal Institute of International Affairs.'

'And?'

'And I was wondering if perhaps you had come across him?'

'I'm listening.'

'Lord Thompson.'

Munro visibly paled.

'What is it?' asked Ellis, trying to keep concern from his voice.

'Lord Thompson,' he said, his hands beginning to shake,

'has been quietly overseeing our security of the President's State visit.'

'On whose authority?'

'The American State Department. He's arranged for private security to shadow the President's limousine on his drive to the American Embassy.'

'Don't tell me – Black Range Rovers.'

'*The fishing lodge!*'

'Oh shit.'

Chapter 35

'No more bangs on the head!' said the Doc sternly, putting the finishing touches to fresh stitches.

'I'll live then?' said Gilmour.

'Brain dead perhaps. By the way, the RSM was in here a couple of times looking for you. Didn't seem very happy.'

'Thanks Doc,' said Gilmour, checking his head in a mirror.

A hot shower, a change of clothes and a large plateful of breakfast later, Gilmour settled himself on the edge of his bed in his small room on camp and slipped a Tomb Raider game into his PlayStation. Thumbing a games pad, he guided Lara Croft down some rocks into a valley surrounded by high cliffs. He didn't have many shotgun cartridges, so he changed to pistols to conserve ammunition before walking his favourite girlie out into the valley. He was tired, but he couldn't sleep. Of the Rovers and Angelina there had been no news.

A dinosaur charged at Lara from a clump of vegetation.

The raptor took a snap and Lara's health bar dropped. The games pad took some heavy thumbing as Lara jumped backwards, blazing away with pistols until the dinosaur let out a roar and dropped dead. Lara sighed with relief as he used a medi-pak and her health returned to normal. He could hear a waterfall somewhere. As he walked towards it, Lara pointed her pistols as another raptor hurtled out of the undergrowth. This time she killed it before it got near her.

Suddenly, the music kicked in and a T Rex stepped round a rock face. The brute spotted Lara and let out a roar that shook the valley. It took a step towards her and the ground trembled. Lara started firing. *Shit!* He'd forgotten to change her back to the shotgun. *Pistols were no good against that bastard thing.*

The T Rex broke into a run and the ground thundered like an earthquake. Its teeth and beady eyes filled the screen. It took a bite and Lara's health bar dropped dramatically.

There was a knock at the door and Ellis walked in.

'Games?' he remarked derisively.

Gilmour quit the game and switched off the PlayStation.

'Tomb Raider,' he said. 'I hope the team who put it together are millionaires.'

'Wasn't that the original?'

'Yep, I bought the new one, but it was crap.'

'Did you find the five secrets for that level?'

'*You play Tomb Raider?*'

'Nightmare in Vegas is my favourite level,' said Ellis.

'Wow,' said Gilmour, impressed. 'I've not found all the secrets to get into that level yet.'

'You should, it's worth it. The Colonel asked me to

come and get you.'

'Is the RSM about?'

'No, but the Brigadier is on his way and he has specifically asked to see you.'

'Me?'

Unease drifted through the corridors of Credenhill like wisps of morning mist. The imminent arrival of the Director of Special Forces was weighing heavily on the camp.

As Gilmour made his way back to the Colonel's office, a young woman marched round the corner of a building. She spotted him and made a beeline. It was Taylor's wife.

'Okay Jamie – where's Andy? Where is the bastard?'

She put her hands on her hips and waited for an answer.

Gilmour looked at her with a haunted expression.

'Look, I know you two went off together!'

'Sue . . . I . . . I . . .'

Suddenly, her anger vanished.

'Jamie?'

Gilmour didn't know what to say.

'Oh God,' she whispered, putting her hands to her mouth. 'Where is he?'

'Intensive care.'

She turned white and ran for her car.

'Sue—!'

Gilmour reached out a hand, but she was gone.

Suddenly, a door burst open and Munro waved him inside.

'I just saw Andy's wife,' said Gilmour, closing the door behind him. 'She doesn't know.'

'We've not been able to find her,' said the Colonel.

'She's staying at her mothers.'

'What about the couple who gave you their Audi?'

'A new car and a small cheque should do it.'

The Colonel made a note in his diary.

Just then, purposeful footfalls echoed down the corridor outside the office. The Colonel stood up awkwardly behind his desk and brushed down his uniform. Munro adjusted his beret and made for the door.

The Brigadier strolled in with a beaming smile.

'Right, gentlemen,' he breezed, glancing quickly round the office. 'Where are the two Range Rovers?'

'We picked them up crossing the Scottish border about two hours ago,' said the Colonel. 'We've a chopper following them down the motorway.'

'What's the situation?' asked the Brigadier.

'We think McCann is tailing the Range Rovers in another car,' said the Colonel. 'One of our lads on the border is convinced he saw McCann drive past his OP in a Cavalier a few miles behind them.'

'Makes sense,' said Ellis. 'Watching their backs.'

'That was good work in Lichfield, Ellis,' said the Brigadier. 'We've arrested Lord Thompson. The President has been informed and there have been a number of arrests in America. The President was shaken, but owing to the enormity of the occasion he has decided to continue with his State visit.'

Ellis nodded with satisfaction.

'So we've just the girl to worry about?'

'Yes, and two Rovers packed with explosives. It would be a shame if the girl were killed now.'

'Apart from McCann,' said the Colonel, 'we have a fairly comfortable situation here.'

'Give me the old Audi and a driver,' said Gilmour. 'Let

me deal with McCann.'

Ellis gave the Brigadier a little nod.

The Colonel was aghast.

'Gilmour, you are on your way back to the Parachute Regiment.'

'Please Colonel,' calmed the Brigadier.

'But I have men—'

'Colonel, Ellis is here at the Prime Minister's behest. We are to extend to him all the resources at our disposal.'

The Colonel slumped back in his chair muttering to himself.

When Mobility troop had finished working on the Audi, they wiped their blackened hands with oily rags and shook their heads sadly. But Gilmour's mind was made up. He sat in the front passenger seat cradling an MP5 sub-machine gun. Hinckley was his driver and he sat beside Gilmour lost in his own thoughts. Hinckley started the engine and wiped the windscreen with a cloth.

'Jamie?' he said in a queer voice.

'What?'

'You ever been afraid of death?'

The question took Gilmour by surprise.

'Hundreds of times.'

'I'm afraid, like.'

'I suppose I don't want to die,' said Gilmour. 'At least, not horribly or painfully. I kinda like the idea of going quietly to sleep when I'm an old man.'

'I don't mean fear like that,' said Hinckley, glancing over at him. 'I mean, death itself.'

'I was scared in Cambodia.'

'Were you over there?'

'With a few Australians. The Khmer Rouge were

something else.'

'I don't mean death in that sense. You know . . . death. One moment you're breathing and the next you're, well, dead, like.'

'That's life,' said Gilmour sardonically.

'I've never been married,' said Hinckley. 'I want a family. I want to go home after work, cuddle a wife and have kids running round me.'

Gilmour wasn't sure if he liked the way the conversation was going.

'Tom . . . shut up.'

'I'm getting out,' said Hinckley. 'Eight years is enough for me. I'm missing something.' His hand swept the sky. 'There must be more to it than this.'

Hinckley visibly relaxed now that he'd made the decision, but Gilmour was not happy. Before he had time to think, the Brigadier and the Colonel strolled over.

'Are you sure you won't use one of the other cars?' asked the Brigadier, fingering the corners of his military trouser pockets.

'No sir, McCann wouldn't suspect this old thing coming up behind him. It'll give me an edge.'

Munro rushed over with a worried frown.

'We might lose them if we don't hurry, Sir, the weather is closing in.'

'You'd best be off then,' said the Brigadier, bending down to look in the window. 'And remember, we don't particularly want this McCann chap alive if it can be at all avoided.'

'I hope you're right about this car,' said Hinckley, as they raced through the main gates.

Serious misgivings disturbed Gilmour. He knew he should have turned back for another driver. But time was pressing and he let it go.

The latest intelligence crackled out of the radio and Gilmour checked his map. The terrorists were less than three miles ahead of them. It was dark and a light drizzle smeared the windscreen. Red taillights appeared dimly through the gloom. Hinckley inched up on the car until Gilmour could make out the registration number through his night glasses. He jotted the number down and picked up the radio. Hinckley eased off on the accelerator and the lights gradually dimmed. The report on the car checked out. Hinckley accelerated and pulled over to the middle lane to overtake. Gilmour felt his palms beginning to sweat on the barrel of his machine gun.

A young woman caught his eye as they drove past her. Someone reported the Rovers' latest position over the radio.

'What makes you so certain about McCann?' asked Hinckley.

'Dunno, just a feeling.'

'If I was him, I'd be out of the country by now, like.'

'You don't know the bastard.'

Gilmour's stomach suddenly knotted.

'Tom, slow down.'

'What is it?'

'I can feel him – he's close.'

Gilmour couldn't help reflecting on how simple and uncomplicated his life had been before McCann. Now it was twisting and writhing like a skewered snake, spitting poison at him every time he tried to get a grip of it. Hinckley didn't slow down quickly enough and red taillights appeared ahead. Gilmour took a long look through the night glasses.

'It's a new Cavalier, but I can't make out the plate. There are two of them in the car. There's dirt or something obscuring the numbers, I can't make it out.'

'Shall I get closer?'

'It's him,' said Gilmour. 'Easy does it. Ease back mate.'

Hinckley kept pace with the lights and then gradually let them pull away.

'How can you be so sure?' he asked.

Gilmour slipped off his night glasses, released the safety catch on his weapon and wound down his window. Light rain blew into the car.

'Let's just take them.'

Hinckley's eyes bulged.

'*Wha . . ?*'

The Audi slowed even more and the taillights ahead began to fade.

'You heard me,' said Gilmour, bracing his legs in the footwell.

'But . . . we can't just—'

'I'm giving the orders here.'

'We need back up! Call the Headshed and get some back up!'

'Get a move on.'

'But the Rovers—?'

'With McCann out of the way, the Rovers will be a piece of piss.'

'*But—!*'

'Tom,' said Gilmour very quietly, his voice taking on a threatening edge. 'Move, or stop the car and get the fuck out.'

'Well, it's your call. Just remember that.'

The Audi surged forward and the taillights reappeared

through the drizzle.

'Keep it steady,' said Gilmour.

Hinckley indicated and pulled out into the middle lane. As they pulled alongside, the driver of the Cavalier turned and their eyes met.

It was McCann.

Gilmour fired a short burst. The Irishman ducked and his bullets hit the passenger. The Cavalier braked and its lights went out. Gilmour fired again and watched in dismay as his rounds tore harmlessly over the bonnet. Hinckley yanked up the handbrake, threw the steering wheel round and the Audi slithered sideways to a halt. Gilmour fired at the retreating sound of spinning tyres and then picked up the radio. Hinckley turned the car and set off after the Cavalier.

'Blue one . . . *contact!*'

'Did you get him?' asked the Colonel.

'We're in pursuit.'

'On the south bound carriageway?'

'Roger that, heading north . . . repeat, heading north.'

'*North?*'

The headlights of an approaching vehicle suddenly swerved violently across the carriageway. Hinckley pulled over onto the hard shoulder.

'I've got him!' he said excitedly.

Another set of headlights approached. Hinckley threw the Audi across the motorway towards the outside lane. He was just in time. The approaching headlights swerved and the driver lost control on the damp road surface. The car spun down the motorway, its headlights stabbing crazy circles through the night. Hinckley rocked backwards and forwards, willing more speed out of the Audi. Another set of headlights approached, briefly silhouetting the Cavalier. The lights flashed past, narrowly missing them. Gilmour reached for the radio to request back up.

'*Watch it!*' screamed Hinckley, stamping on the brakes. 'He's stopping . . . *look out!*'

The wheels locked and the tyres slithered forward on the wet road. Gilmour watched everything go into the now familiar slow motion. He stood up through the open window and searched for a target. Wind and rain lashed into him, watering his eyes.

There was a sharp crack.

Hinckley's head jerked as a bullet caught him in the temple.

The Audi went into a spin.

Gilmour was almost thrown out of the window. Just in time, he pulled himself back into the car. The Audi smashed into the central reservation, somersaulted, crashed down on its roof and scraped along the road spinning wildly. In a shower of sparks, it screeched across the hard shoulder and thumped into the grass bank. Gilmour was thrown forward heavily and then it went very quiet.

Broken glass crunched outside as brown brogues walked slowly round the car. The brogues stopped. One of the laces was undone. Gilmour's fingers clawed round desperately, searching for his machine gun. The brogues seemed to hesitate for a moment, then turned and crunched away. He heard McCann grunt as he pulled the passenger from the Cavalier and dump him on the hard shoulder. A car door slammed, headlights came on and the Cavalier drove off.

Gilmour lay for a while, wondering why he was still alive. Then he cried out of sheer frustration.

'Tom?'

There was no reply.

Why was he covered in lumps of flesh? He screwed his eyes shut and pounded his fists off the crumpled roof until they were bleeding.

He didn't notice other headlights approaching. He didn't notice a car pulling up either. The first he knew of it was when he became conscious of another pair of shoes crunching round the car. Different shoes. Black and polished. A man bent down and a balding, round face with spectacles blinked at him.

'Are you okay?' asked the man, flicking on a torch and shining it into the car.

Gilmour couldn't think of anything to say. Then he saw Hinckley and realised where all the little lumps of flesh on him had come from. They were bits of his head.

The baldy guy got to his feet, crunched back to his car and chattered into a radio. Scrabbling madly, Gilmour pulled himself to the mangled doorframe and wriggled out. The damp wind ruffled his hair as he got unsteadily to his feet. One of the tyres was still turning forlornly. With a shake of his fist, he screamed up the night sky.

'*McCann . . . bastard! You're fucking dead!*'

The baldy guy put his radio down and blinked at him.

'Who are you then?' asked Gilmour.

'Gary Johnson, Mi5.'

His spectacles were misted up, his balding head was glistening with moisture and he was dressed in a dull grey suit that was getting damp. He didn't look like much, with his chubby face, shabby suit and cheap glasses.

'Mi5?'

'Chopper's on its way,' said Johnson, blinking at him.

Gilmour spotted the body further up the motorway. He thought he saw it move.

'You know what I think,' he said. 'I think evil is more than just some nebulous, ethereal concept. I think it has brains, that it's organised, knows what it's doing and has a lot of money.'

'What do you mean?'

Gilmour walked over to the Colombian and stared down at him until he stopped moving.

Suddenly, a searchlight stabbed through the drizzle. A chopper swooped down and men jumped to the road. Someone started barking orders. A couple of blokes ran to the Audi while others cleared debris off the motorway. Another helicopter thundered down out of the black sky. Hinckley was dragged from the wreckage and a wire strop fed through the Audi and shackled to the undercarriage of the chopper. It took the strain and lifted away with the car swaying underneath. An officer recognized Gilmour and ran over.

'Pear shaped again, eh?'

Gilmour stared at him icily.

Hinckley was laid on a stretcher and a blanket was draped over him. Gilmour eyed Johnson's car, but the Mi5 man had been watching.

'You'll need a driver,' he said.

'Eh?'

'You're thinking of taking my car, right?'

'You don't look like you can drive.'

'Get in,' he said quietly.

Gilmour quickly checked over his shoulder and jumped in. Johnson whipped out night glasses from the glove compartment, slipped them on, put his foot down and the car rocketed forward. Gilmour scraped a slimy piece of Hinckley off his trousers and examined it, wondering which part of his head it had come from.

They had gone less than five miles when suddenly the car juddered as a chopper thundered overhead. Johnson braked hard as it pulled up in front of them. Gilmour let his window down as a black figure jumped to the road.

'Yes Brian?' he asked, scraping the piece of Hinckley onto the wing mirror.

Munro scratched his scar.

'Going somewhere?'

'McCann's just up ahead.'

Munro pushed his beret back.

'Is he now?'

A doubt crossed Gilmour's mind.

'How do you do?' said Johnson politely.

'How do I do? Well . . . there's a thing!'

Johnson blinked at him.

'Nice motor,' nodded Munro, stepping back to admire it.

'Custom built to my specifications,' said Johnson proudly. '0 to 60 in 4.3 seconds, top speed 182 mph.'

'Impressive.'

'Okay, what is it?' asked Gilmour.

'McCann,' said Munro after a brief pause, 'broke through the central reservation and headed back up the motorway. He had a good shufty at us on the way past and left the motorway back at Junction 14. We lost him on some country road. He's over fifteen klicks from here, going the other way.'

Gilmour's head fell forward.

'Remember the girl?' said Munro.

Gilmour looked up blankly.

'The girl, wanker, remember the girl?'

Gilmour had been so engulfed in the flames of hatred, he'd completely forgotten about Angelina.

'C'mon, let's go.'

He climbed sheepishly out of the car.

'See and pop up to Creden sometime mate,' said Munro, smiling at Johnson. 'Just tell the gate that Brian said he'd buy you a pint.'

'I'll do that,' said Johnson with an appreciative nod. 'Very kind of you.'

Gilmour sat with his head down and stared morosely at a bit of dirt vibrating on the steel deck of the chopper. Inside he was devastated. The others left him well alone. When they landed at Credenhill, he felt a tightening in his stomach. He didn't want to face anyone, especially not Ellis. The others jumped out and quickly disappeared. Reluctantly, he jumped from the chopper and it lifted off in a flurry of dust.

Although dawn filtered through the clouds, it did little to cheer the morning. A crumpled crisp bag blew across the landing area. Was that all life amounted to? A few brief moments blown around on the winds of life? Where was Hinckley now? The crisp bag skittered along the ground and stopped in a puddle.

A closet skeleton raised a mouldy finger. It had been during a drunken brawl in a pub that someone had screamed the truth at him. His mother had turned white and fainted. She'd been raped before he'd been born and the child given up for adoption. Somewhere out there in the world, he had a big brother. He took his SAS beret from a pocket, looked at the winged dagger and then crumpled it in his fist. He'd had enough. He turned towards the gates.

'You still work for me,' said Ellis, stepping out of a doorway.

Gilmour pulled up with a groan and looked down at his crumpled beret. The winged dagger meant nothing to him anymore. Nothing seemed to matter anymore.

'Look,' said Ellis, 'McCann's getting the better of you because you have no concept of how he thinks.'

'So what's the answer?'

'Would you like a polo?'

'How come you never give me a straight answer?'

'Maybe I don't have one.'

'You know McCann, don't you?'

'Why didn't you take a polo?'

'I didn't want one.'

'Bullshit.'

'What are you on about?'

'You didn't even think about it.'

'What?'

'Precisely,' said Ellis.

Gilmour sighed and waited for an explanation.

'Think about my motivation for offering,' said Ellis.

'You wanted to be friendly?'

'Could it have been a bribe?'

'*What?*'

'Don't *ever* let anything just go by you. You can't afford to miss details. When life comes at you, consider your next move, make a decision and *then* act.'

Gilmour finally had his ears open.

'There's *always* an answer to a problem,' said Ellis, realising he had his attention.

'What's the answer to McCann?'

'McCann is a criminal. He doesn't care how he gets things done. He has no rules. You, on the other hand, work entirely by the rules.'

'What do you mean?'

'He knows all your rules, but you don't understand his. You may have to break the rules to catch him out.'

Gilmour looked at him vacantly.

'Good,' said Ellis, with a little smile and turned on his heels and walked off.

Gilmour looked around him. A small patch of cloud brightened perceptibly and a thin shaft of pale morning light brushed the camp. *Angelina!* She was alive somewhere, scared and alone. And he was her only hope, her pale shaft of light in a sky of emptiness. He pulled himself together and hurried off after Ellis.

The Brigadier sat behind the desk. The Colonel stood by the window, watching the sparrows squabbling over a bacon roll he'd chucked out to them. Ellis took a seat by the wall and crossed his legs.

'What happened this time?' asked the Brigadier with concern, taking great care to keep any hard edges from his voice.

'We had him.'

'And?'

'I missed him and hit the Colombian.'

'And?'

'Once we'd lost the element of surprise, the Audi let us down.'

The Colonel turned from the window.

'You don't seem particularly upset that we've lost another good man,' he reflected sourly.

Gilmour recited a verse from a poem he'd once read.

The storms of winter seem to blow forever on;

I hear the wind, I feel the rain.
But far above the fleeting clouds the sun still shines;
My heart will never be the same.

The Colonel opened his mouth to say something, but the Brigadier stopped him with a wave of his hand.

'Where do you think McCann might be now?' asked Ellis.

'He'll still be shadowing the Rovers.'

'Pah!' retorted the Colonel. 'After being compromised and knowing we're on to him?'

'All he wants is his money, Boss. If the Arabs call it off, he won't get paid. He won't have said a word to them.'

Gilmour noticed everyone was looking at him.

'Can you handle him?' asked Ellis.

'Yes, but I'm doing thing's my way from now on and I'm going alone.'

'That's hardly standard operating procedures,' observed the Brigadier.

'No, Sir.'

'What do you intend to do?'

'Just give me a car and a radio.'

'I think you should have someone with you,' said Ellis after much deliberation.

Gilmour was in no mood for arguing.

'I'm going alone.'

'I don't like it,' frowned the Brigadier.

'You need a driver,' said Ellis.

'I'm going alone.'

'You're not listening again.'

Gilmour checked himself just in time. Hinckley was as good as they came, but he had not been good enough.

Then Johnson blinked at him. The Mi5 man had completely fooled him. Perhaps he could do it again. With McCann.

Gilmour tucked his beret under his arm as he walked through St Martin's church yard looking at the names of dead SAS soldiers engraved in the cold granite of their headstones. Some of the men he'd known. It didn't matter to him now whether he'd beat the clock or not. If he'd done his job back at the Lodge, Mike and Charlie would still be alive. Yet here he was and they were dead. He'd get McCann and then the boys would go in and get Angelina. After that, the clock could have him.

The clouds broke and warm sunshine slanted down. Somewhere, a songbird began to sing. The bird's shrill chirruping was the most beautiful thing he'd ever heard. McCann had no place amongst such beautiful things. Soon, he wouldn't be. The thought comforted him. He looked up and saw a small patch of blue sky.

'Hi,' said Gilmour, jumping into the front seat. He laid his MP5 on the floor and tucked his pistol under his thigh. 'Look Gary, I was a dickhead.'

'Where to?' said Johnson, blinking behind his glasses. 'M5.'

The car lurched forward, slipped through the main gate and headed for the motorway. Gilmour felt a deep respect building for Johnson as he observed how he handled the car. The guy was good and he was glad to have him. When they reached the motorway, Johnson put the boot down. Morning traffic was building up, but he still managed to keep the car up around 140 mph.

'I'm sorry,' said Gilmour at length.

'Forget it,' said Johnson, throwing the car across to the hard shoulder to avoid a throng of traffic. The tyres thumped the cat's-eyes as they hurtled past a row of lumbering lorries.

'It's just that you don't look like much, you know.'

'We're not supposed to, remember?' said Johnson, swerving back across three carriageways.

'I'm going to make it up to you.'

Johnson managed a hint of a smile.

'Forget it,' he said.

'You sure?'

'Yeah . . . why me then?'

'Eh?'

'As your driver? Why not SAS?'

'I asked for you.'

'Get away.'

Gilmour caught the sarcasm.

'McCann knows us too well.'

'So why me then?'

'You fooled me and I reckon you might fool McCann. I need someone who'll react differently to us and maybe catch him out.'

'Hmmm,' mused Johnson, enjoying the compliment. 'That sounds like fun. What's the usual story with you lot on a job like this?'

'Forget the usual story – we're freelance.'

Johnson lapsed into a thoughtful silence and Gilmour noticed one of his fingers was tapping the steering wheel very gently.

The terrorists left the motorway at junction 18 and headed into Bristol along the gorge. The radio traffic increased dramatically at this dangerous development and voices became agitated and edgy. Johnson eased off on the speed as they approached a heavy build up of morning rush hour traffic.

'Let's just stay with the flow,' said Gilmour.

'What about the Rovers?'

'We're after McCann.'

'Won't he be with them?'

'Maybe.'

The needle dropped to forty-five as they moved into the traffic. Gilmour clambered into the back and kept down. They were still miles behind the Rovers, but he was taking no chances. As they approached junction 18, they took the slip road.

The terrorists drove through the city centre and crossed the Avon into Bedminster. Johnson chucked a Bristol A-Z over his head. Gilmour leafed through it and started passing directions. They drove under the Clifton suspension bridge and stopped at traffic lights.

'Cavalier, red, one male, perhaps twenty cars ahead,' said Johnson.

Gilmour peered between the seats, but couldn't be sure. The traffic moved again, and the Cavalier took the flyover towards the A370.

'Stay with it,' said Gilmour.

At the next traffic lights, Gilmour lifted his head and sucked in his breath.

'You need to relax,' said Johnson quietly.

'Eh?'

'You're too wound up about this prick.'

When the lights changed, Johnson darted over a lane, accelerated hard and pulled in again, managing to get four cars closer.

'*Watch it!*' hissed Gilmour. 'He'll see us!'

Johnson dropped a gear, squealed back into the out-side lane and took another two cars. A horn blared an-grily. Johnson lowered his window and gave the driver the middle finger. The horn stayed down.

'*Gary!*'

The Cavalier cleared the filter traffic heading into Ashton and sped off. Johnson parped on the horn as he barged his way forwards.

'*Do you want him to see us?*'

'Yes,' said Johnson, weaving round a gesturing mini driver. 'I do.'

Gilmour slid down in the seat and flicked off the safety catch on his pistol.

'What can I say mate? I didn't realise I'd pissed you off so much.'

'Dickhead,' said Johnson. 'McCann thinks I'm just some idiot who's late for work.'

The radio crackled. The terrorists had turned left off the A38 towards Winford. Gilmour checked the A-Z. They were less than ten minutes away. He peeked over the top of the seat for a quick look. McCann indicated left and took a slip road off the dual carriageway.

'He's cutting across to the airport road,' he said, leaf-ing hurriedly through the A-Z.

Johnson closed right up behind the Cavalier and started pushing him.

'McCann just smiled at me in his mirror,' said Johnson. 'He thinks I'm an asshole. You two share the same attitude problem.'

Gilmour grimaced, but said nothing.

They sped through a tiny village, drove up a narrow hill and approached red traffic lights.

'Get ready,' said Johnson without emotion.

'I'm going to die,' said Gilmour heavily as he grabbed the door handle.

The Cavalier braked gently as it approached the lights. Johnson stuck the boot down and pulled out. As he passed the Cavalier, he swung the wheel round hard. There was huge crunch. The Cavalier careered off the road, went down a bank and smashed through a fence into a wood. Johnson yanked on the handbrake and slew the car to a halt.

Gilmour rolled out and loosed off a few rounds into the side of the Cavalier. Glass shattered as rounds punctured the bodywork. A shadow moved in the trees. Instinctively Gilmour rolled and fired another few shots. A branch snapped. He got to his feet and leapt the fence. Johnson crouched over the bonnet of his car, covering him with a handgun.

'Well,' said Gilmour with a sad shake of his head, 'that certainly did the trick, you mad bastard.'

'Look, blood,' said Johnson, pointing.

Sure enough, there was a bloody smear on the bark of a tree. The passenger door creaked on its hinges as Gilmour leaned inside. A mobile phone lay on the floor but there was no sign of a pistol.

'What now?' asked Johnson.

'You better make yourself scarce before the police show up.'

'I'll see you around then.'

Gilmour took a few steps into the trees, listening hard. This time there was no adrenaline rush. He wasn't afraid. Johnson's little ploy had worked and McCann was bleeding. Now it was just a matter of time.

Chapter 36

Ellis stared at a paper clip on the Colonel's desk, a pulse throbbing at his temples. The Brigadier stood by the window, absorbed in his own dark thoughts.

'Coffee?' suggested the Colonel.

Ellis reluctantly declined. He'd already had four mugs since breakfast. His eyes were red from lack of sleep.

'John, can I ask you a question?'

'Of course Peter,' replied the Brigadier.

'The transit van?'

The Brigadier turned from the window.

'What about it?'

'How did you find it so quickly?'

'A tip off old chap.'

'From Peterson?'

'Remarkable, how did you know?'

'Hmmm.'

Just then, Peterson's Jaguar drew up outside. The Brigadier squared his shoulders as the Colonel stood up behind his desk. The pulse at Ellis' temple intensified.

'Good morning gentlemen,' said Peterson sombrely as he closed the office door behind him.

He looked as if he'd just recently showered after a good night's sleep, which, indeed, wasn't too far from the truth. His fresh complexion though was marred by a heavy frown.

'Good morning,' said Ellis, watching the minister very closely.

The Colonel sat behind his desk and shifted in his seat uncomfortably.

'Is anything the matter?' asked Peterson, noticing something different about Ellis' manner.

'Oh yes,' said Ellis, 'there's a great deal the matter.'

'Coffee Minister?' suggested the Colonel.

'No thank you,' said Peterson. 'McCann? Where is he now?'

The Colonel shrugged.

'And Gilmour?'

'The last we heard, he chased McCann into a wood on foot. We believe McCann to be injured.'

Peterson checked his watch, deeply troubled.

'And just exactly whose bright idea was it to send Gilmour off gallivanting on his own like that?'

'Mine,' said Ellis, sitting in his corner drinking in the heavy mood. 'Have you a problem with it?'

'And why wasn't I informed?'

'Because I specifically asked for you not to be.'

'And the terrorists?' asked Peterson, eyeing Ellis warily.

'Parked up on the shores of Chew Valley Lake,' said the Colonel. 'A few miles South of Bristol. We are planning an assault as we speak.'

Peterson sighed.

'You don't seem too happy Minister,' observed Ellis.

'Excuse me?'

'The polite response is *sorry*, or simply *what*.'

Peterson lowered his voice.

'You presume to teach me etiquette?'

'More to the point, Minister, the Israelis warned your office of a pending terrorist spectacular some time ago. Why have you done nothing about it?'

Peterson studied him for a time and then nodded to the Colonel and the Brigadier.

'Would you excuse us gentlemen?'

Both men looked at each other and then left without a word.

Peterson walked round the office to the window.

'It is an American problem, as you well know.'

'Really? And had you heard that we've taken Lord Thompson into custody?'

Peterson whipped round.

'That's right, Minister. Surprised? We know of the plan to surround the President's limousine with three Range Rovers packed with explosives and detonate them simultaneously in a suicide attack.'

Peterson sat in the Colonel's chair and put his feet up on the desk. A finger stroked his upper lip.

'What are you talking about?'

'In your quest for world domination,' said Ellis, 'and this one world government you all wank over, don't you care how many people die?'

'What are you—?'

Ellis cut him off.

'I know you're one of the Illuminati, Minister.'

Peterson studied him for a moment.

'Minds as small as yours are incapable of comprehension.'

'Ah, spoken like one of the truly enlightened.'

'One World governance,' said Peterson, 'is the only way to bring world peace. Think about it, if you're at all capable of such.'

'So you continue to destabilise country after country, bringing death, poverty and suffering to millions, just so we can all be happy and live in peace?'

Peterson smiled.

'That's one way of looking at it.'

'The end justifies the means eh.'

'That's the philanthropic view.'

'No Minister, that's the view of a few greedy men who want the whole world all to themselves and fuck everybody else. Communism has nothing to do with human rights and world peace, it has everything to do with armed robbery and murder – stealing countries and then murdering the squatters to get them off your new property. I know you and the Illuminati are financing Arab terrorism Minister. I must admit, though, linking the al Qaeda network to you wasn't easy.'

Peterson dropped his feet slowly from the desk and sat up.

'Oh, and how did you make *that* ridiculous link?'

'McConnell.'

Peterson leaned forward and put his elbows on the polished desk.

'Who?'

'I spotted one of his men at Lord Thompson's manor house in Lichfield and it set me thinking. So I tried to contact Pat.'

'Ah yes, Pat,' said Peterson, developing something of a smirk. 'It eventually occurred to you to confirm my story about the tip off at the quarry.'

'Unfortunately, he'd been killed in a traffic accident.'

'Sad.'

'So I got to wondering about what you and McConnell and an English Lord could possibly have in common and I did some checking.'

'And?'

'You were all at a recent meeting of The Royal Institute of International Affairs at Chatham House in London. Of course, that soon led me to The Council on Foreign Relations, The Trilateral Commission, of which you are a prominent speaker, and a host of other subversive organisations which you control.'

'You miss the big picture Ellis, when we have the world we will be able to do so much. Just think, no more hunger—'

'You were a Jesuit priest before moving into politics, were you not?'

'No more wars—'

'Minister, I know you've given your blessing to these Arabs. I know of your plans to undermine British security and social order in your quest for the world.'

Fire suddenly flared in Peterson's eyes.

'You have nothing on me, Ellis, nothing whatsoever. Do you think we are as stupid as that fool Thompson? He did our bidding without even understanding what he was doing. You are all so pathetic. We are in key positions of power and influence the world over, dictating to the public faces of policy how to behave and to the orators what to tell the masses. Your efforts to combat that will be as impotent as your search for truth.'

'Novus Ordo Seclorum,' sighed Ellis, getting to his feet to leave. 'By the way Minister,' he said, almost as an afterthought.

'Yes?'

'There have been a number of attempts on my life and, quite frankly, it's pissed me off.'

'And what has that to do with me?'

'Well, someone had to be following me.'

'Is there a point to this?'

'And then I met a certain Miss Roberts.'

'Intriguing.'

'I did some checking and discovered that in her innocence she was reporting directly to you.'

'Ah yes, *that* Miss Roberts. I had such high hopes for her.'

'I'm sorry Minister, but I'm going to have to liquidate you to prevent a recurrence. For my own peace of mind, you understand.'

The sneer on Peterson's face vanished as Ellis closed the door and headed down the corridor.

Chapter 37

Angelina had long given up caring about the world outside. Life was a slavering beast that bit into her every time she woke. Her only escapes were longer and longer periods of unconsciousness. A tune haunted her. Words seemed to come to her from nowhere and she learned them by heart. Each time the tune came there were new words. She wondered what the words meant and wished the song would end.

The dark night of the soul,
That long and wearisome road.
Entombed inside my own head,
Empty, cold and alone.
Imprisoned in dungeons of time,
Dreams screamed out of tune.
A soul forgotten in thought,
Each thought forgotten too soon.

She thought about the words for a while and then drifted off into unconsciousness. She felt herself slipping away and wished it would be forever.

She woke with a start. There was a warm feeling between her legs. She'd wet herself. She wondered if her mummy would be mad at her. She tried to slip back into her dreams. But it was no use. She was going to have to face reality for a while.

One of the Arabs beside her was urinating into a plastic coke bottle. She watched the viscous yellow liquid dribble inside and slop around the bottom. The driver groaned and held his stomach. She couldn't feel her toes anymore she was so numb. They were all exhausted. Even the older Arab. The driver groaned again and doubled over. He couldn't hold it any longer and shit into his trousers. The Arab wrinkled his nose but refused to let anyone wind down a window. People were wandering around outside and he was taking no chances.

Angelina looked around. They were parked up under trees by the side of a picnic area on the shores of a large lake. The sun shone brilliantly in a clear blue sky. A dog ran around barking. With a laugh, a young girl with dark hair picked up a stick and hurled it towards the lake. The dog bounded after it yapping with delight. The stick bounced and skittered into some reeds by the shore. Shaking water from its shaggy coat, the dog ran back up the bank with the stick in its mouth.

'Please,' begged Angelina, 'please let me out for just a minute.'

'It not possible,' said the Arab. 'Too much people.'

'When will it be over?'

'Tomorrow.'

'The sooner the better,' muttered the driver.

The Arab glanced across at him and poised himself for important words.

'The sword of Islam will strike into heart of enemy. Tomorrow is great victory for Allah.'

The Arab beside her screwed the top back on the coke bottle and sloshed his urine around for something to do. Outside, the dog ran up to the young girl and dropped the stick at her feet. Angelina felt darkness coming. She welcomed it and longed for the night to come. The Arab's words broke her spirit and she slipped back into unconsciousness.

The next time she came to, the Arab was irritably punching buttons on his phone and putting it to his ear. But he wasn't getting any answer.

'They should be 'ere by now,' remarked the driver.

'Your Allah is very cruel,' said Angelina.

There was no answer and she looked out over the lake.

The sun sparkled on the water but she wished it would go away. The branches of the trees waved listlessly in the light breezes. She wondered what it would be like to slip off her shoes and socks and paddle along the shore of the lake.

'My people,' said the Arab, waking her from her thoughts, 'suffer for long centuries by infidels. Soon we strike and West feel bite of sword.'

Angelina had no idea what he was on about. The other Arabs however, were in no mood for such fine talk. They wanted out of that stinking car so they could go home.

'When will you pay us?' asked the one with the urine

bottle.

The older man turned and asked for two briefcases to be passed forward from the boot. They were lifted over Angelina's head. The smaller one the Arab put between his feet, the other he opened. A gasp broke from the lips of the driver. The other Arabs leaned forward expectantly.

'Two million America dollars,' said the Arab.

The others stared at the money until he closed the case and stuck it down between his legs. He glanced at his watch.

'It seem Mr McCann forget us. So tonight we share his money. Tomorrow, we hand the cars over to our martyrs and you go home to your women rich men.'

'What about me?' asked Angelina, 'Will you let me go home?'

The silence told its own story.

A car pulled up on the other side of the picnic area. A young couple got out and wandered down towards the lake holding hands. They stood by the shore looking out over the water and the girl put her head on her boyfriend's shoulder.

Angelina suddenly burst into tears. She didn't want to die. She wanted to live. She wanted someone to hold her and hug her. She wanted to hear her mummy's laughs and to sit on her knee and be cuddled. She wanted to feel warm sunshine on her face and clean rain on her skin. She wanted to see a movie and do some shopping. These Arabs had no right to take her dreams away. *Jamie, where are you?* She threw her eyes desperately round the trees. *Where were the SAS? Didn't they know she was going to die?* Tears burned down her cheeks. Her tongue tasted salt. *Please God, please get me out of this.*

The guy down by the lake turned to his girlfriend, gently lifted her face to his and kissed her. The driver leaned forward, his eyes bulging. The two Arabs in the back looked at each other in astonishment. The older Arab became alarmed and looked over his shoulder at the trees. He dug something out of his pockets and started toying with it. Sweat trickled down his temple. The guy by the lake gently brushed his fingers over his girlfriend's breasts. Gasps filled the car. Suddenly, there was a brilliant flash of white and a bang that burst the sky. Angelina screamed as all the windows in the car exploded.

> *Freed from my dungeon in time,*
> *Dreams sung sweetly in tune.*
> *The peace, oh the peace that is mine,*
> *Forever is never too soon.*

Darkness took her and she slipped away. Her last thought was that she was glad she was finally dead.

Chapter 38

Gilmour crouched in the gloomy twilight under the leafy canopy, unsure of his next move. Rushing straight off into the trees seemed ridiculously like suicide. The forest was deathly quiet. So quiet it was unnerving. Even the traffic noise from the main road seemed muffled and lifeless. He thought he saw pale eyes peeping out at him from a dark hole under a dead branch. Break the rules? What did Ellis mean? What rules could he break here?

A rusty wire fence squeaked a good way off to his right. He spun round but all he could see was tangled undergrowth. It must have been the fence bordering the A38. McCann was getting away. He ran back to the crashed Cavalier, climbed the bank and sprinted up the road towards the traffic lights. Tyres squealed up ahead as a car braked savagely. Cars were slowing down and stopping. A shot rang out. A car door slammed and tyres spun on the road. His chest heaving, he dashed past the lights and out into the middle of the main road.

A light blue Escort disappeared towards Bristol in a cloud of blue exhaust fumes.

The driver of the Escort writhed on the ground, his hands clutching his leg where he'd been shot. Shocked motorists were getting out of their cars and running towards the man to help him. Someone spotted the gun in Gilmour's hand and cowered away. The Escort disappeared round a bend and Gilmour almost collapsed. McCann had beaten him again. His knees trembled and the desire to sit down was overwhelming. People were staring at him. He felt ridiculous standing in the middle of the road holding a gun.

A shiny black 3 series BMW pulled up and a strange thought occurred to him. Then he realised what Ellis had meant.

'*Out!*' he screamed, running over to the sports car and pointing his pistol straight at the driver through the window. '*Get the fuck out!*'

The young executive opened his door and fell out onto the road, his hands over his head. Gilmour jumped in and with a skirl of smoking rubber, he turned the car and sped off.

As he rounded a corner, he caught sight of a petrol station on the left. A car sat awkwardly across the pavement, black skid marks curving across the road behind it. The driver got out gesticulating wildly and slapping the top of his head. A startled woman with a petrol nozzle in her hand stared across the road at the entrance to a small lane. Gilmour stamped on the brakes, slewed the car to a halt facing the lane and just caught sight of the Escort disappearing round a corner in the distance. The back end of the BMW slithered around as the rear wheels struggled to grip the road.

The lane wound steeply up through thick forest. He hit a tight corner and the back end drifted away from him. He steered into the slide and the car juddered as it straightened out. At the top, he sped through a small village, rounded a sharp corner and spotted the Escort. A crazy image from an old Clint Eastwood movie played in his mind as he slammed into the back of it. The BMW coughed and spluttered. Not such a good idea after all. Still, he'd made his point and McCann knew who was behind him. As he nursed the revs back up, a strange kind of detachment settled over him, probably due to all the adrenaline his body had pumped round his system in the last few days.

McCann screamed along in a low gear taking blind corners on the narrow lane with breath-taking reckless-ness. At a junction with a main road, the Escort shot straight out and swerved to the right, narrowly missing a small van. Gilmour didn't risk it and slammed on the brakes. A large petrol tanker thundered down the road, narrowly missing his bonnet as he slithered to a halt.

The main road was narrow and winding, bordered on both sides by high hedgerows. He pulled out behind a slow moving car and thumped his steering wheel in ex-asperation. The road swung left and dropped sharply over the back of the hill, the high hedgrows making over-taking impossible. As they crawled down, they came up behind an even slower moving car. Far below them, he caught sight of the Escort screaming along the nar-row road as it crossed the valley. If he didn't move now he was going to lose him.

Dropping a gear, he pulled out. It was suicide, but he was out of options. The BMW rocketed down the hill. It felt like he was in freefall. He passed the first car, the narrow road still curving between the hedgerows. His teeth ground together. An old tractor appeared chugging up the hill, driven by a farmer with a tweed cap. Black diesel smoke coughed from the exhaust sticking up out of its rusty bonnet. The leading car saw him coming in his mirror and braked. There was a crunch as the car behind slid into it. The farmer took one look and jumped from the tractor into the hedge. Gilmour wrenched the wheel round. How he missed the tractor he had no idea.

Sweat poured from him as he struggled to hold the car into another tight corner. He was pushing himself beyond anything he'd ever done before, even in Northern Ireland. He sped along a straight and raced into a forest. A steep hill dropped away, snaking down through overhanging trees. At the bottom, the road turned sharply to the left. He misjudged it and the back end swung away from him. An evil little humpback bridge leered at him. Somehow, he got the car between the parapets. The car crunched down on its suspension as it hit the hump and the bonnet reared up into the air. When he thumped back to earth, he threw the wheel into a vicious right-hand bend. He just made it and slithered to a halt at a mini roundabout. *Where was McCann?* He pulled out and saw the back end of the Escort disappearing round a corner some way ahead of him.

The road wound dangerously through farmed countryside, the high hedges blocking his view of the road ahead. *Where was the damn Escort?* He squealed round a sharp bend and there it was. Palming his pistol, he pulled out. There was a bang as he swung the wheel hard over. The Escort slid sideways, its rear wing crumpling as it slammed into a stone wall. The car spun down the road and came to rest in a cloud of smoke and dust.

Gilmour managed to control the BMW and skidded to a halt. Rolling out, he came up on one knee, both hands steadying his pistol. McCann staggered from the wreckage, coughing. Blood streaked his grimy face. He had a Browning pistol in his hand.

'*Drop the weapon, arsehole.*'

Gilmour didn't bother waiting for a response and fired. The Browning skittered across the road.

'You . . . you . .' croaked McCann hoarsely, his voice not yet recovered from the blow to his throat back at the petrol station.

He stared disbelievingly at the bones sticking out of his shattered hand. A car came round the corner, screeched to a halt and sped off in reverse, its engine whining. Metal crumpled against metal as another car slid into the back of it. Both drivers got out and fled back up the road. Gilmour never took his eyes from McCann. The Irishman fell to his knees, his face caked with dust, grime and blood. He laughed weakly, wiping grime out of his eyes with the back of his good hand. A fit of coughing racked him and blood dribbled from his mouth.

'What's the target?' asked Gilmour, toying with the trigger.

'Auch, you're a fucker so you are,' croaked McCann. Gilmour thought he heard blood gurgling in his throat.

'Is the girl still alive?'

McCann looked up at him.

'All you wanted was the girl? You mean, if I'd let her go, this wouldn't be happening?' His eyes fell to the road. 'Fuck me.'

Gilmour breathed a little more freely. Angelina was

still alive.

'What's the target?'

'Two million bucks,' said McCann, searching Gilmour's eyes for a moment. 'It's in a briefcase in one of the Rovers. I don't suppose . . ?'

Gilmour shook his head.

'Auch, so that's the crack is it. I guess it's all over then.'

Gilmour knew he was wasting his time. But he didn't want to pull the trigger just yet. McCann heaved up blood as another fit of coughing racked him. He was dying.

'Tell me about the girls.'

'Auch, will you wheesht.'

Gilmour took a step and kicked him in the kidneys. As the Irishman doubled over, he kicked again, catching him full in the mouth, knocking him back against the door of the Escort. McCann fell to the road and spat out a few teeth. In the distance, a police siren wailed. It was time to get out of the area. He needed somewhere quiet.

Gilmour kept himself between the car and the stone wall of a lay-by. On the other side of the wall, waves lapped gently at the shores of a large lake. He yanked open the back door and with a few vicious kicks, roused McCann. Their eyes met and locked. But there was no hate in McCann's eyes, which surprised him. Gilmour pointed the pistol at the Irishman's legs. McCann held up a hand.

'No wait . . .'

Saliva and blood dribbled from his mouth. He coughed weakly and tried to move. But it was too much effort.

His eyes began to roll.

'Not yet you piece of shit,' hissed Gilmour, kicking him awake.

McCann tried to lift his head, but sank back, exhausted.

'I was only wanting my money, so I was.'

Gilmour hesitated. There were a couple of things he just had to know. He looked straight into McCann's eyes. Training the weapon at his forehead, he held his gaze for a few seconds.

'What did you want with me? And why didn't you kill me back at the motorway?'

McCann seemed suddenly very sad.

'Auch, I couldn't.'

Gilmour's eye's narrowed.

'What do you mean?'

McCann slipped a photograph from a pocket of his tweed jacket. It was Gilmour's stolen family portrait.

'And how is our mother?' asked McCann, his eyes filling with tears.

'Eh?'

'I only wanted to meet my kid brother.'

The words didn't register immediately. When Gilmour tried to speak, he couldn't.

A tear trickled slowly down McCann's cheek.

'That SAS thing was hard to take,' he said softly. 'Why did you have to join them fuckers?'

'I could ask you the same thing about the IRA,' grunted Gilmour, his insides wracked with pain.

'If you'd been brought up in Ireland, you'd be one of us.'

'Not me mate. Murdering women and children was never going to be my thing.'

McCann gurgled something unintelligible, no longer able

to clear the blood welling up in his throat.

Two bullets blew the back of his head off.

His dead eyes stared vacantly up at the roof.

The dead girl at the lodge reached out her hand to Gilmour. Her voice called to him and then faded. She drifted out of his mind and floated away on the soft breeze. He stood staring into the car, his mind a whirlwind. Tears stung his eyes. Ellis knew. *He fucking knew!*

Exhaustion swam in his dizzy head. He felt dirty and used. Blood dripped from McCann's lifeless fingers to a sticky red puddle on the carpet. Something in the air made him look up. Suddenly, an explosion rocked the trees half a mile or so down the shore. He threw an arm over his eyes and sank to his knees. It was all over.

Chapter 39

Squadron Sergeant Major Brian Munro sat amongst the array of radios and computers decking the black van that was his mobile command centre and drummed his fingers on his notepad as he listened to the Net. His nerves were tingling, but his emotions were slightly mixed. He'd been relieved as SAS liaison officer overseeing the President's State visit and put in command of the assault on the Rovers, which greatly pleased him; but he was to be nowhere near the sharp end of the action, which didn't please him at all. His trigger finger itched. With philosophical acceptance, he put it from his mind. The success of the assault and the safety of the men were his responsibility now, not charging in all barrels blazing. Still, he couldn't complain – next birthday he'd be forty-six, with almost twenty four years service in the SAS.

He swivelled in his seat, lifted his binos and focused out of the open side door. Through tangled undergrowth and the overhanging foliage of a few large birch trees, he could clearly make out the far shore line of the lake. The sun danced dazzlingly on the blue water, making him squint as he followed the shore. From the two Range Rovers parked up at the edge of the picnic area, a path meandered along the shore skirting the trees. It was such a pleasant day that the lake had attracted a lot of people. Some were out walking dogs; some were out walking themselves or jogging. Others were just sitting around, enjoying the views. A young girl ran around shouting excitedly and a dog scampered about chasing butterflies and anything else that moved.

From one point of view, it was ideal, as the terrorists would feel relaxed with so many people around. But from another, it posed massive problems as no assault could go in until they had somehow first cleared the area without alerting the terrorists. He scratched the scar running from his ear to the side of his mouth and wondered what the Argentinean bastard who'd shot him was up to.

Putting the binos down, he wriggled uncomfortably on the leather seat. It seemed unlikely that the terrorists would move before nightfall, but if they did, they wouldn't get very far. About a hundred yards. An ambush already in place by the track leading from the picnic area to the main road would make sure of that. It wasn't the ideal option but he was satisfied it would do the job. His tongue clicked as he ran various scenarios through his brain.

He found himself with a few minutes to think and put his notepad down. He'd been involved in a number of counter-terrorist operations with the Regiment, but nothing had ever come of them and it severely pissed him off. He badly wanted to see dead terrorists. A few incredibly frustrating tours in Northern Ireland had severely blunted his confidence in British justice. It seemed to him that terrorists were better protected by the government than he was. He was beginning to suspect a conspiracy. The systematic break down of law and order was, after all, just another cog in the terrorist machine. Anyway, he thought with grim satisfaction, here, at last, was an opportunity to actually shoot some of the bastards.

The shimmer from the lake was beginning to hurt his eyes. With everything coming to a head, the clamour on the radio had increased and it was becoming more difficult to break in. He sent out a message that only Troop Commanders were to use the Net unless absolutely necessary. It worked. The clamour died down and things became more controlled.

Four green LED lights glowed on the Bru-22 radio beside him. Each green light meant that snipers had the four terrorists in the front of the two Rovers in their sights. It had been over twenty minutes since he'd last seen a red light. He went through his plan one last time, ticking off the points on his notepad. He knew there was no more he could do. It was time to get things going.

At his order, two men camouflaged in gillie suits wormed through the trees towards the Rovers. When they were in position, they clicked the pressle switches on their radios three times. Munro felt the tension solidify. He gave another order and people wandering around in the woods were approached and quietly led away to safety. The young girl with the dog ran off down a path into the trees and didn't come back.

A black Astra bumped down the track from the main

road and pulled up near the terrorists. A woman got out and wandered casually towards the trees. Mi5 had its uses. Movement was important right now. Everything had to look normal. His stomach tightened. It was time. He got on the radio, but Credenhill advised him to wait.

'*What is it now?*' he hissed, banging a clenched fist into his palm.

Suddenly, one of the green lights on the Bru radio turned to red. He frowned. This was not the time for problems. He got on the radio.

'Gold Two, sitrep over.'

'It's the bloody sun, Boss. It's moved. The light isn't good. I can't see the triangle of his eyes and mouth clearly.'

'Can you see his head?'

'Silhouette only.'

'Why are you fuckers always complaining about your shots? You're trained to take shots at silhouettes, take the shot.'

'But—'

'Gold Two, take the fucking shot! Out!'

The red light on the Bru radio turned back to green.

A red Nova bounced into the picnic area. An SAS soldier and an Mi5 girl posing as a couple clambered out and ambled down towards the lake holding hands. Time slowed right down and Munro became conscious of each second in a tangible sort of way. The couple turned to each other and kissed. The time was right, and Munro knew it.

'We've got to move *now*,' he shouted into his radio.

'Wait one . . . the Minister thinks—'

'*Fuck the minister!*'

A different voice came on the radio.

'Just do it Brian,' said Ellis very calmly.

Munro snatched up his binos.

'*Stand by . . . stand by*' he screamed down his throat mike, '. . . *GO!*'

Stun grenades fired from M203 grenade launchers landed around the Range Rovers and exploded, sending birds screeching into the sky. The snipers found their targets and the terrorists in the front of the Range Rovers were dead before even realising they had been shot. Two cars screamed down the track and rammed the front of the Rovers as the assault teams sprinted from the trees. Dressed completely in black, the SAS men crowded round the vehicles and emptied their magazines into jerking terrorists. It was all over in less than ten seconds.

The Arabs hardly had a head left between them. Spurts of blood gushed from pulped necks. Smoke drifted lazily out through the shattered windows and trailed off on the breeze. Two helicopters bristling with machine guns skimmed across the lake. The assault teams kept their machine guns poking inside the Rovers, unable to grasp the enormity of what they'd just done. The radio had gone deathly quiet. It was the helicopters that broke the spell.

They roared down blowing dust everywhere, landing well away from the danger area. Medics leapt from them and sprinted to the Rovers with a stretcher. The assault teams applied their safety catches, stepped back and then ran for safety. A few cars sped down the dirt track from the main road and blokes spilled out into the bright sunshine brandishing handguns. Munro stared open-mouthed through his binoculars from the door of his van on the other side of the lake. This was the crown jewel of his entire career.

The medics yanked open a door and dragged Angelina from the carnage. Munro felt a twinge of panic as he focused on her lifeless form. If she were dead, his crown jewel would quickly devalue to nothing more than a cheap plastic trinket. Two Chinooks lumbered heavily over the trees and settled down in a clearing. The medics laid Angelina carefully on a stretcher and scampered away from the bombs like frightened rabbits.

And then it went strangely quiet. Four bomb disposal men, ungainly and awkward in their protective Kevlar body armour and steel plated suits, waddled towards the Rovers like Michelin men. They huddled in a little group and had a hasty discussion. One of them pointed at the cars and then at the trees. They seemed to agree on something and then three of them lay down behind a bank for cover. The fourth man took a deep breath, squared his shoulders and waddled to the rear of the nearest Rover. The elation subsided as the seconds ticked by. The sweating man opened the boot gingerly and checked for wires. Pulling a pair of pliers from his pocket, he leaned in to examine the first bomb. Munro put the binos down. With a fingernail, he picked at the dirt engrained on the keyboard of his laptop and waited for the bang. That was no job for sane men.

Gilmour was prepared for the worst. As he approached the turn off to the picnic area, he slowed down. Two soldiers with automatic weapons blocked the road. When they recognised him, they stepped back and allowed him past.

'What's happening?' he asked.

'EOD are dealing with the explosives,' said one of

them.

'Is the girl . . ?'

'Sorry mate, no idea.'

'Who you got there then?' asked the other one, peering inquisitively in the back.

'Oh, just family.'

Gilmour parked up and got stiffly out. He limped down the track, a hand to his head. Ellis and the Colonel were standing off to one side by themselves, watching from the safety of the trees.

'Ah!' exclaimed the Colonel. 'At last.'

'How's the girl?'

The Colonel shrugged.

Gilmour groaned. Now that it was all over, it seemed that every muscle in his body had decided to seize up.

'Where's McCann?' asked Ellis.

Gilmour nodded towards the BMW.

'Dead?'

'Of course.'

Ellis sensed something was wrong and cocked his head to one side inquiringly.

'Did anyone see you . . . er, deal with McCann?' asked the Colonel.

'Don't think so, Boss.'

Gilmour riveted his eyes on Ellis.

'You don't *think* so?' asked the Colonel.

'Well,' explained Gilmour, eyeing Ellis coldly, 'a few people saw weapons, but no one saw me slotting him.'

'Is something the matter?' asked Ellis.

Gilmour clenched his fists.

'Who else knows?' he said, struggling to keep the tremor from his voice.

'Sorry?'

Two of the bomb disposal men waddled towards them whistling different tunes.

'Thought you might like this, Boss,' said one of them, tossing something through the air.

The Colonel caught it deftly.

'What is it?' he asked, turning it over in his hand.

'Remote detonator, Boss. It was on the floor in the front.'

'Good lord.'

'Yeah, the bastard must have been holding it when the sniper took him out.'

'*Good lord!*'

'You also might want these,' said the other Michelin man, putting down two briefcases.

'And what have you got there?'

'A whole lot of money,' he said simply. Well, see you later.'

The two of them sauntered away, still whistling different tunes.

'Who else knows?' asked Gilmour again.

Uncertainty flickered in Ellis' eyes.

'You can give me a straight answer,' said Gilmour, 'or I'm going to punch your fucking lights out.'

'Mi5 dug it up from somewhere,' said Ellis heavily. 'Peterson knows, but you don't have to concern yourself about him.'

'No one else?'

'Everyone knows what happened to your mother, but no one knows about McCann. He was adopted by an Irish couple living in England at the time and never heard of again.'

The Colonel twigged and visibly shrank in horror.

'What about the Police?'

'It wasn't reported to the Police. It was covered up very carefully.'

'Really?' said Gilmour caustically.

'Would you have wanted the whole world to know?'

Gilmour tore his eyes from Ellis and wandered off across the picnic area. Ducks had reappeared from the reeds and were paddling around the lake, diving and chasing each other again as if nothing had happened. A butterfly fluttered across the car park and settled on a small bush. Out in the lake a trout leapt and fell back with a plop sending ripples widening across the surface. Somehow, the beauty and warmth of the moment melted the ice that had formed on his heart.

Life was strange. On the one hand it was simply too beautiful for words. On the other, it was so ugly it was also beyond words. One thing he was sure of though – if there was a God, there was *definitely* a Devil. The butterfly lifted off and fluttered away over the grass. Watching it go made the rest of his life seem somehow worthwhile. He was unaware of the Colonel frowning behind him.

'I'm worried about him,' said the Colonel.

'I wouldn't be,' replied Ellis. 'He'll never be the same again, and may seem a bit laid back, even dozy. But I wouldn't worry about him.'

'I'm sure I don't know what you're talking about.'

'I'm sure I don't either.'

'Missed it mate!' laughed one of the assault team as Gilmour limped over.

They were flushed and laughing, like excited football players after winning a cup final. He searched their faces.

'She's okay, right?'

'Better ask the medic,' replied one of them, nodding to one of the helicopters.

'The RSMs been asking for you,' laughed another of them, cracking a can of beer. 'Heard you're off back to the shitehole Paras.'

The others burst out in good-natured laughter. Gilmour smiled politely and looked over his shoulder. Ellis, with the help of another couple of blokes, was dragging McCann's overweight body out of the BMW. The laughter died.

'What you been up to then?' asked one of them curiously.

'Oh nothing much,' said Gilmour, enjoying his moment. 'While you crap hats were playing yourselves, I was off doing a man's work.'

'*Fuck off!*' they all sang in unison.

Gilmour clambered awkwardly on board the helicopter. Angelina was a mess. Her hair was matted with blood and there were little bits of flesh and bone sticking to her. The smell turned his stomach.

'How is she?'

'Oh . . . it's you,' said the Doc brightly, and then frowned. 'I thought I told you to take it easy for a while.'

'How is she?'

The Doc flicked air out of a hypodermic needle.

'I'm not sure.'

'Is she alive?'

'Hmmm, do you think I should check that first before sticking needles in her?'

Gilmour sat with his back to the fuselage, tucked his knees up and put his relieved head in his hands.

'When we get to Creden,' said the Doc sternly, chucking the used needle into his bag. 'I'm putting you under observation.'

Gilmour had no argument with that. A couple of days in bed sounded good to him.

One of the Chinooks thundered overhead, the very air vibrating to the beat of its rotors. The Colonel stuck his head in the door and then jumped aboard.

'Right, let's go,' he said, giving the thumbs up to the pilots.

The helicopter throttled up and lifted off in a storm of dust. Gilmour sat back enjoying the vibrations as the helicopter strained up into the sky. Through the door, he watched the shoreline receding into the distance. It was hard to believe it was all over. He turned to the Colonel.

'Any word on Andy?' he shouted above the noise.

The Colonel brightened.

'I saw him briefly a short while ago.'

Gilmour felt his pulse race.

'Is he going to be okay?'

'Well,' shouted the Colonel with a sly look, 'I don't know about that. His wife was holding his hand and he was mumbling some crap about never drinking again and taking her and the kids to McDonalds for breakfast on Sundays.'

Andy!

He couldn't wait to see him.

As they approached Bristol, they thundered past a Chinook with one of the Rovers swinging securely underneath. Angelina moaned. Gilmour's heart leapt. How many times had he dreamed of this?

'Hiya,' he smiled, crawling over to her side.

Her eyelids fluttered and opened. She looked bewildered.

'How . . ?' she began, then stared at the strange fuselage.

'Hi you,' he soothed, taking her hand.

'Where . . .?' she tried again, but her voice trailed off. Fear filled her eyes and she tried to sit up.

'Shhh . . .' said Gilmour, gently holding her down.

'But the bomb?' she said, 'how . . ?'

'That wasn't the bomb sweetheart, that was just the boys doing their thing. The bad guys are all dead. You're safe now, on your way to hospital.'

'The bombs were for tomorrow.'

She tried to sit up again, panic chiselled all over her face.

'It's all taken care of.'

'The Arabs?'

'Dead.'

She was quiet for a moment.

'You're a Sheep in Wolf's Clothing,' she smiled bravely.

'A what?'

She lay back.

'I knew you'd come for me,' she said, her fingers tightening in his.

Gilmour gently brushed her cheek with a finger as the aircraft banked somewhere over Bristol and set course for Hereford.

Chapter 40

A few days later, Gilmour was at the hospital in London. He watched through the window of the ward as Angelina approached her mother's bed holding her grandfather's hand. A little uncertainly, she glanced over her shoulder and brushed her long hair from her eyes. Then, with a little smile that Gilmour knew was just for him, she rushed to her mother's side and started chattering away, telling her all about her awful adventure. When she got to the really nasty bit when she thought her finger was going to be cut off, she lifted her hand to emphasize how scared she'd been. Suddenly, she stopped talking and looked back in alarm. Gilmour raised his eyebrows.

'What is it?' he mouthed through the glass.

With a little squeal, Angelina jumped back from the bed. A nurse rushed over.

'*There!*' exclaimed Angelina, pointing. 'She did it again!'

One of her mother's forefingers was gently tapping

the sheets.

'*Mum!*'

Her grandfather collapsed into a chair.

Angelina threw her arms round her mother's neck as her eyes started to flicker.

'Careful there young lady,' said the nurse, trying to ease her away.

A doctor suddenly ran down the corridor and hurried into the ward. Gilmour lost the war to keep his eyes dry and pulled a tissue from his pocket. It was time to go.

There was something deeply poignant about wandering round Credenhill knowing he was no longer part of the SAS. A few sparrows flitted past him. He watched them go and knew he could never go back to the Paras. The Kenyan job was feeling good. One of the boys strolled past and nodded, but nothing was said. The others understood what he was going through. They were just thankful it wasn't them.

The clumping of heavy boots sounded from around the corner of the next building. Instinctively, he turned to run, but stopped himself. Taking a deep breath, he squared his shoulders and waited. The RSM trundled round the corner like a British battle tank and the two men eyed each other solemnly. Gilmour decided to speak first.

'Shove your fucking job Billy.'

The RSM clasped his hands behind his back and started nodding.

'Not many men have had the nerve to swear at me, *mister*.'

Gilmour held his eye.

'Do you still have that travel warrant?' asked the RSM.

'Yes, Billy, I've got your warrant.'

'There is a problem with it. Come to my office.'

Gilmour fell into step behind the RSM, wishing it was all over so he could climb into his Trooper and drive away.

The RSM sat behind his desk, pulled open a drawer and then looked across thoughtfully at his battered four-drawer filing cabinet. Gilmour stood patiently, the travel warrant in his hand. The RSM didn't intimidate him any longer. He doubted he would ever be intimidated by anyone ever again.

'Sit down will you?' said the RSM.

Gilmour stood his ground.

'The warrant please,' sighed the RSM, reaching across his desk for it.

Gilmour watched him crumple it up and throw it in his bin.

'You, Gilmour, are going to Buckingham Palace to pick up a Medal for your part in the assault on the hi-jacked aircraft.'

Gilmour had no answer to that.

'How's the girl?' asked the RSM, managing something of a smile.

'Fine, her mother's going to make it.'

'Yes, I just got a call from the hospital. And it seems Taylor is back to his old cocky self too.'

'The warrant?'

The RSM looked into his bin as if he'd missed something.

'What about it?' he asked.

'Don't take the piss out of me Billy.'

The RSM pushed his chair back with a squeak.

'The truth is Gilmour,' he said, 'you are one almighty

pain in the backside. But I can hardly RTU someone who is going to be scoffing biscuits and slurping tea with the Queen now, can I?'

Gilmour caught his breath.

'Besides, that was a damn good job you did with McCann.'

'*I'm still in?*' said Gilmour pathetically.

'Yes, but we are going to have to do some work on this attitude problem of yours. Have a few days off, and be back here a week Monday.'

'Yes Boss.'

'Now fuck off and don't *ever* swear at me again!'

Gilmour couldn't keep the smile from his face as he left the office and closed the door.

'Ah, Jamie!'

Gilmour couldn't believe his eyes. Ellis marched over to him with a very satisfied grin on his face. Behind him, a brand new, dark green, Aston Martin DB7 Vantage gleamed in the car park.

'Nice eh,' said Ellis, twirling the car keys round his finger.

'Who's that?' asked Gilmour incredulously, staring at the gorgeous girl in the Aston Martin.

Ellis smiled so broadly, his teeth showed.

'That's Chrissy.'

Gilmour laughed.

'By the way,' said Ellis, taking an envelope from his pocket and handing it to him. 'This is for you.'

'P 45?'

'A little bonus.'

'Thanks,' said Gilmour, tearing open the envelope and peering inside at the cheque. He raised his eyebrows in surprise. 'Fifty grand?'

'You did a good job, despite doing my head in. By the way, your little problem is solved.'

'My problem?'

'With the RSM.'

'Er . . . you had something to do with that?'

'Let's just say I have some friends.'

'*The Queen?*'

Ellis laughed at the bemused look on Gilmour's face.

At that moment, two men carried a coffin round a corner and laid it down outside one of the buildings.

'One of us?' asked Ellis, glancing in the coffin's direction.

'It's one of the girls from the lodge.'

'Ah.'

'Her parents are coming to collect her. Do you know who they were?'

'Just some young kids from London. Picked up at a nightclub, wined and dined, drugged and dragged off to be raped.'

'Poor girls. Hey, funny about Peterson getting killed like that,' said Gilmour, turning his attention from the coffin.

'Sorry?'

'Didn't you know?' Gilmour looked at him in astonishment. 'Last night in a traffic accident.'

'The Minister?'

'Don't you read the newspapers? He was drunk and in a right mess apparently.'

'Oh well, such is life. I'd better be going. I've an estate agent to see.'

'In Hereford?'

'No, in Hawaii. I'm thinking of buying a small island in

the South Pacific.'

Gilmour stared with dismay at the state of his back garden. It didn't take long for the bastard weeds to poke their heads up.

'*Scud!*' he shouted, his hand cupped to his mouth.

Roberts laughed.

'*Scud?* You're joking, right?'

'You can forget *Fluffy*,' said Gilmour seriously, strolling down the garden to the trees.

'*Fluffy?*'

Her laughter drifted across his unmown grass like waves of the sea. He turned to scowl, but instead found himself staring open-mouthed at her. She unbuttoned her coat and threw him a wicked smile. That was when he recognised the burgundy scarf around her neck. Forgetting the cat, he marched back up the garden, took her hand and led her into the kitchen.

'What were you doing on that aircraft?' he asked, searching her deep brown eyes.

He pulled her towards him and she didn't pull away. His senses exploded in a flash of bright light as their lips touched. The cat streaked into the kitchen and made for its plate.

'Better go see to Scud,' said Roberts breathlessly, pushing him away as the cat prowled over to the food cupboard.

Gilmour cleared a space on the kitchen table with a sweep of his arm. The laughter in Roberts' eyes flamed with desire as he held her shoulders firmly and pushed her back towards the table.

'Had you anything planned for the rest of your life?' he asked quietly.

George Maciver
Biography

George Maciver was a stranger before he was ten years old. And every new school was filled with more of them. He never really understood why the fun things in life were always illegal. He never did understand why Judges were always so stern looking. Oh well, if one can't have fun, one can always get drunk – at least that's what George thought.

He wasn't sure how long he was drunk. "Falling over a cliff is an exhilarating experience when you have no concept of gravity or its effects. Until you hit the bottom. Why can't you just simply fall up again? Why does gravity only go down? Staring wide eyed into the mirror, digging his nails into his cheeks until blood dripped to the ground, George didn't seem to accomplish much until he found words.

One day he looked up at the towering cliff and surveyed the steep path to the top. There was no easy way back up there. He sat for a while, but no one offered to carry him. Well, he wasn't content to remain at the bottom. But he rejected the call of words and dived off another cliff into the Parachute Regiment.

Holy shit! He even dreamt that. His back was going to break under that load! A rucksack of things and a haversack of history. Running, running, running.

That's all he seemed to do. He just kept on running. *'Move your fucking arse Maciver!'* screamed a corporal. He ran past a recruit lying at the side of the track who looked up with a haunted look of defeat. George never forgot those eyes. They kept him going. They still keep him going. The utter look of fear in defeat – of not being who you are meant to be.

But one gets older and one eventually gets tired of dragging heavy loads over endless hills and mountains. To words? Not exactly: George decided that Sales management might be fun. Like an extra in a Miami Vice take, George cruised through town in a black Mercedes, tinted glass, lowered suspension, spoilers and alloys, Billy Idol blasting from the stereo. Posing kept him amused for a while – driving rather than running – just getting nowhere a lot quicker. But it wasn't to last. He went to work one miserable winter morning to find the front door barred - the receivers were in and George was out. Losing the car and writing off nearly £7,000 in owed commissions introduced him to a few more strange new emotions and another cliff.

Madison Sol was established in order to build a Publishing House of avant-garde writers who dedicate their art to fomenting a 21st Century renaissance in Scottish thinking. Madison Sol is committed to publishing both works of non-fiction and fiction by these great writers; works that uplift the soul and change peoples' lives for the better, for good.

Publishing by its nature must take a long-term view; and Madison Sol does so in the knowledge that greatness only comes with patience and attention to detail.

Madison Sol has never forgotten her Highland roots; she remains true to them whilst never losing sight of the world beyond. Her perspective is global, her spirit Highland.